Magic Study

Magic
Study

MARIA V. SNYDER

mira

mira™

Recycling programs
for this product may
not exist in your area.

ISBN-13: 978-0-7783-6823-6

Magic Study

First published in 2006. This edition published in 2024.

Mira
22 Adelaide St. West, 41st Floor
Toronto, Ontario M5H 4E3, Canada

Printed in U.S.A.

To my children, Luke and Jenna,
a constant source of inspiration and love.
You both are truly magical.

In loving memory of Anthony and Victoria Foster.

THE TERRITORY OF IXIA

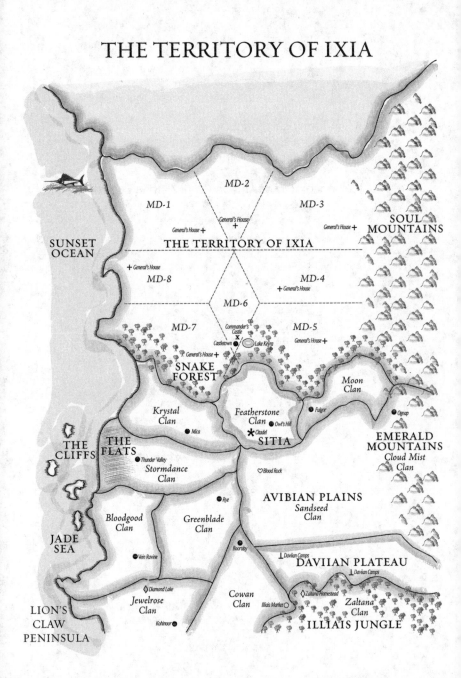

1

"We're here," Irys said.

I looked around. The surrounding jungle bulged with life. Overgrown green bushes blocked our path, vines hung from the tree canopy, and the constant chatter and trill of jungle birds beat at my ears. Small furry creatures, who had been following us through the jungle, peeked at us from their hiding spots behind huge leaves.

"Where?" I asked, glancing at the three other girls. They shrugged in unison, equally confused. In the thick humid air, their thin cotton dresses were soaked in sweat. My own black pants and white shirt clung to my clammy skin. We were tired from lugging our heavy backpacks along snake-thin jungle paths, and itchy from hosting unnameable insects on our skins.

"The Zaltana homestead," Irys said. "Quite possibly *your* home."

I surveyed the lush greenery and saw nothing that resembled a settlement. During the course of our travels south, whenever Irys had declared that we had arrived, we were usually in the midst of a small town or village, with houses made of wood, stone or brick, hemmed in by fields and farms.

The brightly dressed inhabitants would welcome us, feed us

and, amid a cacophony of voices and spicy aromas, listen to our story. Then certain families would be summoned with great haste. In a whirlwind of excitement and babble, one of the children in our party, who had lived in the orphanage in the north, would be reunited with a family they hadn't known existed.

As a result, our group had grown ever smaller as we'd traveled farther into the southern land of Sitia. Soon, we had left the cold northern air far behind, and were now cooking in the steamy warmth of the jungle with no sign of a town in sight.

"Homestead?" I asked.

Irys sighed. Wisps of her black hair had sprung from her tight bun, and her stern expression didn't quite match the slight humor in her emerald eyes.

"Yelena, appearances can be deceiving. Seek with your mind, not your senses," she instructed.

I rubbed my slick hands along the grain of my wooden staff, concentrating on its smooth surface. My mind emptied, and the buzz of the jungle faded as I sent out my mental awareness. In my mind's eye, I slithered through the underbrush with a snake, searching for a patch of sunlight. I scrambled through the tree branches with a long-limbed animal with such ease that it felt as if we flew.

Then, above, I moved with people among the treetops. Their minds were open and relaxed, deciding what to eat for dinner, and discussing the news from the city. But one mind worried about the sounds from the jungle below. Something wasn't right. Someone strange was there. Possible danger. *Who's in my mind?*

I snapped back to myself. Irys stared at me.

"They live in the trees?" I asked.

She nodded. "But remember Yelena, just because someone's mind is receptive to your probing doesn't mean you're permitted to dive into their deeper thoughts. That's a breach of our Ethical Code."

Her words were harsh, the master level magician scolding her student.

"Sorry," I said.

She shook her head. "I forget that you're still learning. We need to get to the Citadel and begin your training, but I'm afraid this stop will take some time."

"Why?"

"I can't leave you with your family like I did for the other children, and it would be cruel to take you away too soon."

Just then, a loud voice from above called out, "Venettaden."

Irys swung her arm up and mumbled something, but my muscles froze before I could repel the magic that engulfed us. I couldn't move. After a frantic moment of panic, I calmed my mind. I tried to build a mental wall of defense, but the magic that ensnared me knocked down my mental bricks as fast as I could stack them.

Irys, however, was unaffected. She yelled into the treetops. "We're friends of the Zaltanas. I'm Irys of the Jewelrose Clan, Fourth Magician in the Council."

Another strange word echoed from the trees. My legs trembled as the magic released me and I sank to the ground to wait for the faintness to pass. The twins, Gracena and Nickeely collapsed together, moaning. May rubbed her legs.

"Why have you come, Irys Jewelrose?" the voice above asked.

"I believe I may have found your lost daughter," she replied.

A rope ladder descended through the branches.

"Let's go, girls," Irys said. "Here, Yelena, hold the bottom while we climb."

A peevish thought about who would hold the ladder for me flashed through my mind. Irys's annoyed voice admonished me in my own head. *Yelena, you will have no trouble getting into the trees. Perhaps I should have them raise the ladder when it's your turn to climb, as you might prefer to use your grapple and rope.*

She was right, of course. I had used the trees to hide from

my enemies in Ixia without the convenience of a ladder. And even now, I'd enjoyed an occasional "walk" through the treetops to keep my skills honed.

Irys smiled at me. *Perhaps it's in your blood.*

My stomach filled with unease as I remembered Mogkan. He had said I was cursed with Zaltana blood. I'd no reason to trust the now-dead southern magician, though, and I'd been avoiding asking Irys questions about the Zaltanas so I wouldn't get my hopes up about being a part of their family. Even while dying, I knew Mogkan would have been capable of pulling one last spiteful trick.

Mogkan and General Brazell's son, Reyad, had kidnapped me along with over thirty other children from Sitia. Averaging two children a year, they had brought the girls and boys north to Brazell's "orphanage" in the Territory of Ixia for use in their twisted plans. All of the children had the potential of becoming magicians because they had been born to families with strong magic.

Irys had explained to me that magical powers were a gift, and only a handful of magicians came from each clan. "Of course, the more magicians in a family," Irys had said, "the greater chance of having more in the next generation. Mogkan took a risk kidnapping children so young—magical powers don't manifest until a child reaches maturity."

"Why were there more girls than boys?" I had asked.

"Only thirty percent of our magicians are males, and Bain Bloodgood is the only one to achieve master level status."

As I steadied the rope ladder that hung from the jungle's canopy, I now wondered how many Zaltanas were magicians. Beside me, the three girls tucked the hems of their dresses into their belts. Irys helped May start up the rope rungs, and then Gracena and Nickeely followed.

When we had crossed the border into Sitia, the girls hadn't hesitated to exchange their northern uniforms for the bright multicolored, cotton dresses worn by some of the southern women. The boys switched their uniforms for simple cotton pants and tunics. I, on the other hand, had kept my food taster's uniform on until the heat and humidity had driven me to purchase a pair of boy's cotton pants and a shirt.

After Irys disappeared into the green canopy, I set my boot on the bottom rung. My feet felt as if they were swollen with water, weighing me down. Reluctance clung to my legs as I dragged them up the ladder. In midair, I paused. What if these people didn't want me? What if they didn't believe I was their lost daughter? What if I was too old to be bothered with?

All the children who had already found their homes had been immediately accepted. Between the ages of seven and thirteen, they had been separated from their families for only a few years. Physical resemblances, ages, and even names had made it easy to place them. Now, we were down to four. The identical twins, Gracena and Nickeely were thirteen. May was the youngest at twelve, and I was the oldest of the group at twenty.

According to Irys, the Zaltanas had lost a six-year-old girl over fourteen years prior. That was a long time to be away. I was no longer a child.

Yet I was the oldest one who had survived Brazell's plans and remained whole. When the other kidnapped children reach maturity, those who had developed magical powers had been tortured until they surrendered their souls to Mogkan and Reyad. Mogkan had then used the magic of these now mindless captives to enhance his own, making the children nothing more than living bodies without souls.

Irys bore the burden of informing the families of these children, but I felt some guilt by being the only one to survive Mogkan's efforts to capture my soul. The effort, though, cost me a great deal.

Thinking about my struggles in Ixia led to thoughts of Valek. An ache for him chewed at my heart. Hooking an arm around the ladder, I fingered the butterfly pendant he had carved for me. Perhaps I could devise a way to return to Ixia. After all, the magic in my body no longer flared out of control, and I would much rather be with him than among these strange southerners who lived in the trees. Even the name of the south, Sitia, felt thick as rancid syrup in my mouth.

"Yelena, come on," Irys called down to me. "We're waiting."

I swallowed hard and ran a hand over my long braid, smoothing my black hair and pulling out the few viney tendrils that clung to it. Despite the long trek through the jungle, I wasn't too tired. While shorter than most Ixians at five feet four inches, my body had transformed from emaciated to muscular during my last year in Ixia. The difference had been in my living arrangements. From starving in the dungeon to tasting food for Commander Ambrose, my situation had improved for my physical well-being, but I couldn't say the same for my mental well-being during that time.

I shook my head, banishing those thoughts and concentrating on my immediate circumstances. Climbing up the rest of the ladder, I expected it to end at a wide branch or a platform in the tree like a landing on a staircase. Instead, I entered a room.

I looked around in amazement. The walls and ceiling of the room were formed by branches and limbs that had been roped together. Sunlight leaked in between the gaps. Bundled sticks had been worked into chairs that had cushions made of leaves. The small room held only four seats.

"Is this her?" a tall man asked Irys. His cotton tunic and short pants were the color of the tree's leaves. Green gel had been combed into his hair and smeared over all his exposed skin. A bow and a quiver of arrows hung over his shoulder. I guessed he was the guard. Why, though, would he need a weapon if he was the magician who had frozen us? Then again, Irys had deflected that spell with ease. Could she turn aside an arrow, as well?

"Yes," Irys said to the man.

"We've heard rumors at the market, and wondered if you would pay us a visit, Fourth Magician. Please, stay here," he said. "I'll get the Elder."

Irys sank into one of the chairs, and the girls explored the room, exclaiming over the view from the single window. I paced the narrow space. The guard seemed to disappear through the wall, but upon investigation, I discovered a gap that led to a bridge also made of branches.

"Sit down," Irys said to me. "Relax. You're safe here."

"Even with that heartwarming reception?" I countered.

"Standard procedure. Unaccompanied visitors are extremely rare. With the constant danger of jungle predators, most travelers hire a Zaltana guide. You've been edgy and defensive ever since I told you we were headed to the Zaltana's village."

Irys pointed at my legs. "You're in a fighting stance, prepared for attack. These people are your family. Why would they want to hurt you?"

I realized that I had pulled my weapon off my back, and was clutching it in the ready position. With effort, I relaxed my posture.

"Sorry." I threaded the bow, a five-foot wooden staff, back into its holder on the side of my backpack.

Fear of the unknown had caused me to clench. For as long as I could remember in Ixia, I had been told my family was dead. Lost to me forever. Even so, I used to dream of finding an adopted family who would love and care for me. I had only given up that fantasy when I had been turned into Mogkan and Reyad's experiment, and now that I had Valek, I felt I didn't need a family.

"That's not true, Yelena," Irys said aloud. "Your family will help you discover who you are and why. You need them more than you know."

"I thought you said it was against your Ethical Code to

read someone's mind." I rankled at her intrusion on my private thoughts.

"We are linked as teacher and student. You freely gave me a pathway to your mind by accepting me as your mentor. It would be easier to divert a waterfall than to break our link."

"I don't remember creating a pathway," I grumbled.

"If there was a conscious effort in making a link, it wouldn't have happened." She watched my face for a while. "You gave me your trust and your loyalty. That was all that was needed to forge a bond. While I won't pry into your intimate thoughts and memories, I can pick up on your surface emotions."

I opened my mouth to reply, but the green-haired guard returned.

"Follow me," he said.

We wound our way through the treetops. Hallways and bridges connected room after room high above the land. There had been no hint of this maze of dwellings from the ground. We didn't see or meet a soul as we passed around bedrooms and through living areas. From glimpses into the rooms, I saw they were decorated with items found in the jungle. Coconut shells, nuts, berries, grasses, twigs and leaves were all artfully arranged into wall hangings, book covers, boxes and statues. Someone had even fashioned an exact replica of one of those long-tailed animals by using white and black stones glued together.

"Irys," I said, pointing to the statue, "what are those animals?"

"Valmurs. Very intelligent and playful. There are millions of them in the jungle. They're curious, too. Remember how they spied on us from the trees?"

I nodded, recalling the little creatures that never stood still long enough for me to study. In other rooms, I spotted more animal replicas made from different colored stones. A hollowness touched my throat as I thought of Valek and the animals he carved out of rocks. I knew he would appreciate the crafts-manship of these stone statues. Perhaps I could send one to him.

I didn't know when I'd ever be able to see him again. The Com-mander had exiled me to Sitia when he had discovered I possessed magical powers. If I returned to Ixia, the Commander's order of execution would be in effect, but he had never said I couldn't com-municate with my friends in Ixia.

I soon found out why we hadn't encountered anyone on our journey through the village. We entered a large, round com-mon room where about two hundred people gathered. It ap-peared the entire settlement was here. People filled the benches of carved wood that circled a huge fire pit made of stone.

Talk ceased the minute we entered. All eyes focused on me. My skin crawled. I felt as if they were examining every inch of my face, my clothes and my muddy boots. From their ex-pressions, I gathered I wasn't meeting expectations. I stifled the desire to hide behind Irys. Regret that I hadn't asked Irys more questions about the Zaltanas thumped in my chest.

At last, an older man stepped forward. "I'm Bavol Cacao Zaltana, Elder Councilman for the Zaltana family. Are you Yelena Liana Zaltana?"

I hesitated. That name sounded so formal, so connected, so foreign. "My name is Yelena," I said.

A young man a few years older than I pushed through the crowd. He stopped next to the Elder. Squinting hard, his jade-eyed gaze bore into mine. A mixture of hatred and revulsion creased his face. I felt a slight touch of magic brush my body.

"She has killed," he called out. "She reeks of blood."

2

A collective gasp sounded from the crowd of Zaltanas. Abhorrence and outrage gripped the now hostile faces in the room. I found myself behind Irys, hoping to block the negative force emanating from so many eyes.

"Leif, you always tend toward the dramatic," Irys admonished the young man. "Yelena's had a hard life. Don't judge what you don't know."

Leif wilted before Irys's gaze.

"I reek of blood, too. Do I not?" she asked.

"But you're the Fourth Magician," Leif said.

"So you know what I've done and why. I suggest you find out what your sister has had to deal with in Ixia before you accuse her."

His jaw tightened. The muscles on his neck pulled taut as he swallowed what might have been a reply. I risked another peek around the room. Now contemplative, worried and even sheepish looks peppered the group. The Zaltana women wore sleeveless dresses or skirts and short-sleeved blouses with bright floral patterns on them. The hemlines reached to their knees. The men of the clan wore light-colored tunics and plain pants.

All the Zaltanas were barefoot, and most had lean builds and bronze skin.

Then Irys's words sank in. I grabbed her arm. *Brother? I have a brother?*

One side of her mouth quirked up. *Yes. A brother. Your only sibling. You would have known this if you hadn't changed the subject every time I tried to tell you about the Zaltanas.*

Great. My luck was holding steady. I had thought my troubles were over when I had left the Territory of Ixia. Why should any of this surprise me? While all the other Sitians lived in villages on the ground, my family resided in the trees. I studied Leif, searching for a resemblance. His stocky muscular build and square face stood out compared to the rest of the lithe clan. Only his black hair and green eyes matched my own features.

During the awkward moments that followed, I wished for an invisibility spell, and reminded myself to ask Irys if there was such a spell.

An older woman about my height approached us. As she neared she shot Leif a powerful glance, and he hung his head. Without warning, she embraced me. I flinched for a heartbeat, uncertain. Her hair smelled like lilacs.

"I've wanted to do this for fourteen years," she said, hugging me tighter. "How my arms have ached for my little girl."

Those words transported me back in time, shrunk me down into a six-year-old child. Wrapping my arms around this woman, I bawled. Fourteen years without a mother had made me believe I could be stoic when I finally met her. During the journey south, I had imagined I would be curious and unemotional. *Nice to make your acquaintance, but we really need to get to the Citadel.* But I was woefully unprepared for the torrent of emotions that racked my body. I clung to her as if she alone kept me from drowning.

From a distance, I heard Bavol Cacao. "Everyone get back to work. The Fourth Magician is our guest. We need a proper feast for tonight. Petal, make up the guest rooms. We'll need five beds."

The buzz of voices filling the common area disbursed. The room was almost empty when the woman—my mother—released me from her arms. It was still difficult to match her oval face to the title of "Mother." After all, she might not be my real mother. And if she were, did I have the right to call her by that name after so many years away?

"Your father will be so pleased," she said. She pulled a strand of black hair from her face. Streaks of gray painted her long braids, and her pale green eyes shone with unshed tears.

"How do you know?" I asked. "I may not be your—"

"Your soul fits the void in my soul perfectly. I've no doubt you're mine. I hope you'll call me Mother, but if you can't you can call me Perl."

I wiped at my face with the handkerchief Irys handed me. Glancing around, I looked for my father. Father. Another word that threatened to ruin what little dignity I had remaining.

"Your father's out collecting samples," Perl said, seeming to read my mind. "He'll be back as soon as word reaches him." Perl turned her head. I followed her gaze and saw Leif standing near us; his arms crossed over his chest and his hands bunched into fists. "You've met your brother. Don't just stand there, Leif. Come give your sister a proper greeting."

"I can't stand the smell," he said. He turned his back on us and stalked away.

"Don't mind him," my mother said. "He's overly sensitive. He had trouble dealing with your disappearance. He was blessed with strong magic, but his magic is..." She paused. "Unique. He can sense where and what a person has been doing. Not specifics, but general feelings. The Council calls on him to help solve crimes and disputes, and to determine if a person is guilty or not." She shook her head. "Those Zaltanas with magical powers have un-usual abilities. What about you, Yelena? I feel the magic coursing through you." A brief smile touched her lips. "My own limited ability. What is your talent?"

I glanced at Irys for help.

"Her magic was forced from her and was uncontrolled until recently. We have yet to determine her specialty."

Color drained from my mother's face. "Forced?"

I touched her sleeve. "It's all right."

Perl bit her lip. "Could she flame out?" she asked Irys.

"No. I have taken her under my wing. She has gained some measure of control. Although, she must come to the Magician's Keep so I can teach her more about her magic."

My mother grabbed my arms hard. "You must tell me *every-thing* that has happened to you since you were taken from us."

"I…" A trapped feeling seized my throat.

Bavol Cacao stepped to my rescue. "The Zaltanas are honored that you have chosen one of ours as your student, Fourth Magician. Please let me escort your party to your rooms so you may freshen up and rest before the feast."

Relief coursed through me, although the determined set to my mother's jaw warned that she was not yet finished with me. Her grip tightened when Irys and the three girls moved to follow Bavol Cacao to our rooms.

"Perl, you'll have plenty of time to spend with your daughter," he said. "She's home now."

She released me, stepping back. "I'll see you tonight. I'll ask your cousin Nutty to lend you some decent clothes for the feast."

I grinned as we worked our way to the guest rooms. With all that had happened today, my mother had still managed to notice the clothes I wore.

The feast that night began as a sedate dinner, but then transformed into a party despite the fact that I might have offended my hosts by first tasting the many fruit dishes and seasoned cold meats for poisons before I ate. Old habits die hard.

The night air filled with the scent of burning citronella mixed with a damp earthy smell. After the meal, various Zaltanas pulled out musical instruments made of bamboo and twine, some jumped up to dance and others sang with the music. All the while, petite furry valmurs swung from the ceiling rafters and hopped from table to table. Some of my cousins had made pets of them. Splashes of black and white and orange and brown sat on their shoulders and heads. Other valmurs tumbled in the corners or stole food from the tables. May and the twins were delighted with the animals' long-tailed antics. Gracena tried to tempt a little tan-and-gold valmur to eat from her hand.

My mother sat next to me. Leif hadn't come to the feast. I wore a bright yellow and purple lily-patterned dress that Nutty had loaned me. The only reason I wore the obnoxious thing was to please Perl.

I thanked fate that Ari and Janco, my soldier friends from Ixia, weren't here. They would be rolling with laughter to see me wearing such a gaudy outfit. But oh, how I missed them. I changed my mind, wishing they were here; it would be worth the embarrassment just to see the glint in Janco's eyes.

"We need to leave in a few days," Irys said to Bavol over the din of voices and music. Her comment caused a mood-dampening ripple in those around us.

"Why do you have to leave so soon?" my mother asked. Dismay creased her eyebrows tight together.

"I need to get the other girls home, and I've been away from the Citadel and the Keep for too long."

The tired sadness in Irys's voice reminded me that she hadn't seen her family for nearly a year. Hiding and spying in the Territory of Ixia had drained her.

Our table was quiet for a while. Then my mother brightened. "You can leave Yelena here while you take the girls home."

"It will be out of her way to come back for Yelena," Bavol Cacao said.

Mother frowned at him. I could see her thoughts whirling behind her eyes. "Aha! Leif can take Yelena to the Citadel. He has business with the First Magician in two weeks."

Emotions rolled through my chest. I wanted to stay, but I feared being separated from Irys. They were my family, yet they were strangers. I couldn't help being wary; it was a skill learned in Ixia. And traveling with Leif seemed as unpalatable as drinking a wine laced with poison.

Before anyone could agree or disagree, Mother said, "Yes. That will do." She ended all discussion on the matter.

The next morning I had a small panic attack when Irys pulled on her backpack. "Don't leave me here alone," I pleaded.

"You're not alone. I counted thirty-five cousins and a whole mess of aunts and uncles." She laughed. "Besides, you should spend some time with your family. You need to learn not to distrust them. I'll meet you at the Magician's Keep. It's within the Citadel's walls. In the meantime, keep practicing your control."

"Yes, sir."

May gave me a big hug. "Your family is so much fun. I hope my family lives in the trees, too," she said.

I smoothed her braids. "I'll try to visit you sometime."

Irys said, "May might be at the Citadel's school this cooling season if she can access the power source."

"That would be great!" May cried out with delight. The twins both gave me a quick hug.

"Good luck," Gracena said with a grin. "You're going to need it."

I followed them down the rope ladder and into the cooler air of the jungle floor to say goodbye. Watching Irys and the girls fight their way through the tight trail, I kept my eyes on them until they were out of sight. In their absence, my body felt paper-thin and in danger of being shredded by the light breeze.

In order to delay my return to the treetops, I studied my surroundings. The jungle's canopy above showed no evidence of the Zaltana dwellings, and the thick vegetation all around prevented me from seeing too far in any direction. Even with the loud clamor of insects, I could hear the faint sound of water rushing and lapping nearby. But I couldn't push past the growth to find the source.

Frustrated, sweaty and tired of being a meal for every mosquito, I gave up and climbed the rope ladder. Back in the warm and dry forest canopy, and among the labyrinth of rooms, I quickly became lost.

Unrecognizable faces nodded or smiled at me. Others frowned and turned away. I had no idea where my room was, or what I was supposed to be doing, and I didn't want to ask. The thought of telling my mother my life story was unappealing. Inevitable, I knew, but too much to bear at this moment. It had taken me almost a year to trust Valek with my history—how could I divulge my struggles to someone I'd just met?

So I wandered here and there, searching for a view of the "river" I had heard on the jungle floor. Large expanses of green filled every vista. Several times, I spotted the gray smoothness of a mountainside. Irys had told me the Illiais Jungle grew in a deep valley. Tucked into the crooks of the Daviian Plateau's edge, the odd-shaped jungle was below the plateau's rim, leaving only one side open for travelers.

"Very defensible," Irys had said. "It's impossible to scale the walls to reach the plateau."

I was fooling around and testing my balance on a rope bridge when a voice startled me and I had to grab the handrail.

"What?" I tried to reestablish my footing.

"I said, what are you doing?" Nutty stood at the end of the bridge.

Sweeping an arm out, I said, "Taking in the view."

I could tell by her dubious expression that I hadn't convinced her. "Follow me if you want to see a real view." Nutty bounded away.

I scrambled to keep up with her as she took shortcuts through the tree branches. Her thin arms and legs reached and grabbed vines with such flexibility that she reminded me of a valmur. When she entered a spot of sunlight, her maple-colored hair and skin glowed.

I had to admit there was one good thing about staying in the south. Instead of being the only person with tan skin, I finally looked as if I belonged. Living in the north with the pale-skinned Ixians for so long, though, had not prepared me for such a variety of brown skin tones. Much to my embarrassment, I had found myself gawking at the deeper mahogany skin colors when we had first entered Sitia.

Nutty stopped suddenly, and I almost knocked into her. We stood on a square platform in the tallest tree in the jungle. Nothing blocked the view.

An emerald carpet stretched out below us, ending at two sheer rock faces that angled toward each other. Where the two cliffs joined, a vast waterfall poured forth, ending in a cloud of mist. Beyond the top edge of the rock cliffs, I saw a flat expanse. A mixture of tans, yellows, golds and browns painted the smooth landscape.

"Is that the Daviian Plateau?" I asked.

"Yep. Nothing lives there but wild prairie grass. They don't get a lot of rain. Beautiful, huh?"

"An understatement."

Nutty nodded, and we stood for a while in silence. Finally, my curiosity broke the lull in conversation. I asked Nutty questions about the jungle, and eventually wove the conversation around to the Zaltana family.

"Why do they call you Nutty?" I asked.

She shrugged. "My real name is Hazelnut Palm Zaltana, but everybody's called me Nutty since I was little."

"So Palm is your middle name."

"No." Nutty swung down over the edge of the platform and into the tree branches that supported it. The leaves shook and after a moment, she climbed back. She handed me a group of brown nuts. "Palm, as in palm tree, is my family's name. Zaltana is the clan name. Everyone who marries us has to take that name, but within the clan there are different families. Here, crack them like this..." Nutty took one of the nuts and banged it on a nearby branch, revealing an inner nib.

"Your family is Liana, which means 'vine.' Yelena means 'shining one.' Everyone is either named after something in the jungle or their name means something in the old Illiais language, which we're forced to learn." Nutty rolled her eyes in exasperation. "You're lucky you missed that." She poked me with a finger. "And you missed having to deal with obnoxious older brothers, too! I once got into trouble for tying mine up in a vine and leaving him hanging... Oh, snake spit! I forgot. Come on." She hurried back through the trees.

"Forgot what?" I asked, scrambling after her.

"I was supposed to take you to your mother. She's been looking for you all morning." Nutty slowed only slightly to negotiate a rope bridge. "Uncle Esau's back from expedition."

Another family member to meet. I considered "accidentally" losing her. But remembering the hostile glares that I had received from some of my cousins, I stayed with Nutty. When I caught up to her, I grabbed her arm.

"Wait," I panted. "I want to know why so many Zaltanas frown at me. Is it the blood smell?"

"No. Everyone knows Leif can see gloom and doom in everything. He's always looking for attention." She gestured at me. "Most of them think you're not really a Zaltana, but a spy from Ixia."

3

"You're joking, right?" I asked. "They don't really believe I'm a spy."

Nutty nodded. Her ponytails, one on each side of her head, bobbed in contrast to her serious face. "That's the gossip. Although, no one would dare breathe a word of that to Aunt Perl or Uncle Esau."

"Why would they think such a thing?"

Her light brown eyes widened as if she couldn't believe my stupidity. "Look at your clothes." She gestured at my black pants and white shirt. "We all know northerners are forced to wear uniforms. They say if you were truly from the south, you wouldn't want to wear pants ever again."

I glanced at Nutty's orange skirt. The hem was tucked up into her brown fur belt and she wore a pair of short yellow pants underneath.

Ignoring my stare, she said, "And you carry a weapon."

That much was true. I had my bow with me in case I found a place to practice, but, so far, the only space big enough had been the common room and that was always too crowded. Now was probably not the best time to tell Nutty about the switch-blade strapped to my thigh.

"Who's been saying these things?" I asked.

She shrugged. "Different people."

I waited. The silence drove the information out of her.

"Leif's telling everyone that you don't feel right to him. He says he would know his own sister." She fidgeted with her sleeve, rolling up the bright cotton fabric. "Sitians are always worried that the Commander will attack us someday, and we think northern spies are gathering information on our ability to defend ourselves. Even though Leif tends to overreact, his magic is strong, so almost everyone believes you're a spy."

"What do you think?"

"I don't know. I was going to wait and see." She looked down at her bare feet. They were tanned and callused.

Another reason I stood out among the Zaltanas. I still wore my leather boots.

"That's very smart," I said.

"Do you think so?"

"Yes."

Nutty smiled. Her light brown eyes lit up. I noticed a sprinkle of freckles across her small nose. She continued to lead the way to my mother.

As I followed, I thought about the accusations that I was an Ixian spy. I wasn't a spy, but I couldn't say that I was a true southerner, either. And I wasn't sure I wanted to be called a Sitian. My reasons for being in the south were twofold: to avoid being executed and to learn how to use my magic. Meeting my family had been a bonus, and I wasn't going to let some petty rumors ruin my time here. I decided to ignore any more sidelong glances for now.

There was no ignoring my mother's fury, though, when Nutty and I reached her residence. Every muscle in her thin arms and long neck was pulled taut. Waves of unspoken anger pulsed from the petite woman.

"Where have you been?" she demanded.

"Well, I saw Irys off, and then…" The explanation seemed weak in the face of her outrage, so I stopped.

"You've been gone from me for fourteen years, and we have only two weeks together before you go again. How could you be so selfish?" Without warning she crumpled into a chair as if all her energy had been pulled from her.

"I'm sorry…" I started.

"No, I'm sorry," she said. "It's just that your speech and manners are so foreign. And your father's back and anxious to see you. Leif's been driving me crazy, and I don't want my daughter to leave here feeling like she's still a stranger."

I hugged myself, feeling guilty and inadequate. She was asking for a great deal; I was sure to fail her in some way.

"Your father wanted to wake you in the middle of the night. I made him wait, and he's been searching the homestead all morning," Perl explained. "I finally sent him upstairs with something to do." She swung her arms wide. "You'll have to forgive us if we go too fast for you. Your arrival was so unexpected and I should have insisted you stay with us last night, but Irys warned us not to smother you." She took a deep breath. "But it's killing me. All I want to do is wrap you in my arms." Instead, her arms dropped into her lap, resting on the blue-and-white fabric of her sleeveless dress.

I couldn't reply. Irys had been right; I needed time before I would feel comfortable with the whole family dynamic, but I could also empathize with my mother. Each day, I missed Valek more than the day before. Losing a child had to be much worse.

Standing by the door, Nutty pulled at her ponytails. My mother seemed to realize she was there. "Nutty, can you fetch Yelena's things from the guest quarters and bring them here?"

"Sure thing, Aunt Perl. I'll have them here faster than a curari bat can paralyze a valmur." In a flash of orange, Nutty was gone.

"You can stay in our extra room." My mother pressed her hand to her throat. "It's your room actually."

My room. It sounded so normal. I had never had a place of my own before. I tried to imagine how I might have decorated it and made it my own, but I came up with a blank. My life in Ixia hadn't included special items such as toys, gifts or art. I stifled a bark of laughter. My only private room had been my dungeon cell.

Perl jumped from her seat. "Yelena, please sit down. I'll get us some lunch. You have no meat on your bones." As she hurried away, she called toward the ceiling, "Esau, Yelena's here. Come down for tea."

Alone, I glanced around the sitting area. The warm air smelled faintly of apples. The couch and two armchairs appeared to be made from ropes woven together, yet they were hard to the touch. The furniture was unlike the other Zaltana chairs I had seen, which were constructed with branches and sticks tied together.

I settled into an armchair; the red leaf-patterned cushions crunched under my weight, and I wondered what had been stuffed inside them. My gaze lingered on a black wooden bowl on a small glass-topped table in front of the couch. The bowl looked to be hand carved. I tried to relax, which worked until I saw a long counter against the back wall.

Stretching across the length of the countertop was a series of odd-shaped bottles connected by loops of tubes. Unlit candles sat under some of the containers. The configuration reminded me of Reyad's lab. The memory of his collection of glass jars and metal instruments unnerved me. Visions of being chained to a bed while Reyad searched for the perfect torture device caused sweat to roll down my neck and my heart to squeeze. I berated myself for my overactive imagination. It was ridiculous that a similar contraption could make me recoil after two years.

I forced myself closer. Amber liquid pooled in a few bottles.

I picked up one and swirled the contents. A strong apple scent filled my nose. The memory of swinging and laughter floated into my mind. The image disappeared when I focused on it. Frustrated, I set the bottle down.

The shelves behind the table were lined with rows of more bottles. The contraption looked like a still for making alcohol. Perhaps the liquid was an apple brandy like General Rasmussen's of Military District 7 in Ixia.

I heard my mother return, and turned around. She held a tray full of cut fruit, berries and some tea. Placing the lunch on the small table before the couch, she gestured for me to join her.

"Found my distillery, I see," she said as if every Zaltana had one in their living room. "Smell anything familiar?"

"Brandy?" I guessed.

Her shoulders drooped just a bit, but her smile didn't waver. "Try again."

Putting my nose over one of the amber-filled bottles, I inhaled. The scent blanketed me in feelings of comfort and safety. It also choked and smothered. Memories of bouncing mixed with the image of lying on my back, clawing at my throat. I suddenly felt light-headed.

"Yelena, sit down." My mother's hand was on my elbow, guiding me to a chair. "You shouldn't have breathed in so deeply. It's very concentrated." She kept her hand on my shoulder.

"What is it?" I asked.

"My Apple Berry perfume."

"Perfume?"

"You don't remember." This time her disappointment showed as her smile faded from her lips. "I wore it all the time when you were a child. It's my best-selling perfume—very popular with the magicians at the Keep. When you disappeared, I couldn't wear it anymore." Her hand touched her throat again as if she were trying to block either her words or emotions.

With the word "magicians" my windpipe tightened. The scene of my brief abduction at the Fire Festival the previous year played in my mind. The tents, the darkness and the smell of Apple Berry mixed with the taste of ashes and the image of Irys ordering four men to strangle me to death.

"Does Irys wear your perfumes?" I asked.

"Oh, yes. Apple Berry is her favorite. In fact, she asked me last night to make her more. Does the scent remind you of her?"

"She must have worn it the first time we met," I said, choosing not to say more. If it hadn't been for Valek's timely arrival, Irys would have succeeded in killing me. It was ironic how both my relationships with Irys and Valek began badly.

"I have found that certain smells are linked to specific memories. It's something Leif and I have been working on as part of his project with First Magician. We've created a variety of scents and odors that we use to help victims of crime remember. These memories are very powerful, and they help Leif get a clearer picture of what happened to them." She moved away from me. Sitting down, she spooned fruit into three bowls. "I had hoped the Apple Berry would trigger your memories of us."

"I did get something, but…" I stopped, unable to put the brief impressions into words. I quelled my growing aggravation at being unable to recall anything from my six years of living here. Instead, I asked, "Do you make many perfumes?"

"Oh, yes," she said. "Esau brings me wonderful flowers and plants to use. I enjoy making new perfumes and scents."

"And she's the best in the land," a booming male voice said behind me. I turned to see a small, stout man enter the room. His resemblance to Leif was unmistakable.

"Her perfumes have been worn by Master Magicians, as well as the Queen and Princess of Ixia when they were alive," Esau boasted. He grabbed my wrists and pulled me upright. "Yelena, my child, look how you've grown." He squeezed me in a bear hug that lasted several seconds.

A strong odor of earth filled my nose. He released me, sat down with a bowl of fruit in his lap and a cup of tea in his hand before I could react. Perl handed me the other bowl as I resumed my seat.

Esau's uncombed gray hair fell to his shoulders. As he ate, I saw that the lines on his hands were stained dark green.

"Esau, have you been playing with that leaf oil again?" Perl asked. "No wonder you took so long to come down. Trying to scrub it off so you wouldn't smear it everywhere."

I could tell by the way he ducked his head without responding that this was an old argument. Esau stared at me in silence, squinting and cocking his head from side to side as if deciding on something. His complexion resembled tea without the milk. Deep lines etched his forehead and fanned out from his eyes. He had a kind face used to laughing and crying.

"Now I want a report on what you've been doing all these years," Esau said.

I suppressed a sigh. No more chances to avoid it. Used to obeying orders in the north, I told them about growing up in General Brazell's orphanage in Military District 5. I glossed over the unpleasant years when I had reached maturity and become Reyad and Mogkan's laboratory rat. My parents were distressed enough just hearing about their plans to use their kidnapped victims' magical power to help Brazell overthrow the Commander; I saw no reason to tell them the brutal details of how they had erased the southern children's minds.

When I mentioned becoming Commander Ambrose's food taster, I failed to tell them that I had been in the Commander's dungeon awaiting execution for killing Reyad. And after I had spent a year there, I had been given the choice of the noose or the poison taster's position.

"I bet you were their best taster," my father said.

"What a terrible thing to say," Perl admonished. "What if she were poisoned?"

"We Lianas have a great sense of smell and taste. The girl's here and safe, Perl. If she wasn't good at detecting poisons, I doubt she would have lasted this long."

"It's not like someone was trying to poison the Commander all the time," I said. "Only once, really."

Perl's hand flew to her neck. "Oh, my. I bet it was his pet assassin that tried to poison him. That loathsome creature."

I stared at her uncomprehending.

"You know, his spy, Valek? Every Sitian would love to see that man's head on a pike. He murdered almost the entire royal family. Only one nephew survived. Without Valek, that usurper would have never gained power and upset Sitia's good relationship with Ixia. And those poor northern children who are born with magic. Slaughtered by Valek in their cribs!"

While she shuddered with revulsion, I gaped. My fingers sought the chain around my neck, and found the butterfly pendant Valek had carved for me. I squeezed it. Guess I wouldn't be telling her about my relationship with him. And I decided not to enlighten her about the Commander's policy on Ixians discovered with magical abilities. Not as gruesome as killing babies, but usually ending in death for the unfortunate man or woman. Valek had not been a fan of that policy, but he wouldn't disobey an order from the Commander. Perhaps, in time, Valek would help the Commander see the benefits of having magicians on his staff.

"Valek isn't as horrible as you think," I said, trying to redeem his reputation. "He was instrumental in uncovering Brazell and Mogkan's plans. In fact, he helped to stop them." I wanted to add "he saved my life twice," but the twin grimaces of loathing on my parents' faces stopped me.

So much for my effort. He was *the* villain of Sitia, and it would take more than words to change his status. I couldn't say I blamed my parents. When I had first met Valek, I feared his reputation, having no clue about the fierce loyalty, sense of fairness and willingness to sacrifice himself for others that lurked beneath his reputation.

I thanked fate when Nutty barged in with my backpack swinging from her hands.

Esau took it from her. "Thanks, Nut," he said, tugging one of her ponytails.

"Welcome, Saw." She punched him lightly in the stomach, and then danced out of reach as he swung to grab her. Sticking her tongue out at him, she skipped toward the door.

"Next time, Nut, I'm going to crack you."

Her laugh echoed. "You can try." And she was gone.

"Let me show you to your room," Esau said to me.

As I turned to follow him, Perl said, "Yelena, wait. Tell me what happened to Brazell's plans?"

"Thwarted. He's in the Commander's dungeon."

"And Reyad and Mogkan?"

I took a breath. "Dead." I waited for her to ask me who had killed them, and I wondered if I would tell her about my role in both of their deaths.

She nodded with satisfaction. "Good."

Esau and Perl's living quarters had two floors, and instead of a ladder or staircase to connect them, Esau used what he called a lift. I had never seen anything like it before. We stood in a closet-size room. Two thick ropes went through holes in the floor and ceiling. Esau pulled on one of the ropes, and the wooden room rose. I put my hand on the wall, but the motion was smooth. Eventually, we ascended to the second floor.

Esau poked his head back into the lift when I failed to follow him out. "Like it?" he asked.

"It's great."

"One of my designs. Pulleys are the key," he explained. "You won't find many in the Zaltana homestead. The others are slow to change, but I've sold a ton at the market."

"Does Perl sell her perfumes at the market, as well?" I asked as I stepped onto the landing.

"Yep. Most of the Zaltanas either sell or exchange goods at the Illiais Market. It's open all year. My inventions and Perl's perfumes have provided us with a plentiful source of income." Esau talked as we walked down the hallway. "A group of Zaltanas will make a trip to the market when enough items have been made or when a special order's due. We aren't the only ones who sell there, either, so if we want something, we'll go and buy. Unfortunately, not everything we need can be found in the jungle. Like your mother's glass bottles and the hardware for my chairs."

"You designed the rope furniture, too?"

"Yep. Except they're not ropes. They're lianas." When understanding failed to brighten my face, he explained, "Vines from the jungle."

"Oh."

"The lianas are a constant source of trouble. Probably why they're our family name." Esau grinned. "They grow everywhere, and they can pull trees over. We have to keep them trimmed or cut them down. One day, instead of burning them, I took a bunch home and tried working with them." Esau pulled back a cotton curtain that covered an entrance on the right side of the hallway. He gestured for me to precede him into a room.

"The vines become very strong when dried. While they're pliable, they can be woven into almost anything."

At first, I thought we had entered a storeroom. The air held a slight musty odor, and rows and rows of shelves holding glass containers of every size obscured the walls. The bottles were filled with various tinted substances. Only when I pulled my gaze away from the colorful collection did I see a small bed made from lianas and a wooden bureau.

Esau ducked his head. He ran a green-stained hand through his hair. "Sorry. I've been using this room to store my samples.

But I cleaned off the bed and desk this morning." He pointed
to a Blackwood desk tucked into a corner.

"It's fine," I said, trying to mask my disappointment. I had
been hoping that this room would help me remember something, anything of my life before Brazell's orphanage.

Laying my backpack on the bed, I asked, "What other rooms
are up here?"

"Our bedroom and my workroom. Come on, I'll show you."

We continued down the hall. There was another curtained
doorway on the left, which led to a big bedroom. This room
had a large bed with a purple flowered quilt, two end tables
and shelves filled with books instead of containers.

Esau pointed to the ceiling, which was made of leather hides
stretched over branches. "I coated it with oil so the rain runs
off," he explained. "No water drips in here, but it does get hot."

Hanging from the middle of the ceiling was a large flower-
shaped fixture made of wood planks. Ropes wrapped around
the base, crossed the ceiling and trailed down the walls. "What's
that?" I asked.

He smiled. "Another invention. Pulleys again and some
weights make the flower spin, cooling the room."

We went out into the hallway. Across from Esau's bedroom
was another bedroom. A plain single bed, dresser and night-
stand were neatly arranged inside. No decorations, inventions
or other signs of its occupant were evident.

"Leif lives at the Magician's Keep most of the year," Esau said.

We continued down the hall, which ended in a spacious
room. I grinned as I looked around. Esau's workroom was
stuffed full with plants, containers, piles of leaves and tools.
Shelves groaned under the weight of many jars filled with
strange items and various liquids. Walking into the room without bumping a shin seemed impossible. The clutter reminded
me of Valek's office and apartment. While Valek had books,

papers and rocks piled everywhere, Esau had invited the jungle to reside with him.

I stood in the doorway for a moment.

"Come in, come in." He walked past me. "I want to show you something."

Taking my time, I threaded my way toward him. "What do you do here?"

"This and that," he said as he searched through a pile of papers on a table. "I like to collect samples from the jungle and see what I can cook up. Found some medicines. Found some foods. Flowers for your mother. Aha!" He held up a white notebook. "Here."

I took the book, but my attention was on the room as I searched for something familiar. The words "my mother" had triggered the feeling of doubt that had plagued me since my arrival at the Zaltana homestead. Finally, I asked Esau the same question I had asked Perl. "How do you know I'm your daughter? You seem so certain."

Esau smiled. "Look in that book."

I opened the cover. On the first page was a charcoal drawing of a baby.

"Keep turning."

The next page had a drawing of a small child. As I turned the pages, the girl grew from a child to an adolescent into someone I recognized. Me. A hard knot gripped my throat as tears threatened to gush from my eyes. My father had loved me even when I was gone and I couldn't even remember anything from my time here. The pictures showed my childhood as it should have been, living here with Esau and Perl.

"It's really fun to flip through the book fast. Watch yourself grow twenty years in a few seconds." Esau took the sketchbook from my hands, and held it open. "See? This is how I know you're mine. I drew your picture every year after your birth, and even after you disappeared." He turned to the last page and studied the portrait there. "I wasn't too far off. It's not perfect, but now that I've seen you I can make corrections."

He tapped the book on his chest. "When you first dis-appeared, your mother carried this book with her, looking through the pictures all day long. Eventually she stopped, but after a couple years, she saw me drawing another picture, and she asked me to destroy it." Esau handed the book to me. "I told her she would never see it again. As far as I know, she hasn't. So let's keep it between us for now. Okay?"

"Sure." I gave each page my full attention. "This is won-derful."

All doubts of my lineage vanished as I took note of the de-tails that my father had put into these pictures. In that moment I knew I was part of the Zaltana clan. A feeling of relief washed through me. I vowed to try harder to make a connection with my parents. Leif, though, was another story.

"You should show your sketchbook to Leif," I said, giving the book back to Esau. "Maybe then he would believe I'm his sister."

"Don't worry about Leif. He doesn't need to see a picture. He knows who you are. It's the shock of your arrival that's thrown him off balance. He had a difficult time with your disappearance."

"Oh, yes. I forgot—I've had it so easy in the north."

Esau grimaced, and I regretted my sarcasm.

"Leif was with you the day you were taken from us," he said in a quiet voice. "You had begged him to take you down to play on the jungle floor. He was eight, which may sound young, but Zaltana children are taught to survive in the jungle as soon as they can walk. Nutty was climbing trees before she took her first steps—it drove my sister crazy."

Esau sat in one of his vine chairs and weariness seemed to settle on him like a coating of dust. "When Leif came home without you, our concern was minimal. A lost child had al-

ways been found within an hour or two. After all, the Illiais
Jungle isn't that big. Predators are not as active during the daytime, and at night we have a few tricks to keep them from our
homestead. But we grew more frantic as the day wore on and
we still hadn't located you. You had disappeared so completely
that everyone thought you had been caught by a necklace snake
or a tree leopard."

"Necklace snake?"

He grinned, and an appreciative glint flashed in his eyes. "A
green-and-brown predator that lives in the trees. Sometimes
fifty feet long, it loops its body over the branches, blending
in with the jungle. When its prey comes close, it wraps itself
around the victim's neck and squeezes." Esau demonstrated
with his hands. "Then it swallows the body whole and feeds
on the carcass for weeks."

"Not pleasant."

"No, and it's impossible to see what is inside the snake unless
you kill them. But their hides are too thick for arrows, and it's
suicide to get close to one. Same with the tree leopard. The cat
drags its kill into its den, another unapproachable site. In the
end, only Leif believed that you were still alive. He thought
you might be hiding somewhere, playing a game. As the rest
of us grieved, Leif searched the jungle for you day after day."

"When did he finally stop?" I asked.

"Yesterday."

4

No wonder Leif was so angry. Fourteen years spent searching, and I hadn't had the decency to let him find me. He alone had believed I was still alive. I regretted every harsh thought I had entertained about him. Until he showed up at the door to Esau's workroom.

"Father," Leif said, ignoring me. "Tell that girl, if she wants to go to the Citadel, I'm leaving in two hours."

"Why so soon?" Esau asked. "You're not due for two weeks!"

"Bavol has received a message from First Magician. Something has happened. I'm needed right away." Leif's chest seemed to inflate with his own sense of importance.

I suppressed the desire to jab him in his solar plexus and knock some of his ego out of him.

When Leif turned on his heel and left, I asked Esau, "Is there anyone else going to the Citadel in the next couple of weeks?"

He shook his head. "It's a long journey. Many days' walk. And most Zaltanas prefer the jungle."

"What about Bavol Cacao? Isn't he our Councilman at the Citadel? Doesn't he have to be there?" Irys had explained that the Council consisted of the four Master Magicians plus a representative from each of the eleven clans. Together they ruled the southern lands.

"No. The Council disbands during the hot season."

"Oh." It was hard to believe they were just starting their hot season. Coming from Ixia during its cold season, the whole southern territory felt as if it were already scorching.

"Can you give me directions?" I asked.

"Yelena, you'll be safer with Leif. Come now, let's pack. Two hours isn't..." Esau stopped, and shot me a glance. "Is that backpack all you have?"

"And my bow."

"Then you need some provisions." Esau began to search his room.

"I don't—" My words were cut short as he handed me a book. It was white like his sketchbook, but inside were drawings of plants and trees with written descriptions beneath.

"What's this?" I asked.

"A field guide. I planned to reteach you how to survive in the jungle, but this will have to do for now."

I found a page with an illustration of an oval-shaped leaf. The instructions below the picture explained that boiling the Tilipi Leaf in water would make a draught that would reduce a fever.

Next, Esau gave me a set of small bowls and some bizarre-looking utensils. "That guide is of little use without the proper equipment. Now let's find your mother." He paused and sighed. "She is not going to be happy."

He was right. We found her working at her distillery and fussing at Leif.

"It's not my fault," Leif said. "If you want her to stay so badly, why don't you take her to the Citadel? Oh, that's right—*you* haven't set your precious little feet on the jungle floor in fourteen years."

Perl spun on Leif with a bottle of perfume clenched in her hand poised to throw. He stepped back. When she spotted

Esau and me standing in the doorway, she went back to filling the bottle.

"Tell that girl I'll be at the bottom of the Palm ladder in two hours," Leif said to Esau. "If she's not there, I'm leaving without her."

When Leif left the room, the silence continued to thicken.

"You'll need some food," my father said, retreating into the kitchen.

Bottles clinking, my mother approached. "Here," she said. "Two bottles of Apple Berry for Irys, and a bottle of Lavender for you."

"Lavender?"

"You loved it when you were five, so I took a chance. We can experiment later and find something else if you'd like."

I opened the cap and sniffed. Again, I experienced no memories of being five, but the scent made me remember the time I had hidden under a table in Valek's office. I had been searching for the recipe to the antidote for Butterfly's Dust, the so-called poison in my body that had been Valek's way to keep me from escaping. Thinking I had needed a daily dose of the antidote to stay alive, I had been intent on finding the cure. Valek had come back early, and discovered me because I had used lavender-scented soap.

I still favored the scent. "This is perfect," I said to Perl. "Thank you."

Unexpected fear flared in Perl's eyes. She clamped her lips and clasped her hands. Taking a deep breath, she declared, "I'm coming with you. Esau, where's my pack?" she asked him as he returned with an armload of food.

"Upstairs in our room," he said.

She rushed past him. If he was surprised by her sudden decision, it didn't show in his expression. I added the bread and fruit he had brought to my pack, and I wrapped the perfume bottles in my cloak. During the journey south, my cloak had been too hot to wear, but it had made a soft place to sleep when we had camped along the road.

"The food will only last so long, and you'll probably need more clothes while you're at the Citadel," Esau said. "Do you have any money?"

I fumbled in my pack. Needing money for food and clothes still seemed odd to me. In the north, we had been provided with all of our basic necessities. I pulled out the bag of Ixian gold coins that Valek had given to me before we parted.

Showing one to Esau, I asked, "Will these work?"

"Put that away." He closed my hand around the coin. "Don't let anyone see that you have them. When you get to the Citadel, ask Irys to exchange them for Sitian money."

"Why?"

"You might be mistaken for a northerner."

"But I am—"

"*You are not.* Most southerners are suspicious of people from Ixia, even the political refugees. You are a Zaltana. Always remember that."

A Zaltana. I worked the name around my mind, wondering if just saying the name would make me one. Somehow I knew it wasn't going to be that easy.

Esau went over to a desk and rummaged through the drawers. I put away Valek's money. With my father's supplies and food, my pack bulged. I made an attempt to organize the contents. Would I need my rope and grapple? Or my northern uniform? While I hoped that I wouldn't have cause to use them, I couldn't bring myself to part with them just yet.

Metal rattled. Esau returned with a handful of silver coins. "It's all I could find, but it should be enough until you get to the Citadel. Now go up and say goodbye to your mother. It's getting late."

"Isn't she coming with us?"

"No. You'll find her on the bed." He said those words with a mixture of resignation and acceptance.

I pondered his words as I pulled the lift up. I found her curled up in a ball on top of the quilt in her bedroom. Perl's body shook as tears soaked into her pillow.

"Next time," she sobbed. "Next time I'm going with Leif to the Citadel. Next time."

"I would like that," I said. Remembering Leif's comment on how she hadn't left the jungle in so long, I added, "I'll come home and see you as soon as I can."

"Next time. I'm doing it next time."

Having decided to delay the trip to the Magician's Keep, Perl calmed. Eventually, she unfurled and stood, smoothing her dress and wiping tears from her cheeks. "Next time, you'll stay with us longer."

It sounded like an order. "Yes, Per... Mother."

The creases of worry disappeared from her face, revealing her beauty. She hugged me tight and whispered, "I don't want to lose you again. Be very careful."

"I will." I meant it. Some hard-learned habits couldn't be broken.

There were only a few exits to the jungle floor. Each exit was named after a family whose residences were nearby. I reached the room that had the Palm ladder. Just as I swung a leg onto the first rung, I heard Nutty's voice. I had already said goodbye to my parents and Bavol Cacao, but hadn't been able to find Nutty anywhere.

"Yelena, wait," Nutty said.

I stopped, looking up in time to see her swinging through the door. She clutched a mass of colorful cloth in one fist.

"I made these—" she paused to catch her breath "—for you."

The light yellow skirt—subdued by Zaltana standards—was

printed with small buttercups, and the shirt was a solid coral color. I eyed the skirt with suspicion. Nutty laughed.

"Look," she said, pulling the skirt apart. "See? It looks like a skirt, but it's really pants. You'll be awfully hot in those black trousers when you cross the plains." She held the waistband up to me as if judging the length. "And this way, you won't stand out so much."

"Clever girl," I said, smiling.

"You like?"

"I like."

She seemed pleased with herself. "I knew it."

"Can you make me some more? Perhaps you can send them with Bavol when he comes?"

"Sure."

I removed my backpack, and searched for some money. "How much?"

Nutty shook her head. "When you get to the Illiais Market, buy some cloth from Fern's stand. Then have her send it to me. I'll need three yards for each set of clothes. I'll make as many as you want."

"But what about wages for your efforts?"

Her ponytails flew as she swung her head no again. "Zaltanas do not charge family. Although…" Her brown eyes glinted. "If anyone should ask who designed your clothes—feel free to give them my name."

"I will. Thanks." I folded my new outfit and stuffed it into my backpack. Then Nutty hugged me goodbye.

The warmth from her body clung to me as I climbed down the ladder. It lasted until the first cold sneer from Leif drove it away.

He waited for me on the jungle floor. Leif had changed into traveling clothes that consisted of a tan cotton tunic, dark brown pants and boots. He carried a large leather pack on his back and a machete hung from his thick belt.

"Keep up or be left behind," he said to the air above my head. Turning his broad back to me, he took off at a brisk clip.

I knew I would soon tire of looking at his back, but, for now, the pace he set was a welcome chance to stretch my legs.

Without another word uttered between us, we traveled on a narrow path through the jungle. Sweat soon soaked my shirt, and I found myself glancing up in search of necklace snakes. Esau had also mentioned tree leopards. I decided I would search Esau's field guide for a picture of the predators when I had some time.

Various birds sang and whistled and animal cries echoed through the leafy canopy. I wanted to know the names of these creatures, but I guessed Leif would ignore my questions.

He stopped once, taking a machete from his belt. Without thought, I grabbed my bow. Snorting in derision, he merely hacked at a small sapling.

"Strangler fig," he huffed over his shoulder.

I made no reply. Should I be honored that he had finally chosen to talk to me?

Leif didn't wait for a response. "A parasite. The strangler fig uses another tree to reach the sunlight. Once there it grows bigger, eventually strangling and killing its host." He pulled the fig's branches away from the tree. "A process I'm sure you're very familiar with." He tossed the plant onto the ground and marched on.

Not a lesson on jungle life, but a jab at me. I contemplated tripping him with my bow. It would be a petty, mean-spirited thing to do. Tempting, but I threaded my staff into its holder on my pack instead.

We arrived at the Illiais Market just as the sun began to set. The collection of bamboo structures had thatched roofs and bamboo shades for walls. Some of the "walls" had been rolled up to allow customers to browse and the light breeze to cool.

Leif and I had been walking downhill, and the trail ended at the market, which stood in a clearing at the edge of the jungle. The mammoth trees of the tropical forest no longer dominated the landscape. Beyond the clearing, I could see woodland that looked similar to the Snake Forest in Ixia.

"We'll camp here tonight and leave at first light," Leif said before heading toward one of the stands.

I had thought that with the setting of the sun, the market would close. Instead, a vast array of torches was lit, and business continued unabated. The sounds of bartering could be heard above the general buzz of a hundred or so customers talking, calling to children and hurrying from stand to stand carrying packages.

Some of the shoppers wore the familiar dress of the Zaltanas, but I also saw a number wearing green leggings and tunics that were the dress of the forest dwelling Cowan Clan. When we had traveled from Ixia, Irys had taught me to recognize the different clans by their clothing.

I also spotted a few women wearing the traditional shimmering silk pants, short beaded tops, and sheer veils of the Jewelrose Clan. The Jewelrose men even sported beads and jewels on their long tunics that hung down to the knees of their pants. When Irys had explained her clan's customs to me, I couldn't imagine Irys wearing anything but the simple linen shirt, pants and wide belt that she always donned.

I wandered through the market, marveling at the variety of goods available for sale. Practical items like food and clothing sat side by side with jewelry and handcrafts. A pine scent from the torches dominated, but it didn't take long for me to discern the smell of roasting meat. I followed the mouthwatering aroma to a fire pit. A tall man covered with sweat spun the meat that sizzled in the flames. His white apron was streaked with soot. I bought some hot beef from him to eat right away and some smoked jerky for later.

Trying to ignore the pointed stares of the other shoppers,

I searched the market for Fern's stand, vowing to change into Nutty's clothes as soon as I found some privacy. Soon a table piled high with bolts of cloth attracted my attention. As I looked through the prints, a small dark woman with large eyes peeked out from behind the collection.

"May I help you?" she asked.

"Are you Fern?"

Her eyes widened in alarm as she nodded.

"Nutty Zaltana sent me. Do you have any solid colors?"

From underneath the table, Fern pulled bolts of plain cloth and added them to the table. Together we matched up colors and patterns for three outfits.

"Are you sure you don't want this Illiais print?" Fern held up a loud pink-and-yellow-flowered pattern. "Solid colors are usually worn by the Zaltana men. This print is very popular with the girls."

I shook my head. Just as I began to pay her for the cloth, I spotted a material that matched the colors of the forest. "Some of this, too," I said, pointing to the green pattern. When we had settled up, I asked her to send the fabric to Nutty, but I found room for the forest print in my pack.

"Who should I say is sending it?" Fern asked; her quill poised above the parchment.

"Her cousin, Yelena."

The quill froze in midair. "Oh, my," she said. "The lost Zaltana child?"

I gave her a weary half smile. "Not lost, nor a child any longer."

Strolling past a few more stands, I stopped at a table displaying statues of jungle creatures. They were constructed of small multicolored stones glued together. I selected a black-and-white valmur statue and bought it for Valek. Not quite sure how I would send it to him, I wrapped the gift in my new green fabric.

Campfires began to blaze behind the market. Commerce slowed as the shop owners rolled the bamboo shades down, closing their stands. Customers either headed into the surrounding forest or toward one of the camps. I spotted Leif seated next to one of the fires. He held a bowl in his lap while he talked to the three young Zaltana men seated near him. Through the shimmering air above the fire, I saw him smile and laugh. His whole face transformed in that instant. Scowl lines smoothed. Cheeks lifted, erasing the impact of his serious face and softening his square jaw. He looked ten years younger.

Remembering that Esau had said Leif had been eight when I was kidnapped, I realized now that my brother was only two years older than me. He was twenty-two instead of my original guess of thirty.

Without thought, I moved to join him. In a heartbeat, the merriment dropped from his face. He scowled with such fierceness that I stopped in my tracks. Where was I to sleep that night?

Someone touched my shoulder. I spun.

"You're welcome to stay at my fire," Fern said. She pointed to a small blaze behind her stand.

"Are you sure? I might be a spy from Ixia." I tried to joke, but the words came out harsher than I had wanted.

"Then you can report to your Commander that I make the finest cloth of all the clans. And if he wants a new uniform made from my famous Illiais print, just have him send me an order."

I laughed at the image of the impeccable Commander Ambrose draped in gaudy hot-pink and yellow flowers.

As the first rays of sunlight touched the straw roofs of the market, I waited for Leif to continue our journey. Fern had been a kind host, treating me to dinner and showing me where I could change in private. As it turned out Nutty was her best customer, supplying all the Zaltanas with clothes.

I fidgeted in the warm morning air, trying to get used to the extra fabric around my legs. The hem just covered the tops of my soft leather boots. Fern had assured me that my boots would blend in better once I reached the Citadel. Only the jungle and forest clans preferred mud between their toes.

Finally, Leif appeared. Refusing to acknowledge my presence, he started down a forest path. After a couple of hours, I grew tired of following him in silence. I pulled my bow and began executing blocks and jabs as I walked. I concentrated on the feel of the wood in my hands, setting my mind into that mental awareness that Irys had claimed was my way of tapping into the magical power source.

To practice control of the magic, I projected my awareness out. At first, I encountered a cold stone wall. Confused, I retreated until I realized the barrier was Leif's mind; closed and unyielding. I shouldn't have been surprised.

Skirting his presence, I sought the calm forest surrounding us. I crept with a chipmunk, looking for nuts. I froze with a young deer, hearing the sound of footsteps. My mind touched different creatures as I reached out. Gradually, I projected my awareness farther and farther away, seeing how far I could go.

Behind me, I could still feel the people at the market, five or six miles away. Thrilled, I pushed ahead to see if a town was close by. At first, I touched only more animals, but just as I was about to pull back, my mind touched a man.

Careful to avoid breaking the Ethical Code, I skimmed the surface of his mind. He was a hunter, waiting for prey, and he wasn't alone. There were many men around him. They crouched in the bushes just off the trail. One sat on a horse with his weapon poised for an attack. I wondered what they hunted. Curiosity made me dip a little deeper into the man's thoughts. An image of his prey appeared, snapping me back to my body.

I stopped.

I must have gasped, because Leif turned and stared at me. "What are you doing?" he demanded.

"The forest. Men."

"Of course. The woods are full of game," he explained as if talking to a simpleton.

"Not hunters. Ambushers. Waiting for us."

5

"Ambushers? Don't be ridiculous," Leif said. Amazement colored his voice. "You're not in Ixia anymore."

"Why would a hunting party hide so close to the path?" I asked, ignoring his tone and hoping that logic would prevail.

"Animals use the forest trails. It's easier than fighting through the underbrush." Leif started to walk away. "Come on."

"No. You're leading us into a trap."

"Fine. I'll go without you."

When he turned his back again, I was gripped with rage. "Do you think I'm lying?" The words growled from between my teeth.

"No. I think you're suspicious of everything and everyone, just like a northerner." His mouth twisted as if he wanted to spit.

"You think I'm a spy," I snapped at him in frustration. "I'll lower my defenses. Project your mind out and see for yourself that I'm not here to spy on Sitia."

"I can't read minds. In fact, no *Zaltana* can."

I ignored the jab. "Can't you at least sense who I am?"

"Physically you're a Zaltana. But just because Irys claims you survived Mogkan's efforts to wipe your mind doesn't mean it's true." Leif pointed an accusing finger at me. "You could be a pawn, an empty vessel that has been provided with a northern host. What better way to have eyes and ears in the south?"

"Ridiculous."

"No. It's not. You've revealed yourself," Leif said with a quiet intensity. Then his eyes dulled and turned vacant as if he peered into another world. "I taste strong loyalty and longing for Ixia emanating from you. You stink of blood and pain and death. Anger and passion and fire buzz around you like a haze." His gaze refocused on me. "My sister would be reveling in her freedom, and wrapped with hatred for her captors. You have lost your soul to the north. You are not my sister. It would have been better if you had died than return to us tainted."

I took a deep breath to calm the sudden fury that threatened to take control. "Wake up, Leif! What you dreamed of finding in the jungle didn't factor in reality. I'm not that innocent six-year-old. I endured more than you can imagine and fought hard to keep my soul." I shook my head. I was *not* going to explain myself to this stubborn fool. "I know who *I* am. Perhaps *you* need to reevaluate your expectations of me."

We stood for a moment, glaring at each other. Finally, I said, "You're walking into an ambush."

"I'm walking *to* the Citadel. Are you coming?"

I weighed my options. If I used my grapple and rope to climb into the trees, I could travel through the forest canopy and move past the ambush while remaining near the trail. But what about Leif; my brother who acted like my enemy? He had his machete. Did he know how to use it in a fight?

What if he were injured in the ambush? It would be his own fault. We were brother and sister by blood alone, and I couldn't imagine Leif and me ever being close. Still, a pang of regret touched my heart. Esau and Perl wouldn't want to see Leif hurt. Then I realized Leif was a magician. Could he defend himself with his magic? I shook my head. I didn't know enough about magic to even contemplate what could be done with it.

"I would have never guessed a hunting party could frighten a northerner away." Leif laughed as he set off down the trail.

That did it. I unslung my backpack and found my switchblade. Cutting a small slit along the outer seam of my new pants, I strapped the thigh-holder to my leg. I pulled apart my single braid, and wrapped my hair up into a bun using my lock picks to hold it in place. Now dressed for a fight, I slipped my pack over one shoulder, and raced after Leif.

As I caught up with him, he gave me an amused grunt. With my five-foot bow in hand, I set my mind into my mental fighting zone. The zone was a concentration technique that allowed me to anticipate my opponent's moves as I fought. This time, I focused on the trail ahead.

The men were poised and ready, six on each side of the road. I knew the instant they heard us, but they waited. They wanted to surround us, attacking only when we had walked into the middle of their group.

I had other plans. Just before we reached the ambush, I dropped my pack to the ground and called, "Wait up!"

Leif spun around. "What now?"

"I think I heard some—"

A shout filled the forest. Birds darted into the sky with a flurry of wings. Men exploded from the bushes with their swords in hand. But the element of surprise was mine. I knocked aside the swords of the first two men who rushed me. Slamming my bow hard against their temples, I sent them to the ground.

As a third man approached, I swept his feet out from under him. Two more men rushed me, I stepped up to engage them, but they jumped to the sides of the trail. My confusion lasted until I felt a deep rumbling through the soles of my boots. Looking up I saw a broad-chested horse charging down the path toward me. I dove out of the way just as a flash of steel bit into my upper left arm. Furious, I attacked the man closest to me, jabbing my bow into his nose. Blood gushed as he cried out in pain.

"Stop her," the man on horseback ordered.

I searched for Leif. He stood in the middle of the road surrounded by four armed men. An astonished look creased his face, but otherwise he appeared unharmed. His machete lay at his feet.

Outnumbered, I had only seconds left. The horseman had turned his steed around, preparing for another charge. The man with the broken nose lay on the ground. I stood on his chest and threatened his neck with the end of my bow.

"Stop or I'll crush his windpipe," I yelled.

The young man halted his horse. But as the others backed away, staring at me in disbelief, he raised his sword into the air.

"Surrender or I'll kill your brother," he said.

How did he know Leif was my brother? I looked at Leif, considering. The point of a guard's sword balanced mere inches from Leif's heart. Fear had bleached my brother's face. Served him right. The soldier under my feet wheezed.

I shrugged. "Seems we're at an impasse," I said to the horseman.

"Indeed." He paused. "What say we stand down and discuss the situation?"

I began to agree when the rider snapped his fingers. I sensed movement, but before I could swing around, I heard a horrible thud, felt a crushing pain at the base of my skull, then nothing.

My head pulsed with pain as if someone were beating two mallets on the sides of my skull. I opened my eyes for a second, but squeezed them shut again. Bobbing brown hide filled my view, causing nausea. As I fought to keep the contents of my stomach in place, I realized I had been hung upside down and was being moved. I risked another peek and confirmed my suspicion that I had been thrown over the back of a horse. I vomited.

"She's awake," said a male voice.

Thank fate the horse stopped.

"Good. We'll stop and make camp here," said the horseman.

I felt a hard push in my side, and I dropped to the ground. A jolt shot through my body on impact. Stunned, all I could do was hope nothing had been broken.

As the sunlight faded, I heard the rustle of men working. When I tried to squirm into a more comfortable position, I started to panic. I couldn't move very well. Then I recognized the familiar stomach clenching sound of manacles clamped on my wrists and ankles. Upon inspection I noticed a foot-long chain hanging between the metal cuffs on my wrists. It took a considerable effort not to scream and flail at my restraints. A few deep breaths calmed my speeding heart and frantic mind.

I assessed the damage to my body. Aside from some bruised muscles, I couldn't feel any broken bones, although my upper left arm burned from the sword cut. I hadn't noticed the pain during the fight and, even now, it seemed a mere nuisance compared to the pounding in my skull. So I lay still and bided my time.

By full dark, the noises of setting up the camp had been replaced by the quiet murmur of voices. When the pain in my head died down to a dull ache, I tried to move again, and succeeded in turning onto my back. My view of the stars was soon obscured by a man's face looking down at me. Small close-set eyes peered around a many-times-broken nose. Moonlight glinted off his sword, allowing me to see that the tip hovered above my throat.

"Make trouble and I'll skewer you with me blade," the man said with a sick smile. "And I'm not talking about me sword." To prove his point, he sheathed his weapon.

I decided not to make trouble. At least not yet. The guard

seemed satisfied with my silence. He crossed his thick muscled arms over his chest, staring at me. I could feel my switchblade holder on my thigh. Whether or not it still held my weapon was another matter, and I couldn't risk checking it while under guard. Instead, I surveyed the area to get my bearings.

My attackers had camped in a clearing. Men surrounded a bright fire, cooking something that smelled like meat. A single tent had been erected. Leif and the horseman were not in sight, but the horse was tied to a nearby tree. I counted ten men in the clearing, including my guard. There might have been more inside the tent. Either way, too many for me to fight.

I tried to sit up. The world spun, and my stomach heaved until there was nothing left inside.

A guard came toward me from the campfire. He was an older man with short gray hairs bristling from his scalp. He held a cup in his hand, which he handed to me. "Drink this," he ordered.

The warm scent of ginger floated from the liquid. "What is it?" My voice rasped.

"It doesn't matter." My guard took a step closer to me, raising his fist. "You do what Captain Marrok says."

"Easy, Goel, she has to be able to walk tomorrow," Captain Marrok said. Then to me, "Your brother made it from some leaves he had in his pack."

Leif was alive. My relief surprised me.

"It's to make your head feel better," the Captain said when my lips hesitated on the rim of the cup. A hint of kindness touched his blue-gray eyes, but he didn't let the feeling alter his stern expression.

Why poison me now when they could have killed me before? Perhaps Leif wanted me dead?

"Drink it or I'll force it down your throat," Goel said.

I believed Goel, so I took a small sip, testing for poisons. It tasted like sweet ginger mixed with lemon juice. Feeling a little better from the one taste, I gulped the rest.

"Cahil said to move her closer to the fire. It's too dark back here. I've assigned four-hour buddy shifts for tonight," Captain Marrok said.

Goel grabbed me under the arms and pulled me to my feet. Preparing for another round of nausea, I braced myself, but nothing happened. My stomach settled, and my head cleared enough for me to wonder how I was supposed to walk with such a short chain between my manacled ankles. At least my wrists and ankles weren't connected together.

The problem was solved when Goel lifted me over his shoulder. When he dropped me near the fire, the other men ceased their conversation. One man glared at me above the bloody bandage that he held to his nose.

Marrok gave me a plate of food. "Eat. You'll need your strength."

The guards all laughed. It was a humorless, frightening sound.

I debated whether or not to eat the meat and cheese bread. It had been only a few minutes since I had emptied my stomach on the ground, but the inviting smell of grilled meat made the decision for me. After tasting for poisons, I gobbled the meal.

With my headache gone, and my body somewhat revived from the food, I contemplated my situation. My biggest question was why had Leif and I been captured, and by whom. Goel still hovered nearby so I asked him.

He backhanded me across my face. "No talking," he ordered.

My cheek stung as unbidden tears welled. I hated this Goel.

I spent the next hours in silence, using the time to search for a way to escape. My backpack wasn't anywhere in sight, but, across the fire, a heavyset man tried to spar another guard with my bow. Sweating with profusion, the big man inexpertly hacked at the other's practice sword and was beaten with ease.

After watching the bout, I decided that these men had to be soldiers even though they wore plain homespun civilian clothes.

Their ages ranged from mid-twenties to late-forties, maybe even fifty. Mercenaries, perhaps? Captain Marrok's command of these men was obvious.

So why had they attacked us? If they needed money, they could have taken what they wanted and been on their way. If they were killers, I would be dead by now. That left kidnapping. For a ransom? Or for something worse?

A shudder shook my shoulders when I thought of my parents receiving word that I had disappeared again and I promised myself that I wouldn't let it go that far. Somehow, I would escape, but I knew it wouldn't be under Goel's zealous watch.

I rubbed my neck. My hand came away sticky with blood. Exploring with my fingertips, I found a deep gash at the base of my skull and a smaller cut above my left temple. I tapped my bun and moved my hand away with what I hoped was a casual motion. My lock picks were still holding up some of my hair, and I prayed Goel didn't see them.

A possible means of escape was within reach. I just needed some time unguarded. Unfortunately, it didn't look like that would happen anytime soon; two men came out of the tent and headed straight toward me.

"He wants to see her," one man said as they hauled me to my feet.

They dragged me toward the tent. Goel followed. I was pulled inside and dumped on the floor. When my eyes adjusted to the dim candlelight, I saw the young horseman sitting at a canvas table. Leif, unchained and unharmed, sat beside him. My backpack was on the table, and my possessions had been spread out.

With effort, I stood. "Friends of yours?" I asked Leif.

Something hard connected with the side of my head, slamming me back to the ground. Leif half rose from his seat, but settled when the horseman touched his sleeve.

"That was unnecessary, Goel," the horseman said. "Wait outside."

"She spoke without permission."

"If she fails to show the proper respect, you may teach her some manners. Now go," ordered the horseman.

I struggled to my feet again. Goel left, but the other two guards remained by the door. By now my patience was gone. If I were quick enough, I might be able to wrap the foot of chain hanging between my wrists around the horseman's neck.

As I was gauging the distance, the horseman said, "I wouldn't try anything stupid." He lifted a long, broad sword from his lap.

"Who the hell are you and what do you want?" I demanded.

"Watch your language or I'll call Goel back," he replied with a smile.

"Go ahead, call him back. Take my manacles off and let us have a fair fight." When he didn't reply, I added, "Guess you're afraid I'd win. Typical ambusher mentality."

He looked at Leif in amazement. Leif stared back with concern, and I wondered what had gone on between them. Friends or foes?

"You failed to mention this bravado. Of course," he turned back to me, "it could all be an act."

"Try me," I said.

The horseman laughed. Despite his full blond beard and mustache, he still looked younger than I. Maybe seventeen or eighteen years old. His eyes were a washed-out blue, and his shoulder-length blond hair had been pulled back into a ponytail. He wore a simple light gray tunic. Even from this distance, I could tell that his shirt's fabric was finer than the guards' clothes.

"What do you want?" I asked again.

"Information."

I gaped at his unexpected answer.

"Oh, come on," he said. "Don't play the simpleton with me. I want military statistics on Ixia. Troop size and location. Strengths. Weaknesses. How many weapons? Valek's precise location. Who and where his other spies are. That type of information."

"Why would you think I know all this?"

He glanced at Leif, and sudden understanding flooded my mind. "You think I'm a northern spy." I sighed. Leif *had* set me up. That's why the horseman knew Leif was my brother. Leif's fear and shock during the ambush had all been an act. He had no business with the First Magician. No wonder he hadn't said a word since I had arrived in the tent.

"All right, since everyone believes I'm a spy, I guess I should act like one." I crossed my arms to achieve a defiant posture. The clang of the manacles didn't help the image, but I sallied forth anyway. "I'm not telling you southern scum anything."

"You'll have no choice."

"Then you're in for a surprise." Meaning I didn't have the answers he sought. If he had wanted to know the Commander's favorite food, I'd be happy to oblige.

"I could have Goel torture the information out of you," he said. "He would enjoy that. But that's rather messy and time-consuming. And I always consider facts divulged under stress to be suspect."

The horseman rose from his chair, and walked around the table, coming closer to me. He clutched his sword in his right hand, trying to be intimidating. He was about seven inches taller than me and he had tucked his dark gray pants into knee-high black leather riding boots.

"You're the one in for a surprise, because I'm going to bring you to the Magician's Keep where First Magician will peel your mind like a banana, exposing the soft center where all the answers lie. Your brain gets a little mashed in the process—" he shrugged his shoulders as if unconcerned about this detail "—but the information is always accurate."

Real fear brushed my skin for the first time since I had awakened a prisoner. Perhaps I'd made a mistake in playing the spy.

"I don't suppose you would believe me if I said I didn't have what you wanted?"

The horseman shook his head. "The proof of your loyalties is in your backpack. Ixian coins and your northern uniform."

"Which really proves I'm *not* a spy, because Valek would never recruit someone stupid enough to carry her uniform on a mission," I said in frustration, but regretted having mentioned Valek's name. A "she-just-gave-herself-away" look flashed between the horseman and Leif.

I tried to stall for time. "Who are you and why do you want this information?"

"I'm King Cahil Ixia. And I want my throne."

6

King of Ixia? This young idiot was claiming to be a king?

"The King of Ixia is dead," I said.

"I'm well aware that your *boss*, Valek, murdered the King and all his family when Commander Ambrose took control of Ixia. But he made what will soon prove to be a fatal mistake." Cahil jabbed his sword into the air. "He didn't count the bodies, and the King's six-year-old nephew was smuggled to the south. I'm the heir to the Ixian throne and I plan to claim it."

"You'll need more men," I said.

"How many more?" he asked with considerable interest.

"More than twelve." My best guess of the number of men in the camp.

He laughed. "Don't worry. The Commander's military and corps of assassins are enough of a threat to Sitia to provide me with plenty of followers. Besides—" he thought for a moment "—once I deliver you to the Citadel, and show them that I've uncovered a dangerous spy, they'll have no choice but to support my campaign against Ambrose. I'll have the whole Sitian army at my command."

He failed to impress me. Instead, he reminded me of a boy

playing with toy soldiers. I did a quick mental calculation. Cahil was a year older than me, making him twenty-one.

"So you're taking me to the Citadel?" I asked.

He nodded. "There, First Magician will reap the information from your mind." He smiled as a greedy glint sparked in his eyes.

Somehow, I had missed the connection of the Magician and the Citadel the first time Cahil had mentioned it. The reference to them mashing my brains must have thrown me off.

"I'm going to the Citadel anyway. Why all the trouble?" I unfolded my arms, showing the manacles.

"You are masquerading as a student. Unfortunately, the Magicians take their Ethical Code very seriously, and won't interrogate you unless you're caught doing something illegal. Without my intervention, they would have invited you in, and taught you all the secrets of Sitia."

So I was to be his proof. He wanted to show them that he had saved the Sitians from a menacing criminal. "Okay. I'll go with you to the Citadel." I offered my wrists. "Remove these, and I won't give you any trouble."

"And what's to stop you from running off?" he asked. There was a hitch of disbelief in his voice.

"My word."

"Your word means nothing," Leif said.

His first verbalization of the night, and I felt a strong urge to quiet him with my fist. I stared at him, beaming the promise of a future confrontation.

Cahil appeared unconvinced.

"How about the twelve men you have guarding me?" I asked.

"No. You're my prisoner. You should be dressed as such." Cahil waved his hand, and the two guards by the tent's entrance grabbed my arms.

Meeting over. I was dragged from the tent and dumped by

the fire, where Goel resumed his hawklike guard. Cahil had left me no choice. I would *not* arrive at the Citadel as his prize.

I lay there, watching and listening to the men as a simple plan formed in my mind. When the camp settled in for the night, two men relieved Goel. I feigned sleep, waiting until the second shift of men had enough time to grow bored.

Magic was the only weapon I had left; yet I was uncertain of my strength and abilities. What I planned to do could be considered a direct violation of the Magicians' Ethical Code, but, at this point, I didn't care. I would have preferred to fight, but I was out of options and time.

Breathing deep, I tried to project my awareness out. Without the aid of my bow, I failed miserably. I couldn't focus. Not wanting to risk any big movements, I rubbed my thumbs along my fingertips. The skin contact helped to center my mind until I could push it away from me.

I had hoped my guards would be drowsy, but one whistled under his breath and the other reviewed military tactics in his head, although I could feel the desire for sleep pulling at their minds.

I used that desire. I gave a mental command to sleep, and crossed my fingers. My knowledge of magic was very limited; I had no idea if it would work. At first, resistance pushed back. I tried again. Soon, the two men sank to the ground, but still remained awake. I had wanted to be subtle, but the night was running out. Sleep, I ordered with force, and they fell over.

The chains clanked when I sat up. Pressing them to my beating chest, I scanned the slumbering men. I had forgotten about the noise. Since I could only use one hand and my mouth, picking the manacles' locks would be difficult and loud, so I revised my plan. Perhaps I could send all the men into a deep sleep where noise would not rouse them.

I projected my awareness, touching each man's mind, putting them into a heavy, dreamless slumber. Cahil slept on a cot in the tent. While I would have enjoyed rifling through his mind, I settled for sending him into an unconscious state. Leif's magical protection prevented me from affecting him. I hoped he was a heavy sleeper.

Working with my diamond pick in one hand and with the tension wrench between my teeth, I managed to pop the locks on my wrist manacles after a fifth attempt. The sky began to brighten a shade. My time was slipping away. I crept into the tent to retrieve my backpack, stuffing my belongings into it. I made more noise then I wanted, but my instincts told me that full dawn would waken the men. As I fled, I grabbed my bow from beside the guard who had claimed it.

Running through the forest, I noticed that the darkness faded with every stride. My thoughts turned sluggish, and I huffed for breath as weakness pulled at my legs. Using magic on the men had drained my energy.

I scanned the treetops, looking for a big leaf variety with lots of branches. Spotting a tree with potential, I halted and took my grapple and rope from my backpack.

By the time I managed to hook a branch, my arms felt like rubber. I had to smile at the irony of my situation, though, as I pulled myself up the rope. This was the third time I had used the treetops for escape, and the climb was becoming almost routine. But the distant shouts of angry men spurred me on.

When I reached the top, I reeled in my rope, and then scrambled to a higher limb for more cover. I wrapped Fern's green cloth around me as I sat with my back to the trunk, my knees drawn to my chest. Leaving a gap to see through, I settled in for a long wait. I hoped my strength would return soon.

Hearing a commotion, I imagined the scene going on at Cahil's camp. The reprimand of the guards who fell asleep during their watch; the discovery that my backpack and effects were missing. I trusted that made Cahil pause, knowing that I had stood only a few feet from him and let him live.

My position in the tree was closer to the camp than I had wanted. Searchers with drawn swords came into view sooner than I had anticipated. I froze in my green cocoon.

Goel led the men. He stooped to inspect a bush, and then called, "This way. She's not far. The sap's still sticky."

Rivers of sweat ran down my skin. Goel was a tracker. I moved my hand, finding the slit in my pants. My switchblade hadn't been confiscated. Grabbing the smooth wood of the handle made me feel a bit better.

He stopped at the bottom of my tree. I shifted my weight forward and crouched on the branch, preparing to flee if needed.

Goel examined the ground around the base of the trunk. His eyes slid up into the branches. My breath locked as cold fear splashed through me. I realized I had made a grave mistake.

A predatory smile spread across Goel's lips. "Found you."

7

I yanked my forest camouflage off my back and shook the material out like a sheet.

"There she is," one of Goel's men cried out, pointing up at me.

Releasing the fabric, I let it float down toward the men. The second the material obscured their view, I launched myself through the treetops, scrambling with a sudden spur of energy from branch to branch in an effort to get myself higher and farther from Goel and his men.

"Hey!" someone yelled from below.

"Stop her!"

I kept moving, hoping that Goel couldn't track me through the trees. My mistake had been to forget that Cahil had searched through my backpack. He knew I carried a grapple and rope. With a good tracker and the hint of my trick, it hadn't taken them long to find me.

Curses and yelling followed below me. I focused all my efforts on finding branches that would hold my weight, and getting away. Once my mind calmed enough for rational thought, I realized I was making a racket. Goel and his men could track me by listening to the rattle of the leaves and the snapping of branches. All they had to do then was wait for me to fall, or exhaust myself.

Once I slowed down, taking care not to make any noise, I could hear the men on the forest floor. They called my position to each other, closing in.

"Hold up!" a voice said right below me.

My muscles jerked in shock.

"She stopped."

I kept climbing. My progress was a nerve-racking snail's pace, but quiet.

"We have you," Goel called. "Come down now and I'll only hurt you a little."

I bit back a sarcastic reply to his "generous" offer. Instead, I continued to move through the trees. The men remained silent, and soon I had no idea where they were. I paused on an upper branch to search for some sign of them, but saw nothing but a sea of green leaves.

Then my imagination kicked in. I felt trapped. My face burned with the sudden belief that Goel's eyes were on me. Panic pumped in my heart until I remembered the instruction Irys had given me back in the jungle—seek with your mind, not with your eyes. Using my magic still wasn't instinctive.

Taking a deep breath, I pulled my bow, concentrated on the smooth wood against my fingers, and projected my awareness down to the forest floor.

The men had spread out. They searched a wide area to my right. I couldn't sense Goel below. With a sick feeling crawling along my skin, I swept the treetops. Goel had climbed into the canopy. He followed the trail I had left in my haste. Black thoughts of inflicting pain colored his mind.

When he reached the place where I had begun to travel with more care, I waited. He hesitated for a heartbeat, but spotted another sign, continuing on toward my location.

It was only a matter of time before Goel found me. I considered using my magic to force him off my trail. Could I make him fall asleep? Probably, but Goel would eventually wake up and track me down. I could try prompting him into forgetting who he searched for, but for that I would need to delve deep into his mind and such an effort would drain my remaining strength.

Think. I had to take Goel out. Unless Cahil had another tracker, my chances of escaping improved without Goel on my tail. A plan began to form in my mind. I slid my bow back through its holder on my pack.

Keeping light contact with Goel's mind, I picked up the pace and continued on my route for a while, making sure to leave a trail. When I reached a small clearing in the forest, I swung down to the ground, landing with a hard jolt. Leaving nice deep boot prints, I walked across the clearing and broke through the underbrush on the other side.

Now came the hard part. Retracing my path, I returned to the tree from which I had jumped. The grapple would leave marks, so I used it to throw the rope over the tree branch, and then I shimmied up. Hopefully, the rub marks on the branch would make it appear that I had gone down to the clearing, not up. Then I looped the rope and hung it around my shoulder and torso so my hands were free.

Goel was now close enough to hear me. I made a small grunt like I had hit the ground hard. With the utmost care, I climbed higher in the tree. Goel came into sight. I froze.

He inspected the branch I had used to drop into the clearing. He leaned over and peered at the forest floor.

"So me prey has gone to ground," Goel said to himself.

He swung down and crouched by my marks. His thoughts focused on how much he would enjoy torturing me. Sleep, I projected into his mind. Sleep. But he was wide-awake and the command raised immediate suspicions. He stood and glanced around the clearing.

Damn. That wasn't working. Don't look up; I projected as I moved to a lower branch. The leaves shook, but Goel didn't notice. Triggering my switchblade, I cut a three-foot section of rope. I wrapped the ends around my hands as Goel turned back to examine my tracks.

I jumped, landing behind him. Before he could move, I looped the rope I held around his throat. I spun. My backpack touched his back, and the rope was now over my shoulder. I dropped to one knee, forcing Goel to bend backward over me. In that position only his fingertips could reach me. Instead, he yanked at the garrote around his neck.

Just when I thought he was unconscious, his head bumped mine, and I felt his full weight on my back. He did a backward somersault over me. I saw his boots hit the ground in front of me.

Damn. Goel knew some self-defense techniques. He straightened and wrenched the rope right out of my hands.

"Got anything else?" he asked. His voice rasped from my strangulation attempt.

I pulled my bow from my back. He drew his sword.

He smiled. "Little girl. Little weapon." Goel pointed to himself. "Big man. Big weapon."

I shifted into a fighting stance, balancing my weight on the balls of my feet. He wasn't going to intimidate me. If I could disarm my friend Ari, who had twice Goel's muscle mass, and Ari's partner, Janco, who was rabbit fast, I could take on Goel.

Sliding my hands along the wood of my weapon, I reestablished my mental link with Goel. When he lunged, I knew it before he moved. I stepped to the side, turning sideways so his sword missed my stomach. In a stride, I was in close. I slammed my bow into his temple. He crumpled to the ground, unconscious.

Thanking fate that Goel hadn't called for his men, I searched his pack. I found brass knuckles, a small whip, a black club, an assortment of knives, a gag, manacles, keys and my camouflage material.

If I killed Goel, I would be doing the south a favor. A shame that Goel's death wouldn't go well in my "I'm not a spy" defense. So I dragged him to a tree and propped him into a sitting position against the trunk. The manacles had just enough chain for me to lock his hands behind the tree. I shoved his gag into his mouth, fastening the strap around his head.

I took my camouflage material and the manacles' keys from his pack. Then I hid his pack and sword in the bushes. Pausing a moment to regain my focus, I sought Goel's men with my mind. Satisfied that they were far enough away, I mentally scanned the forest for Cahil's campsite. Once I knew in which direction to go, I set out.

I couldn't leave Goel to die. Yet, if I released him, he would only track me down. I could find someone to direct me to the Citadel, and hope the few hours it took Cahil to find Goel would be enough time for me to stay ahead of them. That had been my intent when I had first escaped. But now that rankled. It would be the actions of a criminal or a spy, and I wasn't guilty. I *wouldn't* run away.

Perhaps I could use my magic and trick Goel into losing my trail. Then I could follow Cahil, keeping a close eye on him. But would he continue to the Citadel without me as his prisoner? I didn't know.

A sudden intense desire for Valek was swept through my body. Discussing military tactics with him had always helped me work out a problem. I thought about how Valek would handle this situation and, soon after, a rough plan formed.

"You lost her," Cahil repeated. He frowned as he stared at the faces of the four unhappy men who stood in front of him. "Where's Goel?" he asked.

A mumbled reply.

"You lost him, too?" Outrage gripped Cahil's face.

The men cringed and stammered.

I suppressed the urge to laugh out loud. My position near his campsite afforded me a clear view of Cahil and his men, while I remained hidden under my camouflage. I had used the waning daylight and the clamor of the search party's arrival to move closer to the clearing.

"You're a bunch of bumbling fools. Searching a prisoner for weapons and anything that would help an escape, is standard procedure." Cahil glared at his men. "A *complete* and *thorough* search. You don't stop because you found one weapon." Cahil stared at his men until they fidgeted. "Captain Marrok?"

"Yes, my lord." Marrok snapped to attention.

"If Goel doesn't return by first light, I want you to lead a search party to find him. He's our best chance of recovering that spy," Cahil ordered.

"Yes, sir."

Cahil stalked off to his tent. When he was gone, I could see the grim faces of his men as they stood around the campfire. The smell of roasting meat made my stomach complain. I hadn't eaten all day, but I couldn't risk making any noise. With a sigh, I squirmed into a comfortable position, settling in for a long wait.

Keeping alert proved difficult once the men had gone to sleep. Captain Marrok posted two guards, who circled the campsite. Using magic had drained me and I fought my heavy eyelids until I gave up and dozed for a while. The dream image of Goel's hands on my neck jerked me awake in the middle of the night.

The guards were on the far side of the camp. I used my magic to send the sleeping men into a deeper slumber. The guards, though, fought hard. The image of the harsh punishment their comrades had received for falling asleep on guard duty the night before kept them vigilant. So I tried the "don't look" command as I crept toward Cahil's tent.

Upon reaching the back wall of the tent, I triggered my switchblade and cut a slit in the fabric. Then I entered the tent through that small opening.

Cahil was asleep. Leif looked like he hadn't heard my entrance. Curled up on his side with one arm dangling over the edge of the cot, he appeared to be sleeping. Cahil lay on his back, his arms crossed over his stomach. His long sword rested on the floor within Cahil's reach. I moved the weapon away before I sat on his chest.

The instant he awoke, I had my blade pressed against his throat. "Quiet or I'll kill you," I whispered.

His eyes widened. He tried to move his arms, but my weight pinned them down. Cahil could muscle me off, but I pushed the blade's point into his skin. A drop of blood welled.

"Don't move," I said. "Your sword is out of reach. I'm not that stupid."

"So I'm learning," he whispered.

I felt him relax.

"What do you want?" Cahil asked.

"A truce."

"What kind?"

"You stop trying to drag me to the Citadel in chains and I'll accompany you there as a fellow traveler."

"What do I get out of the deal?"

"You get Goel back and my cooperation."

"You have Goel?"

I dangled the manacles' keys over his face.

"How can I trust you when your brother doesn't trust you?"

"I'm offering a truce. So far, I've had two opportunities to kill you. You're a real threat to Ixia. If I were a true spy, your death would make me famous in the north."

"And if I renege on this truce?"

I shrugged. "I'll escape again. But this time, I'll leave Goel's dead body behind."

"He's a good tracker," Cahil said with pride.

"Unfortunately."

"If I say no to your offer?"

"Then I'm gone, leaving you to find Goel."

"Dead?"

"Yes." I bluffed.

"Why come back? You took care of Goel. He was the only threat to you."

"Because I want the chance to prove that I'm not a spy," I said with frustration. "I'm a Zaltana. And I'm not going to run like a criminal, because I'm not guilty. But I don't want to be your prisoner. And…" I couldn't explain anymore. I sighed. He was right. If my own brother didn't trust me, why should Cahil? I had gambled and lost.

Time for plan B. I would run. My safest course would be to find Irys. I withdrew my switchblade from Cahil's throat. After a full day on the lam without food or sleep, a bone-deep fatigue overcame me. I jumped off of Cahil.

"I'm not going to kill anybody." I backed toward the slit I had cut in the tent, keeping my eyes on Cahil.

When I turned to find the rip in the fabric, a sudden wave of dizziness overcame me, and I stumbled to the ground. The tent spun and I lost consciousness for a mere moment as all my energy fled. I regained my wits in time to see Cahil pick up my switchblade.

8

Cahil moved away and lit the lantern on his bedside table. He examined my switchblade in the candlelight.

"My lord?" a voice called through the door.

I braced myself, preparing to be accosted and manacled by a rush of guards.

"Everything's fine," Cahil called.

"Very good, sir."

I heard the guard move away and I looked at Cahil in surprise. Perhaps he wanted me to tell him where Goel was before he "reclaimed" me. I sat up and glanced at Leif. His eyes were closed, but I didn't know if the light and Cahil's voice had roused him.

"These markings are very familiar," Cahil said, referring to the six symbols engraved on the handle of my switchblade. "My uncle's secret battle codes, I believe." His gaze returned to me.

His sleep-tousled hair reinforced my first impression of his youth, but a sharp intelligence danced in his eyes.

I nodded. The codes had been used by the King of Ixia to send secret messages to his captains during battles.

"It's been so long," Cahil said. A brief sadness pulled at his face. "What do they mean?"

"It says, 'Sieges weathered, fight together, friends forever.' It was a gift."

"Someone in the north?"

Loneliness touched my heart as I thought of what I had lost by coming south. My fingers sought the lump under my shirt, Valek's butterfly. "Yes."

"Who?"

An odd question. Why would he care? I searched Cahil's face for some sign of duplicity, and found only curiosity. "Janco. One of my self-defense teachers." I grinned at the memories of Janco singing his rhymes and knocking aside my attacks. "Without him and Ari, I wouldn't have had the skills to escape you and take on Goel today."

"They taught you well." Cahil ran a hand along his neck, smearing the drop of blood.

He seemed deep in thought as he turned my switchblade in his hands. He pushed the blade into the handle then triggered it. The snick from the weapon made me flinch.

"Well made," he said.

Cahil stepped toward me. I scrambled upright and stood in a defensive stance. Even though I was light-headed and weak, I contemplated my chances of getting away. Instead of threatening me, Cahil retracted the blade and gave me the switchblade. I looked at the weapon in my hand with a tired astonishment.

"A truce, then," he said. "But any trouble and I'll have you in chains." Cahil gestured to a corner of the tent. "You're exhausted. Get some sleep. We have a long day tomorrow." Placing his sword back within reach, Cahil lay down on his cot.

"Do you want to know where Goel is?" I asked.

"Is he in any immediate danger?"

"Not unless there are poisonous or predatory animals in this forest."

"Then let him sweat out the night. Serves him right for being caught." Cahil closed his eyes.

I glanced around the tent. Leif hadn't moved since I had arrived, but his eyes were open. He made no comment as he rolled over to his other side, turning his back on me. Again.

I sighed, wondering how much he had heard, and found I was too tired to care. With weariness dragging at my limbs, I spread my cloak on the floor, blew out the lantern and collapsed on my makeshift bed.

The next morning, Leif left the tent without saying a word. Cahil told me to stay inside while he made a show of the fact that Goel hadn't returned.

I heard Cahil question the guards of the previous night.

"All was quiet, my lord," one man replied.

"Nothing unusual?" Cahil asked.

"Just your light, sir. But you said—"

"What if I'd had a knife at my throat, Erant? Would you have believed what I said?"

"No, sir."

"How did you know, then, that I wasn't in trouble?"

"I didn't, sir. I should have checked," Erant said, sounding miserable.

"Should haves lead to death. In war, you don't get a second chance. In a battle with the north, they won't send an army against us. They'll send one man. Without vigilance, we'll all be killed in our sleep."

Someone scoffed. "Surely one man can't get by us."

"How about a woman?" Cahil asked.

"No way," a guard said amid cheers of assent.

"Then explain this. Yelena," Cahil called. An immediate silence filled the forest. "Join me, please."

I didn't like being part of Cahil's lesson, but he was right. An assassin trained by Valek would have had no trouble taking out his guards. I stepped from the tent, holding my bow in case anyone decided to rush me. The morning sun shone in my eyes as I squinted to examine Cahil's men.

Surprise, anger and disbelief peppered their faces. Captain Marrok drew his sword. Leif was nowhere in sight.

"Everything wasn't fine last night, Erant," Cahil said. "Next time, make sure."

Erant hung his head. "Yes, sir."

"Yelena will be traveling with us to the Citadel. Treat her as a comrade," Cahil ordered.

"What about Goel?" asked Captain Marrok.

Cahil looked at me. "Tell him where Goel is."

"You'll keep Goel on a leash?" I asked. There was no doubt in my mind that Goel's desire for revenge would cause trouble. I shuddered at the thought of being at his mercy.

"Captain Marrok, explain the situation to Goel. Before you free him, make sure he gives his word not to harm Yelena."

"Yes, sir."

"Unless I give him permission," Cahil added, staring at me. "Trouble will get you in chains. Treason will get you Goel."

A rumble of appreciation rolled through Cahil's men. His little show had earned him points in their minds. I gave him a bored look. I had been threatened many times before and had learned that the men who didn't make verbal threats were the most dangerous. With that thought, I searched the campsite for Leif. Perhaps he had returned home now that I had delivered myself to Cahil.

I gave Marrok the key to the manacles and instructions as to where to find Goel and his pack. As the Captain left to free him, the rest of the guards began breaking down the campsite. Cahil's men kept a wary eye on me. A couple of hostile glares were thrown my way, especially when they discovered the rip in the tent's fabric.

While waiting for the Captain and Goel to return, I sorted and organized my backpack. I combed and braided my hair, then twisted the long braid up into a bun, using my lock picks to hold the hair in place. It never hurt to be prepared. Cahil might trust me not to cause trouble, but he still believed I was a northern spy.

Goel returned with Marrok and Leif. I was surprised to see Leif, but not surprised by the seething glower on Goel's face. His cheeks had deep red marks where the gag's strap had pressed into his skin. His hair and clothes were unkempt. Wetness stained his pants and his skin was blotchy from multiple mosquito bites. Goel gripped his sword, starting toward me.

Captain Marrok intercepted Goel and pointed across the clearing to a bedroll still lying on the ground. Goel sheathed his sword and headed to the sleeping mat, shooting me a look of venom.

I resumed breathing. Once the camp was packed, Cahil mounted his horse and led us to the forest trail. I stayed close to Marrok in case Goel forgot his promise again.

The Captain grinned at me and said, "Watch now."

Cahil clicked at his horse as he tapped his heels into the animal's sides. The horse increased its stride, and the men began to jog.

"Keep up," Marrok said.

I hadn't run laps since training with Ari and Janco, but I had found some time to exercise while traveling south. Matching Marrok's pace, I asked, "Why does he make you run?"

"Keeps us battle ready."

I had more questions, but I saved my breath, concentrating instead on staying with Marrok. By the time we reached the next campsite, my field of vision had shrunk to a small area on the Captain's back. My efforts to stay in shape hadn't been enough. When we stopped, I labored for air, sucking in huge mouthfuls. Leif, too, seemed winded. Hasn't run with his friends for a while, I thought peevishly.

Once the camp was erected, Cahil offered to let me sleep in

the corner of his tent again. There, I collapsed to the ground without bothering to spread my cloak. In the morning, I ate a light breakfast.

The next three days mirrored the first day of traveling with Cahil, but by the end of the fourth day, I wasn't as exhausted. I could eat dinner, and even stayed by the fire for a while. Goel glared at me whenever I met his eye, so I ignored him. Leif pretended I didn't exist.

I began to think the forest was endless. Day after day we covered many miles, yet met no one on the trail, nor saw any sign of a village. I suspected Cahil avoided the towns. I couldn't be sure if it was for my benefit or his.

Eventually, the men got used to my presence. They bantered and kidded with each other, and practiced sword fighting. The wary glances disappeared, and my arrival at the campfire no longer caused an immediate hush. I found it interesting that the men always sought Captain Marrok's approval prior to doing anything.

After we'd been traveling for seven days, Captain Marrok surprised me. Some of the guards were performing self-defense drills, and he invited me to join them.

"We could use the practice against that staff of yours," he said.

I agreed, showing the men some basic defense moves with my bow. While they used their wooden swords, I demonstrated the advantages of having a longer weapon. My participation in the practice drew Cahil's attention. He usually showed no interest in the training sessions, preferring instead to talk to Leif about his quest to conquer Ixia, but now he approached to watch.

"Wood against wood is fine for practice, but wood against steel is no contest in a real fight," Cahil said. "A sharp sword would reduce that staff to splinters."

"The edges are the sword's danger zone. The trick is to avoid the edges," I said.

"Show me." Cahil drew his sword.

The thick blade extended about three and a half feet from the hilt. An impressive weapon, but heavy. Cahil would need two hands to wield it, slowing him down.

I concentrated on the feel of the bow's wood in my hands, setting my mind into my mental fighting zone.

He lunged forward. Surprised by his quickness, I jumped back. Cahil held the sword one-handed, and I found myself on the defensive. He had some skill with his weapon, but not much. When he swung the massive blade, I dodged, stepped in close, and struck the flat of his sword with my bow. The next time he swung I hit his hand. When he lunged, I kept my bow horizontal and brought it down on the flat tip of the blade, deflecting the weapon toward the ground. My counter-strikes wouldn't disarm him, but all the while, I kept moving, forcing Cahil to chase me.

When he grabbed his sword with both hands, I knew he was beginning to tire. It was just a matter of time before he made a tactical error.

Our match lengthened. His men cheered for him, urging him to take me out. They didn't notice the sheen of sweat on Cahil's forehead, or hear the rasp of his breath.

Soon enough, he swung too wide. I ducked in close, and tapped my bow on his ribs. "Have I proven my point?" I asked, dancing past his next attack.

Cahil stopped. "It's getting late. We'll have to finish this later," he said. Sheathing his sword, he marched off to his tent.

Practice was over. His men were quiet as they put away their equipment.

I sat by the campfire, waiting until Cahil had a chance to cool down. Captain Marrok sat next to me.

"You proved your point," he said.

I shrugged. "With a lighter sword, Cahil would have won."

We stared at the flames in silence.

"Why does he carry that sword?" I asked Marrok.

"It was the King's. We managed to smuggle it south with Cahil."

I studied Marrok. His face had that worn leather look of a man who has been around for a long time and seen it all. I realized his skin was tanned from the sun and wasn't a natural pigmentation. "You're from the north."

He nodded and gestured to the men. "We all are."

I studied the men. They were a mixed crew of dark- and light-skinned. And I remembered that, before the takeover, the border between Ixia and Sitia had been just a line on the map, and people from both countries mingled freely.

Marrok continued, "We're the soldiers who weren't important enough to assassinate, nor willing to switch our loyalties to the Commander. Goel, Trayton, Bronse and I were all part of the King's guards." Marrok shoved a twig into the fire. Sparks flew up into the night sky. "We couldn't save the King, but we saved his nephew. We raised him, and taught him everything we know. And—" he stood "—we plan to give him a kingdom." Marrok barked orders to the men, and then headed to his bedroll.

Weariness settled over me. My eyes grew heavy and I dragged myself to my corner of the dark tent.

Just before I fell asleep, the tent brightened. I felt a presence near me. My eyes snapped open. Cahil loomed over me with his sword in his hand. Anger pulsed from him in waves.

9

I stood slowly and stepped back from Cahil.

"You humiliated me in front of my men," he said in anger.

"You asked me to show you how a bow could defend against a sword. I was only doing what you wanted."

"It wasn't an honest match."

"What?"

"Leif said you used magic during the fight. That you made me tired."

I suppressed my anger and looked Cahil straight in the eye. "I did not."

"Then what did?"

"Do you really want to know why you lost?" I asked.

"Do you really have an answer?" he countered.

"You need to get off your horse and run with your men. You don't have the stamina for a long fight. And find a lighter sword."

"But it was my uncle's."

"You're not your uncle."

"But I'm the King, and this is the King's sword," Cahil said. His brows creased together. He seemed confused.

"So wear it to your coronation," I said. "If you use it in battle, you'll be wearing it to your funeral," I said.

"You believe I'll be crowned?"

"That's not the point."

"What *is* the point?"

"I would have beaten you with my bow. That sword is too heavy for you."

"I always win against my men."

I sighed. Of course his men wouldn't beat him. I tried another tactic. "Have you been in a battle?"

"Not yet. We're in training. And besides, a King doesn't risk himself during a battle. I stay in the base camp and direct the combat."

His comment didn't sound right to me, but, then again, I had no experience with warfare. Instead, I said, "Think about it, Cahil. Your men raised you. They want to reclaim the throne. But do they want it for you or for themselves? Exile in the south isn't as glamorous as being the King's guards."

Cahil snorted with disdain, shaking his head. "You know nothing. Why would you care? You're a spy. You're just trying to confuse me." He returned to his cot.

Cahil was right. I didn't care. Once we reached the Keep and I proved my innocence, I wouldn't have to bother with him again. Leif, on the other hand, had interfered with me one too many times.

I scanned the tent. My brother's cot was empty.

"Where's Leif?" I asked.

"Gone."

"Where?"

"I sent him ahead to notify the Keep of our arrival. Why?"

"Family business." I spat the words out.

Cahil must have seen the murderous glint in my eyes. "You can't hurt him."

"Oh, yes, I can. He's caused me a lot of trouble."

"He has my protection."

"Is that one of the benefits of being a member of your quest for the north?"

"No. When we captured you and Leif, I gave him my word that no harm would come to him in exchange for his full co-operation in dealing with you."

I blinked at Cahil. Had I heard him right? "But Leif set me up."

"No, he didn't."

"Why didn't you tell me before?"

"I thought letting you believe you had been betrayed by your own brother would demoralize you. However, it seems to have had the opposite effect."

Cahil's plan might have worked if Leif and I had had a relationship. I rubbed my face as I tried to decide if knowing the truth changed my opinion about Leif.

Sitting on the edge of his cot, Cahil studied me in silence.

"If Leif didn't set me up, then who did?"

Cahil smiled. "I can't reveal my sources."

Leif had managed to convince many Zaltanas that I was a spy, so the entire clan was suspect. Anyone at the Illiais Market could have overheard our destination, as well.

I couldn't worry about it now, but I wouldn't forget it, either. "You said you sent Leif to the Keep," I said. "Will we be there soon?"

"Tomorrow afternoon—about an hour after Leif arrives. I want to make sure we're met by the right people," Cahil said. "An important day, Yelena. Better get some sleep." He blew out the lantern.

I reclined on my cloak, wondering about the Citadel and Keep. Would Irys be there by tomorrow? Doubtful. I stretched my awareness out, seeking Irys but only encountering wild-life. Without Irys at the Keep would the First Magician peel away the layers of my mind? Apprehension churned inside my stomach. I would rather face Goel than the unknown. Eventually, though, I slept.

Dark dreams of Reyad swirled in my mind.

"Same story, Yelena," Reyad's ghost said, laughing and taunting. "No options. No friends. But you have a knife. Again."

An image of Reyad wrapped in blood-soaked sheets flashed in my dreams. The killing wound in his neck was the result of my desire to protect myself and the other kidnapped children from torture and mindless slavery.

"Will you cut another's throat to save yourself?" he asked. "How about your own?"

I woke to the sound of crying and realized with horror that my face was wet. Brushing away the tears, I resolved not to let my doubts plague me. Reyad's ghost might haunt my dreams, but I wouldn't allow him to haunt my life.

Morning dawned with the smell of sweet cakes, and I joined the men by the fire for breakfast. After we ate, Cahil's men packed up the camp. Their mood was light and their banter friendly, so I was caught off guard when I felt a hand on my shoulder.

Before I could move, the grip tightened, causing pain. I turned my head. Goel stood behind me.

He dug his fingers deeper into my flesh as he whispered in my ear. "I promised not to hurt you while we traveled to the Citadel. Once there, you're mine."

I rammed my elbow into Goel's stomach. He grunted. I stepped forward and knocked his hand off my shoulder with my arm as I spun. Facing him, I asked, "Why warn me?"

He drew in a deep breath and grinned. "Your anticipation will make the hunt more exciting."

"Enough talk, Goel. Let's do it now."

"No. I want time to play. I have all kinds of games planned for when I have you, my sweet."

My body shook with an icy chill of revulsion. Goose bumps

covered my skin. It was a sensation I never thought I would feel in the sweltering south.

"Goel, help take down the tent," Captain Marrok ordered.

"Yes, sir." Goel walked away, glancing back at me with a smirk on his face and a promise in his eyes.

I let my breath out slowly. This didn't bode well.

When the men finished breaking camp, Cahil mounted his horse and we set off through the forest. After several hours, the trees thinned as the trail ascended a hill. At the top of the rise, a vast valley, bisected by a long dirt road, spread out in front of us. Farm fields etched geometric shapes on the left side of the road. An immense plain dominated the landscape on the right side. Across the vibrant valley was another ridge, and I could just make out a white fortress spanning its crest.

"Is that the Citadel?" I asked Marrok.

He nodded. "Another half day's march." His gray eyes slid to the right as if searching for something.

I followed his gaze and watched the long grass stalks sway in the breeze. "Daviian Plateau?"

"No. That's farther southeast," Marrok said. "This is the edge of the Avibian Plains. The plain is huge. It takes ten days to cross it."

"My cousin mentioned traveling through a plain on the way to the Citadel, but we're really just skirting it."

"Crossing Avibian is a shortcut. Zaltanas will cross, but everyone else avoids contact with the Sandseed Clan who calls the plains home. Taking the forest route is the long way, but it's safe."

I wanted to ask more, but Cahil increased the pace as we descended into the basin. He was either eager to reach the Citadel or anxious to put the plains behind him.

We passed laborers working in the farm fields, and a caravan of merchants with their horse-drawn wagons loaded with goods. Nothing but the tall grass moved in the plains.

The Citadel grew massive in appearance as we traveled closer. We stopped only once to water the horse and the men.

When we reached the towering gates, I was awed by the sheer size of the outer bulwark. Green veins streaked the white marble walls. I ran a hand along them, finding it smooth and cool despite the blistering heat. I had thought it was hot in the forest, but that had been nothing compared to being fully exposed to the searing sun.

The two guards at the Citadel's open gates approached Cahil. After a brief conversation, Cahil led us into a courtyard. I squinted in the bright sunlight. The majestic sight before me took a while to sink in. An entire town resided within the Citadel's outer walls. All the structures were made of the same white marble with veins of green that comprised the outer wall. I had visualized the Citadel as one large building, like the Commander's castle in Ixia, but this was far beyond anything I could have imagined.

"Impressed?" Marrok asked.

I closed my mouth and nodded. Our party began to walk through the streets and I realized the place was deserted. "Where is everyone?" I asked Marrok.

"The Citadel's a ghost town during the hot season. The Council is in recess, the Keep is on holiday and only a skeleton crew tends the crops. Everyone who can flees to the cooler climates, and those who are left retreat inside at midafternoon to avoid the sun."

I didn't blame them. My scalp felt as if it were on fire. "How much longer?" I asked.

"Another hour," Marrok said. "See those four towers?" He pointed to the east. "That's the Magician's Keep."

I stared at their height, wondering what dwelled in those lofty chambers.

We trudged on through the empty streets. The road surface alternated between packed dirt and cobblestones. I spotted dogs, cats and a few chickens crouched in bits of shade. When we neared a large square structure with multiple tiers, Marrok said, "That's Council Hall where the Sitian government has its offices and conducts meetings."

The building had long steps that stretched the entire length beneath the first floor and led up to a grand entrance. Jade colored columns bracketed the doorway. A group of people huddled in the Hall's shadow. They approached us as we walked past. A strong odor of urine emanated from them. Filth matted their hair and covered their tattered attire.

One man reached out with a soot blackened hand. "Please, sir, spare a coin?"

Cahil's men ignored them and kept walking. The group followed along, determined.

"Who are...?" I started to ask, but Marrok didn't slow. I tried to catch up, but a small boy pulled on my arm. His brown eyes were rimmed with sores and streaks of dirt lined his cheeks.

"Lovely lady, please. I'm hungry," the boy said. "Spare a copper?"

I glanced around for Marrok. He was half a block away. I couldn't understand why this boy needed money, but I couldn't refuse those eyes. I dug into my pack and pulled out the Sitian coins Esau had given me. I dumped all of them into his palm.

Kneeling down to his level, I said, "Share these with your friends. And take a bath. Okay?"

A joyful expression lit his face. "Thank—"

Before he could finish we were engulfed by a strong stench as the others surrounded us. They grabbed my arms, pulled at my clothes and yanked on my backpack. I saw the boy pocket the coins and slid out of the melee between the others' legs. The putrid smell of so many unwashed bodies made me gag.

"Lovely lady. Lovely lady," filled my ears until their words were cut off by the clatter of hooves on the cobblestones.

"Get away from her," Cahil yelled. He brandished his sword in the air. "Go. Or I'll cut you in half."

In a heartbeat, the crowd disappeared.

"Are you all right?" Cahil asked.

"Yes." I smoothed my hair and reshouldered my pack. "What was that about?"

"Beggars. Filthy street rats." A look of disgust darkened his face. "It was your fault. If you hadn't given them money, they would have left you alone."

"Beggars?"

My confusion seemed to amaze Cahil. "Surely you know what beggars are?" When I didn't answer, he continued, "They don't work. They live on the streets. They beg for money for food. You had to see them in Ixia," he said with frustration.

"No. Everyone in Ixia has a job. Basic necessities are provided to all by the Commander's military."

"How does he pay for it?"

Before I could answer, Cahil's shoulders drooped. "With my uncle's money. He has probably drained the treasury dry."

I bit back my reply. As far as I was concerned, better to have the money helping people than covering the floor of some treasury.

"Come on." Cahil took his foot out of the stirrup, reached down, and held out his hand. "We need to catch up to the others."

"On the horse?" I asked.

"Don't tell me they don't have horses in the north."

"Not for me," I said as I placed my foot in the stirrup and grabbed his arm. He pulled me into the saddle. I sat behind him, not sure what to do with my arms.

Cahil turned slightly. "For who then?"

"The Commander, Generals and high-ranking officers."

"Cavalry?" Cahil asked.

He was fishing for information. I suppressed a sigh. "Not that I saw." The truth, but I ceased to care if he believed me or not.

Cahil craned his head around and studied my face. A wave of heat enveloped me; I suddenly felt too close to him. His eyes sparked a bluish-green color like the water in the sunlight. And I found myself wondering why he wore a beard in such a hot climate. I imagined Cahil without his beard. He would look younger, and it would be easier to see his smooth, tanned skin and hawklike nose.

When he turned back, I shook my head. I wanted nothing more to do with him.

"Hold on," he said. Then he clicked his tongue.

The horse began to move. I clutched Cahil's waist as I bounced in the saddle. The ground seemed so far down and looked so hard. I fought to keep my balance as we caught up to his men. When we passed them, I relaxed, assuming he would stop and let me off. But we kept going, and the men ran behind.

As we wound our way through the Citadel, I focused on the horse beneath me, trying to find a rhythm for my body to match the horse's like Cahil seemed to be doing. He crouched above the saddle, while my legs pounded the leather. I concentrated on the horse's movement and suddenly found myself looking out of the horse's eyes.

The road wrapped around like I was inside a bubble. I could see far forward as well as to each side, and almost all the way behind. The horse was hot and tired, and he wondered why there were two people on his back. Peppermint Man was the only one who usually rode him. But sometimes Straw Boy took him out for exercise back home. He longed for his cool quiet stall filled with hay and a bucket of water.

Water soon, I thought to the horse. I hoped. *What's your name?* I asked.

Topaz.

I marveled at our communication. Contact with other animals had only given me a glimpse through their eyes and a hint of their desires. I never had an actual conversation with an animal before.

My back began to ache. *Smoother?* I asked. Topaz changed his gait. Cahil grunted in surprise, but I exhaled with relief. It was as if I rode on a sled down a snow-covered hill.

With the new gait, we moved faster, and the men fell farther behind us. Cahil tried to slow Topaz down, but the horse was determined to get his water.

We reached the base of a tall tower and stopped in the shade. Cahil jumped down from the horse and inspected Topaz's legs.

"I've never seen him do that before," Cahil said.

"Do what?"

"He's a three-gaited horse."

"Meaning?"

"Meaning he knows how to trot, canter and gallop."

"So?"

"So that wasn't one of his gaits. Some horses can do up to five, but I'm not even sure what that was."

"It was smooth and fast. I liked it," I said.

Cahil looked at me with suspicion.

"How do I get down?" I asked.

"Left foot in the stirrup. Swing your right leg back around to the left, then hop off."

I landed on wobbly legs. Topaz swung his head and looked at me. He wanted water. I took one of Topaz's water bags off the saddle and held it open for him. Cahil narrowed his eyes at me, then at his horse.

"Is this Magician's Keep?" I asked to distract Cahil.

"Yes. The entrance is around the corner. We'll wait for my men, then go in."

It didn't take long for his men to catch up. We walked to the Keep's entrance, where high scalloped arches framed the massive marble doors. Pink columns supported the arches that spanned two stories. The gates stood open, and we entered without any resistance from the guards.

Inside was a courtyard and beyond that was a collection of buildings. Another city within the city. I couldn't believe the sizes and colors. A patchwork of different-colored marble formed the structures. Statues of various animals peeked out from corners and roofs. There were gardens and lawns. My eyes were relieved to view the greenery after enduring the white glare of the Citadel's walls.

I could see that the Keep's thick outer wall formed a rectangle that enclosed the entire area. A tower occupied each of the four corners.

Directly opposite the entrance, two figures stood on the steps that led up to the largest structure. Small blocks of peach marble dotted the predominately yellow-colored building. As we drew closer, I realized the figures were Leif and a tall woman. She wore a sleeveless midnight-blue dress that fell to her ankles. Her feet were bare and her white hair was cropped close to her head. Sunlight disappeared into her almost-black skin.

When we reached the base of the steps, Cahil handed the horse's reins to Marrok. "Take him to the stables and then unpack. I'll meet you in the barracks."

"Yes, sir," Marrok said, turning to go.

"Marrok," I said. "Make sure you give Topaz some milk oats."

He nodded and moved on.

Cahil squeezed my arm. "How do you know about milk oats?"

I thought fast. "Cahil, I've been traveling with you for over a week, I've helped feed him." True to a point, but I didn't think it would be a good idea to tell Cahil that his horse had asked me for some milk oats. And I was certain he didn't want to know that his own horse called him Peppermint Man.

"You're lying. Milk oats are a special treat that the Stable Master bakes. *He* feeds them to the horses, no one else."

I opened my mouth to reply, but a strident voice interrupted, "Cahil, is something wrong?"

Together we glanced at the woman. She and Leif were descending toward us.

"Nothing's wrong," Cahil said.

They stopped a few steps above us.

"Is this her?" the woman asked.

"Yes, First Magician," Cahil said.

"Are you certain about her allegiance to Ixia?" she asked.

"Yes. She carries an Ixian uniform and has Ixian coins," Cahil said.

"Her loyalty and longing for Ixia tastes thick like a rancid soup," Leif said.

The woman stepped closer to me. I looked into her amber eyes. They were shaped like a snow cat's and were just as lethal. Her gaze expanded, encompassing me and my world disappeared as the ground turned to rippling amber liquid. I began to sink. Something circled my ankles, and then pulled me under the surface. My clothes were stripped away, then my skin, then my muscles. My bones dissolved until there was nothing left but my soul.

10

Something sharp scratched my soul, searching for vulnerable spots. I pushed away the intrusive object and began to build a wall of defense in my mind. This magician would not reach me.

Bricks formed and stacked, but they crumbled at the edges. Holes drilled through as I struggled to stay ahead of First Magician. I poured all my strength into that wall. I patched the holes. I added another wall within the first. But the bricks disintegrated and collapsed.

Damn it! No! I scrambled for a while, but it was just a matter of time. In the end, I let the wall dissolve. But, with a sudden rush of energy, I created a curtain of green-veined marble, cutting her off.

I pressed myself to the smooth stone and held on with all my might. Exhaustion pulled at my mind. In pure desperation, I used the last of my power, calling for help. The marble transformed into a statue of Valek. He looked at me in concern.

"Help," I said.

He wrapped his strong arms around me, pulling me close to his chest. "Anything, love."

With nothing left, I clung to him as darkness descended.

★ ★ ★

I awoke in a narrow room; my head throbbing. Looking up at the ceiling, I realized that I was on a bed. It had been pushed against a wall under an open window. When I moved to sit up, my stiff legs protested. I felt raw and violated as though someone had scrubbed off my skin. My throat blazed with thirst. A pitcher of water sweated on a night table, an empty glass beside it. I poured a large drink and downed the cool liquid in three gulps. Feeling a little better, I examined the room. An armoire stood along the opposite wall with a full-length mirror on the right and a doorway on the left.

Cahil appeared in the doorway. "I thought I heard you."

"What happened?" I asked.

"First Magician tried to read your mind," Cahil said. He looked embarrassed. "She was extremely annoyed by your resistance, but she did say you weren't a spy."

"Peachy." Sarcasm rendered my voice sharp. I crossed my arms over my chest. "How did I get here?"

Splotches of red spread on his cheeks. "I carried you."

I hugged myself. The thought of being touched by him made my skin crawl. "Why did you stay?"

"I wanted to make sure you were all right."

"*Now* you're concerned about me? I find that hard to believe." I stood on sore legs. They felt as if I had run too many laps, and my lower back ached. "Where am I?"

"In the students' quarters. Apprentice wing. You've been assigned these rooms."

Cahil retreated into the other room. I followed him into a small sitting area with a large desk, a couch, table and chairs, and a marble fireplace. The walls were made of light green marble. My pack rested on the table with my bow.

There was another door. I crossed the room and opened it. Beyond the threshold was a garden courtyard with trees and statues. Through them I could see the setting sun. I stepped outside, glancing around. My rooms were at the end of a long one-story building. No one was in sight.

Cahil joined me outside. "The students will be back at the start of the cooling season." He pointed to a path. "That leads to the dining hall and classrooms. Want me to give you a tour?"

"No," I said, going back into the sitting room. I turned around in the doorway. "I want you and your toy soldiers to leave me the hell alone. Now you know I'm not a spy, stay the hell away from me." I closed the door and locked it, leaving Cahil outside. Just to be safe, I wedged a chair under the doorknob.

I curled up on the bed. The desire to go home racked my body. Home to Valek. To his strength and his love. Just that brief contact with him made me miss him even more. His absence left an emptiness that burned deep inside me.

I wanted to leave Sitia. I had gained enough control of my magic to avoid a flameout. I didn't need to be here with these horrible people. All I had to do was head north, and I would reach Ixia's border. I planned the journey in my mind, making a list of provisions, and even considered horse-napping Topaz to make my escape. When the room grew dark, I fell asleep.

When the sun woke me, I rolled onto my other side, weighed my chances of escaping the Keep without anyone knowing and realized I knew nothing of the layout of the Keep. I could make a reconnaissance of the area, but I had no desire to see anyone or be seen. So, I stayed in bed all day and went back to sleep that night.

Another day passed. Someone rattled the doorknob then knocked, calling out to me. I shouted for them to go away, and was content when they did.

Eventually, I lay in a stupor. My mind floated and reached some creatures in the garden. I flinched away from even that light contact, seeking a peaceful place.

Then I found Topaz. Peppermint Man had come to visit,

but the horse wondered where Lavender Lady was. I saw a picture of me in Topaz's mind. Lavender Lady must be the name he had given me. It was funny that Topaz called me Lavender Lady. Traveling with Cahil left little time for bathing, but I had managed to find some privacy to freshen up and apply a few drops of my mother's Lavender perfume.

Go smooth and fast, Topaz thought.

Would you take me far away to the north? I asked.

Not without Peppermint Man. Smooth and fast with you both. I am strong.

You are very strong. Perhaps I'll stay with you.

No, you won't, Yelena. You've sulked enough, Irys's voice said in my mind. Her contact was like a thick cool salve rubbed on an open wound.

I'm not sulking.

Then what would you call it? Irys demanded with annoyance.

Protecting myself.

She laughed. *From what? Roze barely got through.*

Roze?

Roze Featherstone, First Magician. And she's been in a rage ever since. You've weathered worse things, Yelena. What's the real problem?

I felt helpless and alone with no one to watch my back. But I buried that thought deep, unwilling to share it with Irys. Instead, I ignored her question. Knowing my mentor was back, I rallied. She was the only person I could trust in the Keep.

I'm coming with some food. You will let me in and you will eat. Irys ordered.

Food? Topaz thought hopefully. *Apple? Peppermints?*

I smiled. *Later.*

My stomach grumbled. As I moved to sit on the edge of the bed, a wave of dizziness overcame me. I had lost track of the days and I was weak from hunger.

Irys came as promised, carrying a tray laden with fruit and cold meats. She also brought a pitcher of pineapple juice and some cakes. As I ate, she told me about her trip to May's home. May was the last of the kidnapped girls to find her lost family.

"Five sisters just like her," Irys said, shaking her head.

I grinned, imagining May's homecoming. Six girls squealing with delight, laughing and crying as they all talked at once.

"Their beleaguered father wanted me to test all the girls for magical potential. May has some, but I want her to wait another year before coming to the school. The others were still too young." Irys poured two cups of juice. "I had to cut my visit short when I felt your call for help."

"When Roze was invading?"

"Yes. I was too far away to assist you, but it seems like you managed on your own."

"Valek helped me," I said.

"That's impossible. *I* couldn't reach you. Valek's not a magician."

"But he was there and I drew on his strength."

Unwilling to believe me, Irys shook her head.

I thought about how Irys had found me in the north. "You felt my power when I was in Ixia," I said. "It's the same distance for Valek to reach me."

She shook her head again. "Valek is resistant to magic so I think you used his image as a shield against Roze. When I felt you last year, you had no control over your powers. Uncontrolled bursts of magic cause ripples in the power source. All magicians, anywhere in the world can feel that, but only Master Magicians will know from which direction it comes."

That worried me. "You felt my call for help when you were at May's home, though. Was I out of control to be able to reach you at that distance?" Loss of control led to flameout, which led to death for the magician and damaged the power source for all magicians.

She looked startled. "No." She frowned and stared at the

wall, considering. "Yelena, what have you been doing with your magic since I left you?"

I told her about the ambush, the escape and the truce with Cahil.

"So you put *all* of Cahil's men into a deep sleep?" she asked.

"Well, there were only twelve. Did I do something wrong? Have I broken your Ethical Code?" There was so much I didn't know about magic.

Irys snorted, reading my mind. *And you wanted to run away with a horse.*

"Better than staying here with Cahil and Leif," I said aloud.

"Those two." Irys frowned again. "The Master Magicians had a discussion with both of them. Roze is furious that they misled her about you. Cahil actually had the audacity to demand a Council session in the middle of the hot season. He'll just have to wait until the cooling season. Perhaps he'll get on the agenda, or perhaps not." Irys shrugged, seeming unconcerned.

"Would the Sitians go to war for Cahil?" I asked.

"We have no quarrel with the north, but no love for them, either. The Council has been waiting for Cahil to mature. If he develops the charisma and strong leadership abilities, his plans to take back Ixia may be supported by the Council." She cocked her head to the side as if considering the prospect of going to war.

"The trade treaty is the first official contact we've had with Ixia in fifteen years," she explained. "It's a good beginning. We have always been worried that Commander Ambrose would try to take over Sitia as he did in the north, but he seems content."

"Would a Sitian army prevail against the north?"

"What do you think?"

"Sitia would have a difficult time. The Commander's men are loyal, dedicated and well trained. To lose a battle, they would either need to be vastly outnumbered or be vastly outsmarted."

Irys nodded. "A campaign against them would have to be launched with the utmost care, which is why the Council is waiting. But that is not my concern today. My priority is to teach you magic, and discover your specialty. You're stronger than I thought, Yelena. Putting twelve men to sleep is no easy task. And having a conversation with a horse…" Irys pulled her hair back from her face and held it behind her head. "If I hadn't been listening in, I wouldn't have believed you."

Irys rose and began to pile the dishes onto the tray. "What you did to Cahil's men would normally be considered a breach of the Ethical Code, but you acted in self-defense, so it was acceptable." She paused for a moment. "What Roze did to you was a clear violation of our ethics, but she thought you were a spy. The Code doesn't apply to spies. All Sitians are united in their intolerance for espionage. The Commander gained power by infiltrating the monarchy and using assassination, so Sitia worries when a spy is uncovered that the Commander is trying to collect enough information to launch another takeover."

Picking up the tray of dirty plates, Irys said, "Tomorrow, I will show you the Keep and start your training. There are candles and flint in the armoire if you need a light, and there's firewood behind the building for when it gets cold. I've assigned you to the apprentices' wing because you're too old for the first-years' barracks. And I think by the start of school, you'll be ready to join the apprentice class."

"What's the apprentice class?"

"The Keep has a five-year curriculum. Students start the program about a year after they reach maturity. Usually around the age of fourteen their magic has grown to a point where they can direct it. Each year of the Keep's curriculum has a title. First year, novice, junior, senior and apprentice. You'll be at the apprentice level, but your schooling will be different since you need to learn about our history and government." Irys shook her head. "I'll figure it out before classes start. You'll probably be with students from different levels, depending on the subject. But don't worry about that now. Why don't you unpack and make yourself at home."

Her words reminded me that I had something for her in my pack. "Irys, wait a moment," I said before she could leave. "My mother sent you some perfume." I dug into my bag. By some stroke of luck, the bottles hadn't been damaged during the trip to the Citadel. I gave Irys the Apple Berry perfume, and put my bottle of Lavender on the table.

Irys thanked me and left. After she was gone, the room felt empty. Taking everything out of my backpack, I hung my old uniform in the armoire and decorated the table with the valmur statue I had bought for Valek, but the rooms still seemed bare. I would ask Irys to exchange my Ixian money. Perhaps I could purchase a few things to brighten up the place.

I found Esau's field guide at the bottom of my pack. Taking a candle into the bedroom, I read his book until my eyes grew heavy. From his vast notes, it seemed that almost every plant and tree in the jungle had a reason for existing. I caught myself wishing there was a page in his guide that had my picture on it with the reason for my existence written underneath in Esau's neat hand.

In the morning, Irys scrunched up her nose when she entered my rooms. "Perhaps I'll show you the bathhouse first. We'll send your clothes to the laundry and get you some fresh ones."

I laughed. "Bad?"

"Yes."

Irys and I went to another marble building with blue columns all around. The bathhouse had separate pools for men and women. Washing the road grime from my skin felt wonderful. The laundry mistress took my tattered and stained clothes. Nutty's outfit, my white shirt and black pants all needed mending.

I borrowed a light green cotton tunic and khaki-colored

pants. Irys told me the Keep had no particular dress code for classes and everyday events, but special functions required an apprentice robe.

After I combed and plaited my hair, we walked to the dining room for breakfast. Gazing around the Keep, I could see a pattern in the inner layout. Paths and gardens wound their way past marble buildings of various size and shape. Barracks and student housing ringed the main campus. The stables, laundry and kennels lined the back wall of the Keep. Horses grazed in a large fenced pasture next to an oval training yard.

I asked Irys about the four towers.

"The Master Magicians live in them." She pointed to the one in the northwest corner. "That one is mine. The one in the northeast corner near the stables is Zitora Cowan's, Third Magician. The southwest one is Roze Featherstone's, and the southeast one is Bain Bloodgood's, Second Magician."

"What if you have more than four Masters?"

"In the history of the Magician's Keep, we have never had more than four. Less, yes, but never more. It would be a wonderful problem to have. The towers are huge so there would be plenty of room to share." She smiled.

Three people sat in the dining room. Rows and rows of empty tables lined the long room.

"When school starts, these tables will be filled with students, teachers and magicians. Everyone eats here," Irys explained.

She introduced me to the two men and one woman eating breakfast. Gardeners on break, they were just a small part of the vast force needed to tend the landscaping.

We ate, I pocketed an apple for Topaz and Irys took me to her chambers. After climbing what seemed like a million steps and passing ten levels of rooms, we emerged at the top. The circular room's windows stretched from floor to ceiling. Curtains, long and lacy, blew in the hot breeze. Colorful cushions and couches in blues, purples and silver decorated the bright area. The place was ringed with bookshelves, and the air held a fresh citrus scent.

"My meditation room," Irys said. "The perfect environment to draw power and to learn."

I walked around, looking outside. She had a magnificent view of the Keep and, through the northeast facing windows, I could see rolling green hills pockmarked with small villages.

"That's part of the Featherstone Clan's lands," Irys said, following my gaze. She gestured to the center of the room. "Sit down. Let's begin." Irys sat on a purple cushion, crossing her legs.

I perched on a blue pillow across from her. "But my bow…"

"You won't need your bow. I'll teach you how to draw your power without relying on physical contact. The power source surrounds the world like a blanket. You have the ability to take a thread from this cloth, pull it into your body and use it. But don't take too much or you'll bunch up the blanket, warping the source and leaving some areas bare and others with too much power. It's rumored that there are places where there are holes in the blanket, areas of no power, but I haven't found any."

I felt her power spread from her like a bubble. She raised her hand and said, "Venettaden."

The power slammed into me. My muscles froze solid. I stared at her in a growing panic.

"Push it away," she said.

I considered my brick wall, but knew it was no match for her strength. Once again, I drew down my marble curtain and severed the flow of power. My muscles relaxed.

"Very good," she said. "I took a line of power and shaped it into a ball. Then, using a word and a gesture, I directed it toward you. We teach the students words and gestures for learning purposes, but really you can use anything you want. It just helps focus the power. And after a while you won't need to use the words to perform the magic. It becomes instinctive. Now, your turn."

"But I don't know how to pull a thread of power. I just concentrate on the feel of my bow's wood and then my mind somehow detaches and I project it out to other minds. Why does that work?"

"The ability to read thoughts is another thread of power linking two minds, forging a connection. Once the link is made, it remains there and reconnecting is easy. For example, consider the link between us, and between you and Topaz."

"And Valek," I said.

"Yes, Valek, too. Although with his immunity to magic, I think your link with him must be on a subconscious level. Have you ever read his thoughts?"

"No. But I haven't tried. Somehow I always knew what he was feeling."

"A survival instinct. That makes sense, considering his position in Ixia, and since he decided if you would live or die on a daily basis."

"That survival instinct saved me a few times," I said, remembering my troubles in Ixia. "I would find myself in a tight spot, and suddenly it seemed another person had taken control of my body and impossible things would happen."

"Yes, but now you have control and you can *make* those things happen."

"I'm not so sure—"

Irys raised her hand. "Enough of that. Now concentrate. Feel the power. Pull it to you and hold it."

I took a deep breath, and closed my eyes for good measure. Feeling a little silly, I focused on the air around me, trying to sense the blanket of power. For a while nothing happened. Then, I felt the air thicken and press against my skin. I willed the magic to gather closer. Once the pressure grew intense, I opened my eyes. Irys watched me.

"When you release it toward me, think of what you want the power to do. A word or gesture will help and can be used as a shortcut for the next time."

I pushed the power, and said, "Over."

For a moment nothing happened. Then Irys's eyes widened in shock, and she fell over.

I ran to her. "I'm sorry."

She peered up at me. "That was odd."

"Odd how?"

"Instead of pushing me over, your magic invaded my mind, giving me a mental command to fall." Irys settled herself back on the pillow.

"Try again, but this time think of the power as a physical object like a wall and direct it toward me."

I followed her directions, but the results were the same.

"It's an unorthodox method, but it works." Irys tucked a loose strand of hair behind her ear. "Let's work on your defenses. I want you to deflect my power before it can affect you."

In a blur of motion she aimed a ball of energy toward me. "Teatottle."

I jumped back and put my hands up, but I wasn't fast enough. My world spun. Streaks of color swirled around me before I could position my defenses. I was flat on my back, looking up at the sloped ceiling of the tower. An owl slept on a nest in the rafters.

"You need to keep your defenses up at all times," Irys said. "You don't want to be caught unaware. But then again..." Irys smoothed her shirt. "You kept Roze from going deep into your mind."

I shied away from that subject. "What does Teatottle mean?" I asked.

"It's a nonsense word," Irys said. "I made it up. No sense alerting you to what I planned to do. I use those words for attacks and defensive moves. But for practical matters like fire and light, I use real words."

"I can make fire?"

"If you're strong enough. But it's tiring work. Using magic is draining, some types more than others. You seem to be able to connect with other minds without a lot of effort," Irys said. "Perhaps that is your specialty."

"What do you mean by specialty?"

"Some magicians can only do certain things. We have magicians who can heal physical injuries and others who can help with mental trauma. Some can move large objects like statues, while others can light fires with minimal effort." Irys played with the tassels on her cushion. "Sometimes, you'll find someone who can do two or three things, or a hybrid talent like Leif who can sense a person's soul. For you, we've discovered that not only can you read minds, but you can also influence a person's or animal's actions. A rare talent. That's two abilities."

"Is that the limit?" I asked.

"No. Master Magicians can do everything."

"So why is Roze called First Magician and you're Fourth?"

Irys gave me a tired smile. "Roze is stronger than I am. We can both light fires. While I can only make a campfire, she has the ability to set a two-story structure ablaze."

I thought about what she had said. "If a magician only has one talent, what do they do when they finish their training?"

"We assign magicians to different towns and cities, depending on what is needed. We try to have a healer in every town at all times. Other magicians cover several towns, traveling from place to place to help with projects."

"What would I do?" I asked, wondering if a useful place for me existed. But, at the same time, I wasn't sure if I wanted a useful place in Sitia.

Irys laughed. "It's too soon to tell. For now you need to

practice collecting power and using it. And practice keeping up your defenses."

"How do I keep my wall up without draining myself?"

"I imagine my defensive wall, which resembles this tower room. I make it solid and strong, and then I make it translucent so I can see out of it, and then I don't think about it anymore. But when magic is directed toward me, my barrier solidifies and deflects the attack before my consciousness is even fully aware of it."

I followed her instructions and created an invisible barrier in my mind. Irys tested it at unexpected times throughout the morning and it held. The rest of the time I practiced gathering magic, but, no matter how hard I tried, my magic could only affect two things. Irys and the owl sleeping in the rafters.

Irys's patience amazed me, and, for the first time since coming to Sitia, I felt hopeful that mastering my powers might be within my abilities.

"That was a good start," Irys said as lunchtime neared. "Go eat, and then rest this afternoon. We'll work in the mornings and you can practice and study at night. But tonight you need to see the Stable Master and pick out a horse."

Did I hear her right? "A horse?"

"Yes. All magicians have horses. Occasionally you'll be needed somewhere fast. I had to leave my horse, Silk, here during my mission in Ixia. When you called for help, I had to borrow a horse from May's father. How else do you think I got here so fast?"

I hadn't even thought about it. I had been so wrapped up in my own misery at the time. Following Irys's directions, I located the dining hall. I ate lunch then went back to my rooms where I collapsed into bed and fell asleep.

That night after dinner, I sought out the Stable Master. I found him at the end of a row of stalls, cleaning a leather saddle. A small stocky man, his wild brown hair fell past his shoulders like a horse's mane. When he glared up at me, I suppressed my smile.

"What do you want? Can't you see I'm busy?" he asked.

"I'm Yelena. Irys sent me."

"Oh, right, the new student. I don't know why Fourth Magician couldn't wait until everyone's back to start your lessons," he muttered to himself as he put the saddle down. "This way."

He led me past the stable. Topaz poked his head out of his stall.

His big brown eyes looked hopeful. *Apple?* he asked.

Irys had been right. I reconnected with Topaz without any conscious effort. Or had he connected with me? I would have to ask her about that. I gave him the apple in my pocket.

The Stable Master turned around. "You just made a friend for life," he said, snorting in amusement. "That horse loves food. I never saw a horse take such pleasure in eating before. You can train him to do just about anything for a peppermint."

We went past the hay barn to the pasture. The Stable Master leaned against the wooden fence. Six horses grazed in the field.

"Pick one out. Makes no difference which one, they're all good. I'll go find your instructor."

"You don't teach?" I asked before he could go.

"Not in the middle of the hot season when everyone but me is gone," he said with annoyance. "I'm too busy mucking out stalls and fixing tack. I said to wait, but Fourth Magician wanted it right away. Good thing one of my instructors came back early." He mumbled some more as he headed toward the stable.

I studied the horses in the field. Three were dark brown like Topaz, two were black, and one was copper with white on the legs from the knees down. Knowing nothing of horses, I guessed it would come down to color. The copper-and-white horse looked over at me.

Like her, Topaz said. *She go smooth and fast for Lavender Lady.*
How do I get her to come over? I asked.

Peppermints. Topaz looked lovingly at a leather bag hanging near his stall. The Stable Master had disappeared. I went back to the stable. Taking out two mints, I gave one to Topaz, and took the other back to the field.

Show Kiki peppermint.

I held out the mint. Kiki glanced at the other horses, and then moved toward me. When she came closer, I could see she had a white face with a patch of brown around her left eye. Something about her eyes seemed strange. It wasn't until she sucked the peppermint from my palm that it struck me. Her eyes were blue. I had never seen that before, but that didn't mean much. I knew next to nothing about horses.

Scratch behind ears, Topaz suggested.

The mare's long copper ears were cocked forward. I stood on tiptoes and rubbed my fingernails behind them. Kiki lowered her head and pressed it against my chest.

"What do you think, girl?" I asked out loud. I couldn't hear her like Topaz. While rubbing her ears, I pulled a thread of power and projected my mind to her. *Be with me?*

She nudged me with her nose. *Yes.*

I felt Topaz's pleasure. *We go smooth and fast together.*

I jumped when I heard the Stable Master behind me.

"Found one already?" he asked.

I nodded without looking at him.

"That one came from the plains," he said. "Good choice."

"She must pick another," said a familiar voice.

I turned. Dread curled in my stomach. Cahil stood next to the Stable Master.

"And why would I listen to you?" I demanded.

He smirked. "Because I'm your instructor."

11

"No," I said. "You will *not* be my instructor."

"No choice," said the Stable Master. He glanced at Cahil then me, looking puzzled. "There's no one else and Fourth Magician insists you start right away."

"What if I help you muck out the stables and feed the horses? Will you have time to teach me then?" I asked the Stable Master.

"Young lady, you already have plenty to do. You'll be mucking and caring for your own horse, as well as studying your lessons. Cahil's been a stable rat since he was six. No one, other than me..." He grinned. "...knows more about horses."

I planted my hands on my hips. "Fine. As long as he knows more about horses than he does about people."

Cahil cringed. Good.

"But I keep this horse," I said.

"She's a walleye," Cahil said.

"A what?" I asked.

"She has blue eyes. That's bad luck. And she's been bred by the Sandseed Clan. Their horses are difficult to train."

Kiki snorted at Cahil. *Mean Boy.*

"A silly superstition and an unfair reputation. Cahil, you

should know better," the Stable Master said. "She's a perfectly good horse. Whatever's going on between you and Yelena, you'll have to work it out. I've no time to babysit." With that, he stalked away, once more muttering to himself.

Cahil and I glared at each other for a while until Kiki nudged my arm, looking for peppermints.

"Sorry, girl, no more," I said, holding out my empty hand. She tossed her head, and resumed grazing.

Cahil stared at me. I crossed my arms over my chest, but they seemed an inadequate barrier between us. I would have preferred thick marble walls. He had exchanged his traveling clothes for a plain white shirt and tight-fitting jodhpurs, but he still wore his black riding boots.

"You'll have to live with your decision about the horse. But if you're going to fight me every time I try to teach you something, let me know now, and I won't waste my time."

"Irys wants me to learn, so I'll learn."

He appeared satisfied. "Good. First lesson starts now." He climbed over the pasture's fence. "Before you learn how to ride a horse, you must know everything about your horse from the physical to the emotional." Cahil clicked his tongue at Kiki, and when she ignored him, he approached her. Just as he came up beside her she turned, knocking him over with her rump.

I bit my lip to keep from laughing. Every time he tried to get near, Kiki either moved away or bumped into him.

His face red with frustration, Cahil finally said, "The hell with this. I'm getting a halter."

"You hurt her feelings when you said she was bad luck," I explained. "She'll cooperate if you apologize."

"How would you know?" Cahil demanded.

"I just know."

"You didn't even know how to dismount a horse. I'm not that stupid," he said.

When he started to climb over the fence, I said, "I know the same way I knew Topaz wanted milk oats."

Cahil stopped, waiting.

I sighed. "Topaz told me he wanted the treat. I connected with his mind by accident, so I asked him to go smoother because my back hurt. It's the same with Kiki."

Cahil pulled at his beard. "The First Magician said you had strong magical abilities. I guess I should have known it before, but I was too focused on the spy thing." He looked at me as if noticing me for the first time.

For a second, I thought I witnessed cold calculation slide through Cahil's blue eyes, but it disappeared, leaving me to wonder if I had seen anything at all.

"Her name's Kiki?" he asked.

I nodded. Cahil returned to Kiki and apologized. I felt a sudden peevish annoyance. He should have been apologizing to me for all the pain he had caused. Spy thing, my ass.

Push Mean Boy? Kiki asked.

No. Be nice. He's going to teach me to care for you.

Cahil gestured for me to join him near Kiki. I clambered over the fence. As Kiki stood her ground, Cahil pointed to and lectured about the different parts of her body. Starting with her muzzle, he didn't stop until he had lifted her right back hoof and showed me the underside.

"Same time tomorrow," he said, ending the lesson. "Meet me in the stable. We'll go over horse care."

Before he could head back to the barn, I stopped him. Now that my annoyance that he was my instructor was gone, I wondered why he was here. "Why are you teaching me? I thought your campaign for the Ixian throne would take up most of your time."

Well aware of how I felt about his quest, Cahil studied me, seeking for signs of sarcasm.

"Until I receive the full support of the Sitian Council, I can only do so much," he said. "Besides, I need money to pay for my expenses. Most of my men are employed at the Keep as guards or gardeners, depending on what's needed." He wiped his hands on his pants, staring at the horses in the pasture. "When the Keep is on hiatus during the hot season, I focus all my efforts on gathering support. This season I thought I would finally get the Council's backing." Cahil looked at me. "But that didn't work out. So I'm back to work and back to begging the Council to put me on their agenda." He frowned and shook his head. "Tomorrow, then?"

"Tomorrow." I watched Cahil as he walked to the stable. He had been counting on catching an Ixian spy to influence the Council. I wondered what he would try next.

Kiki nudged my arm and I scratched behind her ears before I returned to my rooms. Rummaging around for some paper, I sat at my desk and drew a crude sketch of a horse. I labeled the parts that I could remember. Topaz and Kiki helped me with the rest.

The connection I had formed with the two horses was odd yet comforting. It was as if we were all in the same room, doing different tasks and minding our own business and having our own private thoughts. But when one of us would "speak" directly to the other, we would "hear" it. I only had to think about Kiki and her thoughts would fill my mind. The same was true with Irys. I didn't need to pull power and project it to Irys. All I needed to do was think about her.

Over the next week, my days fell into a pattern. Mornings spent with Irys to learn about magic, afternoons spent napping, studying and practicing my self-defense techniques. Evenings were spent with Cahil and Kiki. As I moved throughout the campus, I kept a wary eye out for Goel. I hadn't forgotten his threat.

Not long into my magical training, Irys began testing me for other abilities.

"Let's see if you can start a fire," Irys said one morning. "This time, when you pull in the power, I want you to concentrate on lighting this candle." She placed a candlestick in front of me.

"How?" I asked, sitting up. I had been reclining on the pillows in her tower room, thinking about Kiki. It had been a week, and I still hadn't ridden her. So far, Cahil had spent every lesson teaching me about horse care and tack. What an annoying man.

"Think of a single flame before you direct your magic." Irys demonstrated. "Fire," she said. The candle flared and burned before she blew it out. "Your turn."

I focused on the candle's wick, forming a flaming image in my mind. Pushing magic toward the candle, I willed it to light. Nothing happened.

Irys made a strangled sound and the candle burned. "Are you directing your magic to the candle?"

"Yes. Why?"

"You just ordered me to light the candle for you," Irys said in exasperation. "And *I* did it."

"Is that bad?"

"No. I hope you know how to light a fire the mundane way, because, so far, it seems that's not part of your magical skills. Let's try something else."

I tried to move a physical object with no success. Unless making Irys do it for me could be considered a magical skill.

She raised her mental defenses, blocking out my influence. "Try again. This time focus on keeping control."

As I pulled in power, Irys threw a pillow at me. The pillow struck me in the stomach. "Hey!"

"You were supposed to deflect it with your magic. Try again."

By the end of the session, I was glad Irys had chosen a pillow. Otherwise, I would have been covered with bruises.

"I think you just need to practice your control," Irys said, refusing to give up. "Get some rest. You'll do better tomorrow."

Before leaving, I asked something that had been on my mind for several days. "Irys, can I see more of the Citadel? And I need to exchange my Ixian coins for Sitian so I can buy some items and clothes. Is there a marketplace?"

"Yes, but it's only open one day a week during the hot season." She paused for a moment, considering. "I'll give you market days off. No lessons. You can explore the Citadel or do whatever you want. It'll be open in two days. In the meantime, I'll exchange your money."

Irys couldn't pass up the opportunity to lecture me on spending money wisely. "Your expenses are covered while you're in the Keep. But once you graduate, you'll be on your own. You'll earn wages as a magician, of course," Irys said. "But don't give your money away." She smiled to ease the reprimand. "We don't like to encourage the beggars."

The image of the dirty little boy rose in my mind. "Why don't they have any money?" I asked.

"Some are lazy, preferring to beg instead of work. Others are unable to work because of physical or mental problems. The healers can only do so much. And some gamble or spend their money faster than they can earn it."

"But what about the children?"

"Runaways, orphans or the offspring of the homeless. The hot season is the worst time for them. Once school starts and the Citadel is populated again, there are places they can go for food and shelter." Irys touched my shoulder. "Don't worry about them, Yelena."

I mulled over Irys's comments on my way back to my rooms. That evening, while teaching me to saddle and bridle Kiki in her barn stall, Cahil asked, "What's gotten into you? You've been snapping at me all night."

Lavender Lady upset, Kiki agreed.

I sucked in a deep breath, preparing to apologize, but an unbidden torrent of words poured from my mouth instead. "You want Ixia so you can be king. So you can collect taxes, sit on a throne and wear a crown of jewels while the people suffer like they did under your uncle. So your henchmen like Goel can kill innocent children when their parents can't pay the taxes for your fine silk clothes, or so they can kill the parents, leaving their offspring homeless and beggars." My outburst ended as fast as it had begun.

Cahil gaped in shock, but recovered fast. "That's not what I want," he said. "I want to help the people of Ixia. So they have the freedom to wear whatever clothes they want instead of being forced to wear uniforms. So they can marry whomever they want without securing a permit from their district's General. Live wherever they want, even if it's in Sitia. I want the crown so I can free Ixia of the military dictatorship."

His reasons sounded superficial. Would the people be any freer with him as their ruler? I didn't believe his answer was the real reason. "What makes you think the Ixian people want you to free them? No government is perfect. Did it ever occur to you that the Ixians might be content under the Commander's rule?" I asked.

"Were you content with your life in the north?" Cahil asked. An intensity held his body rigid while he waited for my response.

"I had unusual circumstances."

"Such as?"

"None of your business."

"Let me guess," Cahil said with a superior tone.

I clutched my arms to keep from punching him.

"A kidnapped southerner with magical abilities? That is unusual. But do you think you were the first person that Fourth Magician had to rescue? Northerners are born with magical powers, too. My uncle was a Master Magician. And you *know* what the Commander does to anyone found with power."

Valek's words echoed in my mind. Anyone found in the Territory of Ixia with magical power was killed. Magicians might be hunted in Ixia, but the rest of the citizens had everything they needed.

"We're not that different, Yelena. You were born in Sitia and raised in Ixia, and I'm an Ixian raised in Sitia. You have returned home. I'm only trying to find mine."

I opened my mouth to reply, but snapped it shut when Irys spoke in my mind. *Yelena, come to the infirmary right away.*

Are you all right? I asked.

I'm fine. Just come.

Where's the infirmary?

Have Cahil show you. Then her magical energies withdrew.

I told Cahil what Irys required. Without hesitation, he removed Kiki's saddle and bridle. We hung them in the tack room before we headed for the center of the Keep. I had to jog to keep up with him.

"Did she say what this was about?" he asked over his shoulder.

"No."

We entered a one-story building. The marble walls were a soothing pale blue, resembling ice. A young man in a white uniform moved about the lobby, lighting lanterns. The sun's rays had begun to disappear for the day.

"Where's Irys?" I asked the young man.

He looked puzzled.

Cahil said, "Fourth Magician."

"She's with Healer Hayes," he said, and when we failed to move, the man pointed to a long corridor. "Down the hall. Fifth door on the left."

"Few call her Irys," Cahil explained as we hurried down the empty hallway.

We stopped at the fifth one. The door was closed.

"Come in," Irys called before I could knock.

I opened the door. Irys stood next to a man dressed in white. Healer Hayes perhaps. A figure lay under a sheet spread over a bed in the center of the room. Bandages shrouded the face.

Leif hunched in a chair in the corner of the room, looking horrified. When he spotted me, he asked, "What's she doing here?"

"I asked her to come. She may be able to help," Irys said.

"What's going on?" I asked Irys.

"Tula was found in Booruby near death. Her mind has fled, and we can't reach her," Irys explained. "We need to find out who did this to her."

"I can't feel her," Leif said. "The other Master Magicians can't reach her. She's gone, Fourth Magician. You're just wasting time."

"What happened?" Cahil asked.

"Beaten, tortured, raped," the healer said. "You name something horrible, and it's probably been done to her."

"And she was fortunate," Irys said.

"How can you call that fortunate?" Cahil demanded. His outrage evident in the sudden tautness of his shoulders, the strident tone in his voice.

"She escaped with her life," Irys replied. "None of the others were so lucky."

"How many?" I asked, not really wanting to know, but unable to stop the words.

"She is the eleventh victim. The others were all found dead, brutalized in the same manner." A look of disgust etched Irys's face.

"How can I help?" I asked.

"Mental healing is my strongest power, yet you reached the Commander and brought him back when I couldn't," she said.

"What?" Cahil cried. "You helped the Commander?"

His outrage focused on me. I ignored him.

"But I knew the Commander. I had an idea of where to look," I said to Irys. "I'm not sure I can help you."

"Try anyway. The bodies have been discovered in different towns throughout Sitia. We haven't been able to find a reason for the killings and we have no suspects. We need to catch this monster." Irys pulled at her hair. "Unfortunately, this is the kind of situation you will be asked to deal with when you become a magician. Consider this a learning experience."

I moved closer to the bed. "May I hold her hand?" I asked the healer.

He nodded and pulled the sheet back, revealing the girl's torso. Between the blood-soaked bandages, her skin looked like raw meat. Cahil cursed. I glanced at Leif; his face remained turned to the wall.

Splinted with pieces of wood, each of the girl's fingers must have been broken. I gently took her hand, rubbing my fingertips along her palm. Pulling a thread of power, I closed my eyes and projected my energy to her.

Her mind felt abandoned. The sense that she had fled and would never come back filled the emptiness. Gray intangible ghosts floated in her mind. Upon closer examination, each specter represented Tula's memory of a specific horror. The ghosts' faces twisted with pain, terror and fear. Raw emotions began to sink into my skin. I pushed the ghosts away, concentrating on finding the real Tula who was most likely hiding some place where her horrors couldn't reach her.

I felt a sensation along my arms as if long grass tickled my skin. The clean earthy scent of a dew-covered meadow lingered in the air, but I couldn't follow the source. I searched until my energy became depleted and I could no longer hold the connection.

At last, I opened my eyes. I sat on the floor with the girl's hand still clutched in mine. "Sorry. I can't find her," I said.

"I told you it was a waste of time," Leif said. He rose from his corner. "What did you expect from a northerner?"

"You can expect me not to give up as easily as you have," I called before he stalked out of the room.

I frowned at his retreating form. There had to be another way to wake Tula.

The healer took the girl's hand from mine and tucked it back under the sheet. I remained on the floor as he and Irys discussed the girl's condition. Her body would heal, they thought, but she would probably never regain her senses. It sounded as though she would be mindless like the children Reyad and Mogkan had created in Ixia when they had siphoned their magical power, leaving behind nothing but empty soulless bodies. I shivered at the memory of how the two evil men had tried to break me.

I brought my mind back to Tula's problems. How *had* I found the Commander? He had retreated to the place of his greatest accomplishment. The place where he felt the happiest and in the most control.

"Irys," I interrupted. "Tell me everything you know about Tula."

She considered for a moment. I could see questions perched on her lips.

Trust me, I sent to her.

"It's not much. Her family operates a profitable glass factory right outside Booruby," Irys said. "This is their busy season, so they keep the kilns going all the time. Tula was to keep the fire hot during the night. The next morning when her father came out to work, the coals were cold and Tula was gone. They searched for many days. She was finally found twelve days later in a farmer's field barely alive. Our healer in Booruby tended her physical wounds. But her mind was unreachable, so they rushed her here to me." Irys's disappointment shone on her face.

"Does Tula have any siblings?" I asked.

"Several. Why?"

I thought hard. "Any close to her age?"

"I think a younger sister."

"How much younger?"

"Not much. A year and a half maybe." Irys guessed.

"Can you bring her sister here?"

"Why?"

"With her sister's help, I might be able to bring Tula back."

"I'll send a message." Irys turned to the healer. "Hayes, let me know if Tula's condition changes."

Hayes nodded and Irys marched out the door.

Cahil and I followed. He said nothing as we left the infirmary and stepped into the twilight. With the sun almost gone, the air cooled and a faint breeze touched my face. I sucked in the freshness, trying to dilute the bitter smell of the girl's horror.

"Pretty bold," Cahil said, glancing at me. "To think you can reach her when a Master Magician could not." Cahil strode away.

"Pretty stupid," I called after his retreating form. "To give up before all possible solutions have been tried."

Cahil continued to walk without acknowledging my comments. Fine. He had given me another reason to prove him wrong.

12

Dreams of Tula's hideous ordeal swirled in my mind that night. Over and over, I fought her demons until, at last, they transformed into my own demon's mocking face. Vivid memories of my own torture and rape at Reyad's hands haunted my sleep. I awoke screaming. My heart hammered against my chest. My nightshirt was drenched with sweat.

I wiped my face, focusing on reality. There had to be a way to help Tula. Wide-awake, I dressed and went to the infirmary.

In Tula's room, Healer Hayes slumped half-asleep in a chair. He straightened when I stepped closer to the bed.

"Something wrong?" he asked.

"No. I wanted to…" I cast about for the right explanation. "Spend some time with her."

He yawned. "Can't hurt, and I could use some rest. I'll be in my office at the end of the hall. Wake me if anything changes."

I sat in Hayes's chair and held Tula's hand. Reestablishing our link, I was once again inside her vacant mind. The ghosts of her horrors flickered past. I studied them, looking for weakness. When Tula came back, she'd have to deal with each of these ghosts, and I planned to help her banish them.

Irys woke me the next morning. I had rested my head on the edge of Tula's bed.

"Have you been here all night?" she asked.

"Only half." I smiled, rubbing my eyes. "I couldn't sleep."

"I understand all too well." Irys smoothed the sheets on Tula's bed. "In fact, I can't stay here doing nothing. I'm going to fetch Tula's sister myself. Bain Bloodgood, Second Magician has agreed to continue your training while I'm gone. He usually teaches history, and likes to lecture about famous and infamous magicians." Irys smiled. "He'll give you a ton of books to read, and will quiz you on them, so be sure to finish each of your assignments."

Hayes entered the room. "Anything?"

I shook my head.

When he started to change Tula's bandages, Irys and I left the room.

"I'm leaving this morning," Irys said. "Before I go, I'll introduce you to Bain."

I followed her from the infirmary. We headed toward the large building with the peach-and-yellow marble blocks that was located across from the Keep's entrance.

The structure housed offices for the Keep's administrative staff. It contained various-size conference and meeting rooms, and an office for each Master Magician. According to Irys, the Masters preferred to meet with outsiders and officials in these rooms rather than in their towers.

Irys led me into a small meeting room. Four people huddled over a map that was spread open on a conference table. Other maps and charts were hung on the walls.

Of the four, I recognized Roze Featherstone and Leif. Roze wore another long blue dress and Leif wore his customary scowl. Beside them stood an elderly man in a navy robe and a young woman with braided hair.

Irys introduced me to the man. He had curly white hair that stuck out at odd angles.

"Bain, this is Yelena, your student for the next week or so," Irys said.

"The girl you rescued from the north?" He shook my hand. "Strange mission that."

A failed mission. Roze's cold thoughts stabbed my mind. *Yelena should have been killed, not rescued. She's too old to learn.*

Yelena's linked to me. She can hear your thoughts. Irys's annoyance was clear.

Roze gazed at me with her amber eyes. *I don't care.*

Unflinching, I stared back. *Your mistake.*

Irys stepped between us, breaking our eye contact. "And this is Zitora Cowan, Third Magician," Irys said, gesturing to the young woman.

Zitora's honey-brown braids hung to her waist. Instead of shaking my hand, she hugged me.

"Welcome, Yelena," Zitora said. "Irys tells us you may be able to help us find Tula's attacker."

"I'll try," I said.

"Tula's from my clan, so I would appreciate whatever you can do to help her." Zitora's pale yellow eyes shone with tears. She turned away.

"As you can see," Bain said, indicating the room's contents, "we are trying to deduce the methods and means of this killer. A very cunning and shrewd fellow. Unfortunately, that's all we know. Perhaps fresh eyes can spot something we missed." Bain pointed to the map on the table.

"She shouldn't be here," Leif said. "She knows nothing about this."

Before Irys could speak in my defense, I said, "You're right, Leif, I haven't dealt with this before because a horror like him would not have survived in Ixia for long."

"Why don't you just run back to your precious Commander

and your perfect Ixia and keep your nose out of our troubles?" Leif spat the words at me.

I drew breath to counter, but Irys put a warning hand on my sleeve.

"Yelena and Leif, that's quite enough," Irys said. "You're wasting time. Catching this killer is imperative."

Chastised, I peered down at the map on the table. The Sitian lands were divided into eleven territories, one for each clan. City and town locations were marked, as well as the places where the other girls had been found. Some towns had two victims, while others had none. I failed to see a pattern.

"The only consistency has been in the victims," Bain said. "All are unmarried females fifteen to sixteen years old. All were missing for approximately twelve to fourteen days. All were taken during the night. Some were stolen right from the very bedrooms they shared with siblings. And no witnesses. None."

My initial gut feeling indicated that magic had been involved, but I didn't want to say as much in front of four Master Magicians.

"We have considered a rogue magician," Irys said. "And while we have confirmed the alibis of the magicians who have graduated from our school, we are unable to question those who have one-trick powers."

"One-trick?" I asked.

"There are some who have just enough magic to do one thing like light a candle, but are unable to use magic for anything else," Irys explained. "One-tricks do not come to the Keep, but they normally use their gift in beneficial ways. Some, though, do use their ability for crime. Mostly petty. It's possible this killer's one-trick is to turn himself invisible, or be able to walk without making a sound. Something that gives him the upper hand when kidnapping a girl."

Irys's face hardened into an expression of serious determination. A look I recognized with a queasy feeling deep in my stomach. She had worn it when she had tried to kill me in Ixia.

"But only for the moment," she vowed.

"We have not ruled out a rogue magician," Bain said. "History is full of them. And I include recent history." He nodded to me. "Some day, you must tell me of the misdeeds of Kangom in Ixia, and how he met his end. I wish to add his folly to the history books."

Confused at first, it took me a moment to remember that Kangom had changed his name to Mogkan upon fleeing to Ixia.

"Speaking of books," Bain said to me, "I have some for you in my office." He turned to Roze. "Are we finished here?"

She gave a curt nod.

The other magicians made to leave, but Zitora stayed by the table, tracing a finger over the map of Sitia.

"Irys?" she asked. "Did you mark Tula's location?"

"No." Irys picked up a quill and dipped it into a bottle of red ink. "With all the commotion, I forgot." She placed a mark on the map and stepped back. "I'll be back in ten days. Please send word if something happens. Yelena, keep practicing your control."

"Yes, sir," I said.

Irys smiled then left the room. I glanced down at the map to see how far Booruby was from the Citadel. The red ink had not yet dried. Tula's town resided on the western edge of the Avibian Plains. I had thought Captain Marrok exaggerated when he had said the plains were huge, but the map showed that the plains dominated the eastern Sitian landscape.

When my eye caught the other red marks, I must have made a sound because Zitora clutched my arm.

"What is it?" she asked.

"A pattern. See?" I pointed to the map. "All the marks are near the border of the Avibian Plains."

The others returned to the table.

"Fresh eyes," Bain said, nodding to himself.

"It's obvious, now that the map's been updated," Roze said. Annoyance made her voice sharp.

"Did anyone search the plains when the girls went missing?" I asked.

"No one goes into the plains," Zitora said. "The Sandseed Clan doesn't like visitors, and their strange magic can befuddle the mind. It's best to circumvent them."

"Only the Zaltanas are welcomed by the Sandseeds," Roze said. "Perhaps Yelena and Leif could visit and determine if anything is amiss."

"No need to rush," Bain said. "Better to wait until Irys returns with Tula's sister. If Tula awakes and identifies her assailant, we would have the advantage."

"What if another girl goes missing in the meantime?" Leif asked. His scowl had deepened, and he seemed upset either by the thought of another victim or the prospect of traveling with me again.

"Then, welcome or no, we will send armed searchers into the plains," Bain said.

"But you might be too late," I said.

"We have some time." Zitora pulled at one of her braids. "That was another pattern we were able to discern. He has the victims for two weeks and then waits four weeks before claiming a new one."

The thought of another victim filled me with dread and led to a horrible scenario. "What if he comes to the Keep to finish what he started? Tula could be in danger!"

"Let him come." Roze's voice turned icy with determination. "I *will* take care of him."

"First we would have to apprehend him." Bain tapped the table with a bony finger. "We must post guards in Tula's room."

"But it's the hot season, and we're short-handed," Zitora said.

"I will tell Cahil to assign some of his men," Roze said. "He owes me."

"Get them right away, Roze," Bain said. "Not a moment to lose. Come now, Yelena, we have work to do."

Bain led me out of the room and down the hallway.

"Nice observations, young lady. I see why Irys chose not to kill you."

"Has Irys ever chosen to kill?" I asked. Cahil's comment that I had not been the first person Irys had rescued from Ixia weighed on my mind.

"Unavoidable at times. Nasty choice overall, but Irys is well suited to that role. She has a unique ability to cease a heart without pain or fear. Roze has the skill, too, but she's much too harsh. She works best with criminals and their ilk. Leif helps her with those unfortunate criminal investigations. During his schooling at the Keep, the Masters determined that would be the best use of his unusual power. Zitora, on the other hand, would die rather than harm another. I have never met a sweeter soul."

Bain stopped to unlock a door. He gestured for me to precede him into his office. Entering the room, I was greeted by a riot of color, a jumble of contraptions and shelves upon shelves of books.

"And you, sir?" I asked. "What place do you hold in this group of magicians?"

"I teach. I guide. I listen." He stacked books into a pile. "I answer questions. I let the younger magicians go on missions. I tell stories of my eventful past." Bain smiled. "Whether or not my companions wish to hear them. Now, we'll start you with these few books."

He handed me the stack. I counted seven texts. Few? Obviously, my definition of few was different than his. At least most of the books were slim.

"Tomorrow is market day. An extra day for study." Bain's

voice held a touch of reverence. To him it seemed an extra day to study was similar to receiving a pouch of gold. "Read the first three chapters in each book. We'll discuss them the day after tomorrow. Come to my tower after breakfast."

He bustled around a table, looking for something. He pulled a leather pouch from beneath an immense tome. "Yours from Irys."

The pouch jingled as I opened it. Irys had exchanged my Ixian coins for Sitian.

"How do I find the market?" I asked.

Bain rummaged around his desk until he found a sheet of paper. It was a map of the Citadel.

"Use this." Bain pointed to the market square located near the center of the Citadel.

"May I keep this?"

"Yours. Now, go. Read." With the indulgence of a father sending his child off to play, he shooed me out the door.

I read the book titles as I made my way back to my rooms. *The Source of Magic; Magical Mutations; The History of Sitian Magic; Master Level Magicians Throughout the Ages; Misuses of the Power Source; The Magician's Ethical Code* and *Windri Bak Greentree: A Biography.*

I had to admit the titles seemed fascinating, so I started my reading assignments as soon as I reached my rooms. The afternoon flew by, and only the incessant growling of my stomach made me stop to find some food.

After dinner, I visited the stables. Topaz's and Kiki's heads appeared over their stall doors the moment I arrived.

Apples? Both horses looked hopeful.

Have I ever come without? I asked.

No. Lavender Lady nice, Topaz said.

I fed Topaz and Kiki their apples. After wiping apple juice and horse slobber from my hands, I realized Cahil was late.

Deciding not to wait for him, I took Kiki's bridle and riding saddle from the tack room.

Practice? Kiki sounded as bored as I by the repetitive lessons.

How about a walk? I asked.

Fast?

No. Slow and steady so I don't fall off.

I bridled and saddled Kiki without incident, surprising myself with how much I had learned.

Before I could mount, Cahil arrived, his face red, and his beard matted with sweat. He looked as though he had run to the stables. I wondered how far he had run, which led me to wonder where he lived in the Keep, which led me, ultimately, to wonder about his childhood. What had it been like to grow up in the Magician's Keep without any family?

Cahil, oblivious to my curiosity, inspected every inch of Kiki's tack. Probably searching for a mistake. I smiled in satisfaction when all he found was a crooked stirrup.

"All right then, since she's saddled, why don't you try mounting?" Cahil said, reminding me to always mount on the horse's left side.

I placed my left foot in the stirrup and grabbed the saddle. When he moved to give me a boost up, I stopped him with a look. Kiki stood at sixteen hands, tall for a horse, but I wanted to mount her without help. Pushing off with my right foot, I launched myself up and swung my leg over the saddle.

Once settled, I looked down at Cahil from what now felt like an uncomfortable height. From this vantage point, the ground at his feet seemed to transform from plush grass to hard and unyielding earth.

Cahil lectured about the reins and the proper way to hold them, and how to sit in the saddle. "If you think you're going to fall, grab her mane. Not the saddle."

"Why not?"

"You could pinch a finger. Don't worry. You won't hurt the horse."

Cahil continued to lecture about the correct way to steer the horse and the best way to give stop and go commands. He also repeated his advice to grab Kiki's mane if I felt myself falling at least a half dozen more times. Eventually, I tuned him out, gazing around the pasture from my new perspective. I admired the way the sun reflected off a stallion's coat near the far fence, until a change in Cahil's tone caused Kiki's ears to cock forward.

"...listening to me?" Cahil demanded.

"What?"

"Yelena, this is very important. If you don't know how to—"

"Cahil," I interrupted. "I don't need commands. All I have to do is ask Kiki."

He stared at me as if I had spoken another language.

"Watch." I held the reins in front of me as Cahil had instructed. Kiki's left ear cocked back, the other pointed forward. She turned her head slightly to the left so she could see me fully.

Walk around the pasture? I asked her. *Near the fence.*

Kiki started to move. Her steps rocked me from side to side. I let her find the path as I enjoyed the view.

As we circled the pasture, I heard Cahil yell, "Heels down! Straighten up!"

Eventually, we moved out of his sight.

Fast? Kiki asked.

Not yet.

A glint of sunlight and a blur of motion from outside the fence caught my eye. Kiki shied, turning sharply to the right. I flew left.

Bad smell. Bad thing.

Instinctively, I grabbed her mane, stopping my fall. My right leg stretched across the saddle as I hung from Kiki's side, clutching her coarse brown hair.

Kiki's muscles bunched and she danced to the side. I caught a glimpse of what had startled her. *Stop. A man.*

She held still, but her legs trembled in terror. *Bad man. Shiny thing.*

I yanked myself upright in the saddle. *Bad man. Run.*

13

Kiki took off.

I held on to her mane, and tried to stay in the saddle. After a few strides, I looked behind just in time to see Goel's sword flash in the sunlight.

When Cahil saw us racing across the pasture, he raised his arms and shouted, "Whoa! Whoa!"

Kiki galloped straight for him, her mind so focused on survival that I had to wait for Goel's scent to disappear before she would respond to my calming thoughts.

Man gone. It's okay, I said to her. I patted her on the neck and whispered the same thing into her ear. She settled and halted mere inches from Cahil.

"At least you stayed on the horse." He grabbed Kiki's reins. "What happened?"

I jumped down from the saddle and examined Cahil. He didn't look surprised. In fact, he seemed mildly amused.

"What do you think happened?" I countered.

"Kiki spooked at something. I told you horses are skittish, but you had to go off before you were ready."

Something in Cahil's eyes made me suspicious. "Did you send Goel to ambush me?" I demanded.

"Goel?" Cahil seemed taken aback. "No, I—"

"You set that up. You wanted Kiki to panic."

Cahil frowned. "I wanted you to learn. Horses are prey animals and will react to the slightest noise, scent or movement
long before any logic can kick in. And if you'd fallen, you would
know it's not terrible. Then you wouldn't be afraid to fall or
bail off a horse when you need to."

"How nice for you that you've already forgotten I've fallen
off a horse. Actually, shoved off a horse. *Your* horse to be exact.
It's a memory I wish I could forget so easily."

Cahil had the decency to look contrite.

"So sending Goel was a lesson?" I asked. "I don't believe it,
Cahil. He was armed."

Fury flashed across Cahil's face. "I asked Erant to help me.
Goel is supposed to be guarding Tula. I'll deal with him."

"Don't bother. I can take care of Goel. At least *he* had the
decency to warn me of his plans. Unlike others." I glared at
Cahil, snatched the reins from his hands and strode back to
the stable with Kiki. It had been a mistake to go to my lesson
unarmed. I had foolishly assumed Goel wouldn't try to attack
me while I was with Cahil. Lesson learned. Cahil should be
proud, even if it wasn't the lesson he intended.

The next morning, I set out to find the market. I kept a
wary eye on the people in the streets of the Citadel. All seemed
headed toward the center square. Amazed by the number of
people crowding around the market stands, I hesitated. I didn't
want to push my way through them, yet I needed to shop.

I spotted a few of the Keep's workers, and had decided to
ask one of them for assistance when I felt a tug on my sleeve.
Spinning around, I reached for my bow on my backpack. The
small boy flinched. I recognized him as the beggar I had given
my Sitian coins to on my first day in the Citadel.

"Sorry. You startled me," I said.

He relaxed. "Lovely Lady, can you spare a copper?"

Remembering what Irys had said about the beggars, I thought of an idea. "How about you help me and I'll help you?"

Wariness filled his eyes. In that instant he seemed to grow ten years older. My heart broke, and I wanted to empty my purse into his hands. Instead, I said, "I'm new here. I'm looking to buy paper and ink. Do you know a good merchant?"

He seemed to catch on. "Maribella's has the finest stationery," he said, his eyes alight. "I'll show you."

"Wait. What's your name?"

He hesitated, and then lowered his eyes to the ground. "Fisk," he mumbled.

I dropped to one knee. Looking him in the eyes, I offered my hand. "Greetings, Fisk. I'm Yelena."

He grasped my hand with both of his, his mouth agape with astonishment. I guessed he was close to nine years old. Fisk recovered with a shake of his head. He then led me to a young girl's table at the edge of the square. I purchased writing paper, a stylus and some black ink, then gave Fisk a Sitian copper for his help. As the morning wore on, Fisk guided me to other stands for more supplies and soon other children were "hired" to help carry my packages.

When I finished shopping, I surveyed my entourage. Six grubby children smiled at me despite the heat and searing sun. I suspected that one boy was Fisk's younger brother; they had the same light brown eyes. The other two boys may have been his cousins. Greasy strands of hair hid most of the two girls' faces so it was impossible to tell if they were related to Fisk.

I realized then that I was reluctant to return to the Keep.

Sensing my mood, Fisk asked, "Lovely Yelena, would you like a tour of the Citadel?"

I nodded. The midday heat had emptied the market, but as I followed the children through the deserted streets, a feeling of unease settled over me. What if they were leading me into a trap? My hand sought the handle of my switchblade. Concentrating, I pulled a thread of power and projected my awareness.

My mind touched life all around me. Most of the Citadel's citizens resided inside, their thoughts focused on finding a cool spot or a quiet activity while they waited for the sun to set. No threats. No ambushes.

I heard the sound of water before I saw the fountain. With squeals of delight, the children put down my packages and ran to the spray. Fisk stayed by my side, though, taking his role as tour guide seriously.

"That's the Unity Fountain," he said.

A circle of waterspouts surrounded a huge stone sphere with large holes spaced evenly across its surface. Nestled inside the sphere, I could see another smaller sphere with holes of its own. The deep green color of the fountain wasn't veined like the marble of the Citadel's walls, yet the stone hinted that it held something else within.

"Marble?" I asked Fisk.

"Jade mined from the Emerald Mountains. This is the largest piece of pure jade ever found. It took a year to get it here and, because jade is so hard, it took over five years to carve it with diamond-tipped chisels. There are eleven spheres and all of them were carved inside that one stone."

Amazing. I moved closer to the fountain so I could see the other spheres. The cool mist felt good against my hot skin.

"Why eleven?" I asked.

Fisk stood next to me. "One sphere for each clan. And one waterspout for each clan. Water represents life," he explained. "See the carvings on the outer circle?"

I risked getting soaked to examine the intricate lines on the fountain.

"Mythical creatures. Each represents one Master Magician. Ying Lung, a sky dragon for First Magician. Fei Lian, a wind leopard for Second. Kioh Twan, a unicorn for Third. And Pyong, a hawk for Fourth."

"Why those creatures?" I asked, remembering that Irys had worn a hawk mask when she had visited Ixia as part of the Sitian delegation.

"When magicians reach the Master level, they endure a series of tests." Fisk sounded as if he quoted a schoolbook. "During that time, they travel through the underworld and meet their guide. This creature not only shows them through the underworld, but guides them throughout life."

"Do you believe that?" It sounded like a fairy tale to me. When the Commander had taken power in Ixia, superstitions and religious beliefs had been discouraged. If anyone still believed, they kept quiet and worshipped in secret.

Fisk shrugged. "I know something happens to the Magicians during the test because my father's seen it. He used to work at the Keep."

A hardness settled on Fisk's face, so I didn't ask any more questions. But I wondered about the creatures. Irys had disguised herself as a hawk mistress in Ixia. She wore the proper uniform to blend in with the Ixian. Perhaps she also worked with the Commander's hawks.

"It's good luck to drink from the fountain," Fisk said. Then he ran to his friends who played in the water, opening their mouths to catch the spray.

After a moment's hesitation, I joined them. The water tasted fresh as if laced with strong minerals like an elixir of life. I drank deeply. I could use a little good luck.

When the children finished playing, Fisk led me to another fountain. This one was carved from rare white jade. Fifteen horses frozen in motion circled a large spout of water.

Although Fisk didn't complain, I could see that the heat had finally worn him out. Still, when I offered to carry my purchases back to the Keep, all the children refused, saying they would take them as promised.

On the way back, I sensed Topaz's worry the moment before I saw Cahil rounding the corner. My parade of children stepped to the side of the road as Cahil advanced, stopping Topaz in front of us.

"Yelena, where have you been?" he demanded.

I glared at him. "Shopping. Why? Do you have another surprise test for me?"

He ignored my question, staring instead at my companions. The children shrank against the wall, trying to make themselves as small as possible.

"The market has been closed for hours. What have you been doing?" he asked.

"None of your business."

His gaze snapped to me. "Yes, it is. This is your first trip into the Citadel alone. You could have been robbed. You could have gotten lost. When you didn't come back, I thought the worst." Cahil's eyes slid back to the children.

"I can take care of myself." I glanced at Fisk. "Lead on," I said.

Fisk nodded and started down the street. The other children and I followed him.

Cahil snorted and dismounted. Taking Topaz's reins, he walked beside me. But he couldn't remain quiet.

"Your choice of escorts will lead to trouble," he said. "Every time you go into the Citadel, they'll descend on you like parasites, sucking you dry." Loathing filled his face.

"Another lesson?" I asked, not hiding my sarcasm.

"Just trying to help." Anger tightened his voice.

"You can stop. Stick to what you know, Cahil. If it doesn't involve horses, then I don't need your assistance."

He let his breath out in a long huff. From the corner of my eye, I saw him swallow his temper. Impressive.

"You're still mad at me," he said.

"Why would I be?"

"For not believing you about being a spy."

When I didn't say anything, he continued, "For what happened with First Magician. I know it must have been awful—"

"Awful!" Stopping in the middle of the street, I rounded on Cahil. "What do you know? Has she done it to you?"

"No."

"Then you have no idea what you're talking about. Imagine being helpless and stripped bare. Your thoughts and feelings exposed to a ruthless intimate scrutiny."

His eyes widened in shock. "But she said you fought her off. That she couldn't fully read you."

I shuddered at the thought of Roze going deeper, understanding why Cahil had claimed that her interrogation left some people with mental damage.

"It's worse than being raped, Cahil. I know. I've suffered both."

He gaped. "Is that why?"

"What? Go ahead. Ask." I wasn't about to spare him to make him feel better.

"Why you stayed in your room those first three days?"

I nodded. "Irys told me I was sulking, but I couldn't stand the thought of anyone even looking at me."

Topaz put his head over my shoulder. I rubbed my cheek on his soft face. My anger at Cahil had blocked out the horse's thoughts. Now I opened my mind to him.

Lavender Lady safe. Topaz's pleasure filled my mind. *Apple?*

I smiled. *Later.*

Cahil watched us with a strange expression on his face. "You only smile at the horses."

I couldn't tell if he was jealous or sad.

"What Roze...I...did to you. Is that why you keep everyone at arm's length?" Cahil asked.

"Not entirely. And not everyone."

"Who else do you smile at?"

"Irys."

He nodded as if he had expected that answer. "Anyone else?"

My fingers touched the bump my chest made by the butterfly pendant under my shirt. Valek would get more from me than a smile. But I said, "My friends in the north."

"The ones who taught you to fight?"

"Yes."

"How about the person who gave you that necklace?"

I jerked my hand away. "How did you know about my necklace?" I demanded.

"It fell out while you were unconscious."

I frowned, remembering Cahil had carried me to my room after Roze's interrogation.

"Guess I shouldn't have reminded you about that," he said. "But I was right about it being a gift, wasn't I?"

"It's none of your business. Cahil, you're acting like we're friends. We're not friends."

The children waited for us at an intersection. I started toward them.

Cahil caught up. We walked on in silence. When we reached the Keep, I took my packages from the children and paid them each two coppers.

I grinned at Fisk, and then glanced at Cahil, feeling self-conscious about my smiles.

"See you on the next market day," I said to Fisk. "And tell your friends they'll each get an extra copper if they show up clean."

He waved. I watched the group of children disappear; they probably knew all the back alleys and secret ways inside the Citadel. That knowledge might be useful one day. I would have to ask Fisk to show me.

Having grown up in the Citadel, Cahil probably knew the

shortcuts, too, but I wouldn't ask him. Not when he had such a dour expression.

"What now?" I asked.

He sighed. "Why do you always have to make things so difficult?"

"You started this. Remember? Not me."

He shook his head. "Why don't we start over? We've been at odds from the start. What can I do to receive one of your rare smiles?"

"Why do you want one? If you're hoping that we'll become friends and I'll confide in you all the military secrets of Ixia, don't bother."

"No. That's not what I want. I want things to be different between us."

"Different how?"

Cahil looked around as if searching for the right words. "Better. Less hostility. Friendlier. Conversations instead of arguments."

"After what you put me through?"

"I'm sorry, Yelena." The words tore from his throat as if it pained him to say them. "I'm sorry I didn't believe you when you said you weren't a spy. I'm sorry I asked First Magician to—" He swallowed. "To rape your mind."

I turned my face away from him. "That apology is weeks old, Cahil. Why bother now?"

He sighed. "Plans are being made for the New Beginnings feast."

Some hitch in Cahil's voice caused me to look at him. He wrapped and unwrapped Topaz's leather reins around his hands.

"It's a feast to celebrate the beginning of the cooling season and the new school year. A chance for everyone to get together and start anew." Cahil's blue eyes searched mine. "In all these years, I have never wanted to take anyone with me. I never had anyone who I wanted to have by my side. Yet when I overheard the cooks discussing the feast's menu this morning, your image filled my mind. Come with me, Yelena?"

14

Cahil's words struck me like a physical blow. I jerked back a step.

His face saddened at my reaction. "I guess that's a no. We'd probably just fight all night anyway." He began to walk away.

"Cahil, wait," I said, catching up to him. "You surprised me." An understatement for sure.

I had believed that the only thing Cahil wanted from me was information about Ixia. This invitation might still be a ploy, but for the first time I saw a softness behind his eyes. I put my hand on his arm. He stopped.

"Does everyone go to this New Beginnings feast?" I asked him.

"Yes. It's a good way for the new students to meet their teachers, and a chance for everyone to get reacquainted. I'm going because I'll be teaching the senior and apprentice classes about horsemanship."

"So, I'm not your first student?"

"No, but you've been my most stubborn one." He smiled ruefully.

I smiled in return. Cahil's eyes lit up.

"Okay, Cahil, in the spirit of this New Beginnings feast, let's start over. I'm willing to accompany you to the feast as the first step in our new *friendship*." Besides, the thought of going alone to meet my fellow students seemed daunting.

"Friendship?"

"That's all I can offer."

"Because of the person who gave you that butterfly pendant?" he asked.

"Yes."

"And what did you give him in return?"

I wanted to snap that it was none of his business, but I controlled my temper. If we were going to be friends, he needed to know the truth. "My heart." I could have added my body, my trust and my soul.

He looked at me for a moment. "Guess I'll have to be content with friendship." He grinned. "Does this mean you won't be so difficult anymore?"

"Don't count on it."

He laughed and helped me carry my market purchases back to my rooms. I spent the rest of the night reading the chapters Bain had assigned, stopping on occasion to think about Cahil's new role as friend in my life.

I enjoyed my fascinating mornings with Bain Bloodgood. Sitian history extended back for centuries. The eleven Sitian clans fought with each other for decades until Windri Greentree, a Master Magician, united them and formed the Council of Elders. I realized to my dismay, and to Bain's delight, that I had a great deal of study ahead of me to learn the full history. And their mythology alone, populated with creatures, demons and legends, would take years of lessons to know them all.

Bain also explained the structure of the school. "Every student has a magician as a mentor. That mentor oversees the student's learning. He teaches. He guides. He schedules classes with other magicians who have more expertise in certain subjects."

"How many students are in each class?" I asked.

Bain swept his hand through the air, indicating the room, empty except for us. We sat in an open circular chamber at the base of his tower. Books lined the walls in neat piles, and writing projects covered each of Bain's four ink-stained work-tables. The metal rings of Bain's astrolabe glowed in the morning sunlight.

I perched on the edge of his wide desk. Small writing tools and piles of papers rested on the top in an organized arrangement. A white seashell appeared to be his only decoration. Sitting across from me, Bain wore a deep purple robe that drank in the light. His diverse collection of robes amazed me. So far, he was the only magician I'd seen that wore a formal robe on a daily basis.

"We are a class," he said. "There can be up to four students, but no more. You will not see rows upon rows of students listening to a lecturer in this school. We teach using hands-on learning and small groups."

"How many students does each mentor have?"

"No more than four for those who have experience. Only one for the new magicians."

"How many do the Master Magicians teach?" I was dreading the day when I would have to share Irys.

"Ah…" He paused. For once Bain seemed at a loss for words. "The Masters do not mentor students. We are needed in Council meetings. We aid Sitia. We recruit prospective students. But occasionally a student comes along that piques our interest."

He gazed at me as if deciding how much he should tell me. "I have grown weary of Council meetings. So I have transferred all my energies to teaching. This year I have two students. Roze has chosen only one since she became First Magician. Zitora has none. She is adjusting—she only became a Master last year."

"And Irys?"

"You're her first."

"Just me?" I asked in amazement.

He nodded.

"You said Roze chose one. Who?"

"Your brother, Leif."

Evidence that the Keep prepared for an invasion of returning students mounted as the week progressed. Servants scurried to air out rooms and dorms. The kitchen buzzed with activity as the staff prepared for the feast. Even the Citadel's streets hummed with life as residents returned. In the evenings, laughter and music floated on the cooling air.

As I waited for Irys to return from fetching Tula's sister, I spent my mornings with Bain, my afternoons studying and my evenings with Cahil and Kiki. My riding had advanced from walking Kiki to trotting, a bone-jarring gait that left me stiff and sore at the end of the day.

Every night I sat with Tula, connecting with her and lending her my support. Her mind remained vacant, but her brutalized body healed by leaps and bounds.

"Do you have healing powers?" Hayes asked me one night. "Her physical progress has been amazing. More like the work of two healers."

I considered his question. "I don't know. I've never tried."

"Perhaps you've been helping her heal without realizing it. Would you like to find out?"

"I don't want to hurt her," I said.

"I won't let you." Hayes smiled as he picked up Tula's left hand. The splints on her right hand were gone, but the fingers on her left were still swollen and bruised. "I have only enough energy to mend a few bones a day. Usually we let the body heal on its own. But for serious injuries, we speed up the process."

"How?"

"I draw power to me. Then I focus on the injury. Skin and muscles disappear before my eyes, revealing the bones. I use the power to encourage the bone to mend. It works the same for other injuries. My eyes will only see the wound. It is truly wonderful."

Hayes's eyes glowed with purpose, but when they shifted to Tula they dimmed. "Unfortunately, some injuries just can't be healed, and the mind is so complex that any damage is usually permanent. We have a few mind healers. Fourth Magician is the strongest of these, but even she can only do so much."

As Hayes focused on Tula, I felt the air around me thicken and pulsate. Drawing a breath became an effort. Then Hayes closed his eyes. Without thinking, I linked my mind with his. Through him I saw Tula's hand. Her skin became translucent, showing the battered pink fibrous muscles attached to the bones. I saw strands of power, thin as spiderwebs, wrapped around Hayes's hands. He wove the webs around the crack in Tula's bone. As I watched, the crack disappeared and then the muscles healed.

I broke the mental connection to Hayes and looked at Tula. The bruises had faded from her now straight index finger. The air thinned as the power faded. His forehead shone with sweat and his breath puffed from the effort he'd just expended.

"Now, you try," he said.

I moved closer to Tula and took her hand from Hayes. Holding her middle finger, I rubbed it lightly with my thumb as I pulled power to me, revealing the bone. Hayes gasped. I paused.

"Go on," he said.

My strands of power were rope thick. When I applied the strands to the bone, they wrapped around it like a noose. I pulled back, fearing her finger would snap in half.

Placing her hand back on the bed, I looked at Hayes. "Sorry. I don't have full control of my magic yet."

He stared at Tula's hand. "Look."

Both fingers appeared to have been healed.

"How do you feel?" he asked.

Using magic usually left me tired, but I really hadn't used any. Or had I? "About the same."

"Three healings and I need to nap." Hayes shook his head. His dark hair fell into his eyes. He swiped his bangs back with an impatient hand. "You just mended a bone effortlessly. Fate be with us," he said. Awe and fear roughened his voice. "Once you have full control, you may be able to wake the dead."

15

Fear surged through me, leaving my muscles trembling.

"No," I said to Hayes. "You must be mistaken. No one can wake the dead."

Hayes rubbed a hand over his tired eyes, reconsidering.

"Perhaps I spoke rashly," he agreed. "Only one person in our history could revive the dead." He shuddered. "And the results were truly horrible."

I wanted to ask more questions, but Hayes bolted toward the door, insisting he had work to do.

Feeling odd and unsettled, I peered at Tula's motionless form. Through her blanket and skin, I could see each of her injuries. It seemed now that I had learned this new ability, I couldn't turn it off. The fractures, sprains, bruises all pulsed with an urgent red light. The more I studied the light the more it drew my mind in, and I felt Tula's physical pain soak into me. In sudden agony, I collapsed onto the floor.

Curling into a ball, I squeezed my eyes shut. A small part of me knew the pain was imaginary, but, in panic, I still tried to push the torment away. I pulled power from the source. Magic filled me. The buildup crackled across my skin like fire. I released the power.

My scream resounded through the room as cool relief swept through me, quenching my pain. Drained of energy, I remained on the floor, panting.

"Yelena, are you all right?"

I opened my eyes. Hayes hovered over me in concern. I nodded. "Tula?"

He left my side. "She's fine."

I sat up. The room spun for a moment but I forced myself to focus.

"What happened?" Hayes asked.

I wanted to say that I had lost control, to explain that my old survival instincts had kicked in, reacting to the pain without conscious thought. But it hadn't felt quite like that, and to admit that I had lost control would be dangerous. Uncontrolled magicians could damage the power source and the Masters would be forced to kill me. Instead, I clamped my lips together, trying to bring some order to my jumbled thoughts.

Before I could speak, Hayes said, "You healed her other two fingers."

He stood next to Tula's bed, and held her left hand up. Hayes inspected her fingers before laying her arm across her stomach.

Then he turned to me with a frown. "You shouldn't have tried that without me. No wonder you screamed. You gathered too much power and had to release it." Hayes gestured to my prone form. "A beginner's mistake, and now you're exhausted. You really need to work on your control."

While helping me to my feet, Hayes's frown softened into what might have been relief. "You have the ability to heal, but need guidance. I misjudged you at first, thinking you might be a Soulfinder." Hayes huffed out a laugh. "Next time, wait for me. Okay?"

Not trusting myself to speak, I nodded.

Hayes guided me toward the door. "Get some rest. You'll probably be weak for a few days."

As I shuffled to the apprentice's wing, I replayed the events in my mind, and by the time I collapsed into my bed, I managed to almost convince myself that Hayes's explanation was correct. Almost.

Fatigue dogged me all through the next day. Bain's morning lesson passed in a blur. Instead of reading, I napped the afternoon away, and fought to stay awake while riding Kiki that night. Cahil's bellowing eventually pierced the fog in my mind.

"Yelena!"

I looked at him as if seeing him for the first time that evening. Coated with dirt and horse hair, his once-white cotton shirt clung to his muscular frame. Annoyance creased his forehead. His mouth moved in speech, but it took me a moment to discern his words.

"...distracted, exhausted, and you're going to get hurt."

"Hurt?" I asked.

"Yes, hurt. When you fall asleep in the saddle and slide off the horse." Cahil controlled his frustration, but I could see by the way he pumped his clenched fists that he wanted to shake some sense into me.

Lavender Lady tired. Kiki agreed. *Forgot apples.*

"Yelena, go home." Cahil took Kiki's reins to hold her steady while I dismounted.

Home? Unbidden, the image of my small room in the Commander's castle jumped into my mind, followed by the memory of Valek's smiling face. I could use some of his energy right now.

"Are you all right?"

I gazed into Cahil's light blue eyes. They were pale in comparison to Valek's vibrant sapphire color. "Yes. I'm just a little tired."

"A little?" Cahil laughed. "Go get some sleep. I'll take care of Kiki. You'll need your energy for tomorrow night."

"Tomorrow?"

"The New Beginnings feast. Remember?"

"I didn't realize it was so soon."

"Prepare yourself for an invasion of students and magicians. Come morning, our peace and quiet will be gone."

Cahil led Kiki toward the stable. I promised her extra apples before our next lesson as I headed to my rooms.

Apprehension about the feast, though, gnawed through my fatigue even as I climbed into bed. Half-asleep, the shock of realizing that I didn't own the proper attire for a feast nearly jolted me awake. What did one wear to a feast anyway? Would I have to don my formal apprentice robe? I wondered, then sighed. Too tired to worry about things like clothes, I rolled over. More important worries such as the need to take control of my magic pushed out all others.

A frenzy of activity filled the campus the next morning. I skirted groups of people carrying parcels as I walked to Bain's tower.

Opening the door to his study, I started to ask Bain about the arriving students, but stopped when I saw he had two visitors.

From behind his desk, Bain gestured me in. "Yelena, these are my students. Dax Greenblade, a fellow apprentice, and Gelsi Moon, a novice." With an open hand, he pointed to each in turn.

They nodded in greeting. Their serious expressions looked out of place on such young faces. I guessed that Dax was eighteen years old, while the girl must have been about fifteen.

"Have you chosen another student, Master Bloodgood?" Gelsi asked. She tugged absently on the white lace at the end of her sleeve. Violet and white swirls patterned both her blouse and long skirt.

"No, Yelena is working with another," Bain said.

I had to suppress a grin as each relaxed. Dax flashed me a smile.

Gelsi, though, seemed intrigued with me. "Who is your mentor?" she asked.

"Irys...ah...Master Jewelrose."

The two students seemed as surprised as I had been when Bain told me about Irys.

"What's your clan?" Gelsi asked.

"Zaltana."

"Another distant cousin of Leif's?" Dax asked. "You're a little old to start training. What strange power do you have?"

His tone implied curiosity and humor, but Bain said, "Dax, that's inappropriate. She's Leif's sister."

"Ahhhh..." Dax studied me with keen interest.

"Do we have a lesson this morning?" I asked Bain.

The magician perked up at my question. He instructed Dax to go unpack, but he asked Gelsi to remain. Her heart-shaped face paled for a moment before she steadied herself, smoothing her shoulder-length copper curls.

"I fear Irys will be back soon and reclaim you," Bain said to me with a smile. "Gelsi's focus for this semester is to learn how to communicate magically with other magicians. Irys has told me this is your strongest ability. Therefore, I would like your assistance with introducing this skill to my student."

Gelsi's eyes widened. Her long thick eyelashes touched her brows.

"I'll do what I can," I said.

Bain rummaged through one of his desk's drawers and pulled a small burlap sack from it. He set the bag on the desk and opened it, taking out two brown lumps.

"We'll use Theobroma for the first lesson," he said.

The lumps triggered memories of my time in Ixia. Theobroma was the southern name for Criollo, a delicious sweet that had the unfortunate effect of opening a person's mind to magical influences. General Brazell had used the nutty flavored dessert to bypass the Commander's strong will so Brazell's magician, Mogkan, could gain control of the Commander's mind.

Bain handed me one of the Theobroma pieces and he gave the other to Gelsi. Then he told us to sit in the two chairs that faced each other. While I would have enjoyed eating the mouth-coating sweet, I thought it unnecessary.

"Can we try without it first?" I asked.

Bain's bushy gray eyebrows rose as he considered my question. "You don't need it to make an initial connection?"

I thought about the different people and horses I had linked with. "So far, no."

"All right. Yelena, I want you to try to connect with Gelsi."

Dredging some energy from my tired body, I pulled a thread of power and directed it to the girl, projecting my awareness to her. I sensed her apprehension about working with this strange woman from Ixia in her mind.

Hello, I said.

She jumped in shock.

To help her relax I said, *I was born in the Illiais Jungle. Where did you grow up?*

Gelsi formed an image of a small village wrapped in fog in her mind. *We reside in the foothills of the Emerald Mountains. Every morning our house is enveloped in the mist from the mountains.*

I showed her my parents' dwelling in the trees. We "talked" about siblings. A middle child, Gelsi had two older sisters and two younger brothers, but she was the only one in her family to develop magical powers.

Bain watched us in silence, then he interrupted, "Break the connection now."

Sapped of energy, I dragged my awareness back.

"Gelsi, it is your turn to make contact with Yelena."

She closed her eyes, and I sensed her seeking my mind. All I would need to do was tug on her awareness.

"Do not help her," Bain warned me.

Instead, I kept my mind open, but she failed to reach me.

"Not to worry," Bain consoled her. "The first time is the hardest. That is why we use Theobroma."

Bain's gray eyes studied me with kindness. "We will try again another time. Gelsi, go unpack and get settled."

After she left Bain's tower, he said, "No doubt you wore yourself out yesterday. Hayes mentioned something to me. Tell me what happened," he instructed.

I told him about the pain and the power. "It seems I don't have full control yet," I offered, waiting to see if he would chastise me. If my actions had truly been an uncontrolled burst, I knew the other Master Magicians would have felt it. And certain that Roze would have acted without hesitation on that knowledge.

"A lesson learned," Bain said. "Repairing injuries takes immense effort. Enough for today. I'll see you tonight at the feast."

The feast! I had forgotten. Again. "What should I..." I stopped, feeling awkward and silly to be asking about clothing.

Bain smiled in sympathy. "No expertise in that matter," he said, seeming to read my mind. "Zitora will enjoy helping you. She's at loose ends this year and will welcome some company."

"I thought she was busy with Council business."

"She is, but she's transitioning from five years of being a student to being on her own. Having no time to be a mentor doesn't mean she won't have time to make a friend."

I left Bain's tower and headed toward Zitora's in the northeast corner of the Keep. Lively groups filled the campus walkways and people hurried past me in every direction. My quiet walks through the Keep were at an end, yet I felt energized by all the activity.

Zitora greeted me with a bright smile that only dimmed when we discussed Tula's condition. Talk eventually turned to the upcoming festivities, and I inquired about appropriate dress.

"The formal robes are only for the boring school functions," Zitora said. "Do tell me you have something pretty to wear."

When I shook my head, she transformed into a mother hen and set about finding me some clothes.

"Thank fate you're my size," Zitora said with glee.

Despite my protests, she dragged me up two flights to her bedroom and loaded my arms with dresses, skirts and lacy blouses. Zitora propped her hands on her hips, considering my boots. "Those will not do."

"They're comfortable and I can move easily in them," I said.

"A challenge then. Mmm. I'll be right back."

She disappeared into another room, while I waited in her bedroom on the third floor of her tower. Soft pastel paintings of flowers hung on the walls. Oversize pillows graced her canopy bed. The room oozed comfort like open arms wrapping me in a hug.

With a triumphant shout, Zitora sauntered into the room, a pair of black sandals raised high for admiration.

"Rubber soles, soft leather and a small heel. Perfect for dancing all night long." She laughed.

"I don't know how to dance," I said.

"Doesn't matter. You have a natural grace. Watch the others and follow." Zitora added the sandals to the top of my pile.

"I really can't take all of this." I tried to give the clothes back. "I came for advice, not your entire wardrobe." I planned to go to the market. With the return of the Citadel's residents, the shops remained open every day.

She shooed me away. "Hardly made a dent in my armoire. I'm a collector of clothes. I can't pass a dress shop without finding something I must have."

"At least let me pay—"

"Stop." She raised her hand. "I'll make it easier for you. Tomorrow I'm leaving on a mission for the Council, and—much to my chagrin—I will have an escort of four soldiers. Irys and

Roze can gallivant all over Sitia by themselves, and they're assigned all the fun, secret missions. But the Council worries about me. So I'm limited to escorted missions." She huffed with frustration. "I've seen you practicing with your bow near the stable. How about I exchange my clothes for some lessons in self-defense?"

"Okay. But why didn't you learn how to defend yourself while a student here?"

"I hated the Master of Arms," she said with a deep frown. "A bully who turned the teaching sessions into torture sessions. He enjoyed inflicting pain. I avoided him at all costs. When the Masters realized I had strong powers, they focused more on my learning."

"Who's the Arms Master?"

"One of the northerners with Cahil. Goel's his name." Zitora shuddered with revulsion. "Although he wasn't as bad as the Master test…" She paused as a cringe of horror crossed her face. Then she jerked her head as if dislodging unwanted memories.

"Anyway, Roze offered to teach me, but I'd rather have you as my instructor." She flashed me a conspiratorial smirk.

Having agreed to the exchange, I maneuvered down Zitora's tower steps with the bundle of her clothes heaped in my arms. So burdened, I headed toward my rooms. On the way, I wondered about the Master test. Fisk, the beggar boy had also mentioned it. I would have to ask Irys.

The courtyard across from my quarters buzzed with students. A few boys tossed a ball, while others lounged on the grass or talked in groups. Hampered by Zitora's clothes, I fumbled at my door.

"Hey, you!" someone called.

I looked around and spotted a group of girls gesturing at me.

"The first year barracks are that way." One of the girls with long blond hair pointed. "This is for apprentices only."

"Thanks, but this is my room," I called, turning back.

I managed to get the door open before I felt a prickle of power along my spine. Tossing the clothing on to the floor, I spun around. A group of students stood mere inches from me.

"You don't belong here," said the long-haired girl. A dangerous shine lit her violet eyes. "You're new. I know everybody, and new students go to the first-year barracks. You have to *earn* a room here."

Persuasive magic emanated from her. A strong desire to pack my belongings and move to the first-year dorms coursed through my mind and pressed against my body. I deflected her magical command by strengthening my mental defenses.

She grunted in outrage. A look passed among her companions. Power built as they readied to join in. I braced for another attack, but before they could use their combined power, another voice cut through the throng.

"What's going on here?"

The power dissipated in a stiff wave as Dax Greenblade pushed his lean muscular body through the group, staring down at the others with his bottle-green eyes. In the sunlight, his honey-brown skin made his face appear older.

"She doesn't belong here," the girl repeated.

"Yelena is Fourth Magician's student," Dax said. "She's been assigned to this wing."

"But that's not fair," the girl whined. "You have to *earn* the right to be here."

"And who's to say she hasn't?" Dax asked. "If you believe Fourth Magician is in error, I suggest you take it up with her."

An uncomfortable silence followed before the group returned to the courtyard. Dax stayed beside me.

"Thanks," I said. The group huddled in a tight pack, casting nasty looks my way as they talked. "Guess I haven't made any friends."

"Three points against you, I'm afraid. One." Dax held up a long slender finger. "You're new. Two. Fourth Magician's your mentor. Any student selected by a Master is guaranteed to be the subject of jealousy. If you're looking for friends, I'm afraid Gelsi and I are your only choices."

"What's the third point?"

He smiled sardonically. "Rumors and speculation. The students will dig up every bit of information they can on you and why you're here. It doesn't matter if the information is true or not. In fact, the stranger the tidbits the better. And I have a feeling from what I already heard your tidbits are quite juicy and should inflame the gossip all the more."

I studied his face. Lines of concern creased his forehead, and I saw no signs of deceit. "Tidbits?"

"You're Leif's lost sister, you're older than all the students and you're extremely powerful."

I looked at him in surprise. Me? Powerful?

"I didn't come over to help you. I came to protect them." He inclined his head toward the group in the courtyard.

Before I could comment, Dax pointed to a room, five doors down from mine. "Come anytime for any reason. Gelsi is in the novice barracks near the west wall."

Dax waved goodbye and strode toward his room. The group's hostility transferred briefly to his back before returning to me. I closed my door.

Great. Day one and already the outcast. But did I care? Here to learn and not to make friends, I thought it wouldn't matter once lessons started. By then, the students would be too busy to pay any attention to me.

I sorted through Zitora's clothes, choosing a long black skirt and a red-and-black V-neck blouse. The shirt had two layers of material. A pattern of fine black lace over red silk.

I tried on the outfit. Deciding to leave my bow behind during the feast, I cut a slit in one of the skirt's pockets for quick access to my switchblade. The sandals were a little big, so I poked another hole in the strap.

Until I looked at myself in the mirror I hadn't realized I wore Commander Ambrose's colors, the same combination as my northern uniform. I considered another outfit, even tried on different clothes, but felt the most comfortable in my first choice.

Pulling my hair from its braid, I scowled at the limp mess. The year before I had cut out the snarls and tangles, and now the ends had grown in ragged. My black hair now reached past my shoulders. It would need a good trim and washing.

I changed back into my day clothes and left my rooms to feed the promised apples to Topaz and Kiki. Conversation in the courtyard ceased as I emerged. Ignoring them, I set out for the stable. I would stop by the baths on my return.

The time for the feast came quicker than I expected. Once again, I stood in front of the mirror in my bedroom, assessing my clothing with a critical eye. I pushed a stray curl from my face.

An assistant at the baths had fussed over my awkward attempts to cut my own hair. She had commandeered my scissors and proceeded to trim the ends, then had rolled my hair with hot metal tubes.

Instead of being pulled into a bun, my hair now fell to my shoulders in big soft curls. I looked ridiculous. But before I could rearrange it, someone knocked on my door.

I grabbed my bow and peeked out the window. Cahil waited outside. His hair and beard appeared white in the moonlight.

Opening the door, I said, "I thought we agreed to meet…" I gaped.

Cahil wore a long silk tunic of midnight-blue. The collar stood up and silver piping followed the edge of the fabric to form a vee far enough below his throat to allow a glimpse of his muscular chest. The piping also went across his shoulders and dropped down the outside seam of his full sleeves. A silver mesh belt studded with gemstones cinched the tunic around his narrow waist. His trousers matched his shirt, and, once again, silver piping traced the outside seam of his pants, carrying my eyes down to a pair of polished leather boots. Royalty incarnated.

"I pass your rooms on the way. Seemed silly not to stop," Cahil said.

He squinted into the lantern light that glowed behind me, and I realized he couldn't see my openmouthed stare.

"Ready?" he asked.

"Give me a moment." Returning to the sitting area, I gestured Cahil toward a chair as I went into my bedroom, where I secured my switchblade then smoothed my skirt. With no time to fix my hair, I settled for tucking it behind my ears. Curls! Living in Sitia had made me soft.

Cahil smiled broadly when he saw me in the light.

"Don't laugh," I warned.

"I never laugh *at* a beautiful woman. I'd much rather laugh and dance *with* her."

"False flattery won't work on me."

"I meant every word." Cahil offered his arm. "Shall we?"

After a slight hesitation, I linked my arm in his.

"Don't worry. I'm only your escort tonight. I would offer to protect you from the drunken attentions of the other men, but I know all too well that you're quite capable of holding your own. You're probably armed. Right?"

"Always."

We walked in companionable silence. Groups of students and other couples headed in the same direction soon joined us. Lively music pulsed through the air, becoming louder as we approached.

The dining room had been converted into a ballroom. Orange, red and yellow velvet streamers twisted along the ceiling and draped the walls. Laughter and conversation competed with the music as some people drank and ate, while others danced on the wooden dance floor. Everyone appeared to be wearing their finest clothes. The room sparkled with jewelry in the candlelight.

Our arrival went unnoticed. But as Cahil pulled me through the crowd toward the back of the room, a couple of surprised glances marked our passing.

A jolt snapped through me as we cleared the crowd and I spotted Leif. I hadn't seen him since Irys had left, and I had assumed since he had graduated from the Keep he was no longer involved with the students or classes. But there he stood, next to Roze and Bain. Cahil aimed for them.

I almost fainted when Leif smiled at me as we approached, but when he recognized me it turned into a scowl. I wondered what I would have to do to get a true smile from Leif. I dismissed the thought; I didn't want to earn his goodwill, and I certainly didn't need it. Now, if I could keep saying that over and over in my mind, I might just start to believe it.

When we joined the group, Bain complimented my hairstyle, while Roze ignored me. Our group only truly came alive when Zitora joined us.

"Perfect! Absolutely perfect!" Zitora exclaimed over my outfit.

The talk soon turned to Council business and Cahil pressed Roze to get him on the agenda. Having no interest in discussing politics, my attention wandered as I scanned the crowd. I saw only a few of Cahil's men. They wore dress uniforms and stood awkwardly to the side as if on duty instead of being there for pleasure. Perhaps they were.

I watched the dancers for a while. They circled the floor in pairs. After eight beats, they stopped and then took four steps into the center, then four steps back and continued around the circle. The pattern was then repeated. Similar to some of my self-defense katas, the dance resembled a prescribed set of moves.

Dax and Gelsi appeared. Bain's students greeted the three Master Magicians with a stiff formality. Gelsi wore a soft green gown that shimmered in the lantern light. The gown's color matched her big eyes. Studded with gold buttons, Dax's red shirt had a mandarin collar. Gold piping lined the outside seam of his black pants.

"Hey, we match," Dax said to me. I could just hear him over the music. "Would you like to dance?"

I glanced at Cahil, debating with Leif. "Sure."

Dax smiled and pulled me into an opening on the dance floor. Watching had been easier than doing, but with Dax's steady guidance, I soon caught the rhythm.

As we circled the floor, Dax said, "Remember when I said you had three points against you?"

I nodded.

"Now there are five."

"What now?" I asked in exasperation. It was hard to believe I'd had time to make anyone else mad.

"You came to the feast on Cahil's arm. Everyone will assume two things. One. That you're his girlfriend. And two. That you're an Ixian sympathizer, which is the greater of the two evils."

"Well, they would be wrong. Who comes up with all these points and assumptions?" I demanded.

"Not me, that's for sure," Dax said. "If I were in charge, we'd have more desserts at dinner, more feasts and much more dancing."

We danced for a while in silence. I mulled over the implications and decided not to waste my time worrying about what everyone else thought, or to bother attempting to change their perceptions. My time at the Keep was just a stopover. Let them wonder. My nervousness about the evening dissipated with my decision. I smiled at Dax.

"You have a mischievous glint. What are you planning?"

"Only five points against me?" I narrowed my eyes in mock concern. "Such a small number. I say we try for eight or ten."

A wolfish grin spread across Dax's face. "My lady, you are far too modest. You're more than capable of handling fifteen or twenty."

I laughed with genuine pleasure. Dax and I twirled around the dance floor for a few more songs before rejoining the group. Cahil met our return with a sour look. Before he could say anything or go back to debating with Leif, I grabbed Cahil's hand and pulled him toward the dancers.

"Tonight is not for business," I said as we followed Dax and Gelsi around the floor. "Tonight is for fun. Dancing instead of fighting."

He laughed. "You're right."

The evening flew by as I danced with Cahil, Dax and Bain. Even the Stable Master swung me around for a rowdy foot-stomping song. If Cahil hadn't insisted, I wouldn't have stopped to eat.

Irys's arrival should have made the evening perfect, but I could see exhaustion etched in her face. Wearing a simple light blue gown instead of traveling clothes, she must have taken the time to bathe and to decorate her regal bun with rubies and diamonds before coming to the feast.

"Is everything okay? Did you find Tula's sister?" I asked.

Irys nodded. "Her sister, Opal, is with Tula now." She gave me an odd look.

"Should we try to help Tula tonight?"

Irys shook her head. "Let Opal spend some time with her sister. It's the first she's seen her since Tula was kidnapped." Again, Irys flashed me that strange look.

"What then? There's something you're not telling me."

"I warned Opal of Tula's condition—both mental and physical." Irys rubbed a hand along her cheek. "But when we arrived, it seemed a miracle had occurred." Irys peered with a deep intensity into my eyes.

"Is Tula awake?" I asked in confusion. Irys's news contradicted her body language.

"No, her soul is still in hiding, but her body is completely healed."

16

"How?" I asked Irys. Hayes had said he could only heal a few bones at a time. Perhaps another healer had come to help him with Tula.

"You tell me," Irys demanded. "What did you do that day? Hayes has been in a state ever since. He's terrified of you."

"Me?"

Bain came to my temporary rescue. "Perhaps you ladies would like to go outside."

I looked around. Several people had stopped talking and gawked at us.

"I forget myself," Irys apologized to Bain. "Now is not the time to discuss this."

She headed toward the buffet. Everyone returned to their conversations. But she wasn't finished with me.

Yelena, she said in my mind. *Please tell me what happened with Tula.*

Sudden dread churned in my stomach. Was Irys upset because I had lost control of my magic and had accidentally healed Tula, or because I could have jeopardized Tula's life? With reluctance, I told her everything that had happened that day in Tula's room.

You were in pain and you pushed the pain away from yourself?
Irys asked.

Yes. Did I do something wrong?

*No. You did something impossible. I thought you tried to heal her,
which would have been dangerous, but it sounds as if you assumed her
injuries and then healed yourself.*

I stared at Irys with pure amazement. She sat across the room,
eating her dinner.

Could you do it again? she asked.

I don't know. It must have been an instinctive reaction.

There is only one way to find out. I felt Irys's weary sigh. *For
now, I want you to get a good night's rest. Meet me in Tula's room
tomorrow afternoon.* Irys broke her magical connection to me.

Confusion creased Cahil's face, and I realized he had been
watching me. "What's the matter?" he asked. "Shouldn't Fourth
Magician be pleased that you healed that girl? That would
mean... Oh, my sword!" He gaped.

Before I could press him for details, the music stopped.

"Midnight," Bain declared. "Time to go. The students have
a full day tomorrow." His delighted anticipation of a full day
of learning caused a ripple of smiles around him.

Obediently, everyone streamed out into the darkness, heading off to dorms and apartments. As he passed, Dax caught my
eye. He grinned and held up seven fingers. I looked forward
to hearing from him about my additional two points of gossip-
inspiring behavior.

Cahil walked me to my rooms. He was unusually quiet.

Finally, I couldn't stand it anymore. "Oh, my sword what?"
I demanded.

"I realized something," he said, trying to shrug me off.

Not content with his vague answer, I prompted, "Which
was..."

"If I told you, you would be angry. I don't want to end the
evening with a fight."

"And if I promised not to get upset?"

"You would anyway."

"Tomorrow, then?"

"Ask me the next time we're fighting."

"What if we don't fight?"

Cahil laughed. "With you, there is always a next time."

Then with a speed that surprised me, he grabbed me around the waist and pulled me in for a quick kiss on the cheek before releasing me.

"Till tomorrow," he said over his shoulder as he strode away.

It was only after watching him disappear into the darkness that I realized I stood with my switchblade clutched in my right hand. But I hadn't triggered the blade. The south was making me soft. First curls, now this. Shaking my head, I opened my door.

At Tula's room the next afternoon, I had to squeeze my way in. Tula's bed occupied the center. Leif and Hayes stood on the right side of her bed, and Irys and a young girl stood on the left. Tula's guard, one of Cahil's men, looked uncomfortable wedged in a corner.

Hayes paled when I looked at him. Irys introduced me to Opal, Tula's sister. Opal's long brown hair was pulled into a ponytail, and her red-rimmed eyes looked swollen from crying.

I hadn't expected an audience. "Irys," I said. "I need to spend some time with Opal before I can try to bring Tula back."

Leif muttered something about grandstanding on his way out, and Hayes just aimed for the door.

"Do you need me?" Irys asked.

"No."

"We don't have much time," Irys warned as she left the room.

She didn't need to remind me that Tula's attacker still roamed free, possibly hunting for another victim. However, I knew in my heart that if I rushed this, I wouldn't succeed.

I asked Opal to tell me about her sister. In halting sentences, the young girl told me only a couple stories of their childhood.

"Tula once made me a large glass tiger to protect me from nightmares." Opal smiled at the memory. "It worked and the tiger looked so lifelike that Tula started making other glass animals." She glanced from her sister's still form to the guard in the corner.

Opal seemed hesitant and distracted by her sister's condition. So I changed the subject and asked about her trip to the Citadel.

Her dark brown eyes widened. "Fourth Magician woke us all up in the dead of night."

At the word dead, the young girl glanced with dread at Tula.

"I was barely awake. Before I knew it, I was on the magician's horse, riding flat out for the Keep." Opal clutched her arms to herself. "When Tula was found, the healers rushed her to the Citadel. My parents had to find people to work the kilns and take care of us before they could follow her. They're on the road somewhere." Opal began to ramble. "We didn't pass them. They don't know I'm here. It's my first trip away from home, and we stopped only to eat. I slept in the saddle."

That would explain Irys's exhaustion. Even today she had dark circles under her eyes. That also explained why Opal seemed so distressed. I switched tactics and invited Opal to take a walk. She appeared reluctant to leave her sister until I assured her that Tula would be fine.

I showed her the campus. The air temperature felt comfortable. With warm afternoons and chilly evenings, the weather during the cooling season was my favorite.

Eventually, we wandered out into the Citadel. I guided Opal toward the market. Fisk appeared with a ready smile and led us to a dress shop. I bought Opal a change of clothes and Fisk played tour guide for her.

When Opal seemed more relaxed, my questions about Tula grew more specific. As she remembered more stories, I pulled a thread of magic and linked my mind with Opal's, witnessing her memories as she spoke. I smelled the hot furnace of their family's glass factory, and felt the coarse sand in my hands.

"Tula and I used to hide from Mara, our older sister. We had found the perfect spot. Mara still doesn't know where it is," Opal said, smiling.

The image of an awning of tree limbs and sun-dappled grass filled Opal's mind as the cool scent of moist earth reached my nose.

"That's it." I grabbed Opal's arm. "Hold that place in your mind. Concentrate on it."

She did as I asked. I closed my eyes and put myself into the memory. Blades of grass brushed my arms as I lay in the small hollow behind a row of overgrown bushes. The smell of sweet honeysuckles hung heavy in the fresh air. Dewdrops sparkled in the morning sunlight. Instinctively, I knew this place hid Tula's soul.

"Come on." I pulled Opal toward the Keep, waving good-bye to Fisk. A guard stood outside Tula's door. He nodded to us as we went inside.

"Shouldn't we wait for Fourth Magician and the others?" Opal asked.

"No time. I don't want to lose the image." I took one of Tula's hands and held my other out to Opal. "Take my hand. Now, I want you to imagine yourself in your hiding spot with Tula. Close your eyes and really concentrate. Can you do that?"

Opal nodded, her pale face drawn.

I linked with Tula. The ghosts of her horrors still floated in the emptiness, but they seemed less tangible than before. Connecting with Opal, I followed the smell of honeysuckles and dew through Tula's mind.

The ghosts thickened with a sudden fury, flying at me, blocking my passage. The air pressed and clung like molasses. I pushed past them only to be ensnared in a row of thorn bushes. My clothing snagged on branches and the barbs dug into my skin.

"Go away," Tula called. "I don't want to come back."

"Your family misses you," I said.

Vines began to wrap around my arms and waist, anchoring me.

"Go away!"

I showed her Opal's memories of what her family suffered when Tula had disappeared.

The thorny bushes thinned a bit. Through their branches I spotted Tula curled up in her childhood hiding spot.

"I can't face them," Tula said.

"Your family?"

"Yes. I've done...things. Terrible things so he wouldn't hurt me." Tula shuddered. "But he hurt me anyway."

The vines climbed up my arms and circled my neck.

"Your family still loves you."

"They won't. He'll tell them what I did. They'll be disgusted. I was his slave, but I didn't try hard enough for him. I couldn't get anything right. I didn't even die for him."

I controlled my anger; my desire to slaughter the beast would have to wait. "Tula, *he* is the disgusting one. *He* is the one who should die. Your family knows what he did to your body. They only want you back."

She drew her body into a tighter ball. "What do you know? You know nothing about what I went through. Go away."

"You assume too much," I choked out as the vines around my throat squeezed tight. I struggled to breathe. Could I face my own horrors again? To find this monster, I would. I opened my mind to hers and showed her Reyad. His delight in torturing me. My willingness to make him happy so he wouldn't harm me. And the night I slit his throat after he had raped me.

Tula peeked at me through her arms. The vines lessened

the pressure. "You killed your torturer. Mine is still out there, waiting."

I tried again. "Then he is free to make someone else his slave. What if Opal is his next victim?"

Tula jumped up in horror. "No!" she screamed.

I linked Opal's mind with ours. For a moment, Opal stood stunned, blinking in surprise. Then she ran to Tula and hugged her. Together they wept. The vines withdrew, and the bushes died away.

But this was just the beginning. The grassy hollow soon faded and Tula's ghosts hovered around us.

"There are too many," Tula said in defeat. "I will never be rid of them."

I drew my bow from its holder on my back and broke it into three pieces. Handing one to Tula and the other to Opal, I said, "You're not alone. We'll fight together."

The ghosts attacked. They were tenacious and quick. I swung at them over and over until my arms felt like lead. A few of Tula's horrors disappeared, others shrank, but some seemed to grow as they fought.

My energy drained at an alarming pace. I felt my bow become stuck inside one of the ghosts. The spirit expanded and consumed me. I screamed as the pain of being whipped racked my body.

"You're weak. Tell me you'll obey and I'll stop," a voice whispered in my ear.

"No." Near panic I reached out for help. A powerful presence formed and handed me a full-size bow that pulsed with energy. Strength returned to me and I beat at the horror until it fled.

We had repelled the attack, but I could see that Tula's ghosts prepared for another.

"Tula, this is merely the first battle in an ongoing war. It will take time and effort to be free of your fears, but you'll have plenty of help from your family. Are you coming with us?" I asked.

She bit her lip, gazing at the piece of bow in her hands. Opal added her bow to Tula's. Tula clutched them both close to her chest. "Yes. I'll come."

Tula's mind filled with memories of her life. Vertigo twirled in my stomach as I broke my mental links with Tula and Opal. Relief descended, and I sank into blackness.

When I came to my senses, I felt hard stone against my back. For the third time I had collapsed on Tula's floor. This time I had no hope of moving. My energy was completely depleted. After a while I noticed that someone gripped my hands. Strong fingers wrapped around mine, encompassing them with warmth.

With effort I opened my eyes to see who held me. Then I closed them tight. I must still be asleep. But after hearing Irys's insistent calls, I looked again. And there sat my brother, holding my hands and sharing his energy with me.

17

Weariness lined Leif's face. "You're in big trouble," he said.

His words didn't seem malicious, just factual, and, as expected, past his shoulders, I saw Irys, Roze, Hayes and Bain all frowning at me. Leif released my hands, but remained on the floor beside me.

Roze eyed him, her displeasure evident in the tight twist of her lips. "You should have let her die," she scolded him. "One less magician to taint our land with her incredible stupidity."

"A little too harsh, Roze," Bain said. "Though I agree about the stupidity. Child, why did you try that alone?" Bain asked.

I couldn't even speak in my defense for I hadn't the energy to form words, let alone try and explain myself.

"Cocky and stupid," Roze said for me. "Since she cured Tula of her physical injuries, she must have believed she was an all-powerful magician and could do anything. The fool will probably be asking to take the Master level test next." Roze snorted with disgust. "Maybe she'll feel differently after we assign her to the first year's barracks. There she can learn the basics of magic while scrubbing the floors, like every new student."

I glanced at Irys. Roze's punishment sounded horrible. Irys

said nothing. Disapproval pulsed off her. I braced for an outburst.

Instead, Opal called, "Tula's awake!"

I closed my eyes in relief as everyone focused on Tula. When I opened my eyes, the magicians had all disappeared from my view.

"You're still headstrong and reckless—an out-of-control strangler fig," Leif said. "I guess Ixia didn't change everything about you." He stood on shaking legs, and I watched him join the others by Tula's bedside.

I puzzled over his comment. Good or bad? I couldn't decide. But then Roze's harsh voice jarred me out of my reflection. She bombarded Tula with questions about her attacker, but Tula wouldn't answer. I cringed, knowing that Tula wasn't up to Roze's interrogation. Thank fate, Hayes intervened.

"Give her some time," he said.

"There is no time," Roze replied.

A thin raspy voice asked, "Who are all these people? Where's Yelena? I can't see her."

"She's here," Opal said. "She's just exhausted from helping you, Tullie."

"Hayes, get some assistants and go dump the fool girl into another room," Roze instructed. "She's done enough damage for one day."

When Hayes moved to obey, Tula said, "No. You leave. All of you. I won't tell you anything. Yelena stays with me. I'll talk to her."

A mummer of irritation and discussion rumbled through the magicians before Roze agreed with reluctance to bring a bed in for me. Hayes and Irys hoisted me off the floor and dropped me without fanfare onto the mattress. Irys still hadn't said a word, and her silence scared me.

"Child," Bain said to Tula. "I understand your fear. You have awakened to a room full of strangers." He then introduced everyone in the room. "First Magician and Leif are the ones you need to tell about your abduction. They will find your kidnapper."

Tula pulled the sheet up to her chin. "I'll tell Yelena. No one else. She'll take care of him."

Roze's harsh laughter scraped in my ears. "She can't even talk! If your attacker walked into this room, he would kill you both." She shook her head in disbelief. "You're not thinking clearly. I'll be back in the morning, and you *will* talk to me. Come, Leif." Roze strode out the door with Leif on her heels.

Hayes shooed everyone else out. As the door closed, I heard Bain tell Irys to assign an extra guard for the evening. A good idea. If Goel came in, I couldn't prevent him from carrying out his promises to torture me.

Apprehension about being so helpless crawled along my spine. A similar situation that haunted Tula. One of her many ghosts was being at the mercy of another. Her promise to tell me everything weighed on my mind; I had just gotten rid of my own ghost. Though, I hated to admit, Reyad still retained some power. Whenever I had doubts, he seemed to enjoy visiting my nightmares. Or did he cause them? Or did I invite him?

To distract myself from such troublesome thoughts, I tried to muster some energy to talk to Tula, but exhaustion claimed me instead and I sank into a deep dreamless sleep.

I felt a little better in the morning, but had only enough strength to sit up in bed. At least I could ask Tula how she felt.

She closed her eyes. Pointing to her temple she said, "Come."

I sighed with regret. "I don't have the energy to link our minds, Tula."

"Perhaps I can help," Leif said from the doorway.

"No! Go away." Tula shielded her face with her arms.

"If you don't talk to me, First Magician will come and take the information she needs from you," Leif explained.

Tula peeked out at me in confusion.

"It won't be pleasant," I said. "It's almost as bad as what your attacker did to you. I know."

Leif averted his eyes. I hoped he felt guilty. Studying him closer, I wondered why he had aided me the day before. What had happened to his smirk? Where was his derision and condescension? I realized I barely knew this man.

Not wanting to guess his motives anymore, I demanded, "Why did you help me?"

A scowl gripped his face, but, with a sigh, he smoothed his features, shuttering his emotions. "Mother would kill me if I had let you die," he said.

He turned to Tula, but I refused to let him get away with such a flippant response. "What's the real reason?"

Hatred blazed in Leif's jade eyes, but a second later his posture softened, as if someone had blown out a candle. He whispered, "I couldn't bear to do nothing and lose you again."

Then, his mental defenses dropped and I heard his thoughts. *I still hate you.*

His trust surprised me, though his petulant comment failed to concern me. An emotion, even hatred, was better than apathy. Could this be a first step in bridging the distance between us?

"What did he say?" Tula asked.

"He wants to help you," I said. "Tula, this is my brother. Without him we wouldn't have gotten you back. If you want me to find your attacker, I'll need his strength."

"But, he'll see. He'll know about..." Tula squeezed her arms together.

"I already know," Leif said.

He pulled Tula's arms away from her face with a gentleness that amazed me. I thought back to my mother's comments about Leif's magic. She had said he helped with crimes, sensing a person's guilt and history. Now, as I watched him with Tula, I wanted to know more about him and how he used his magic.

"We need to find him and stop him from hurting another girl," Leif explained.

She swallowed and bit her lip before nodding. Leif stood between our beds, took Tula's hand and reached for mine. I reclined on the mattress and grabbed his hand. Then, using his energy, I formed a mental link with Tula.

In her mind, the two of us stood by a gray stone furnace. Leif's power roared around us like the fire under the kiln.

"I was here, putting coal into the furnace. It was close to midnight when..." She clutched her apron. Black soot streaked the white fabric. "A dark cloth wrapped around my face. Before I could scream, I felt a sharp stab in my arm. Then...then..." Tula stopped speaking.

On our mental stage, she stepped toward me. I hugged her trembling body, and within the space of a breath I became Tula, witnessing my own abduction.

Numbness spread from the stab wound, freezing my muscles. Dizziness was the only indication I'd been moved. Time passed. When the cloth was removed from my face, I was lying inside a tent. Unable to move, I stared up at a lean man with short brown hair that was streaked with gold. He wore only a red mask. Strange crimson symbols had been painted all over his sand-colored skin. He held four wooden stakes, rope and a mallet. Feeling returned to my limbs.

"Tula, no. I can't," I said in my mind. I knew what horrors threatened to come. I lacked the strength to endure them with her right now. "Just show him to me."

She froze the image of the man so I could study the symbols. The circular patterns resided within bigger patterns of animals. Triangles traced down his smooth arms and legs. Though thin, he radiated power.

A complete stranger to Tula, everything about him seemed foreign to her. Even the harsh way he pronounced her name, emphasizing the la, sounded odd. But he knew her. Knew the names of her sisters and parents. Knew how they melted sand, working it into glass.

Then, in a whirl of sound and color, she showed me the man at different times. She wasn't permitted to leave the tent, but whenever he entered or left, Tula caught a glimpse of the outside, a tease of freedom. Long thick grass filled the whole view.

When he came to her, he always wore a mask. Letting the numbness in her body wear off before beating or raping her. Letting her feel the pain he applied with seeming reverence. After he finished the torture, he took a thorn and scratched her skin.

Puzzled at first by this action, Tula soon learned to dread and to crave the ointment he would rub into the thorn's bleeding gash. It was the numbing lotion that would paralyze her, taking away all her pain and any chance she might have to escape.

The ointment, though, had a strong crisp scent, similar to the sharp smell of alcohol mixed with a citrus perfume. The aroma remained around me like a poisonous fog as Leif's energy waned. He broke the magical connection to Tula.

"That smell..." Leif said as he perched on the edge of my bed. "I couldn't get a good whiff. All my effort went into keeping you and Tula connected."

"It's horrible," Tula said, shuddering. "I shall never forget it."

"What about those symbols?" I asked Leif. "Did you recognize them?"

"Not really. Though there are some clans that use symbols for rituals."

"Rituals?" Dread coiled in my stomach.

"Wedding ceremonies and naming rituals." Leif scowled in concentration. "Thousands of years ago, magicians used to perform intricate rituals. They believed that magical power came from a deity, and if they tattooed their bodies and showed the proper respect, they would be granted greater power. Now we know better. I've seen some symbols painted on faces and hands before, but not like the ones on Tula's attacker."

Leif pulled his black hair back behind his head with both hands. With his elbows jutting out past his face, his posture seemed so familiar. I felt like I could transport back to a time when my concerns only focused on what game to play next. The faint childhood memory dissolved with my efforts to concentrate on it.

Tula covered her eyes, silent tears spilling down her cheeks. Reliving the kidnapping and the torment had to be grueling.

"Get some rest," Leif told her. "I'll come back later. Perhaps Second Magician will know something about those symbols." He left the room.

The morning's events had drained my own small supply of energy. I knew words would give no comfort to Tula, so I was relieved when Opal came in. Seeing her sister's concern, Tula sobbed loudly, and Opal crawled into the bed with her, held Tula close and rocked her like a baby. I fell asleep listening to Tula purge her body of the masked man's poison.

We had visitors throughout the rest of the day. Cahil came, smelling of the barn.

"How's Kiki?" I asked, missing her. Even though my connection with her remained, I couldn't produce enough power to hear her thoughts.

"A little agitated. All the horses are. The Stable Master's been in one of his tempers. Horses take their cues from people's emotions. If a rider is nervous, then the horse will be, too." Cahil shook his head. "I still have a hard time believing you can communicate with them. Guess today is just one of those days where my notions are proven wrong."

"Why's that?"

"I thought you were an overconfident braggart when you said you could help Tula. But you did it." Cahil studied me.

I conceded the overconfidence title. My rescue of Commander Ambrose's soul had seemed easy in comparison to Tula's, but I had forgotten that Irys had been with me in the Commander's room, and it had been his superior fighting skills and determination that had gotten us free of his demons.

"You almost killed yourself saving Tula, though," Cahil said. "Was it worth the risk to prove me wrong again?"

"My motivations weren't selfish," I snapped at him. "I wanted to help her. I understood what she's been through and I knew she needed me. Once I had an idea about how I could find her, I didn't stop to think. I just reacted."

"And the danger to yourself never entered your mind?"

"Not this time." I sighed at his aghast expression.

"You have put yourself in danger for others before?"

"I *was* the Commander's food taster." This was common knowledge, unlike my role in stopping Brazell.

Cahil nodded. "A perfect position to overhear the Commander's plans. He used you as a shield. You should want to help overthrow him. Why do you hold such loyalty for him?" Frustration roughened his voice.

"Because of my position, I saw through his reputation. I witnessed kindness and a deep concern for his people. He didn't abuse his power, and, while he is far from perfect, he always stayed faithful to his beliefs. Reliable and true to his word, you never had to guess at hidden meanings or suspect duplicity from him."

His stubbornness refused to soften. "You've been brainwashed, Yelena. Hopefully, you'll regain some sense after living in Sitia for a while." Cahil left without waiting for a reply.

Our conversation had drained me. I drifted in and out of an uneasy sleep the rest of that afternoon. The masked man invaded my dreams, hunting me through a thick jungle.

Toward evening Dax Greenblade surged into the room, energizing the air.

"You look like hell," he said to me in a low voice. Tula and Opal had fallen asleep in Tula's narrow bed.

"Gee, Dax, don't coat it with honey. Tell me what you really think," I said.

He covered his mouth to mute his laughter. "I figured I'd hit you while you were down, because once you hear the rumors that have been flying through the campus like bare feet on hot sand, your ego will think it's a compliment." In a grand gesture, Dax swept his arms into the air. "You have become a legend!"

"A legend? Me?" Disbelief colored my voice.

"A scary legend," he amended, "but a legend all the same."

"Come on! How gullible do you think I am?"

"Simple enough to think you can find someone's consciousness alone." Dax waved a hand over my bed. "Although, it's not so stupid if this was an attempt to get out of class. But if you see your fellow students scurrying to get out of your way, now you know why. Here comes Yelena, the all powerful Soulfinder!"

I threw my pillow at Dax. His magic brushed my skin as the pillow veered to the right and struck the wall with a soft thump before sliding to the floor. I glanced at the girls. They appeared to be asleep.

"Now you're exaggerating," I said.

"Can you blame me? Cursed with the ability to read and speak archaic languages, Master Bain has me translating ancient history. Very dry and dull." Dax retrieved my pillow and even fluffed it before returning it to me.

When Leif entered the room carrying a large square box, Dax leaned close to me and whispered, "Speaking of dull..."

I suppressed a chuckle. Dax left as Leif began to unpack small brown vials. The clink of glass woke Tula and Opal. Tula eyed the bottles with obvious alarm.

"What are those?" I asked Leif.

"Scent vials," he said. "Each one contains a specific odor. Mother and Father helped me make these. Smells trigger memories, which aid me in finding criminals. But I figured I could use this kit as a start in determining the ointment that Tula's attacker used."

Interested, Tula tried to sit up. Opal got off the bed to help her. Leif rummaged through his collection of about thirty vials until he had lined up ten of them.

"We'll try these first." He uncorked one and passed it under my nose. "Breathe normally."

I wrinkled my nose and sneezed. "No. That's awful."

A small smile touched Leif's face as he put that vial away.

"Leif?" Tula asked. "What about me?"

He hesitated. "You've done so much already. I didn't want to exhaust you."

"I want to help, too. Better than lying here doing nothing."

"All right." He had us sniff three more vials. Tula and I each smelled different ones, and then we took a break for dinner.

"Too many scents will give you a headache, and you won't be able to tell the difference between them after a while," he explained.

Leif spent the evening with us. My interest began to wane, but he kept at it even when he neared the bottom of the box. I was on the edge of sleep when a sharp odor jolted me.

Leif held an uncorked bottle. Tula cowered in her bed, her hands raised as though she tried to deflect a blow. Leif squinted in confusion.

"That's it," I cried. "Can't you smell it?"

He passed the vial under his nose, breathing in the pungent scent. Then he shoved the cork back in, flipped the bottle over, and read the label. He stared at me in shock.

"It makes perfect sense!" His mouth opened in horror.

"What?" I demanded. "Tell me."

"It's Curare." When he saw my confusion he continued, "Comes from a vine that grows in the Illiais Jungle. It paralyzes the muscles. It's great for numbing toothaches, and for relieving minor pain. To freeze a whole body, the medicine would have to be very concentrated." Leif's eyes flashed in dismay.

"Why are you so upset?" I asked. "Now you know what it is. Isn't that good?"

"Curare was rediscovered just last year. Only a handful of Zaltanas know about its properties. Our clan likes to know everything about a substance before selling it to others."

Understanding flooded my mind. Leif believed that the red-painted man could be from our clan.

"Who found the Curare?" I asked.

Still upset, Leif turned the vial in his hands.

"Father," he said. "And the only person I can think of who has the skills to concentrate the Curare enough to paralyze a whole body, is Mother."

18

I sat up in bed. "Leif, you don't really believe…" I couldn't bring myself to conjecture aloud. To say that Esau and Perl, our parents, might have some connection to this horrid murderer.

Leif shook his head. "No. But someone close to them, perhaps."

Another dreadful thought came to mind. "Are they in danger?"

"I don't know." Leif began to pack his scent vials into their box. "I need to talk to our clan leader. Somehow, the Curare must have been stolen. That one of our clan is…" Seeming lost for words, Leif banged the box's top down. "Compromised? Saying we have a spy sounds too dramatic even for me." Leif gave me a rueful grin. "I doubt our leader will even believe me." He grabbed his kit and rushed from the room.

Tula, who had remained quiet during our conversation, asked, "Could Ferde…" She swallowed. "Could my attacker be from the Zaltana Clan?"

"Ferde? Is that his name?"

She covered her face with a hand. "No. That's just what I named him. I hid that from you. I was embarrassed." She stopped and took a deep breath, glancing at her sister.

Opal yawned and said she needed to get some sleep. She kissed Tula on the cheek and pulled the covers up to Tula's chin before leaving.

After a few moments of silence, I said, "You don't have to explain."

"I want to, talking helps. Ferde is short for Fer-de-lance. A poisonous viper that hunts for prey by seeking heat. We used to get them in our factory all the time. They were drawn to the kilns. One killed my uncle. Anytime one of us would go out to the factory, my mother would say, 'Be careful. Don't let Ferde get you.' My older sister and I used to scare Opal by telling her Ferde was coming for her." Tula made a small sound as tears tracked down her face. "I have to apologize to Opal for being so mean. It's funny..." She choked out. "I was the one taken by Ferde, but if I'd had a choice, I would have rather been bitten by the real snake."

I couldn't find any words of comfort for Tula.

Later that night, Bain arrived. He carried a lantern, and Dax, ladened with a large leather-covered book and rolls of paper, followed him into the room. Yet another roll of paper was tucked under Bain's arm. He lit the lanterns in the room until the air blazed with candlelight. Bain wore the same purple robe he had worn the day before. Without preamble, he spread the paper across my bed. My stomach clenched when I looked at the scroll. The symbols I had seen tattooed on Ferde's body covered the parchment.

Bain watched my reaction closely. "These, then, are the right symbols?"

I nodded. "Where..?"

Bain took the book from Dax, and for once the young man's face held a serious expression.

"This ancient text written in the Efe language tells of magic symbols from long ago. It reports that these symbols were so powerful that they could not be drawn in the book, for to do so would call the power. But, fortunate for us, they describe them in detail. And fortunate, too, Dax was able to translate the Efe language into these." Bain gestured to the paper.

"That's some progress," I said.

Dax flashed a smile. "My talents are *finally* being used for a good cause."

Bain gave Dax a stern look. Dax sobered.

"The order of the symbols is very important," Bain explained, "for they weave a story. If you can tell us where they were on the killer's body, we might be able to discern what motivates him."

I studied the sheet, trying to remember where Ferde had painted the markings on his body. "There are some patterns on him that aren't on this paper," I said.

"Here," Tula said. Her eyes were closed. Even though her arm trembled, she held out her right hand. "I know them by heart."

Bain handed her the paper as Dax put his rolls on the floor. Unrolling one, he began to sketch an outline of a man on the sheet with a slender piece of charcoal. Tula stared at the symbols for a moment then she recited their order. Starting with Ferde's left shoulder; she worked her way across his body to his right shoulder, then continued left to right like lines of words in a book.

When Tula came to a symbol that wasn't on Bain's sheet, I drew it on a piece of scrap paper for Dax. Even though my drawings looked clumsy compared to his, he was able to duplicate my efforts on his paper.

Tula stuttered in embarrassment when she reached Ferde's groin. Bain squeezed her hand and made a comment about how the man must have suffered for his art. A single chuckle burst from Tula. By her expression, I knew the brief laugh had surprised her. I suppressed a smile; Tula had started on the long road of recovery.

Tula had memorized the symbols on her attacker's back. I cringed, remembering that she had spent almost two weeks as his prisoner. She also recalled other things about him—the scars on his ankles, the size of his hands, the red dirt under his fingernails, the shape and soft fabric of his red mask, and his ears.

"Why his ears?" Bain asked.

Tula shut her eyes and, even though her voice quavered, explained that each time he had staked her to the ground and thrust deep inside her, he turned his head to avoid looking into her eyes. To block out the pain, Tula focused on his ear. The first time he raped her, Tula bit him on the right ear. She recalled feeling a moment of satisfaction when the hot metallic taste of his blood filled her mouth.

"A tiny victory for me," Tula said then shuddered so fiercely her bed shook. "I never did it again."

Dax, who had been drawing Tula's every description from his spot on the floor, smoothed his horrified expression before giving her his sketch.

After some minor corrections, Tula handed the paper to Bain. "That's him," she said.

The effort had sapped so much of her strength that Tula fell asleep before Dax could gather his supplies.

I touched Bain's sleeve. "Can I ask you something?"

The magician glanced at his apprentice.

"I'll wait for you in your tower," Dax said to him. He left.

"You can always ask. No need to get permission, child."

I shook my head at the endearment. With only a bit of my strength returning, I felt ancient. I had no energy to correct him, though I doubt it would do me any good. He tended to call everyone child, even Irys, and she was twice my age.

"Irys hasn't come to visit. Is she still angry with me?"

"I would not use the word angry. Furious or livid comes closer to the truth."

My face must have reflected my terror because Bain laid a soothing hand over mine.

"You must remember that you are her student. Your actions reflect her skills as a teacher. What you did with Tula was extremely dangerous. You could have killed Tula, Opal, Leif and yourself. You did not consult Irys or seek her help, relying solely on yourself."

I opened my mouth to defend myself, but Bain raised a forestalling hand. "A skill, I am sure, you learned in Ixia. No one to help you. No one to trust. You did what you had to do to survive. Am I not correct?" Bain didn't wait for my reply. "But you are not in the north anymore. Here you have friends, colleagues and others to guide you and to help you. Sitia is very different from Ixia. No one person rules. We have a Council that represents our people. We debate and decide together. This is something you need to learn, and Irys needs to teach you. When she understands why you acted as you did, she will not be so upset."

"How long will that take?"

Bain smiled. "Not long. Irys is like the volcanoes in the Emerald Mountains. She might emit some steam, spit some lava, but she is quick to cool. She probably would have visited today, but a messenger arrived from Ixia this afternoon."

"A messenger?" I tried to get out of bed, but my legs wouldn't hold my weight. I ended up on the floor.

Bain *tsked* at me, calling Hayes to help me into bed.

When Hayes left, I asked again, "What messenger? Tell me."

"Council business." The magician made a shooing motion with his hand as if the entire topic bored him. "Something about an Ixian ambassador and his retinue requesting permission to visit Sitia."

An Ixian ambassador coming here? I mulled over the implications, as Bain, anxious to translate the killer's tattoos, hastened to leave the room.

"Bain," I called as he opened the door. "When are the Ixians coming?"

"I do not know. I am sure Irys will tell you when she comes."

When. At this point, I felt *if* was the better word. Waiting for her became intolerable. I hated just lying there, being so helpless. Irys must have sensed my agitation.

Yelena, I heard her voice in my mind. *Relax. Conserve your strength.*

But I need—

To get a good night's sleep. Or I shall tell you nothing. Understand? Her firm tone left me no chance to argue. *Yes, sir.*

I tried to settle my mind. Instead of obsessing about when the northern delegation would arrive, I thought about who Commander Ambrose would send as his ambassador. He wouldn't risk one of his generals; sending an aide seemed more logical.

Valek would be my choice, but the Sitians wouldn't trust him, and he would be in too much danger. Cahil and his men would try to kill him for assassinating the former King of Ixia. But would they succeed? That would depend on how many attacked him at one time.

I imagined Valek countering strikes with his typical grace and speed, but huge green leaves began to obscure the image in my mind. The leaves blocked my view and soon vegetation surrounded me. I fought my way through the dense jungle, searching for Valek. My pace increased as the awareness of being chased pressed on my back. Glancing over my shoulder, I spotted a long tan snake with red markings slithering after me.

Catching glimpses of Valek through the trees, I shouted and called to him for help. But thick vines from the jungle had ensnared his torso and legs. He hacked at them with his sword, but the vines continued to wrap around him until they covered his arms, as well. I pushed toward him, but a sharp pinch in my thigh stopped me.

The viper had wrapped around my leg. His fangs dripped

Curare. Blood welled from the two small holes in my pants.
The drug spread through my body. I screamed until the poison froze my voice.

"Yelena, wake up."

Someone shook my shoulder hard.

"It's just a dream. Come on, wake up."

I blinked at Leif. A frown anchored his face. His short black
hair stuck out at odd angles, and he had dark smudges under his
eyes. I glanced at Tula. Propped up on one elbow, she looked
at me with concern in her brown eyes.

"Is Valek in trouble?" she asked me.

Leif's gaze jumped to Tula. "Why are you asking about
him?" he demanded.

"Yelena was trying to help him when she was bitten by the
snake."

"You saw it?" I asked.

She nodded. "I dream of the snake every night, but Valek's
new. He must be from your dreams."

Leif turned back to me. "You know him?"

"I…" I closed my mouth. Choosing my words with care, I
said, "As the Commander's food taster, I saw him every day."

Leif blinked. The red flush of annoyance drained from his
face. "I know nothing about your life in Ixia," he said.

"That was entirely your choice."

"I don't think I could stand the extra guilt." Leif turned his
face away, staring at the wall.

"You shouldn't feel any guilt now that you know I was kidnapped. There was nothing you could do," I said, but he refused to meet my questioning gaze.

"Isn't she your sister?" Tula asked into the silence. She wrinkled her nose, squinting in confusion.

"It's a long complicated story," I said.

Tula settled her head on the pillow, and then squirmed

around under the covers as though she were seeking a more comfortable position. "We have plenty of time."

"We have no time," Irys said from the doorway. "Leif, are you ready?"

"Yes."

Irys took a step inside the room. "Then go help Cahil with the horses."

"But I was going to—"

"Explain what is going on," I demanded, sitting up.

"No time. Bain will fill you in."

Irys and Leif turned to leave.

Fury bloomed in my chest. Without thought, I pulled power and directed it toward them. "Stop."

They both froze in place until I released them. I slumped in bed. My outburst had sapped what little strength I had.

Irys returned to my bedside. An odd mixture of anger and admiration on her face. "Feeling better?"

"No."

"Leif, go," Irys said. "I'll catch up in a moment."

He shot me a rueful glance on his way out. Leif's way of saying goodbye, I guessed.

Irys perched on the edge of my bed and pushed me back onto the pillow. "You'll never get better if you keep using magic."

"I'm sorry. I just can't stand being so—"

"Helpless." A wry smile bent Irys's mouth. "It's your own fault. At least, that's what Roze keeps telling me. She wants me to assign you to a season of kitchen duty as punishment for rescuing Tula."

"She should be rewarded, not punished," Tula said.

Irys held her hand up. "Advice I won't be taking. In fact, I believe that your current situation is bad enough that you'll think twice next time you're tempted to use more magic than you can handle. And being stuck here while Cahil, Leif and I travel to the Avibian Plains to visit the Sandseed Clan is sufficient punishment."

"What happened?" I asked.

Irys softened her voice, her words just louder than a whisper. "Last night Leif and I asked Bavol, the Zaltana's Councilman about the Curare. It did come from your parents. They made a large batch and had it delivered to the Sandseed Clan."

My heart skipped a beat. "Why?"

"According to Bavol, Esau had read about a substance that paralyzes muscles in a history book about the nomadic tribes of the Avibian Plains. So, Esau traveled to the Sandseed Clan and found a healer named Gede who knew a little about this substance. In the Sandseed Clan, information is orally passed down from one healer to the next, and sometimes knowledge is lost. Esau and Gede searched the jungle for the Curare vine and, once found, they had Perl help them extract the drug. It's a time-consuming process so Gede returned to the plains, and Esau promised to send him some Curare as a gift for helping him." Irys stood. "So, now we are going to find out what Gede did with his Curare since Councilor Harun Sandseed didn't know."

"I must come!" I struggled to sit up, but my arm refused to hold my weight.

Irys watched me impassively. When I stopped, she asked, "Why?"

"Because I know the killer. I've seen him in Tula's mind. He might be with the clan."

She shook her head. "We have Dax's drawing and Leif caught a glimpse of the man when he helped you connect your mind to Tula's." Irys reached out and smoothed my hair from my face. Her hand felt cool against my hot skin. "Besides, you're not strong enough. Stay. Rest. Grow strong again. I have a great deal to teach you when I return." She hesitated, then leaned over and kissed me on the forehead.

My protests froze on my lips. My reason for being at the Keep was to learn, and already I felt as if I had gone off course, but visiting the Sandseeds could be an educational experience. Why wasn't anything simple?

Irys reached the door when I remembered to ask her about the Ixian delegation.

Pausing at the threshold, she said, "The Council has agreed to a meeting. The messenger left this morning to deliver our reply to Ixia."

She shut the door, leaving me to ponder all that she had told me.

"Ixia," Tula said with wonder. "Do you think Valek will escape the vines and come with the delegation?"

"Tula, that was a nightmare."

"But it seemed so real," she insisted.

"Bad dreams are ghosts of our fears and worries, haunting us while we sleep. I doubt Valek is in trouble."

My thoughts, though, lingered on the image of Valek trapped. It had seemed real. I gritted my teeth in frustration and impatience. Irys had been right, lying here unable to do anything was far worse than scrubbing the kitchen.

Taking some deep breaths, I calmed my mind, cleansing out my worries and irritation. I focused on my last night with Valek in Ixia. A cherished memory.

I must have drifted off to sleep because I felt Valek's presence. A strong cloud of energy surrounded me.

You need help, love? he asked in my dream.

I need you. I need love. I need energy. I need you.

His regret pulsed in my heart. *I can't come. You already have my love. But I can give you my strength.*

No! You'll be helpless for days! The image of Valek tangled in vines leaped into my mind.

I'll be fine. The power twins are with me. They'll protect me. Valek showed me an image of Ari and Janco, my friends in Ixia,

guarding his tent. They camped in the Snake Forest, partici-
pating in a military exercise.

Before I could stop him, power washed over me, soaking
into my body.

Good luck, love.

"Valek," I yelled out loud. He disappeared.

"What was that?" Tula asked.

"A dream." But I felt rejuvenated. I stood on my now steady
legs, marveling.

Tula stared. "It wasn't a dream. I saw a light and—"

I made a sudden decision and bolted for the door. "I have
to go."

"Where?" Tula demanded.

"To catch up with Irys."

19

The two men guarding our room jumped in surprise when I sprinted out the door. I raced toward the stable before my mind could slow me down with logic, but I arrived too late. The yard was empty.

Kiki poked her head out of her stall. *Lavender Lady better?*

Yes, much better. I stroked her nose. *I missed the others. When did they leave?*

Some chews of hay. We catch up.

I studied Kiki's blue eyes. She presented an interesting idea. Even if I had caught up to Irys before they left, there was no guarantee that she would have let me go with them to the Avibian Plains.

Kiki pawed the ground with impatience. *Go.*

I thought fast. Perhaps it would be better if I followed Irys and Leif to the plains, revealing myself only when we traveled too far for her to send me back to the Keep.

I need supplies, I told Kiki. On the way to my room, I made a mental list of everything I would need. My backpack and bow, my switchblade, my cloak, some clothes and food. Money perhaps.

After gathering what I could from my room, I locked the door, turned to go and bumped into Dax.

"Look who's vertical," he said. A wide smile spread across his lips. "I don't know why I'm surprised. After all, you are a living legend."

Shaking my head, I said, "Dax, I don't have time to exchange barbs with you."

"Why?"

I paused, realizing that taking off on my own would be yet another black mark against me. An Ixian decision. But getting information from the Sandseeds was too important for me to worry about the consequences. I told Dax about my plans. "Can you tell Second Magician where I've gone? I don't want Bain combing the Keep for me."

"You're on the fast path to expulsion," Dax warned. "I've lost count of points against you." He paused, considering. "Doesn't matter now. How long of a head start do you want?"

I glanced at the sky. Midafternoon. "Till dark." The timing still left Bain a slight chance to send someone to retrieve me, but I hoped he would wait until the morning.

"Done. I'd wish you good luck, but I don't think it would help."

"Why not?"

"My lady, you make your own luck." Then he shooed me away. "Go."

I hurried to the kitchen and grabbed enough bread, cheese and dried meat to last for ten days. Captain Marrok had said the Avibian Plains were vast and it took ten days to cross them. If the Sandseed Clan lived on the far side, I would have enough food to reach them, and I hoped I could buy more for the return trip.

With my thoughts focused on supplies, I raced toward the barn. As I approached, Kiki snorted in agitation, and I opened my mind to her.

Bad smell, she warned.

I spun in time to see Goel rush me. Before I could react, the point of his sword stopped mere inches from my stomach.

"Going somewhere?" he asked.

"What are you doing here?"

"Little birdie told me you flew the coop. It wasn't hard to track you."

The guards outside Tula's room must have alerted Goel. I sighed. My distraction while collecting supplies had made me an easy target.

"Okay, Goel. Let's make this quick." I took a step back and reached for my bow, but Goel moved forward. The point of his sword cut through my shirt and pricked my skin just as my hands found the smooth wood of my staff.

"Freeze!" he shouted.

I huffed more in annoyance than fear. I didn't have time for this. "Too scared for a fair fight? Ow!" The sword's tip jabbed into my stomach.

"Drop your bow to the ground. Slowly," he ordered.

He nudged his sword tip deeper when I hesitated. In slow motion, I pulled my bow from its strap, keeping Goel's attention on me because out of the corner of my eye I saw Kiki open the latch on her stall's door with her teeth.

The door thumped open. Goel turned his head at the noise. Kiki spun, aimed her hind legs. I scurried back a few paces.

Not too hard, I told her.

Bad man. She kicked him.

Goel flew through the air and slammed against the pasture's wooden fence. Then he crumpled in a heap. When he didn't move, I approached and felt for a pulse. Still alive. I had mixed feelings about his survival. Would he ever give up or would he keep coming after me until he had caught me or until I had killed him?

Kiki interrupted my thoughts. *Go.*

I retrieved her tack and began to saddle her. As I tightened the girth straps around her chest, I asked, *Could you always open your door?*

Yes. Fence, too.

Why don't you?

Hay sweet. Water fresh. Peppermints.

I laughed and made sure to take some mints from Cahil's supply, packing them into my bag. I hooked five feed bags and water bags for her onto the saddle along with my own food and water skins.

Too heavy? I asked.

She looked at me with scorn. *No. Leave now. Topaz scent going.*

I mounted. We left the Magician's Keep and headed through the Citadel. Kiki stepped with care as she walked along the crowded streets of the market. I spotted Fisk, my beggar boy, carrying a huge package for a lady. He smiled and tried to wave. His clean black hair shone in the sun and the hollow smudges under his eyes were gone. A beggar no longer. Fisk found a job.

When we passed under the massive marble arches that marked the gateway of the Citadel, Kiki picked up her pace, breaking into a gallop. The view sped past as we traveled along the main valley road that led from the Citadel to the forest.

Harvest activity buzzed in the fields to our right. On the left, the Avibian Plains flowed out to the horizon. The colors of the tall grasses had transformed from the greens and blues of the hot season into reds, yellows and oranges as though someone had taken a giant paintbrush and swabbed large bands of color across the landscape.

The plains appeared deserted, and I saw no signs of wildlife. Only the colors rippled in the wind. When Kiki turned to enter the plains, I spotted a faint trail cutting through the grass.

The long blades rubbed against my legs and Kiki's stomach. Kiki relaxed her pace. I touched her mind. We were on the right path, and the strong scent of horses filled her nose. She picked out each one by their smell. *Silk. Topaz. Rusalka.*

Rusalka?

Sad Man's.

Confused at first, it took me a moment to realize Sad Man was Kiki's name for Leif. From what I had gathered from Kiki, when a horse meets someone for the first time their immediate impression becomes that person's horse name and they relayed it to other horses. Apparently it doesn't change. To the horses, it made sense. They gave us names just like we had given them names.

Other horses? I asked.

No.

Other men?

No.

Surprised that Cahil hadn't taken some of his men with him, I wondered why. Cahil had skirted the plains on our trip to the Citadel, afraid of the Sandseeds even when traveling with twelve men. I guess he felt safer having a Master Magician accompany him. Either that, or Irys had insisted he leave his watchdogs at the Keep.

As we advanced farther into the plains, I realized that the surrounding grassland hid many things. Despite appearing flat, the terrain rolled like a messy blanket. I looked back the way we had come and couldn't see the farmland. Clusters of gray rocks peppered the plains, an occasional tree rose up from the grass, and I glimpsed field mice and small animals darting away from Kiki's hooves.

We passed a strange crimson-colored rock formation. White veined the single stone, whose top tier loomed above my head. The thick squarish profile of the structure reminded me of something. I scanned my memory and realized the rock resembled a human heart. The fact that I had recalled my lessons surprised me. Biology at Brazell's orphanage had been my least favorite subject. The teacher had delighted in making his students sick to their stomachs.

When the light over the plains began to fade and the air chilled, the thought of spending a night in such an exposed place made me uneasy.

Catch up? Kiki asked.

Are we close?

The pungent smell of horses mixed with a thin scent of smoke. Through Kiki's eyes, I could see a distant fire.

They stop.

I weighed my options. A night alone or the possibility of facing Irys's anger if I joined her. Not used to sitting in the saddle for more than an hour, my legs and back ached. I needed a break. Kiki, though, could travel much longer. Pulling power, I projected my awareness, feeling for the overall mood of the campsite.

Cahil gripped the handle of his sword; the wide-open sky alarmed him. Leif lounged on the ground almost asleep. Irys—

Yelena! Her outrage seared my mind.

Decision made. Before she could demand an explanation, I showed her what had happened between Valek and me.

Impossible.

The word triggered a memory. *You said the same thing when I reached out to Valek to help me against Roze's mental probing. Perhaps there is something connecting us that you haven't encountered?*

Perhaps, she conceded. *Come, join us. It's too late to send you home. And you can't go back to the Keep without me to help you against Roze's wrath.*

With that sobering thought, I told Kiki to find the campsite. She felt glad, though, when we reached Topaz. He grazed with the other horses near the camp.

I removed Kiki's tack, rubbed her down and made sure she had enough food and water. Reluctance and sore muscles made my movements slow.

When I finally joined Irys in the small clearing where they had stopped for the night, she only asked me if I needed dinner. I glanced at the others. Leif stirred a pot of soup cooking over the flames. He wore a neutral expression. Cahil's hand now hovered near his sword handle; he seemed more relaxed about the night sky. He grinned when he met my gaze. He was either glad about my arrival, or was anticipating the entertainment from the reprimand I was certain to receive from Irys.

Instead, Irys lectured Cahil and me on the proper way to interact with the Sandseed Clan members.

"Respect of the elders is a must," she said. "All requests are to be made to the elders, but only after they invite us to speak. They don't trust outsiders and will watch for any sign of disregard or any indication that you are spying on them. So don't ask questions unless given permission and don't stare."

"Why would we stare?" I asked.

"They don't like to wear clothes. Some members will dress when outsiders are visiting, but others won't." Irys smiled ruefully. "Also they have a few powerful magicians. They aren't Keep trained, they teach their own. Although a few of their younger magicians have come to the Keep, seeking to enhance their knowledge. Kangom was one of these, but he didn't stay at the Keep for long." Irys frowned.

Unfortunately, I knew where he had gone from there. He changed his name to Mogkan and started kidnapping children, smuggling them into Ixia.

Before Cahil could voice his questions about Mogkan, I asked Irys, "What about the Sandseed magicians that stay with the clan?"

"They call them Story Weavers," Irys explained. "They hold the clan's history. The Sandseeds believe their history is a living entity, like an invisible presence that surrounds them. Since the clan's story is always evolving, the Story Weavers guide the clan."

"How do they guide them?" Cahil asked with concern.

"They mediate disputes, help in decision making, they show

the clan members their past and aid them in avoiding the same mistakes. Very similar to what the Master Magicians do for the people of Sitia."

"They soothe a troubled heart," Leif said, staring into the flames. "Or so they claim." Then he stood abruptly. "The soup's done. Who's hungry?"

We ate in silence. After we arranged sleeping areas for the evening, Irys informed us that we would be on the road for one more night before we reached the clan's dwellings.

Cahil wanted to make a night watch schedule. "I'll take the first shift," he offered.

Irys just looked at him.

"It makes sense," he said in his defense.

"Cahil, there is nothing to fear. And if trouble heads in our direction, I will wake you long before it arrives," Irys said.

I hid my smile as I watched Cahil pout. I wrapped my cloak around me against the cold night air and lay on the soft sandy ground of the clearing. I checked with Kiki. *Everything okay?*

Grass sweet. Crunchy.

Bad smells?

No. Nice air. Home.

I remembered now that Kiki had been bred by the Sand-seeds. *Nice to be home?* I thought of Valek in the Snake Forest, and hoped he had regained some of his strength.

Yes. Nicer with Lavender Lady. Peppermints? Hopeful.

In the morning, I promised.

I gazed up at the night sky, watching the stars dance while waiting for sleep. Kiki's view of life sounded right. Good food, fresh water, an occasional sweet and someone to care for. That's what everyone should have. A simplistic and unrealistic view I knew, but it soothed me.

My thoughts, though, drifted into strange dreams. I ran through the plains, searching for Kiki. The knee-high grass grew until it reached above my head and impeded my forward motion. I pushed through the sharp blades, trying and failing to find a way out. My foot snagged on something and I fell. When I rolled over, the grass transformed into a field of snakes and they began to wrap around my body. I struggled until they immobilized me.

"You belong with us," a snake hissed in my ear.

I jerked awake in the weak light of dawn. My ear tingled from the dream snake, and I shivered in the cold morning air, trying to shake off the horror of my nightmare.

Irys and the others milled around the small fire. We ate a breakfast of bread and cheese and saddled our horses. My muscles had stiffened during the night, and they protested each movement. By midmorning, the sun warmed the land and I shed my cloak, stuffing it into my backpack.

As we traveled, the soft ground turned into hard stone and the grasses thinned. Small sandstone outcroppings sprinkled the area. By lunch the outcroppings rose higher than our heads, and I felt as if we rode inside a canyon.

During a brief stop, I noticed streaks of red on a pair of sandstone pillars some distance away. "Tula's attacker had something red under his fingernails," I told the others. "Could it be from here?"

"It's possible," Irys agreed.

"We should get a sample," Leif said. He rummaged in his pack until he found a short glass vial.

"We need to keep going." Irys squinted at the sun. "I want to find a campsite before dark."

"Go. I'll catch up," Leif said.

"Yelena, help him, make sure it's the color you remember," Irys ordered, then turned to Cahil before he could voice the objections behind his frown. "Cahil, you stay with me. If Yelena can find us hours after we left the Citadel, she'll have no problem catching up today."

Irys and a still-scowling Cahil mounted their horses and

headed toward the sun, while Leif and I found a path to the pillars. They were farther away than I had thought. Then, it took us longer than we had anticipated to collect a sample. The streaks turned out to be a layer of red clay. The exposed clay had hardened, and we chipped through it to reach the softer material underneath. We placed both the hard chips and soft clay into the vial.

By the time we returned to our starting point, the sun hovered halfway to the horizon. Kiki found Topaz's trail, and we nudged the horses into a run.

I felt unconcerned when the sky began to darken. Topaz's pungent scent filled Kiki's sensitive nose, which meant we were getting close. But when full dark descended and I could not see a fire, I began to worry. When the moon rose, I halted Kiki.

"Are we lost?" Leif asked. He had been following me without comment since we had discovered the trail. I could just make out his annoyed frown in the faint moonlight.

"No. Kiki says Topaz's scent is strong. Perhaps they decided to travel longer?"

"Can you reach Irys?" Leif asked.

"Oh, snake spit! I forgot!" I took a deep breath and gathered a string of power, chastising myself for failing to remember my magic again. I wondered when using magic would become instinctive.

I felt a surprising rush of power. The source seemed concentrated in this area. Projecting my awareness, I searched the surrounding land. Nothing.

Alarmed, I extended my reach, seeking farther. Then I realized that my mind hadn't even touched field mice or any other creatures. I stopped in frustration. If I could connect to Valek in the Snake Forest, I should be able to find Irys; after all, her horse had just passed this way.

Topaz smell always strong, Kiki agreed.

Always?

Yes.

"Well?" Leif asked with impatience.

"Something's wrong. I can't find Irys." I told him what Kiki had just said.

"But that's good, right?"

"There should have been a gradual buildup of scent from faint to sharp. Instead, it's been the same since we found their trail." I turned in a circle; magic pulsed in the air all around us. "Someone is trying to trick us."

"Finally!" A deep voice barked from the darkness.

Kiki and Rusalka reared in surprise, but a soothing strand of magic calmed them. I pulled my bow and scanned the few faint shapes I could see in the weak light.

"Not very quick, are you?" the voice taunted from my left.

I spun Kiki around in time to see a man coalesce out of a blue ray of moonlight. Tall enough to meet my gaze without having to look up, the naked man's skin was indigo and hairless. His bald head gleamed with sweat and I could see strength coiled in his powerful muscles. But his round face held amusement, and I sensed no immediate threat from him. Pure magical energy emanated from him, so I thought he might be influencing my emotions.

I drew my bow. "Who are you and what do you want?" I demanded.

Bright white teeth flashed as he smiled. "I am your Story Weaver."

20

I glanced at Leif; his alarmed expression had turned to fear.
Color leaked from his face as he looked from me to the large
indigo-colored man. The man's painted skin and lack of clothes
made me think of Tula's attacker, but his body was more muscular and scars crisscrossed his arms and legs. But no tattoos.

With my mental barrier in place, I held my bow ready, but
the man stood relaxed. I would be relaxed, too, if I had access
to the amount of magical power within his control. He had no
need to move; he could kill us with a word. Which begged the
question, why was he here?

"What do you want?" I asked.

"Go away," Leif said to the man, "you cause only trouble."

"Your stories have tangled and knotted together," Story
Weaver said. "I am here as a guide to show you both how to
untangle them."

"Banish him," Leif told me. "He has to obey you."

"He does?" That seemed rather easy.

"If you wish me to leave, I will go. But you and your brother
will not be allowed to enter our village. His twisted soul causes
us pain and you are linked to him."

I stared at the Story Weaver in confusion; his words didn't make sense. Friend or foe?

"You said you were here to guide. Guide us where?"

"Banish him now!" Leif yelled. "He will deceive you. He's probably in league with Tula's kidnapper and is trying to delay us."

"Your fear remains strong," Story Weaver said to Leif. "You are not ready to face your story, preferring instead to surround yourself with knots. Some day, they will strangle you. Your choice was to decline our help, but your tangles threaten to squeeze the life out of your sister. This must be corrected." Extending his hand to me, he said, "You are ready. Leave Kiki and come with me."

"Where?"

"To see your story."

"How? Why?"

Story Weaver refused to answer. He radiated calm patience as if he could stand there with his arm extended all night, waiting.

Kiki looked back at me. *Go with Moon Man,* she urged. *Hungry. Tired. Want Topaz.*

Smell? Bad? I asked.

Hard road, but Lavender Lady strong. Go.

I returned my bow to its holder and dismounted.

"Yelena, no!" Leif cried. He clutched Rusalka's reins tight to his chest.

I paused in shock. "That's the first time you've called me by my name. *Now* you care what happens to me? Sorry, it's too late in the game for that to work. Frankly, I don't want to deal with your troubles. I have enough of my own. And we have to find Tula's attacker before he takes another, so it's imperative that we meet with the clan elders. If this is what I need to do, then so be it." I shrugged. "Besides, Kiki told me to go."

"And you would listen to a horse instead of your brother?"

"Until now *my brother* has refused to acknowledge any connection with me since I have arrived in Sitia. I trust Kiki."

Leif snorted in exasperation. "You spent your life in Ixia. You know nothing of these Sandseeds."

"I learned who to trust."

"A horse. You're a fool." He shook his head.

There was no sense telling him about how I had trusted an assassin, a magician who had tried to kill me twice and two soldiers who had jumped me in the Snake Forest. All four now dear to my heart.

"When will I be back?" I asked Story Weaver.

"With the sun's first ray."

I unsaddled Kiki and gave her a quick rubdown while she ate some oats. Then I exchanged her feed bag for water. She drained it, and I placed the empty sacks near her tack.

Apprehension about this strange trip began to crawl along my stomach. *Wait for me?* I asked Kiki.

She snorted and whacked me with her tail, moving away to search for some sweet grass to graze on. Ask a dull-witted question.

I met Leif's stony gaze for a moment, then walked over to Story Weaver. He hadn't moved. Kiki had called him Moon Man. Before I took his hand, I asked, "What's your name?"

"Moon Man will do."

I studied his colored skin. "Why indigo?"

A slow grin spread over his lips. "A cooling color to help soothe the fire between you and your brother." Then, a sheepish look. "It is my favorite."

I laid my hand in his. His palm felt like velvet. His warmth soaked into my bones and flowed up my arm. Magic shimmered and the world around us melted. I began to uncoil, feeling my body loosen and elongate as if it transformed into a string. The individual strands that entwined within my life's story began to separate and diverge so I could see the many events that had formed my life.

Some of my history was familiar; I sought the pleasant memories, watching them as if I stood outside a window.

This is why you need me, Moon Man's voice floated through the scene before my eyes. *You would stay here. My job is to guide you to the proper thread.*

Memories blurred around me. I closed my eyes as the visions swirled. When the air settled once more, I opened them.

I sat in the middle of a living area. Couches constructed of lianas and a glass-topped table surrounded me. A young boy about eight or nine years old reclined across from me on the wooden floor. He wore a pair of green short pants. With his hands behind his head and his elbows jutting out, he stared at the leaf-covered ceiling. About ten bone dice littered the ground between us.

"I'm bored," the boy said.

The appropriate response popped into my mind. "How about Onesies? Or Two Through the Skull?" I scooped up the dice and shook them.

"Baby games," he said. "Let's go down to the jungle floor and explore!" Leif jumped to his feet.

"I don't know. How about we go swinging with Nutty?"

"If you want to play silly baby games with Nutty, go ahead. I'm going to explore and probably make a big discovery. Maybe I'll find the cure to the rotting disease. I'll be famous. They'll probably elect me the next clan leader."

Not wanting to miss any important discoveries and ensuing fame, I agreed to go with him. With a quick call to our mother, we left our tree dwelling and climbed down the Palm ladder into the cooler air of the jungle's floor. The soft ground felt spongy under my bare feet.

I followed Leif through the jungle, marveling at the youthful energy pumping through my six-year-old body. A part of me knew the truth, that I was older and not really here, that this was a vision. Yet I found I didn't care, and I cartwheeled down the jungle path just for fun.

"This is serious," Leif scolded. "We're explorers. We need to collect samples. You gather some leaves while I search for flower petals."

When he turned his back, I stuck my tongue out at him, but I grabbed some tree leaves all the same. A quick movement among the branches distracted me. I froze, scanning the area. Clinging to a sapling hung a young black-and-white valmur. Brown eyes bulged from its small face, peering at me.

I smiled and whistled at the creature. It scampered a bit higher, then turned its gaze back to mine and flicked its long tail. The animal wanted to play. I followed, copying its movements through the jungle. We climbed vines, swung and dodged around the big buttress roots of a Rosewood Tree.

I stopped when I heard a distant voice. Straining to listen, I heard Leif calling for me. I would have ignored him, playing was more fun than collecting leaves, but I thought he said something about a Ylang-Ylang Tree. Mother would bake us star fruit pies if we brought her Ylang-Ylang Flowers for her perfumes.

"Coming," I shouted, jumping down to the jungle floor. When I turned to wave goodbye to the little valmur, it startled and dashed high up into the Rosewood Tree. A feeling of unease settled over me like a mist. I searched the nearby branches, looking for necklace snakes—the main predator of valmurs. With my gaze focused on the tree canopy, I almost tripped over a man.

I jumped back in surprise. He sat on the ground with his right leg splayed out and the other tucked in close. His hands gripped his left ankle. Torn and stained with dirt and sweat, his clothing hung in tatters. Leaves and tendrils clung to his black hair.

The adult part of my mind screamed. Mogkan! Run! But my young self remained unafraid.

"Thank fate!" Mogkan cried as relief smoothed the worry from his face. "I'm lost. I think I broke my ankle. Can you help?"

I nodded. "I'll go get my brother—"

"Wait. Just help me up first."

"Why?"

"To see if I can walk. If my ankle is really broken, you'll have to get more help."

My adult consciousness knew he lied, but I couldn't prevent my child self from stepping closer. I reached out a hand; he grasped it then yanked me down. In one swift motion he grabbed me and muffled my cry with a damp cloth. He pressed it tight against my mouth, forcing a sweet aroma into my nose.

The jungle spun around me. Stay awake! Stay awake! I yelled to my body, but the blackness crept closer.

Struggling in Mogkan's arms, my adult self knew what would happen next. Mogkan would take me to Ixia, and I would be raised in the orphanage of Reyad's father, General Brazell, so when I reached maturity they could try to take the magic out of me as if milking a cow. All so Mogkan could increase his magical powers and help Brazell take over control of Commander Ambrose and Ixia. Even knowing the ending didn't make me feel any better about my abduction.

Leif's face in the bushes was the last thing my young self saw before the darkness claimed me. And that was truly horrifying.

The vision faded. I stood with Moon Man on a dark plain. "Did Leif really see what happened to me?" I asked Story Weaver.

"Yes."

"Why didn't he tell our parents?" They could have sent a rescue party, or tried to get me back. Better for them to know their child's fate than to guess and wonder for years.

As I thought about Leif, my resentment grew. He had robbed me of the chance to have a childhood, to have a bedroom and loving parents, to learn about the jungle with my father and distill perfumes with my mother, to swing through the trees with Nutty and to play games instead of memorizing Ixia's Code of Behavior.

"Why?" I demanded.

"That is a question you must ask him."

I shook my head. "He must have hated me. He was glad to see me kidnapped. That explains his anger when I returned to Sitia."

Moon Man said, "Hate and anger are some of the emotions that strangle your brother, but not all. The easy answer is never the right answer. You must untangle your brother before he chokes himself."

I thought about Leif. He had helped me with Tula, but he could have lied when he told me why, just like he had lied to our parents for fourteen years. My interactions with him since my return to Sitia had almost all been unpleasant. And the single memory I now owned of Leif before my time in Ixia made my blood boil with fury. Perhaps if I had more memories of my childhood.

"Why can't I remember my life before Mogkan kidnapped me?" I asked.

"Mogkan used magic to suppress all your memories, so you would believe him and stay in the orphanage."

That made sense. If I had remembered a family, I would have tried to run away.

"Do you want those memories back?" he asked.

"Yes!"

"Promise you will help your brother and I will unlock them."

I considered his offer. "How do I help him?"

"You will find a way."

"Cryptic, aren't we?"

He smiled. "The fun part of my job."

"What if I refuse to help him?"

"That is your decision."

I huffed in frustration. "Why do you care?"

"He sought relief from his pain in the Avibian Plains. He tried to kill himself. His need for help drew me to him. I offered my services, but fear twisted his heart and he refused. His pain reaches me still. A job unfinished. A soul lost. While there is time left, I will do what I can even if I have to bargain with a Soulfinder."

21

"Soulfinder?" Fear brushed up my spine. "Why do I keep hearing that name?" I asked Story Weaver. We still stood on the featureless expanse. Not unlike the surface of a frozen pond.

"Because you are one," he said in a plain, matter-of-fact tone.

"No," I protested, remembering the loathing and horror that had crossed Hayes's face when he had first mentioned that title to me. He had talked about waking the dead.

"I will show you."

The smooth plain under our feet turned transparent and, through it, I saw my Ixian friend, Janco. His pale face grimaced in pain as his blood gushed from the sword lodged in his stomach. The scene switched to Commander Ambrose lying motionless on a bed; his eyes vacant. Then I saw my own face as I stood over an unconscious General Brazell. My green eyes took on a sudden intensity as if I'd had an epiphany. A brief image of Fisk, the beggar boy, carrying packages and smiling. Then a picture of Tula, lying broken on her bed. The images faded as the ground returned.

"You have found five souls already," Moon Man said.

"But they weren't—"

"Dead?"

I nodded.

"Do you know what a Soulfinder is?" he asked.

"They wake the dead?" When he raised an eyebrow without commenting, I said, "No, I don't."

"You need to learn."

"And telling me would be too easy. Right? Takes all the fun out of being a mysterious Story Weaver."

He grinned. "What about my bargain? Childhood memories for your help with Leif."

Just hearing his name sent waves of anger through my body. My reasons for coming to Sitia had been so simple. First for survival, fleeing the Commander's order of execution. Second had been to learn how to use my magic and meet my family. Perhaps along the way I might develop a kinship with this southern world. Or perhaps not.

My plans had seemed straightforward, then my road kept dipping and turning and I kept getting caught in its traps. Now I felt mired in mud in the middle of nowhere. Lost.

"Your path is clear," said Moon Man. "You need to find it."

And the best way to find something you had lost was to return to the last place you remembered having it. In my case, I needed to start at the very beginning.

"I promise to try to help Leif," I said.

Smells and softness flooded my mind as memories of my childhood came to life. Apple Berry perfume mixed with the musky scent of earth. Laughter and the pure joy of swinging through the air followed an argument with Leif over the last mango. Playing hide-and-seek with Leif and Nutty, crouching on branches to ambush Nutty's brothers during a mock battle. The sharp sting of hazelnuts on my bare arms as her brothers discovered our hiding spot, launching an attack. The slap of mud as our clan leader dug a grave for my grandfather. The sound of my mother's soothing voice as she sang me a lullaby.

The lessons with Esau on different species of leaves and their medicinal properties.

All the happiness, sadness, pain, fear and thrills of childhood came rushing back. I knew some would fade with time, but others would stay with me forever.

"Thank you," I said.

Story Weaver inclined his head. He held out a hand and I grasped it. The dark plain faded and shapes grew from the ground. Colors returned as the sun's first light crested the horizon.

I blinked, trying to orient myself. The clearing where I had left Kiki and Leif had changed. Large circular tents ringed a huge fire pit. Brown animal shapes had been painted on the white canvas of the tents. Dark-skinned people milled about the roaring fire. Some cooked while others tended children. Some wore clothes while others wore nothing. The clothes were all made of white cotton. The women wore either sleeveless dresses that reached to their knees or a tunic and short pants like the men.

Near the fire, Irys and Cahil sat cross-legged with two older men and a woman. They were intent on their discussion and didn't see me. I couldn't spot Leif or his horse, but Kiki stood next to one of the tents. A woman wearing short pants groomed her. Her brown hair bobbed to her neck.

I jumped when I realized Moon Man no longer stood beside me. In fact, I couldn't see him anywhere in the small village. Perhaps he'd gone into one of the tents.

Not wanting to interrupt Irys, I checked on Kiki. She whickered at me in greeting. The woman stopped brushing the dust off her coat. She studied me in silence.

Who's this? I asked Kiki.

Mother.

"Is this your horse?" the woman asked. The inflection in

her voice rose and fell with each word, and there was a slight pause between them.

I reviewed Irys's lecture about the Sandseeds from the night before. The woman had spoken first so I guessed it would be all right to answer her. "I'm hers."

She snorted a short laugh through her nose. "I raised her, taught her and sent her on her journey. It's a pleasure to see her again." She kicked at her saddle on the ground. "She doesn't need this. She will float under you like a gust of wind."

"That's for me." And for our supplies.

Another huff of amusement. She finished brushing her. Kiki turned her blue eyes toward her and understanding flashed on the woman's face. She whooped and jumped up on Kiki's back.

Have fun, I told Kiki as she raced through the tall grass.

"Is that wise?" Cahil asked. He watched Kiki disappear over a hill. "What if that woman doesn't come back?"

"I don't care if she comes back or not." I shrugged, looking past Cahil. Irys and the three Sandseeds stood next to the fire. They were still in deep conversation. One of the men gestured in what appeared to be anger.

"You don't care if she steals Kiki?"

Instead of trying to educate Cahil on my relationship with Kiki, I searched his face. Tension had pulled his eyes into an intent expression. His gaze darted around the campsite as if he expected to be attacked.

"What's been going on?" I asked him, tilting my head toward Irys.

"Last night, we made camp and waited for you and Leif. *I* worried when you failed to catch up, but Irys seemed amused. Then this group of Sandseeds arrived at our site. These are the clan leaders. They travel from village to village, settling disputes, bringing news and goods. It's very convenient that they found us. I think they're hiding something."

Cahil's frown reminded me of my brother. "Where's Leif?"

Worry lined his face. "*They* said he went back to the Keep. Why would he do that?"

Because he, too, felt afraid. But, I said, "He probably wanted to get the red soil samples to Bain."

Cahil appeared unconvinced. Before I could ask more questions, Irys ended her conversation and moved to join us.

"They're upset," she said.

"Why?" I asked.

"They think we're accusing them of giving the Curare to Tula's attacker. And Cahil's attempts to recruit them to his cause have inflamed them." Irys scowled at Cahil. "I thought you wanted to come along so you could see another part of our culture. Your selfish obsession to raise an army has jeopardized our mission."

Cahil didn't look remorseful. "I wouldn't have to raise an army if the Council supported me. You—"

"Silence!" Irys sliced her hand through the air and I felt a brush of magic.

Bright red blotches grew on Cahil's cheeks as he tried to speak.

"Despite all my diplomatic training, I can't get them to tell me anything. Cahil has offended them. They will now talk only to you, Yelena."

"Should we plan our escape route now?" I asked.

She laughed. "We'll push Cahil into their path to slow them down."

Cahil shot Irys a venomous glare.

"You have a slight advantage, Yelena," she said. "I might be a Master Magician and member of the Council, but you're a blood relative. In their eyes, a relative is more important than a Master." Irys shook her head in frustration.

"Relative?" I asked.

"About five hundred years ago a group of Sandseeds decided to move into the jungle. The Sandseeds are wanderers by nature, and there have been many groups that have broken from the main clan to find their own way. Most don't stay in communication with the main clan, but some, like the Zaltanas, do. Just try and discover some information without implying that these Sandseeds are involved. Choose your words carefully."

Irys must have read the skepticism on my face because she added, "Consider it your first lesson in diplomacy."

"Seeing how well you did with them, I'm surprised that I don't feel more confident."

"Avoid sarcasm."

"How about coming with me? So when I start to say something stupid you can wave your hand and silence me, too."

A sardonic smile flashed on her face. "I've been asked to leave and to 'take that annoying puppy' with me. You're on your own. I won't be able to reach your mind through this bubble of Sandseed magic, so we'll meet you at the edge of the Avibian Plains next to Blood Rock."

Irys formed an image in my mind of that white-veined structure that Kiki and I had passed two days ago.

Cahil waved his arms and tapped his throat. Irys sighed again. "Only if you promise not to talk about armies until we're back at the Citadel."

He nodded.

"Yelena, I'll let you release his voice," she said.

Another lesson. I calmed the nervous thoughts about my meeting with the elders before I opened my mind to the magic. Magical energy pulsed all around me, but I saw a thin thread of power wrapped around Cahil's throat. Pulling the power to me, I unlocked his voice.

"Well done," Irys said.

Cahil's ears were still bright red, but he had the sense to speak in an even tone. "If I may point out the obvious," he said. "Leaving Yelena alone is dangerous."

"I don't have a choice," Irys said. "I could force them to tell me what they know, but the Sandseeds would consider that an act of war. Then you'll never get your army, Cahil, because we'll be too busy trying to prevent the Sandseeds from taking a blood vengeance from everyone in Sitia." She turned to me. "Yelena, good luck. We'll have a lot to discuss when you catch up with us. Cahil, go saddle Topaz." Irys strode away, whistling for her horse.

A stubborn expression gripped Cahil's face, and he crossed his arms over his chest. "I should stay. Someone needs to watch your back. Basic military tactics. Always have a partner."

"Cahil, there is so much magic in the air around here that the Sandseeds could close my windpipe and there isn't a damn thing you or I could do about it."

"Then come with us."

"What about Tula or the killer's next victim? I have to try."

"But the risk—"

"Living is a risk," I snapped at him. "Every decision, every interaction, every step, every time you get out of bed in the morning, you take a risk. To survive is to know you're taking that risk and to not get out of bed clutching illusions of safety."

"Your view of life doesn't sound comforting."

"It's not supposed to. That's the whole point." Before Cahil could launch into a discussion on philosophy, I tried to shoo him away. "Get going before Irys loses her patience with you again." I swept my hand through the air as Irys had done.

He grabbed my wrist. "No, you don't!" He held my hand for a moment. "If the Sandseeds hurt you, they'll see some of my blood vengeance. Be careful."

I pulled my hand away. "Always."

All those worried thoughts about offending the Sandseeds came flooding back as I watched Irys and Cahil ride away. I reviewed Irys's last-minute instructions about dealing with the clan elders. I glanced around, wondering what I should do.

The Sandseeds worked in their temporary village with a calm efficiency. My hunger flared when I caught a whiff of roasting meat, and I realized I hadn't eaten since we had stopped for lunch the day before. I laid my pack next to Kiki's saddle and rummaged for something to eat, but sitting down proved to be a bad decision as exhaustion pulled at my body. I let my new memories of childhood circle in my mind, and I contented myself with reliving some of them. Using the saddle as a pillow, I stretched out on the grass, not bothering to spread my cloak. Strange that I felt so safe here.

But I wasn't safe from my nightmares. Hunted by a slithering mass of snakes, I scrambled through the jungle. They wrapped around my ankles, yanking me down. Unable to move, they sank fangs, dripping with Curare deep into my flesh. "Come with us," the snakes hissed.

"Cousin?" a timid voice asked.

I awoke with a loud cry. A petite woman with large eyes stepped back in alarm. Her brown hair was streaked with yellow and tied back with a leather cord. Stains lined the white fabric of her dress.

"The elders will see you now."

I peered at the sky, but sheets of clouds obscured the sun. "How long was I asleep?"

The woman smiled. "All day. Follow me please."

I looked at my bow, knowing it would be an insult to bring it, yet wanting it anyway. With reluctance, I left it on the ground and followed the woman. Questions swirled in my mind as we passed the tents, but I bit my lip to prevent myself from voicing them. Wait, wait, I thought, quelling my impatience. Unfortunately, diplomacy was a dance I needed to learn.

The woman stopped at the largest tent. The animal patterns almost covered the white fabric. She swept back a panel and gestured for me to enter. I stepped into the tent, waiting in the muted light for my eyes to adjust.

"You may approach," said a male voice from the far side of the tent.

I surveyed the interior as I crossed to the back. Maroon-and-tan rugs woven with intricate geometric patterns covered the floor of the round tent. I spotted some sleeping mats and colorful pillows on the left. Bigger pillows on the right surrounded a low table, and candleholders with long red tassels hung from the ceiling.

Sitting cross-legged in a row on an ebony-and-gold mat were two men and a woman. One I recognized. Moon Man smiled at me from between the man and woman. His skin was now painted yellow. Wrinkles creased the face of the other man, and the woman's hair was peppered with gray. Both wore red robes.

I halted in shock as the sudden image of my red prison robe, tattered and bloody, rose in my mind. I hadn't thought of that garment since Valek offered me the option of being executed or becoming the Commander's food taster. I had cast it aside and accepted the Ixian uniform without a backward glance. Odd that I should think of it now. Or had Story Weaver pulled those thoughts from my mind? I peered at Moon Man with suspicion.

"Sit," said the woman. She gestured to a small round rug on the floor in front of them.

I settled into the same position as my hosts.

"A Zaltana who has traveled far. You have returned to your ancestors to seek guidance," the man said. His dark eyes brimmed with knowledge and his gaze pierced my soul.

"I seek understanding," I said.

"Your journey has twisted and bent. Your journey has stained you with blood and pain and death. You must be cleansed." The man nodded to Story Weaver.

Moon Man rose. From under the mat, he pulled a scimitar. The sharp edge of the long blade gleamed in the candlelight.

22

Moon Man advanced. He rested the curved blade of the scimitar on my left shoulder with the sharp edge dangerously close to my neck.

"Are you ready to be cleansed?" he asked.

My throat tightened. "What? How?" My mouth stumbled over the words. All logic fled.

"We take the stains of blood, pain and death from you. We take your blood and cause you pain. You will atone for your misdeeds with your eventual death and be welcomed into the sky."

One word cut through the jumble of fear in my mind. Sudden clarity focused my thoughts. I stood with deliberate care, trying not to jostle the weapon, and stepped back. The blade remained poised in midair.

"I have no misdeeds to atone for. I hold no remorse for my past actions and, therefore, do not need to be cleansed." I braced for their reaction. Diplomacy be damned.

Moon Man grinned and the two elders nodded in approval. Confused I watched him replace the scimitar under the mat and settled back into his position. "That is the correct response," he said.

"What if I had agreed?"

"Then we would have sent you away with only a few cryptic remarks to puzzle over." He laughed. "I must admit I am slightly disappointed. I worked all afternoon on those remarks."

"Sit," the woman ordered. "What do you seek to understand?"

I chose my words with great care as I sat on the mat. "A beast has been preying on young women throughout Sitia. To date, he has killed ten and injured one. I want to stop him. I seek to understand who he is."

"Why come to us?" the woman asked.

"He has been using a certain substance as a weapon. I'm concerned that he might have stolen it from one of your clan members." I waited, hoping the word "stolen" would not imply guilt.

"Ah, yes, this substance," the old man said. "A blessing and a curse. A package from Esau Liana Sandseed Zaltana arrived at one of our villages near the Daviian Plateau. That village was raided soon after by the Daviian Vermin." The old man spat on the dirt floor. "Many things were stolen in that raid."

His scorn for these Vermin was obvious, but I asked anyway. "Who are these Vermin?"

The elders tightened their jaws, refusing to reply.

Frowning, Moon Man explained them to me. "They are young men and women who have rebelled against our traditions. They have broken from the clan and settled on the Plateau. The Plateau does not give up its bounty without a fight. The Vermin prefer to steal from us rather than work to grow their own food."

"Could one of them be the monster I seek?"

"Yes. They have perverted our art of magic weaving. Instead of benefiting the clan, they seek to increase their power, enriching only themselves. Most of them do not have the gift, but there are a few who are very powerful."

Moon Man's fierce expression gave me a mental image of

how he would look when swinging his scimitar in battle. I held
a picture of Ferde, Tula's attacker, in my mind.

"Is he one of them?" I asked. Moon Man's magic coursed
through me.

Moon Man grunted, then growled deep in his throat. Looking at the elder man, he said, "They are practicing the old evil.
We must stop them."

Horrified, the man replied, "We will try again to pierce
their magic screen. We will find them." He stood with grace
and dignity, bowed once to me, then gestured to the woman.
"Come. We must make plans."

They left the tent. Moon Man and I remained. "The old
evil?" I asked.

"An ancient horrible ritual of binding a victim's soul to you,
then killing him. When the victim dies, his magic flows into
you, increasing your strength. The red markings on that beast
are part of the ritual." Moon Man's brow furrowed for a moment before his eyes widened with concern. "You said one
woman was injured. Where is she now?"

"In the Magician's Keep."

"Guarded?"

"Yes. Why?"

"The one you seek will not be in the Daviian Plateau—he
will be in the Keep, waiting for another chance to take her life.
He can not bind another soul until she dies."

"I must go back." I jumped up from the small mat intent
on leaving.

Moon Man grabbed my shoulder and turned me to face him.
"Do not forget your promise."

"I won't. Tula first, then Leif."

He nodded. "May I ask another favor?"

I hesitated. At least, he didn't want a promise. "You can ask."

"When your training with Master Irys is complete, will you

return to me so I may teach you the magical arts of the Sand-seeds? It is part of your heritage and of your blood."

The proposition sounded appealing, but would be yet another curve in my journey. At this rate, I doubted I would even finish my training. If history served as guidance, my future tended to go in unanticipated directions. "I will try."

"Good. Now go!" He bowed to me, then shooed me from the tent.

A frenzy of activity encompassed the camp. Dismantled tents littered the ground as the clan members prepared to leave. Twilight crept closer as I searched for my pack. I found Kiki instead. She was saddled and ready to go. Her short-haired "mother" offered her reins to me.

As I took the leather straps, she said, "Do not sit on the saddle. Crouch over it and shift your weight forward. And she will fly home for you."

"Thank you." I bowed.

She smiled. "You are well matched. I am pleased." With a final pat to Kiki's neck, the woman turned to join the clan in their packing efforts.

I mounted Kiki, and tried to follow her directions. We would lose the light soon. Kiki turned her head to the left, peering at me with a blue eye.

Catch Topaz? Silk? she asked.

Yes. Let's fly!

Kiki moved. The long grasses blurred past my feet until I could no longer see them in the darkness. I held my position as we traveled over the plains. It felt as if I rode on top of a wind storm rather than a horse.

When the moon reached its apex, I felt the Sandseed's magic thin, then disappear. No longer surrounded by their power, I used my magic to search for Irys.

I'm here, she said in my mind and I saw through her eyes that they had made camp by Blood Rock.

Wake Cahil, I told her. *We have to return to the Keep as fast as we can. Tula's still in danger.*

She is well guarded.

He has powerful magic.

We're on our way.

I sent my awareness toward the Keep, hoping to warn them. My mind touched Hayes dozing in his office. He flinched away from me in horror and raised a stronger barrier. The other Master Magicians' defenses were as well constructed as the towers in which they slept. Growing weary with the effort, I pulled back.

Kiki overtook Irys and Cahil on the Citadel road just as the sky began to lighten. I had only a moment to wonder how she had managed a two day journey in one night before we sped past the others.

Need rest? I asked her, glancing behind in time to see Irys and Cahil wave me on.

No.

But my legs burned as if they were on fire. I aimed blue cooling thoughts at them, and they numbed.

We were within sight of the marble gates of the Citadel when all desire to rest fled my mind. A sudden and intense feeling of terrified helplessness pressed on my body. Tula. I launched my awareness toward the Keep, searching for someone, anyone to warn. The guards with Tula didn't have any magic. While I could read the minds of non-magicians, they had no power to "hear" me. Desperate, I kept hunting.

My mind found Dax. He was in the middle of a practice bout, learning to parry and lunge with a wooden sword.

Tula, I screamed in his mind. *Danger! Get help!*

He dropped his sword in surprise and was whacked in the ribs by his opponent.

Yelena? He spun around, looking for me.

Tula's in danger! Go. Now, I ordered. Then my connection

to him severed. It felt as if someone had drawn a stone curtain down between us.

Time slowed to drips of molasses as we entered the Citadel and navigated the busy streets. It seemed as if the entire population walked in the streets. Their unhurried pace clogged the roadway.

The air sparked with the perfect cooling season temperature. And a perfect contrast to the fire in my heart. I wanted to scream at the crowd to move. Kiki, sensing my urgency, stepped up her pace and nudged the dawdlers out of our way.

A few curses followed us. Kiki startled the guards at the Keep's entrance when she refused to stop. She headed straight to the infirmary and even climbed the stairs, stopping only when we had reached the door.

I slid from her saddle. Racing toward Tula's room, I feared the worst when I spotted her guards lying in the corridor. I jumped over them and burst into her room. The door slammed against the wall. The noise echoed off the cold marble, but failed to rouse Tula.

Her lifeless eyes stared at nothing. Her bloodless lips were frozen in a grimace of horror and pain. My fingers sought a pulse; her skin felt icy and stiff. Black bruises ringed her neck.

Too late, or, was I? I placed my hand on her throat, pulling power to me. In my mind's eye, I saw her crushed windpipe. She had been strangled. I sent a bubble of power to reinflate it, sending air into her lungs. I focused on her heart, willing it to pump.

Her heart beat and air filled her lungs, but the dullness refused to leave her eyes. I pushed harder. Her skin warmed and flushed. Her chest rose and fell. Yet, when I stopped, her blood stilled and she failed to take another breath.

He had stolen her soul. I couldn't revive her.

A heavy arm rested on my shoulder. "There is nothing more you can do," Irys said.

I glanced around. Behind me stood Cahil, Leif, Dax, Roze and Hayes. They crowded the small room and I hadn't even noticed their arrival. Tula's skin cooled under my fingers. I pulled my hand away.

A sharp, bone-crushing exhaustion settled over me. I dropped to the floor, closed my eyes and rested my head in my hands. My fault. My fault. I should never have left her.

The room erupted with sound and activity, but I ignored them as tears poured down my face. I wanted to dissolve into the floor, mixing myself with the hard stone. A stone had a single purpose: to be. No complicated promises, no worries and no feelings.

I lowered my cheek to the smooth marble. The cold stung my fevered skin. Only when the noise in the room faded did I open my eyes. And saw a scrap of paper lying under Tula's bed. It must have fallen off when I had tried to put life into her body. I reached for it, thinking it had been Tula's.

The words written on the paper cut through the fog of my grief like Moon Man's scimitar.

The note said: *I have Opal. I will exchange Opal for Yelena Zaltana at the next rising of the full moon. Send Tula's grief flag up First Magician's tower as a sign of agreement and Opal will not be harmed. More instructions will follow.*

23

"We'll send Tula's grief flag up, but we're not exchanging Yelena for Opal," Irys insisted. "We have two weeks until the full moon. That should give us enough time to find Opal."

Again, loud arguments echoed through the magician's meeting room. Zitora had returned from her mission for the Council so all four Master Magicians were there, as well as Tula's family, Leif and the Captain of the Keep's guard.

Leif had tried to ask me about the Sandseeds before the meeting started, but I cut him off with an angry response. I still couldn't look at him without seeing his eight-year-old face in the bushes, watching my kidnapping and doing nothing.

The events that had occurred after I discovered the ransom note felt as if they happened in a dream. Once everyone settled down, the killer's movements prior to attacking Tula were uncovered.

He obtained a position with the Keep's gardeners. Unfortunately, the people he worked with couldn't agree on his facial features and Bain had drawn four completely different men from their descriptions. They also failed to remember his name.

With ten magical souls, Ferde obtained enough power to

equal a Master Magician. He concealed his presence in the
Keep with ease and confused those he worked with.

Tula's guards were shot with tiny darts dipped in Curare.
They could only recall seeing one of the gardeners delivering some medicinal plants to Hayes before their muscles froze.
The fact that Ferde had infiltrated the Keep had put the Keep's
guards in serious trouble.

"He was living in the Keep and we had no clue," Roze said.
Her powerful voice rose over the din. "What makes you think
we can find him now?"

Tula's mother and father drew in horrified breaths. They had
arrived the day before. The news of her passing had shocked
them to their core. I could see in their drawn faces and in their
haunted gazes that knowing the same man held Opal made
their lives a living nightmare. Just like mine.

"Give him Yelena," Roze said into the now quiet room.
"She was able to animate Tula. She has the power to handle
this killer."

"We don't want anyone else harmed," said Tula's father. He
wore a simple brown tunic and pants. His large hands were
rough with calluses and burn scars; evidence of a lifetime of
working with molten glass.

"No, Roze," Irys admonished. "She doesn't have full control
of her magic yet. Probably the main reason he wants her. If he
stole her magic, think how powerful he would then be."

Bain, who had translated the markings on the killer's skin,
told the group in the meeting room that the purpose of the
man's quest was written in his tattoos. Bain's information
matched what Moon Man had told me.

Ferde performed an ancient Efe binding ritual that used in-
timidation and torture to turn a victim into a willing slave.
When all free will had been surrendered, the victim was murdered and her soul's magic was directed into Ferde, increasing

his own power. He had targeted fifteen- and sixteen-year-old girls because their magic potential was just beginning.

Sour bile churned in my stomach as I listened to Bain's explanation. Reyad's and Mogkan's tactics in Ixia to increase Mogkan's magic had been sickeningly familiar. Although, they hadn't raped or killed their thirty-two victims, they tortured their souls from them, leaving them mindless. Just as horrible.

Ferde had gained eleven souls. According to the ritual, the twelfth soul must go to him willingly. No kidnapping for the final ritual, which, when completed, would give him almost unlimited power.

Debate on why Tula survived the initial attack led to a guess that Ferde had been close to being discovered and fled before finishing the ritual.

"Yelena should be protected at all times," Irys said. Her words brought me back to the meeting. "If we can't find him, we'll set up an ambush near the exchange site and apprehend him that way."

The magicians continued to argue. It seemed as if I would have no say in the plans. It didn't matter. I would either find Ferde or be at that exchange site. I had failed Tula; I wasn't going to let Opal suffer the same fate.

A messenger from the Council arrived as the meeting ended. He handed Roze a scroll. She read it then thrust the paper at Irys in what appeared to be disgust. Irys's shoulders drooped when she scanned the document.

What else has gone wrong? I asked her.

Another situation to deal with. This one is not life threatening, though, just bad timing, she said. *At least this will be another chance for you to practice your diplomacy.*

How?

An Ixian delegation is expected to arrive in six days.

So soon? I had thought the messenger with the Council's reply had just left.

Yelena, it's been five days. It's a two-day ride to the Ixian border and a half a day to the Commander's castle.

Five days? So much had happened in those five days that I felt as if I lived one endless day. Difficult, too, to believe I had been living in Sitia for only two and a half seasons. Almost half a year gone in what seemed like a fortnight. My ache for Valek hadn't dulled, and I wondered if meeting the northern delegation would cause me to miss him more.

I followed the others from the room. In the hallway outside, Zitora linked her arm in mine.

"I need some help," she said, guiding me from the Keep's administration building, and toward her tower.

"But I need to—"

"Get some rest. And *not* go searching the Citadel for Opal," Zitora said.

"I will anyway. You know that."

She nodded. "But not tonight."

"What do you need?"

A sad smile touched her face. "Help with Tula's flag. I believe asking her parents would only increase their grief."

We entered her tower and climbed two flights of stairs to her workroom. Comfortable chairs and tables littered with sewing and art supplies filled the large chamber.

"My seamstress skills are limited," Zitora said. She moved around the room, adding fabric and thread to the one empty table near the chairs. "But not for the lack of practice. I can sew and embroider, but I'm better at drawing. When I have the time, I've been experimenting with painting on silk."

Satisfied with her collection, Zitora dug through another pile of cloth and pulled out a sheet of white silk. She measured and cut off a five-foot-by-three-foot rectangle.

"The background will be white for Tula's purity and innocence," Zitora said. "Yelena, what should I put in the foreground?" When she saw my confusion, she explained, "A grief flag is our way of honoring the dead. It's a representation of the person. We decorate it with the things that made up a person's life, and when we raise the flag high, it releases their spirit into the sky. So what would best represent Tula?"

My thoughts went immediately to Ferde. A poisonous snake, red flames for pain and a jar of Curare all came to mind. I scowled, unable to imagine Tula's spirit free. She had been trapped in the blackness of Ferde's soul because of my stupidity.

"He's a cunning demon, isn't he?" Zitora asked, as if reading my mind. "To have the boldness to live in the Keep, to have the skill to kill under our roof and to have you blame yourself for it. A masterful trick, I'd say."

"You're starting to sound like a certain Story Weaver I know," I said.

"I'll take that as a compliment," Zitora replied. She sorted through colorful squares of silk. "Let's see. If you had listened to Irys and remained behind, the killer would have gotten Tula *and* you."

"But I had gotten my energy back," I said. Irys had thought it best not to mention Valek's help.

"Only because you wanted to follow Irys." Zitora raised a thin eyebrow.

"But I wouldn't have gone with Ferde willingly."

"Truly? What if he had promised not to kill Tula in exchange for you?"

I opened my mouth, then closed it, considering. She had a point.

"Once you say the words or move with intent, it's done. What follows after will not change that, and he would have killed Tula anyway," Zitora said. She lined the colored squares along the table's edge. "If you had stayed behind, you would both be gone, and we wouldn't have the information from the Sandseeds."

"Are you trying to make me feel better?"

Zitora smiled. "Now, what should we put on Tula's flag?"

The answer came to mind. "Honeysuckles, a single drop of dew on a blade of grass and glass animals."

Opal had told me about Tula's glass animals. Most of them Tula had either sold or given away as gifts, but Tula kept a small collection of them near her bed. The unwelcome thought of what we would sew on to Opal's flag rose in my mind. I suppressed it, squashing the image into a small corner of my brain. I would not let Ferde murder Opal.

Zitora drew shapes on the silk and I cut them out. When the pile met her approval, we arranged them on the white silk. Honeysuckles bordered the flag, while the blade of grass rose in the center surrounded by a ring of animal sculptures.

"Beautiful," Zitora said. Her eyes shone with grief. "Now comes the tedious part—sewing all these bits of cloth onto the background!"

I threaded needles for her, the extent of my sewing ability. After a while, she told me to go back to my room and get some sleep.

"Don't forget about our agreement," Zitora called as I started down the steps.

"I won't."

Now that she was back, I could begin teaching her some self-defense. With my thoughts preoccupied with scheduling her training, I was startled by two guards who waited for me outside Zitora's tower.

"What do you want?" I demanded, pulling my bow.

"Orders from Fourth Magician. You're to be protected at all times," said the larger of the two men.

I huffed with annoyance. "Go back to the barracks. I can take care of myself."

The men grinned.

"She told us you would say that," the other man said. "We follow *her* orders. If our unit fails to protect you, we'll be assigned to clean chamber pots for the rest of our days."

"I could make your job very difficult," I warned them.

The stubborn stiffness of their shoulders never softened.

"There is nothing you can do that's worse than cleaning chamber pots," said the large man.

I sighed; giving them the slip to search for Opal would be hard. Which was probably why Irys had assigned them to me. She knew that I would go hunting as soon as I could.

"Just stay out of my way," I growled.

I turned my back on the guards and headed for the apprentice's wing. The dark campus seemed to mourn, and an uneasy quiet filled the air. The raising ceremony for Tula was scheduled for dawn.

Then life would continue. I would have my afternoon lesson with Irys. Cahil had already reminded me of our evening ride. I would attempt to keep my promise to Moon Man. All these events would occur despite the threat to Opal. Or should that be in spite of the threat?

My guards refused to let me enter my rooms until one of them searched for intruders. At least they remained outside afterward and didn't insist on staying with me. But Irys had informed them that I would attempt to "escape," because when I looked out my bedroom window, I saw one of the guards standing there. I closed and locked the window shutters.

The guards blocked both exits. I could see Dax's grin in my mind, knowing he would delight in telling me the gossip and rumors from the other students about my protectors.

I sat on the bed in annoyance and sealed my fate. The soft comfort of my pillow called to me. I would rest only a moment, clearing my head so I could plan a way to lose my two shadows.

★ ★ ★

During the next five days, I had only one successful escape. The morning after I had helped Zitora with Tula's grief flag, I stood next to Irys for Tula's raising ceremony.

Tula's body had been wrapped in white linen strips and covered with her flag. The leader of the Cowan clan spoke kind words over her body as her parents wept. All four Master Magicians attended. Zitora soaked a handkerchief with her tears, but I clamped down on my emotions and focused on Opal, hardening my resolve to find her.

Tula's body was to be taken home and buried in her family's graveyard. But, according to Sitian beliefs, during this farewell ceremony her spirit transferred to the flag. The people surrounding me believed that when this pennant of white silk fluttered above Roze's tower, Tula's spirit would be released into the sky.

But I knew better. Tula's spirit was trapped inside Ferde and only his death would release her. For me, Tula's flag not only signaled Ferde that we had agreed to his exchange, but also symbolized my determination to find and stop him.

The morning after Tula's ceremony, I led my guards to the baths. The pools and changing rooms bustled with students getting ready for classes, and despite the assortment of wary looks aimed my way, I managed to pay a few novices to create a diversion near the back entrance.

The ruse worked. I dashed out of the baths and out of the Keep before the soldiers at the gate could recognize me. The guards stationed at the Keep's gate monitored who came in, and, unless there was a crisis, they only paid a passing interest to those who left.

Once out of sight, my first task included finding Fisk and his friends. The market was just stirring to life. Only a few customers wandered through the stands at this early hour. I found Fisk playing dice with a group of children.

He ran over to me. "Lovely Yelena, how can I assist you today?" His smile lit up his face.

The other children surrounded me, waiting for instructions. They appeared clean and cared for. They earned money for their families, and I thought that once I finished this ugly business with Ferde, I would give them more help. I remembered to tell them about the Keep's need for another gardener, though, and was rewarded to see one girl run home to tell her father.

"I need guides," I told Fisk. "Show me all the shortcuts and hidden areas of the Citadel."

While they took me through back alleys and forgotten quarters, I questioned them about the people. Anybody new? Anybody acting strange? Had they seen a young, frightened girl with a man? They regaled me with wild stories, but the information was not what I needed. As we moved, I searched the surrounding homes with my magic, seeking Opal, or the wisp of someone else's magic, or anything that might give me a clue as to her whereabouts.

The day was well spent and only my hunger could stop me. Fisk led me to the best meat griller in the Citadel's market. As I ate the juicy beef, I decided I would continue my search late into the night and then find a place to sleep. I would have plenty more days to spend hunting Opal.

At least that had been my intention until Irys and my guards ambushed me. Hidden behind a shield of magic, she prevented me from sensing them until too late. The instant the two soldiers grabbed my arms; she seized control of my body, pushing aside what I had thought to be a strong mental barrier. The full power of a Master Magician reduced my own defenses to dust. Unable to move or to talk, I stared at her in complete surprise.

Even though I had missed Irys's morning lesson and blocked her efforts to find me with her magic, I thought she would understand my mission. I was unprepared for the severity of her anger.

My guards, looking grim and scared, clung to me.

You will not *leave the Keep again. You will not lose your guards again. Or I will lock you in the Keep's prison. Understand?*

Yes. I'm—

I'll be watching.

But—

Irys severed our mental connection with a head aching abruptness. Yet her magic still gripped my body.

"Take her back to the Keep," Irys ordered the guards. "Take her to her rooms. She may leave them only for lessons and meals. Do not lose her again."

The guards flinched under her searing gaze. The larger one picked me up and threw me over his shoulder. I suffered the indignity of being carried through the Citadel, across the Keep's campus and dumped onto my bed.

Irys didn't relinquish control of my body until the next morning, although I still felt a band of her magic wrapped around my throat. By then, I was ready to throttle anyone who dared to get in my way. Avoided as if I carried a disease, I could only vent my ill humor on the guards as they escorted me through the campus.

After three days of this hell, I stood next to Irys in the great hall of the Council building, waiting for the Ixian delegation to arrive. Irys had used my lesson time to lecture me on proper Sitian protocols and diplomacy. She had refused to let me talk to her about anything other than the lecture topic. My frustration at not knowing about the search for Opal seized my chest like a vise.

The great hall was decorated with large silk banners representing each of the eleven clans and each of the Master Magicians. Hung from the ceiling, these colorful banners flowed down three stories of marble walls until they reached the floor. Tall slender windows separated the banners, allowing the sunlight to stripe the floor with gold. The Council members wore formal robes of silk, embroidered with silver thread. Irys and the other Masters wore their ceremonial robes and masks.

I remembered Irys's hawk mask from when she had visited the Commander in Ixia, and I looked at the others with interest. Roze Featherstone, First Magician wore a blue dragon mask. Bain Bloodgood, Second Magician had donned a leopard skin mask. And a white unicorn covered Third Magician, Zitora's face.

According to Fisk, these animals acted as the magicians' guides through the underworld and throughout their life. They had found them while enduring the Master level test, which, from the little bits of information I could gather, seemed a horrible ordeal.

Cahil had donned the midnight-blue tunic with the silver piping that he had worn to the New Beginnings feast. The color complemented his blond hair and he looked regal despite his hard expression. Present to assess his enemy for weakness, he promised to keep quiet and not draw attention to himself; otherwise, the Council members would have banned him from the greeting ceremonies.

Fidgeting, I twisted the wide sleeves of my formal apprentice robe around my arm. Pale yellow in color, the hem of the plain cotton garment touched my feet and revealed the black sandals Zitora had given to me. I plucked at the skin on my neck and pulled at the robe's collar.

What's wrong? Irys asked. Her rigid posture radiated disapproval.

It was the first time since my house arrest that she had mentally communicated to me. I wanted to ignore her. My anger at her punishment still sizzled in my blood. Even now, Irys's magic wrapped around my neck. She hadn't been kidding when she had said she'd be watching. The power I would need to remove her magic would exhaust me, and I didn't possess enough nerve to provoke her again.

Your leash chafes. My thoughts were cold.

Good. Maybe now you'll learn to listen and to think before you act. To trust others' judgments.

I've learned something.

What?

The harsh tactics of the Commander are not unique to Ixia.

Oh, Yelena. Irys's stiff demeanor melted. The hard band of magic around my throat disappeared. *I'm at my wit's end. You're so focused on action. You have a single-minded determination that barrels through situations. You've been lucky so far, and I don't know how to make you understand that if Tula's killer absorbs your power, he will be unstoppable. Sitia will be his to rule. This goes beyond you and your desire for revenge. This affects us all. All options must be carefully considered before any action is taken. That is the Sitian way.*

She shook her head, sighing. *I have forgotten that you're a grown woman. Once you have complete control of your magic and when this killer is found, you can do as you like, go where you please. I had hoped you would have become a part of our efforts to keep Sitia a safe and prosperous place to live. But your unpredictability will only jeopardize our community.*

Irys's words cut through my anger. To be free to do anything I wanted seemed a foreign concept. The first time in my life that I had been offered such a choice.

I envisioned traveling all over Sitia with Kiki and with no worries or promises to keep. To be unconnected. Moving from one town to the next, experiencing the culture. Or climbing through the jungle with my father, learning about the medicinal properties of some leaf. Or sneaking into Ixia to meet with Valek. She presented an attractive option.

Perhaps I would take her up on it, but not until *after* I captured Ferde and fulfilled my promise to Moon Man.

Deciding I would try harder to work in the Sitian way, I said, *Irys, I would like to help find Opal.*

Sensing my intentions, she turned to me and studied my expression. *There's a meeting scheduled after the formalities with the Ixians. You're welcome to come.*

I smoothed out the sleeves of my robe as the row of trumpet players sounded the arrival of the northerners. An immediate hush fell over the great hall as a stately parade of Ixians entered the room.

The Ambassador led the procession. The tailored cut of her black uniform lent her an air of importance. Two diamonds sparkled from her collar. The Commander must have shown her great favor in allowing her to wear the precious stones for this mission. Her long straight hair was fading toward gray, yet her almond-shaped eyes held a powerful vitality.

Sudden recognition pierced my heart.

24

I quickly scanned the rest of the Ambassador's retinue, searching for the person who had to be there. Her aide, walking one step behind her, wore the same uniform as the Ambassador except the red diamonds on his collar had been stitched with thread. His bland face was unremarkable, so I moved my gaze to the others.

Some of the guards looked familiar, but two captains near the middle caught my eye. Ari's massive muscles strained the seams on his uniform. His tight blond curls looked almost white in the sunlight. His face remained impassive when he glanced at me, but I could see two red blotches spreading on his cheeks as he fought to keep from smiling.

Janco sauntered next to him, looking much healthier than when I had said goodbye to him in Ixia. Then his pale face had been tight with pain and he hadn't the strength to stand. The results of defending Irys against Mogkan's men. Now he moved his lean build with an athletic grace and his skin was tanned. Straight-faced, he peered at me, but I could see pure mischievous glee dancing in his eyes.

It was wonderful to see them, but I kept searching. Clutching my butterfly pendant through my robe, I scrutinized all the guard's faces. He *had* to be here. If the Commander was here, posing as the Ixian Ambassador, then Valek *had* to be close by.

But Valek didn't know about Commander Ambrose's secret. Only I knew about what the Commander called his mutation, having been born a woman with a man's soul. Since Valek didn't know the Ambassador was the Commander, he probably would be with whoever was posing as the Commander in Ixia.

Unless the Commander had sent Valek on another mission, or, even worse, maybe Valek still hadn't recovered from giving me his strength. Maybe he had been injured while weak. Or dead. Horrible scenarios chased through my mind as the delegation exchanged formal greetings.

I willed the pleasantries to move faster. My need to question Ari and Janco about Valek grew with every second.

With my thoughts on Valek, I found my eyes lingering on the Ambassador's aide. His straight black hair fell to his ears and clung limply to his head. A soft fat nose sat above colorless lips and a weak chin. He appeared to be bored as he scanned the Councilors and magicians in the room with no hint of intelligence in his blue eyes.

Our gazes met for a moment. Sapphire-blue lightning struck my heart. That rat. I wanted to slug Valek and kiss him at the same time.

His expression never changed. He gave no sign of having seen me at all as his attention refocused on the Councilors. I could hardly bear the rest of the meeting.

Too impatient to wait until the meeting concluded, I tried to link with Valek's mind. I encountered a formidable barrier stronger than any of the Master Magicians'. Valek sensed the magic and glanced at me.

When the introductions and formalities came to an end, the Ixian delegation was served refreshments and everyone milled about in small groups.

I headed for Ari and Janco, who stood near the Ambassador

as if they had metal rods strapped onto their backs, but Bavol Cacao, my clan leader, stopped me.

"I have a message from your father," Bavol said. He handed me a small scroll.

I thanked him. This was only the second time I had talked to him since he had arrived at the Citadel. He had delivered the clothes Nutty had sewn for me. Even though I wanted to talk to my friends, I inquired after the clan.

"Dealing with the usual petty problems, and trying to combat some fungus that is eating through the wood on a few walls." He smiled. "I've no doubt that Esau'll figure it out. Now if you'll excuse me, I need to check to make sure the Ambassador's suite is ready."

Before Bavol could walk away, I touched his sleeve. "What does the suite look like?" I asked him.

Puzzled, he said, "Our most opulent chambers. The Citadel's guest suites have every convenience. Why?"

"The Ambassador doesn't like opulence. Perhaps you could have some of it removed? Simple elegance would suit her better."

Bavol considered. "She's a cousin of Commander Ambrose. Have you met her?"

"No. But I know most Ixians agree with the Commander's dislike for extravagance."

"Your concern is noted. I'll see to the changes." Bavol hurried away.

I broke the wax seal on the scroll. Unrolling the paper, I read the note then closed my eyes for a moment. In my mind's eye I saw my story line twist into a big complicated noose-like knot. According to the letter, Esau and Perl were on their way to the Keep to visit me. They planned to arrive five days before the full moon.

Who else could come? If I had gotten a message from the underworld announcing Reyad and Mogkan's arrival, I wouldn't have been surprised.

Tucking the note away, I shook my head. I had no control over these events and I would deal with my parents when they arrived. I approached the Ixians. The Ambassador chatted with Bain, Second Magician.

Her gold eyes flicked to me and Bain stopped speaking to introduce us. "Ambassador Signe, this is Apprentice Yelena Liana Zaltana."

I clasped her cool hand in the Ixian greeting, and then bowed formally in the Sitian salutation.

She returned the bow. "I have heard much about you from my cousin. How are your studies progressing?"

"Very well, thank you. Please extend my best wishes to Commander Ambrose," I said.

"I will." Signe turned toward her aide. "This is Adviser Ilom."

I held my face in a neutral expression as I shook his limp hand. He mumbled a greeting then ignored me as someone not worth his time or attention. I knew Valek had to be acting, yet his complete disregard made me worry if his feelings for me had changed.

I didn't have much time to brood, though. When Bain led Signe and Ilom to meet another Councilor, Ari grabbed me in a quick bear hug.

"What's with the dress?" Janco asked.

"Better than that wrinkled uniform," I countered. "And is that gray hair in your goatee?"

Janco smoothed a hand over his facial hair. "A little present from my run-in with a sword. Or should I say from when the sword had a run-in with me?" His eyes lit up. "Want to see the scar? It's cool." He started pulling his shirt out of his pants.

"Janco," Ari warned. "We're not supposed to be fraternizing with the Sitians."

"But she's not Sitian. Right, Yelena? You haven't gone south on us, have you?" Janco's voice held mock horror. "Because if you have I can't give you your present."

I took my switchblade out, showing the inscription to Janco. "What about 'Sieges weathered, fight together, friends forever'? Does that change if I become an official southerner?"

Janco rubbed the hair on his chin, considering.

"No," Ari said. "You could change into a goat and it would still apply."

"Only if she made us some goat's cheese," Janco said.

Ari rolled his light blue eyes. "Just give her the gift."

"It's from Valek," Janco said, digging into his pack. "Since he was unable to accompany the delegation."

"Suicide," Ari said. "The Sitians would execute Valek if they caught him in their lands."

Concern for Valek coursed through me, and I glanced around the hall, looking to see if anyone else had recognized him. Everyone seemed to be engaged in conversation except Cahil. He stood alone, watching the Ixians. He met my gaze and frowned.

At Janco's triumphant grunt I turned back to my friends. Once I saw what Janco had in his palm, all thoughts about Cahil disappeared. A black stone snake with glints of silver twisted four times around his fingers. The snake's scales had been carved with a diamond pattern along its back, and two tiny sapphires gleamed from its eyes. One of Valek's carvings.

"It's a bracelet," Janco said. He took my hand and slipped the snake over it until it fit onto my forearm. "It was too small for me," Janco joked. "So I told Valek he should give it to you. Looks like it fits you perfectly."

I marveled at my gift. Why had Valek chosen a snake? Apprehension coiled in my stomach.

"Things have been quiet since you left," Ari said. "Even though we're not part of his corps, Valek made Janco a fox statue and a horse for me. They're the nicest things we own."

We talked until Ari and Janco had to follow the Ambassador to her suite. They told me they would have rotating shifts to guard Signe and Ilom and would have some time to talk to me again. I offered to show them around the Citadel and perhaps the Keep.

Irys found me before I left the great hall and she accompanied me through the Citadel's streets to the meeting to discuss the ongoing efforts to find Opal. My ever-present guards, who had been discreet during the ceremonies, followed us.

"Janco looks great," Irys said. "That was a quick recovery from such a severe injury. I'm glad."

Irys's words reminded me of something Story Weaver had said. With all the commotion surrounding Opal and the delegation, I hadn't discussed Moon Man's claims with her.

"Irys, what is a Soulfinder? My—"

Don't say anymore aloud, Irys's voice admonished in my mind. *That's not something you want anyone to overhear.*

Why not? Why all the fear? My hand sought Valek's bracelet. I twisted it around my arm.

She sighed. *Sitian history is full of wonderful and brave magicians who have joined the clans together and stopped the wars. Unfortunately, those tales aren't told in the taverns and to the children. The tales of the few magicians who have caused harm seem to be the ones whispered by the fireside. With Mogkan's corruption and now this beast that has Opal, I don't want rumors and stories to circulate about a Soulfinder.*

Irys fiddled with the brown feathers on her hawk mask that she carried. *About a hundred and fifty years ago, a Soulfinder was born. He was considered a gift from the underworld. His strong magic affected people's souls, healing both emotional and physical pain. Then he discovered he could pluck a soul from the air before it could float to the sky, waking the dead.*

But something happened. We don't know what, but he became bitter and he went from helping people to using them. Keeping the souls for himself, he woke the dead without their souls. These emotionless creatures followed his orders and had no remorse for their actions. That ability is considered an aberration and is against our Ethical Code. With his soulless army, he had control of Sitia for many many dark years before the Master Magicians could stop him.

Before I could ask for details, Irys continued her story. *Yelena, you have all the abilities of a Soulfinder. When you breathed for Tula, you shocked me and alarmed Roze. That's why I was so harsh with you about losing your guards. I had to show Roze I could control you. But today you made me realize that was wrong. It was probably the same type of panicked response that pushed the Soulfinder over the edge. We need to discover the extent of your abilities before we categorize you. Who knows? You could be a Master Magician.*

I laughed, thinking of how easy it had been for Irys to ambush me and break through my magical defenses. "Highly doubtful," I said. And also doubtful was Moon Man's claims that I was a Soulfinder. Tula's soul was stolen. I could breathe for her, yet I couldn't wake her without it. I shared some abilities with a Soulfinder, but obviously not all.

As we drew closer to the Keep's entrance, I noticed a small beggar wearing a dirty cloak huddled by the wall, shaking a cup. Annoyed that I was the only one to notice, I walked over and dropped a coin into the cup. The beggar looked up, and I saw a flash of Fisk's smile before he hid his face again.

"We have news about the one you seek. Come to the market tomorrow."

"Hey, you! Stop bothering the lady," said one of my guards.

I spun to glare at the guard. When I turned back, Fisk was gone.

I mulled over Fisk's message. My first instinct involved ditching my guards tomorrow and meeting with him, an Ixian response, but I decided to try the Sitian approach and see what the others had found regarding Opal.

Leif leaned over a table in the meeting room, studying a map. He greeted my arrival with a surprised expression, but I refused to acknowledge him and had to suppress a sudden fury that welled in my throat. I had no idea how I would fulfill my promise to Moon Man when all I wanted to do was shake Leif and demand an explanation.

Irys broke the silence and filled me in on the group's efforts so far. They had divided the Citadel into sections and one magician was assigned to search each quarter. Councilor Harun, the Sandseed's Councilman, had taken his people to hunt for Opal in the part of the Avibian Plains that bordered the Citadel. No clues had been found.

"We'll send guards to search every building in the Citadel," Roze said, sweeping into the meeting room with Bain on her heels.

"Which will cause Opal's immediate death," I said.

Roze sneered at me. "Who invited you?" She gave Irys a poisonous glare.

"She's right, Roze," Irys said. "News of the searches would spread like a barn fire and he would be alerted."

"Does anyone have a better idea?"

"I do," I said into the silence.

All eyes turned toward me. Roze's gaze froze my blood.

"I have friends in the Citadel who can get information without calling attention to themselves. Seems they might have already learned something, but I need to meet them at the market tomorrow." Under my sleeve, I twisted Valek's snake around on my wrist, waiting for their response.

"No," Roze said. "It could be a trap."

"Now *you're* concerned for my welfare? How touching. Although I think jealousy is the real emotion," I shot back.

"Ladies, please," said Bain. "Let us focus on the task at hand. Do you trust this source, Yelena?"

"Yes."

"It would not look unusual for Yelena to go to the market to shop. Her guards would be with her," Irys added.

"The guards would scare away my source," I said, which was true enough for my purposes. "Also my source might lead me somewhere, so I'll have to move quick."

"But you'll need protection. We could disguise your guards," Irys offered.

"No. They're not the protection I need. I can defend myself against a physical threat, but I need to defend against a magical one." Irys was a powerful ally.

Irys nodded, and we made plans for the next day.

After the meeting, I went to the dining room to grab something to eat and I picked up a few apples for Kiki and Topaz. My guards continued to follow me, and it felt odd how I had grown used to their presence. At least I didn't need to worry about Goel trying another surprise attack. Especially when I had so many other things to occupy my thoughts.

I hadn't been able to ride since my house arrest, and, even if I couldn't leave the Keep, at least I could practice riding. Kiki's mother had sneered at my saddle, so I wanted to learn how to ride bareback. Besides, it could be a useful skill to learn. In an emergency I wouldn't have time to saddle her.

And I needed the distraction. Bad thoughts of losing my guards and sneaking into a certain Adviser's room in the Citadel's guest quarters kept surfacing. I drowned the dangerous impulse. I wouldn't risk Valek's life for my own selfish reasons. Pulling up my sleeve, I examined Valek's gift in the late afternoon sunlight, running a finger along its back. The bracelet even felt like a snake, although its body language seemed to indicate a protective rather than an aggressive stance.

Again, I wondered at his choice. Perhaps he had somehow witnessed my nightmares about snakes, but why make one as a present? Wouldn't a mongoose make a better gift?

Kiki waited for me by the pasture's gate. She nickered in greeting, and I fed her an apple before climbing over the fence.

My guards took up positions outside the gate, close but not too close. They were learning.

As Kiki ate, I checked her over. She had nettles snarled in her tail, and dried mud on her belly and caked around her hooves.

"Didn't anyone groom you?" I asked aloud, *tsking*.

"She wouldn't let anyone near her," Cahil said. He held a bucket of brushes and combs over the rail. "Seems only you can do the honors."

I took the handle. "Thanks." I pulled out a currycomb and began to loosen the mud on her coat.

Cahil rested his arms on the fence. "Saw you talking to the northerners today. You know some of them?"

I glanced at Cahil. A serious expression gripped his face. So his timely arrival with the supplies hadn't been a coincidence. He had waited to ambush me with questions about the Ixians.

Choosing my words with care, I said, "Two of the guards are my friends."

"The ones who taught you how to fight?" Cahil tried to sound casual.

"Yes."

"What division do they belong to?"

I stopped brushing Kiki and stared at him. "Cahil, what do you really want to know?"

He stammered.

"You're not thinking of jeopardizing the delegation are you? Planning to sabotage the meetings? Or are you more interested in ambushing them on their way back to Ixia?"

He opened his mouth, but no words came out.

"That would be unwise," I continued. "You'll make both Sitia and Ixia your enemy, and besides…"

"Besides what?" he demanded.

"The Commander's elite guards surround the Ambassador. It would be suicide to make a kidnapping attempt."

"Aren't you just full of wisdom today," Cahil said with a

sharp jab of sarcasm. "Your concern for the welfare of my men is truly heartwarming. Are you sure you're not just protecting your northern friends? Or perhaps protecting your heart mate?"

He had to be guessing. I called his bluff. "What are you ranting about?"

"I was watching you when the delegation arrived. Although your face never moved, I saw your hand fly to that butterfly pendant under your robe. I know the one who gave that to you is here. In fact, he gave you another gift today."

I turned back to work on Kiki, hiding my face from Cahil. "If you know so much then why are you asking *me* questions?"

"Who is he?" When I refused to answer, Cahil continued, "It's the man who's missing half of his right ear. The one who gave you the snake."

Cahil wore such a smug expression that I laughed. "Janco? We bicker like brother and sister. No. He was just delivering the gift."

"I don't believe you."

I shrugged. "Here." I handed a wire brush to Cahil. "You can get the nettles out of her tail." When I saw him hesitate, I added, "Don't worry, she won't kick you."

We worked for a while in silence.

Cahil, though, wasn't content with the quiet. "You're happier now that your northern friends are here."

"I missed them," I agreed.

"Would you want to go back to Ixia?"

"Yes. But that's impossible because I'm a magician." And there was a signed order for my execution, but I thought it prudent not to mention that.

"Nothing's impossible." Cahil finished Kiki's tail and began combing her mane. "When I gain control of Ixia and free the people, you would have a place by my side if you chose to accept it."

Avoiding his unspoken question, I gave him a dubious look.

"Do you still believe Sitia will support you even after they've been making nice with the northern delegation?"

With the passion of a mystic, Cahil said, "All my life I have been told I would rule Ixia one day. Every lesson, every interaction and every emotion was tailored to that single purpose. Even the Council encouraged me to plan and train and wait for the perfect moment to attack." Cahil's blue eyes radiated such a pure intensity that I almost stepped back.

"Then the north agrees to a trade treaty and they visit Sitia." He spat the words out. "Suddenly the Commander is the Council's friend, and my reason for existing is no longer supported. The Council has failed to realize that the Commander is deceiving them, and when he tips his hand, I'll be there. I have many loyal followers who are equally unhappy about the Council's dalliances with the north."

"You're going to need a trained military if you plan to go against the Commander's forces," I said. "And if Valek—"

"What about Valek?" Cahil grabbed my arm. His fingers pressed my bracelet into my skin. I winced in pain.

Kiki cocked an ear. *Kick?*

No. Not yet.

"If Valek discovers what you're planning, he'll stop you before you can rally your men."

"Do you really think he can stop me?" he asked.

"Yes." I pulled my arm out of Cahil's grasp, but he caught my wrist with his other hand and yanked my sleeve up with his free hand, exposing the snake circled around my arm. Before I could stop him, he let go of my sleeve and tugged my collar down. My black stone butterfly pendant swung free. The silver spots on its wings glinted in the sunlight, matching the silver on the snake's body.

"And you would know," Cahil said, releasing me. His face took on a stunned expression as he made a sudden realization.

I staggered back.

"As the Commander's food taster, you worked with Valek every day. He had to teach you about poisons and poisoning techniques." He stared at me in revulsion. "Marrok told me that when the royal family members were assassinated, the assassin would leave behind a black statue that glittered with silver. It was the assassin's calling card. Only after the Commander took control of Ixia was Valek named the assassin."

I returned to brushing Kiki. "That's a big leap in logic, Cahil. Based on a bedtime story, which I'm sure gets more interesting with each telling, and a couple of trinkets. Valek is not the only person who carves things out of those rocks. Think about that before you leap to conclusions."

Refusing to meet Cahil's gaze, I put the grooming equipment back into the bucket and led Kiki to her stall. By the time I finished filling her water pail, Cahil had gone.

My guards trailed me to the baths, and stayed outside while I washed off the horse hair and dust that coated my skin. The sun had set by the time we reached my rooms. I waited outside, shivering in the cold night air while one guard searched inside. Given the all clear, I entered my dark living room. I shuttered and locked my windows against the chilly wind, then lit a fire in the hearth.

"That's better," said a voice that set my soul on fire.

I turned. Valek lounged on a chair with his booted feet propped up on the table.

25

Valek held the valmur statue I had bought for him long ago, admiring it in the firelight. He wore a simple black shirt and pants. The clothes did not appear to be as tight fitting as his hooded sneak suit, but seemed snug enough not to impede his movements.

"How did you—"

"Fool your guards? They're not very good. They forgot to check the ceiling for spiders." Valek grinned. His angular face softened.

Startled, I realized he wasn't in disguise. "This is dangerous."

"I knew falling for you was dangerous, love."

"I meant coming to Sitia. Being here in the Magician's Keep with guards just outside my door." I gestured wildly.

"It's only dangerous if they know I'm here. According to them, I'm just Ambassador Signe's lowly and dull-witted aide." Valek stood; his movements liquid. The black fabric of his clothes clung to his lean build. He stretched his arms out to the side. "See, I'm not even armed."

He made a weak attempt to look innocent, but I knew better. "Should I guess how many concealed weapons you have or should I strip search you?"

"A strip search is the only way to be absolutely certain." Valek's deep blue eyes danced with delight.

I took three steps and was wrapped in his arms, where I belonged. No confusion here. No worries here. No troubles here. Just Valek's scent, an intoxicating combination of musk and spice.

During our short trip to the bed, I found two knives strapped to Valek's forearms, darts and other throwing implements tucked inside his belt, a switchblade strapped to his right thigh and a short sword in his boot.

I knew more weapons hid within his clothes, but once I touched his skin, the game ceased to matter as we became reacquainted. With his body next to mine, I felt all the empty places inside me fill with his essence. Home.

It wasn't until deep into the night that we stopped to talk. Lying next to him under the blanket, I thanked him in a low voice for the snake bracelet and told him about Tula, Opal and the reason for the guards.

"And you said it was dangerous for me," Valek said, pointing out the irony. "Good thing I'm here. You'll need backup that can't be influenced by magic."

Valek's immunity to magic could be considered another concealed weapon. Hope of recovering Opal unharmed bloomed in my chest for the first time since her capture. "How can you provide backup? You're supposed to be with the Ambassador."

He grinned. "Don't worry. I've got that covered. This is not the first time, nor will it be the last time, I've been in Sitia. Keeping tabs on our neighbors has always been one of my duties as security chief. Fun stuff."

"Until you're caught," I said. My mood soured, but Valek seemed unaffected by my comment.

"There's always that chance. Part of the allure, I suppose." He nuzzled my neck and sighed with regret. "I better get back.

It'll be dawn soon." He rolled out of bed and began to dress. "Besides, I don't want to be here when your boyfriend arrives."

"Who?" I sat up.

"The blond that follows your every move with his lovesick eyes," Valek teased.

"Cahil?" I laughed, dismissing him. "He thought Janco was my heart mate. I think you should feel more jealousy toward my horse. She's the one who has stolen my heart."

Valek stilled as the amusement dropped from his face. "What's his name?"

"*Her* name is Kiki."

He shook his head. "Not the horse. The blond."

"Cahil."

"Cahil Ixia? The King's nephew? He's alive?" Valek seemed confused.

"I thought you knew," I said.

I had imagined Valek had let Cahil live once he had reached Sitia. But now Cahil's comment about Valek forgetting to count the bodies when he had assassinated the royal family came to mind. With a growing horror, I realized my mistake.

"Valek, don't kill him."

"He's a threat to the Commander." A dead flatness covered Valek's eyes. He wore his stone face. Unyielding. Uncompromising.

"He's my friend."

Valek's cold killer's gaze met mine. "The second he becomes more than a potential threat, he's dead."

Valek had pledged to protect the Commander, and only his love for me kept him from assassinating Cahil that night. Valek's loyalty was without fail. If the Commander had given him a direct order to kill me, Valek would have. Lucky for us that the Commander hadn't given Valek that order.

"I'm glad the Commander is safe within Ixia's borders." Valek's face softened and he laughed. "He's taking a vacation.

He's the only person I know who thinks hunting sand spiders is relaxing."

"Aren't you worried he'd get stung?" My skin crawled just thinking about the poisonous spiders. They were the size of a small dog and jumped with a lethal quickness. But then I remembered that the Commander was really in the Citadel's guest quarters.

"No. I still can't beat the Commander in a knife fight. His skills are more than adequate to handle a sand spider. Plotting royalty is another matter, though. I'll have to keep an eye on this Cahil."

I knew it was a matter of time before Valek found out about Cahil's plans to regain his kingdom. Then what would I do? Those thoughts reminded me about something Cahil had said that hadn't sounded right.

"Valek, did you used to leave your carvings behind when you assassinated someone?"

"Have you been listening to Sitian rumors?" He smiled.

I nodded. "But I don't necessarily believe all that I hear."

"Good. Although, I'm embarrassed to admit that one is true. I was young, cocky and stupid, enjoying being known as the Death Artist. I even started leaving a carving before I began a job, letting my victim find it." Valek shook his head at the memory. "That nonsense almost got me killed, so I stopped it altogether."

Valek finished dressing. "I'll be at the market today in case anything happens."

He kissed me and I clung to him for a moment, wishing we could run away and forget about soul-stealing magicians and Cahil. But that wasn't for us. Dealing with poisoners, schemers and killers seemed to be our lot in life. Besides, we would probably grow bored living in safety without any problems to worry about. But still I wished for it.

With reluctance, I let Valek go. He nodded toward the door.

I opened it and distracted the guard. When I returned to the living room, the heavy darkness pressed on my skin as the icy air soaked into my bones. Valek was gone.

Irys and I walked to the market that morning. The bleak, overcast sky reflected my mood. I huddled in my cloak. It was the first time I needed to wear it during the daytime.

People crowded the market. They hurried to get their shopping done before the dark rain clouds that hovered on the horizon could descend on the Citadel.

I made a few small purchases before I felt a familiar tug on my sleeve. Fisk stood next to me. He flashed me a smile. His face no longer held the gauntness of malnutrition, and I could see his busy gang of children carrying packages for the shoppers.

"You wanted to find a strange man living with a young girl?" he asked.

"Yes. Have you seen them?"

He grinned, holding out his hand. "Information costs money."

"I see you're branching out into a new trade. Very wise," I said as I handed him a Sitian copper. "But watch who you deal with. Some won't take kindly to your inquiries."

He nodded with understanding and I saw a wisdom far beyond his nine years in his light brown eyes. I suppressed a sigh. In Ixia, Fisk's intelligence would be encouraged. He would grow up to be an Adviser or a high-ranking officer, but in Sitia he had grown up on the street, begging for food and money. But not anymore.

I smiled. "What do you know?"

"I'll show you." Fisk pulled on my hand.

Irys, who had remained silent during our exchange, asked, "Can I come with you?"

Fisk ducked his head, looking at the ground. "If it pleases you, Fourth Magician," he mumbled.

A wry grin touched Irys's face. "So much for my disguise."

Fisk glanced up in surprise. "Only the beggars who work

near the Council's Hall would recognize you, Fourth Magician. With not much to do all day, they study the Council members. It's a game to be the first to recognize one of the Master Magicians."

Irys considered Fisk's comments. He squirmed under her scrutiny until he couldn't stand it any longer and turned away from her stare.

"Come. This way," he said.

We followed him through the Citadel. Cutting across back alleys and empty courtyards, I wondered if Valek followed us. The residents seemed intent on their chores and hardly noticed our passage.

Fisk stopped before we reached an open plaza. A large jade statue of a tortoise with intricate carvings on its shell occupied the middle of the square. The dark green turtle shot water out of its mouth and into a pool of water.

Pointing to a building on the opposite side of the plaza, Fisk said, "On the second floor lives a man with red lines on his hands. He's new and no one knows him. He wears a cloak that hides his face. My brother has seen a young girl enter the building, carrying packages."

I looked at Irys. *Was this quarter searched with magic?* I asked her with my mind.

Yes. But not by a Master.

She stretched out her awareness and my mind's eye went with her. Our minds touched a young woman nursing a baby on the first floor. Her thoughts on getting the baby to nap after he'd eaten his fill. Another woman on the third floor worried about the possibility of rain. We could feel no one on the second floor, but Ferde's magic matched Irys's in strength and he would not be easy to detect.

I could push harder, but he would know we were here, Irys said. *I will come back with some reinforcements.*

Who?

Roze and Bain. Together we should be able to subdue him. And once he's unconscious, he'll be easier to transport to the Keep's prison.

Why unconscious?

A magician is helpless when unconscious.

Sleeping? I asked in alarm.

No. Only if it's a drugged sleep or you get knocked out.

What happens once he wakes? Won't he be able to use his magic to escape?

The Keep's prison cells contain a power loop. If a magician tries to use magic within the cell, the loop absorbs the magical power and directs it back into the cell's defenses until the magician is exhausted.

Fisk, who had been staring at us in fascination, cleared his throat. "Do you think the one you seek is living here?"

"Could the young girl your brother saw be the one with the baby?" Irys asked Fisk.

He shook his head. "That's Ruby. Sometimes she hires me to watch Jatee."

I grinned. "You're turning into quite the entrepreneur."

"I bought my mother a new dress," he said with pride.

Rain began to fall as we made our way back to the market. With a wave, Fisk joined his friends and disappeared. The market emptied as the vendors packed up their wares. One woman bumped into me in her haste to get out of the rain. She shouted an apology, but never slowed her pace. Rumbles of thunder echoed off the hard marble walls of the Citadel.

I'll find Roze and Bain. You return to the Keep, Irys instructed.

But I want to be there when you search that building.

No. Stay at the Keep, Yelena. He wants you. And if something goes wrong and he threatens to hurt Opal, you know you'll give yourself up. It's too dangerous.

I wanted to argue. But Irys was right, and, if I followed her despite her instructions, she wouldn't trust me again.

Irys headed toward the Council Hall to find Roze, who had an appointment with the Ixian Ambassador. A meeting I would have loved to eavesdrop on. The arrogant Master Magician against the powerful Commander.

The rain began to fall in sheets, soaking my cloak. When I tucked my cold, wet hands into the pockets, my fingers touched paper. I couldn't remember putting anything there. I hadn't worn my cloak since coming to Sitia, although, I had used it to sleep when we had camped on the Avibian Plains. Perhaps the paper contained a cryptic message from Story Weaver. I laughed; it seemed to be something he would enjoy doing, leaving a puzzling note in my cloak. However, the mystery would have to wait until I found some shelter from the rain.

My guards waited at the Keep's entrance. They followed me as I headed toward my room. After they searched the interior, I invited them inside, but they declined, citing some military regulation.

After I started a roaring fire and hung up my sodden cloak, I extracted the paper. It *was* a message for me. My hands turned to ice as I read the words, and even the heat from the hearth couldn't warm them up.

"What does the message say?" Valek asked, coming from the bedroom.

I had ceased to be amazed by his abilities. Dripping wet, he must have come in through the bedroom window past one of my guards.

He plucked the paper from my hand. "She had some rudimentary skills. Probably a pickpocket hired to give you this note. Did you get a good look at her face?"

I made the belated connection between the woman who had bumped into me in the market and the message. "No. Her hood covered most of her head."

Valek shrugged, but his gaze pierced me after he scanned the note. "Interesting development."

Yes, Valek *would* think this turn of events interesting. However, I found myself conflicted.

"Seems the killer is one step ahead of the magicians," he said. "He knows they won't exchange you for Opal. So he has taken matters into his own hands. How important is Opal's life to you?"

Valek had, as usual, gotten to the heart of the matter. Ferde's note specified a location and a new date for the exchange. Three nights before the full moon, which was four days from now. I guessed that he needed some time to get me ready for the Efe ritual. My skin crawled with dread and I forced horrible images of being raped and tortured from my mind.

I could tell Irys and the others. They would set a trap for Ferde. But they wouldn't let me near the site, so the trap was bound to fail.

Or I wouldn't tell Irys about the note and would go to the meeting site alone. Irys's warnings of what would happen if Ferde absorbed my magic filtered through my mind. He would then be powerful enough to control Sitia.

Let Opal die to save Sitia? I had promised myself that I wouldn't let that happen to her. And what would stop Ferde once Opal died from tricking another magician into giving him her soul? Nothing.

I would need to keep this new situation tucked deep beneath my surface thoughts. Irys had been true to her word to not pry into my mind, but with the fate of Sitia at stake, I wouldn't be surprised if she broke her promise.

My gaze met Valek's. Magic couldn't detect him.

"Her life is important," I said, answering his question. "But capturing the killer is vital."

"What do you need, love?"

26

Valek and I made some initial plans for rescuing Opal. When he returned to the Ixian delegation, I felt a renewed sense of purpose. The next day I used my free time to practice controlling my magic and to do some physical training in preparation for my encounter with Ferde.

Irys, Roze and Bain had raided the apartment where, according to Fisk, the man with the red hands lived. The rooms were empty, and, by the mess that was scattered on the floor, the occupants had left in a hurry. Either someone had tipped him off, or he had felt the Masters' approach. A dead end either way, which made Valek and my plans critical.

I also began demonstrating self-defense techniques to Zitora, finally keeping my side of our bargain to trade the Third Magician's pile of clothes for defense training. The review helped in my training, as well.

The rain from the day before puddled in the training yard, and splattered us with mud as we worked on basic self-defense techniques. An apt student, Zitora quickly grasped the concepts.

"I pull my wrist out of your grasp through your thumb?" Zitora asked.

"Yes. It's the weakest part." I grunted as she yanked her arm from me. "Perfect. Now I'll show you how to not only free your wrist, but twist your hand so you can grab your attacker's arm and break it."

Her eyes lit up with glee and I laughed. "Everyone thinks you're so sweet and nice. I almost feel sorry for the first person to try and take advantage of that. Almost!"

We worked for a while until her moves became more instinctive.

"That's a good start," I said. "Those moves will help you against someone stronger than you, but if you go against a well-trained opponent, you'll have to use different tactics."

Zitora looked past my shoulder and her tawny eyes grew wide. "You mean *I* could take on someone like *him*?"

I turned. Ari strode into the training area with Janco at his heels. Wearing his sleeveless training shirt and short pants, his powerful physique was apparent. While Janco might be leaner than his partner, I knew his speed could match Ari's strength. They carried bows and broad smiles. My Keep guards looked queasy and undecided. I waved them off.

"Yes," I said to Zitora. "With the proper training, you could escape from him. You wouldn't last in a sparring match, but that's not what self-defense is all about. Remember what I told you? Hit and—"

"Git!" Janco added. "Run like a bunny with a wolf on its tail. I see you're passing our wisdom on, Yelena." Janco turned to Zitora, and said in a conspiratorial whisper, "She was trained by the very best instructors in all of Ixia."

"Another rule of self-defense is never believe everything you hear," Ari said when Zitora appeared to be impressed by Janco's words.

"How did you get past the Keep's guards?" I asked Ari.

He shrugged his massive shoulders. "The guard asked for our names and our reason for visiting. We told him and he went into the guardhouse to consult with someone. When he came out he told us where to find you."

There must be a magician posted at the gate who could communicate by magic to others in the Keep. That was good to know.

"Can we join you?" Janco asked. "I learned a few new self-defense moves. They're nasty, too!"

"We were just finishing up," I said.

Zitora wiped her face with a towel. "I need to get cleaned up before my Council meeting." She hurried off with a wave.

"Are you too tired for a match?" Janco asked. "I want to make sure you're at your best when I beat you." He smiled sweetly.

"He's been getting into trouble all day," Ari said. "Too much time spent standing around, guarding Ambassador Signe and Adviser Ilom as they sat through one meeting after another."

"Boring!" agreed Janco.

The fact that Valek had managed to fool Ari and Janco with his Ilom disguise made me feel a little better about his presence in Sitia.

"I could be half-asleep and still beat you, Janco," I countered with my own boast.

He spun his bow and stepped back into a fighting stance. I picked my bow up and set my mind into my zone of concentration. I attacked.

"Good to know you're keeping fit," Janco puffed. He retreated a few feet, but counterattacked with determination. "She's strong and spry, but can she fly?" Janco chanted.

I smiled, realizing how much I had missed his fighting rhymes. A second before he moved, I knew that he would feint high to draw my guard up so he could strike my exposed ribs. My failure to take the bait and to counter the rib strike shocked Janco into silence. Laughing, I drove him back, swept his feet out from under him and scooted back to avoid the splash of mud when he dropped into a puddle.

Wiping his eyes with the back of his hand, Janco said, "Gee, Ari, and *you* were worried about *her.*"

"She's learned a new trick since coming to Sitia," Cahil said. He was leaning on the training yard's fence, and must have watched the match.

Ari's posture turned defensive and alert as Cahil moved to join us. Armed with his long sword, Cahil wore a loose sand-colored tunic and brown pants.

After I introduced Cahil, Ari still didn't relax. He kept a wary eye on him. I hoped Ari and Janco didn't recognize Cahil's name. Names of the dead King's family were not mentioned in the Commander's history books of the takeover, and if the older citizens of Ixia remembered, they kept it to themselves.

"What trick?" Janco asked.

"A magic trick. She anticipated your every move by reading your mind. Devious, isn't she?" Cahil asked.

Before Janco could respond, I said, "I didn't read his mind. I kept my own mind open and picked up on his intentions."

"Sounds like the same thing to me," Cahil countered. "Leif was right when he accused you of using magic to beat me that time we sparred in the forest. Not only devious, but a liar, too."

I placed a hand on Ari's arm to keep him from throttling Cahil. "Cahil, I didn't need to read your mind. Truth is you're not as skilled as Ari and Janco. In fact, they taught me to find that zone of concentration, or else I never would have the chance to win against them. There is only one person I know who could take them on and win without any help," I said.

Janco considered. "One?" He scratched at the scar in his right ear, thinking.

"Valek," Ari said.

"Oh, yes. The infamous Valek. I'm sure his lover *would* think that highly of him. Or should I call you his spy?" Cahil stared at me in challenge.

"I think you should leave. Now," Ari said. His voice rumbled close to a growl.

"This is my home. Thanks to Valek. You leave," Cahil said to Ari, but his eyes never left my face.

Janco stepped between us. "Let's see if I have this right," he said to Cahil. "Yelena beats you, so you want a rematch, but you think she'll use her magic instead of her fighting skills to win. That's quite the quandary." Janco pulled at his goatee. "Since *I* taught her everything she knows, and I don't have any magic, thank fate, how about you fight me? Your long sword against my bow."

"*You* taught her everything?" Ari asked.

Janco waved away his comment. "Details, details. I'm thinking big picture here, Ari."

Cahil agreed to the match. With a confident expression, Cahil assumed a fighting stance then attacked. Janco's bow blurred and he unarmed Cahil within three moves. His mood didn't improve when Janco told Cahil he needed to use a lighter sword.

"She helped you," Cahil said to Janco. "I should know better than to trust a bunch of northerners." Cahil stalked away with the promise of a future encounter flaming in his eyes.

I shrugged his comments off. Cahil wouldn't ruin my time with my friends. Challenging Janco to another match, I swung my bow toward him, but he blocked it with ease and countered with one of his lightning-fast jabs.

The three of us worked together for a while. Even connected to my mental zone, Ari still beat me twice.

Ari grinned. "I'm trying not to project my intentions," he said after dumping me in the mud.

The daylight disappeared in a hurry. Tired, covered with

layers of mud and sweat and smelling as if I could attract dung beetles, I longed for a bath.

Before Ari and Janco headed back to the Citadel, Ari put a large hand on my shoulder. "Be extremely careful. I don't like the way Cahil looked at you."

"I'm always careful, Ari." I waved and aimed my sore body toward the bathhouse.

The cooling season was ending; I could see the Ice Queen constellation glittering in the clear night sky. The half-moon glowed like a jewel. Only six days until the full moon. I shivered in the cold air. The puddles would be frozen by morning.

My thoughts lingered on Cahil and how fast our relationship had changed back to those first days when he had believed I was a northern spy. A full circle. I reached for my snake bracelet, spinning it around my arm.

Only when I noticed that the campus seemed strangely empty and quiet did I look around for my guards. Used to their presence, it took me a few moments before I realized that they no longer followed me.

Pulling my bow, I searched for attackers. I saw no one. I drew power to project my awareness out, but a bug bit me on the neck, and, distracted, I slapped at it. My fingers found a tiny dart. The hollow metal end dripped with my blood.

I lied to Ari. I wasn't careful. I had trusted my guards to keep me safe. Hundreds of excuses for my lapse churned through my mind as the world around me began to spin. No one to blame but myself.

Unfortunately this acknowledgement of my own stupidity didn't prevent the blackness from claiming me.

27

A sharp pain and a burning numbness in my shoulders roused me from sleep. With a rank taste in my dry mouth, I glanced around. Nothing looked familiar. And why was I standing? Not standing, but hanging. Looking up, I spotted the reason for my position. My wrists were manacled to the ends of a long chain that hung from a thick wooden beam in the ceiling. Once I put my weight on my feet, the pain in my shoulders eased somewhat.

Studying my surroundings, I saw rusted shovels and dirt encrusted hoes lining the wooden walls. Spiderwebs clung to dull-edged scythes. Dust coated the tools. Sunlight filtered in through small cracks and holes, illuminating what I guessed to be an abandoned shed with a muted light.

My confusion about how I had gotten here disappeared the moment I heard his voice behind me.

"We'll start your lessons now." Goel's satisfied tone caused my stomach to lurch.

"Turn around and see what I have planned for you," he said.

My skin prickled with fear, but I forced my face into a neutral expression before I spun. A smirk lit Goel's face as he gestured to a table on his right. Weapons and exotic instruments of torture covered the top. A wagon containing an empty burlap sack was to the left of Goel. The structure was bigger than I had thought. The shed's door loomed behind him, appearing impossibly far to me, but in reality only ten feet.

Goel followed my gaze and smiled. "Bolted and locked. We're in a forgotten place far away from the Keep." He picked up a small black leather whip that had metal spikes on the ends.

The Keep! I pulled some power to me and projected a desperate mental call. *Irys.*

"How're the ribs?" I asked, trying to distract him.

He frowned and touched the side of his chest. "That horse is gonna make a tasty stew." He smacked his lips. "But that's later." He raised the whip.

Yelena! Thank fate you're alive. Where are you? Irys's worried voice sounded in my mind.

A shed somewhere.

Goel stepped closer to strike me with the whip. I kicked him in the stomach. He jumped back more from surprise than pain.

"Me mistake," he said, retreating to his table. "Not to worry. I'll fix." He picked up a dart, dipping it in a vial of liquid.

The sleeping potion. I thought fast.

I need more information. Is Ferde with you? Irys asked.

Not Ferde. Goel.

Goel?

No time. I'll explain later.

Goel loaded the dart into a hollow pipe. He aimed. I laughed. The pipe wavered as he squinted at me in confusion.

"I can't believe it," I said.

"Believe what?" He lowered the weapon.

"That you're afraid of me. No, not afraid. Terrified." I laughed again. "You can't beat me in a fair fight so you ambush and drug me. And even when I'm chained, you're still scared."

"Am not." He exchanged the pipe for a pair of manacles then dove for my feet.

I struggled, but he outweighed me. In the end, my ankles were manacled together. Goel then staked the six-inch chain between the cuffs to the floor. No more kicking, but I remained awake, and I had another trick. Magic. My mind raced through options.

I could try and freeze the muscles in his body, but I didn't know how. Goel chose another whip from his table. This one was longer with braided leather and small metal balls tied into the fringes on the end.

His arm blurred. I projected a confusing array of images into his mind.

Goel lost his balance and fell to the ground. "Huh?" He seemed confused.

As he regained his feet, I caught a slight movement behind Goel. The bolt moved and the knob turned. The door burst open with a rush of light. Two figures stood in the doorway. They pointed their swords at Goel's heart. Ari and Janco.

"Yelena, are you all right?" Ari asked. His eyes never left Goel's surprised face.

Janco came over and inspected the chains. "Keys?" he asked Goel, who pressed his lips together. "Guess I'll have to do it the hard way." Janco pulled his lock picks from his pocket.

My first rush of relief at seeing my friends cooled. This rescue wouldn't stop Goel from trying again. Even if he was arrested for kidnapping, Goel would harbor his grudge until freed and years from now, I might be in the exact same position. *I* had to deal with him. He needed to know that he couldn't win against me.

I shook my head at Janco. "I've got the situation under control. Go back to the Keep, I'll meet you there."

Janco stared at me in astonished silence. Ari, though, trusted me. "Come on, she doesn't need our help." Ari sheathed his sword.

Janco recovered. He flashed me one of his mischievous grins.

"I'll bet you a copper that she'll be free in five minutes," he said to Ari.

Ari grunted in amusement. "A silver on ten minutes," he countered.

"I'll bet you both a gold coin that she kills him," Valek said from behind them. They moved aside and he entered, still dressed in his Adviser Ilom disguise. "The only way to take care of your problem. Right, love?"

"No killing," I said. "I'll manage."

"He's my man. I'll handle this," Cahil said from the doorway.

Valek spun, but Cahil just stared at him for a moment before coming inside. "Goel, stand down," Cahil ordered.

Valek disappeared from sight. The crowded shed seemed to shrink in size and, by this point, I wouldn't be surprised to see Irys and the other Masters following Cahil. We could all have a festival.

During the conversations and arrivals, Goel's face had transformed from stunned to horrified and finally settled into stubborn determination. "No," he said to Cahil.

"Goel, you were right about her. But this isn't the way to deal with her. Especially not with her two henchmen nearby. Release her."

"I don't take orders from you. Everyone else can pretend you're in charge. I won't."

"Are *you* challenging my authority?" Cahil demanded.

"You don't have any authority with me," Goel shot back.

Cahil's face turned bright red as he sputtered. "How dare—"

"Gentlemen!" I shouted. "You can fight it out later. Everyone leave. Now! My arms are killing me."

Janco pulled Cahil from the shed. Ari shut the door. Goel stood there blinking in the sudden darkness.

"Where were we?" I prompted.

"You can't expect me..." He gestured toward the door.

"Forget about them. You have more to worry about in here than outside."

He sneered. "You're not really in the position to be boasting."

"And you don't fully understand what it's like to go against a *magician*."

The sneer faded from his lips.

"You think I'm just some girl to be taught a lesson. That I should fear you. You're the one who needs the lesson." I gathered power to me and reached my awareness out to Goel's.

The word "magician" had only caused a brief feeling of doubt in Goel's mind. *After all,* he thought, *if she was a good magician, she wouldn't have been so easy to catch.*

"A momentary lapse," I said. Since he had no magical power, he couldn't hear my thoughts, but I might be able to control him. I closed my eyes and projected myself into Goel, taking the chance that if I could do it with Topaz I should be able to do it with a person.

He jumped as if struck by lightning when I entered his mind. Although glad that my transfer worked, being closer to Goel's slimy thoughts made me wish for Topaz's clean mind.

When I focused Goel's eyes on me, I understood why he thought so little of me. My hair hung in messy clumps. The combination of closed eyes, dirt-streaked face and mud covered clothes made me seem pathetic. A helpless figure in need of a bath.

I felt his panic when he realized he had lost control of his body. He could still think, see and feel. I marveled at his physical strength, but I encountered some difficulty moving his body around. The proportions felt strange and balancing his body took a concentrated effort.

He tried to regain control, but I pushed his weak efforts aside. I searched for the key to the manacles and found them in his pack under the table. Then I unlocked and removed the manacles from my body's feet. Supporting myself with one of Goel's arms, I unlocked the wrist cuffs. I grabbed my body before it could fall to the ground and lifted it up.

It felt light as a pillow. My body breathed and blood pulsed. I carried it and laid it gently on the ground near the door. Using Goel's thumb, I raised my left eyelid. Although my body lived, the spark of life was gone. Unnerved I stood and backed away.

When the feeling of utter helplessness overcame Goel, I let him experience that sensation for a long while. Picking up a knife from the table, I cut a shallow line along his arm. I felt his pain from the cut, but it was muted and distant. Resting the tip of the blade on his chest, I wondered if I plunged the knife into his heart, would I kill us both?

An interesting question that would have to be answered at another time. Kicking off his boots, I snapped the manacles around Goel's ankles then I shortened the chain hanging from the overhead beam before locking his wrists into the cuffs. I savored the combination of fear, discomfort and chagrin that coursed through his mind before I projected myself back toward my own body.

The shed spun for a moment when I opened my eyes. Fatigue coursed through my limbs. I stood in slow motion, but managed a smug smile at Goel's new predicament. As I headed for the door, I thought I probably wouldn't have discovered that magical skill working with Irys or the other magicians. And what exactly had I done? Transferred my magic? My will? My soul? I shied away from those disturbing thoughts. Taking control of someone's body and forcing him to move must be in violation of the Ethical Code. But when Goel kidnapped me he became a criminal. The Ethical Code didn't apply to him. I almost laughed. I guess I should be grateful Goel attacked me. Now I knew another defensive magical move.

Ari and Janco waited for me in the overgrown field that surrounded the shed. I saw a dilapidated fence and a collapsed barn and guessed we stood on an abandoned farm outside the Citadel. Valek and Cahil hadn't waited for me.

Ari smiled as Janco slapped a silver coin into his huge hand.

"Your problem?" Ari asked me.

"I left him hanging."

"What took you so long?" Janco complained.

"I wanted to prove my point. Where's…ah, Adviser Ilom and Cahil?"

"Why the sudden concern for Ilom?" Janco asked with mock sincerity. "He's a grown man with surprising abilities. That stuffy old bore appeared out of nowhere, did a dead perfect impression of Valek's voice and disappeared as if by magic. The man's a genius! I should have known he would come along. Valek wouldn't miss all the fun."

The smile dropped from Ari's face. "Valek's going to get caught. Cahil made a beeline for the Citadel, probably to tell the Council members about Valek."

"Great disguise, though," Janco said. "He had us fooled."

"Cahil already suspected Valek was here," I said, shivering in the cold morning air. Now he knew for certain. "I'm sure Valek can handle it." My tired mind, though, couldn't produce a good solution.

Ari went over to the shed and picked up my backpack from where it leaned against the side. "I thought you might need this." He handed it to me.

I found my cloak inside. Wrapping the warm garment around me I moved to sling the pack onto my back, but Ari took it from me.

"Let's go," Ari said.

He and Janco led me through the fallow fields. We passed an empty farmhouse.

"Where are we?" I asked.

"About two miles east of the Citadel," Ari said.

I stumbled just at the thought of walking two miles. "How did you find me?"

"We followed your guards last night to make sure they knew what they were doing. By the time we realized they had been hit, you had disappeared," Ari said.

Janco grinned. "The magicians were frantic. Search parties were sent." He shook his head as if amazed by the uproar. "We had no idea what they would find in the dark. We just hoped they wouldn't ruin the trail. Once the sun was up, it took us no time to follow the tracks. Goel used a wagon to wheel you out of the Keep and Citadel."

I thought of the burlap sack lying in the wagon. Goel must have hidden me in that sack.

"I guess Cahil followed us," Janco said. Scratching his scar, he added, "Of course, you didn't want our help. Now I have to go beat up some soldier just to keep my ego intact."

As we reached the east gate of the Citadel, I spotted a commotion near the guardhouse. A loose horse was giving the guards some trouble. Kiki.

She stopped when we crossed through the gate. *Lavender Lady tired. Need ride.*

How did you find me?

Follow scent of Strong Man and Rabbit Man.

She referred to Ari and Janco. I apologized to the gate's guards about Kiki's disruption. Ari helped me onto her back and gave me my pack.

"We'll catch up with you later," Ari promised.

Before Kiki and I headed toward the Keep, I thanked my friends.

"For what? We didn't do anything," Janco grumbled.

"For caring enough to follow my guards. And the next time, I might need the help."

"There better not *be* a next time," Ari said, giving me a stern look.

"How touching," Janco said, pretending to wipe his eyes. "Get going, Yelena. I don't want you to see me cry." He faked a sniffle.

"I'm sure your ego can handle it," I said. "Or will you need to beat up some trainees to feel like a man again?"

"Very funny," he said.

I waved and asked Kiki to take me home. On the way, I connected to Irys and updated her on what had happened. She promised to send some guards out to arrest Goel.

If I don't make it to my room, I'll be asleep in the barn, I said, yawning. I felt her hesitate. *Now what?*

Your parents arrived this morning.

Oh, no!

Oh, yes. Esau is here with me, but when your mother found out you were missing, she climbed a tree and we can't convince her to come down. She's hysterical and won't listen to us. You'll have to talk to her.

I sighed. *I'm on my way. Where is she?*

Perl was in one of the tall oak trees next to the pasture.

Kiki took me to the base of the tree. A handful of orange and brown leaves still clung to the branches. I spotted my mother's green cloak near the top. I called to Perl, telling her I was fine. "You can come down now," I said.

"Yelena! Thank fate! Come up here where it's safe," she said.

I resigned myself to the fact that getting Perl down would be difficult, and took off my cloak and backpack, dropping them to the ground. Even standing on Kiki's back, I still had to stretch to reach the lowest branch. My mother's climbing ability was impressive.

As Kiki grazed, I hauled myself higher, climbing until I reached my mother. I settled on a branch below her, but she appeared next to me in an instant, hugging me tight. When her body started shaking with sobs, I had to grab the tree's trunk to keep us both from falling.

I waited for her to calm before gently pulling her away.

She sat next to me, leaning against my shoulder. Her face was streaked with dirt where her tears had mixed with the dried mud on my clothes. I offered the one clean spot on my shirt, but she shook her head, taking a handkerchief from her pocket. Her dark green cloak had many pockets, and the garment had a slim tailored cut, eliminating the bulky excess of material. It wouldn't make a good blanket, but it was perfect for keeping warm while traveling through the tree tops.

"Is this one of Nutty's designs?" I asked her, fingering the cloth.

"Yes. Since I hadn't left the jungle in fourteen years…" She gave me a rueful smile, "I needed something for the cooler weather."

"I'm glad you came," I said.

Her smile fled. A look of terror touched her eyes before she took a few deep breaths. "Your father gave me some Eladine to keep me calm during the trip, and I was doing so well, until…" She put a hand to her neck, grimacing.

"Bad timing," I agreed. "But I'm fine, see?" I held out an arm. My mistake.

She gasped, staring at the bloody bruises around my wrist. I pulled my sleeve down to cover them.

"They're just scratches."

"What happened? And don't sugarcoat it for me," she ordered.

I gave her a condensed version with only a slight dusting of sugar. "He won't be bothering me again."

"It won't happen again. You are coming home with us," she declared.

After this morning, I wanted to agree. "What would I do there?"

"Help your father collect samples or help me make perfumes. The thought of losing you again is too much to bear."

"But you have to bear it, Mother. I'm not going to run or

hide from difficult or dangerous situations. And I've made some promises to myself and others. I have to see things through, because if I ran away, I couldn't live with myself."

A breeze rustled the leaves, and the sweat on my skin felt like ice. My mother pulled her cloak tight. I could sense her emotions as they twisted into knots around her. She was in a strange place, dealing with the realization that her daughter would willingly put herself in harm's way for others, and she could lose her again. She struggled with her fear, wanting nothing more than the safety of her family and the familiarity of home.

I had an idea. "Nutty's cloak reminds me of the jungle," I said.

She glanced down at the garment. "Really?"

"It's the same color as the underside of an Ylang-Ylang Leaf. Remember that time when we were caught in a sudden downpour on our way home from the market, and we huddled under a big Ylang-Ylang Leaf?"

"You remembered." She beamed.

I nodded. "My childhood memories have been unlocked. But I wouldn't have them now, if I hadn't taken a risk and followed Irys to the Avibian Plains."

"You've been to the plains." The horror on her face transformed to awe. "You're not afraid of anything, are you?"

"During that trip, I could list at least five things I was afraid of." Especially getting my head chopped off by Moon Man's scimitar, but I was smart enough not to tell *that* to my mother.

"Then why did you go?"

"Because we needed information. I couldn't let my fear stop me from doing what I needed to do."

She considered my words in silence.

"Your cloak can protect you from more than the weather," I said. "If you fill the pockets with special items from home, you can surround yourself with the jungle whenever you're feeling overwhelmed or afraid."

"I hadn't thought of that."

"In fact, I have something you can put into your pocket now that will remind you of me. Come on." Without waiting to see if she followed, I climbed down. I hung from the lowest branch before dropping to the ground.

As I searched my backpack, I heard a rustling and I looked up in time to see my mother shimming down the tree's trunk. I found my fire amulet in one of the pack's pockets. Considering my recent run of troubles, the amulet would be safer with my mother.

"I won this during a time in my life when fear was my constant and only companion." I handed it to her. It was the first place prize for an acrobatic competition at Ixia's annual Fire Festival. What followed after was the worst time of my life, but I would have competed for the amulet again, even knowing the outcome.

I handed the amulet to my mother. "This is one of only four items I hold dear. I want you to have it."

She examined the fire amulet. "What are the other three?"

"My butterfly and snake." I pulled out my necklace, and I showed her my bracelet.

"Did someone make those for you?"

"Yes. A friend," I said before she could ask more.

She raised a slender eyebrow, but only asked, "What's the last thing?"

I rummaged in my pack while I decided if my mother would be shocked to know I held a weapon dear. Far from being the perfect daughter, I figured she wouldn't be surprised at all. Handing her my switchblade, I explained what the silver symbols on the handle meant.

"Same friend?" she asked.

I laughed and told her about Ari and Janco. "They're more like older brothers than friends."

My mother's smile felt like the sun coming out after a storm.

"Good to know there are people in Ixia who care about you." She tucked my fire amulet into a pocket of her cloak. "Fire represents strength. I will keep it with me always."

Hugging me tight for a moment, Perl pulled away and declared, "You're freezing. Put your cloak on. Let's get inside."

"Yes, Mother."

Esau and Irys waited for us in the Keep's guest quarters on the west side of the campus. I endured a bone-crushing hug from my father, but had to decline an invitation to dinner with my parents. My desire for a bath and sleep overrode my hunger. I had to promise to spend most of the next day with them before they allowed me to leave.

Irys accompanied me to the bathhouse. Dark smudges lined her eyes and she looked as tired as I felt. She seemed in a contemplative mood.

"Did you use magic on your mother?" she asked.

"I don't think so. Why?"

"She seemed at peace. Perhaps you did it instinctively."

"But that's not good. I should have complete control. Right?"

"I'm beginning to think that not all the rules apply to you, Yelena. Perhaps it was your upbringing or the fact that you started controlling your magic at an older age that has made your powers develop in an unusual way. Not to worry, though," she added when she saw my expression. "I believe it will be to your benefit."

Irys and I parted at the baths. After a long hot soak, I dragged myself to my rooms. My last thought before drifting off to sleep was to marvel over the fact that Irys had trusted me enough not to assign more guards to me.

It seemed a mere moment that I had sunk into a dreamless slumber when Irys's mental call woke me. I squinted in the bright sunlight, trying to orient myself.

What time? I asked her.

Midmorning, Irys said.

Morning? That meant I had been asleep since yesterday afternoon. *Why did you wake me?*

An emergency Council session has been called, and your presence is required.

Emergency session?

Goel was murdered, and Cahil is claiming Adviser Ilom is Valek in disguise.

28

Goel murdered? Valek caught? My groggy mind couldn't quite
understand Irys's comment and her attention pulled away before
I could question her. I changed as fast as I could and ran toward
the Council Hall.

Did Valek kill Goel? And if Valek really was in custody, he
just gave the Sitians one more reason to execute him. Should I
act surprised by Valek's presence or admit I knew about him?
Would I be considered an accomplice to Goel's murder? Perhaps they suspected me. I only told Irys where to find him; I
hadn't mentioned the others to her.

Questions without answers swirled in my mind. I paused before the steps to the Council Hall, smoothed my braid and adjusted my clothes. I wore one of the new shirts and skirt/pants
that Nutty had sewn for me. Glancing at my surroundings, I
checked to make sure no one had followed me. Irys trusted me
to take care of myself. I couldn't let her down.

The Council's members, four Master Magicians, a handful
of the Keep's guards and Cahil had assembled in the great hall.
The noise of their various arguments reached deafening levels,
and I spotted Cahil gesturing wildly to the Sandseed's Councilman. Cahil's flushed face contorted in anger as he replied.

Roze Featherstone, First Magician pounded a gavel to bring order to the meeting. Conversations ceased as the Councilors took their seats. The decorations from the greeting ceremony had been removed, and a U-shaped table had been brought in. Roze and the other three Magicians sat at the bend, while the clan Elders sat along the straight sides. Six on one side, five on the other with Cahil taking the sixth seat. A wooden podium had been placed in the middle of the U. I stood with the Captain of the guard and his men near the side wall, hoping to blend in with the white marble.

"Let us address the matter of Lieutenant Goel Ixia," ordered Roze.

I glanced at Irys in surprise.

All the northern refugees are given Ixia as their clan name, Irys explained in my mind. *Cahil is considered their clan leader. It is an honorary clan and title. He has no lands and no power to vote in the Council.*

That explained Cahil's resentment toward the Council and his continuing frustration of not getting their support for his campaign against the Commander.

"Lieutenant Ixia was found dead in a fallow field east of the Citadel in Featherstone Clan lands," Roze recited. "The healers have determined that he was killed with a sword thrust through his heart."

Murmurs rippled through the Council members. Roze stopped them with a cold stare. "The weapon was not found at the scene, and a search of the surrounding fields is currently in progress. According to Fourth Magician, Yelena Liana Zaltana was the last person to see him alive. I call her to the witness stand."

Sixteen pair of eyes turned toward me. Hostile, concerned and worried expressions peppered the group.

Don't worry, Irys said. *Tell them what happened.*

I walked to the podium, guessing that was the witness stand.

"Explain yourself," Roze demanded.

I told them about the kidnapping and my escape. A collective gasp sounded when I explained about taking control of Goel's body. Whispers about the Ethical Code started to spread.

Irys stood and said, "There is nothing illegal about using magic to defend yourself. In fact, she should be commended for extracting herself without harming Goel."

The Council members asked an endless amount of questions about Goel's motives. Only after the guards that had been assigned to protect me confirmed they had been drugged did the Council run out of inquiries.

"You left Goel chained in the shed, and that was the last time you saw him?" Roze asked.

"Yes," I said.

"She's telling the truth." By Roze's sour expression, I knew that statement had been hard for her to say. "The investigation into Goel's murder will continue. Yelena, you may sit down." Roze gestured to a bench located behind her and the other Master Magicians. "That leaves us with the other matter. I call Cahil Ixia to the witness stand."

As I moved toward the bench, I passed Cahil. His blue eyes held a hard determination and he refused to meet my gaze. I sat on the edge of the wooden bench, and, even though I braced myself for his accusations, Cahil's words made my heart squeeze with fear.

"—and compounding Valek's deception is the fact that his soul mate and master spy is Yelena Zaltana."

The room erupted with a cacophony of voices. Roze pounded her gavel, but no one listened. I felt the force of her magic when she ordered everyone silent. She held them quiet for only a moment, but it was enough to get her point across.

"Cahil, where is your evidence?" Roze asked.

He motioned to one of the Keep's guards. The guard opened a door in the back wall and Captain Marrok and four of Cahil's men entered the hall, dragging Adviser Ilom with them. Ilom's arms were manacled behind his back and the four guards had their swords pointed at him. Ambassador Signe and a handful of Ixian soldiers followed the grim procession.

I strained to catch Valek's eye, but he looked at the Council members with an annoyed frown.

Ambassador Signe was the first to speak. "I demand an explanation. This is an act of war."

"Cahil, I told you to release the Adviser until this matter was settled," Roze said. Fury flared in her amber eyes.

"And let him escape? No. Better to bring him here and unmask him in front of everyone." Cahil strode to Ilom and yanked on his hair.

I cringed, but Ilom's head jerked down as he cried out in pain. Undaunted, Cahil pulled Ilom's nose then clawed at the flesh under his chin. Ilom yelped and blood welled from the scratches on his neck. Cahil stepped back astounded. He reached toward Ilom's face again, but Marrok grabbed him and held him. Cahil's mouth hung open with astonishment.

"Release the Adviser," Roze ordered.

Ilom's manacles were removed as Cahil, his face red with rage, and his men were escorted from the room. The session ended and Roze rushed to make amends and apologize to the Ambassador and Ilom.

I stayed on the bench, watching as Signe's anger and Ilom's pout transformed into more agreeable expressions by Roze's words. I was afraid to call attention to myself, hoping no one would remember Cahil's other accusations about me.

Cahil's shock over Ilom had matched my own. Even knowing his tricks, Valek continued to surprise me. I scanned the Ixian guards, and, sure enough, one blue-eyed soldier looked mighty pleased with himself. Ilom probably dressed as a guard when Valek disguised himself as the Adviser, and they probably switched places when Valek needed to sneak around Sitia.

Eventually, the Council members and Ixians began to leave. Irys joined me on the bench.

Tell Valek to leave, Irys said. *The danger is too great.*

You know.

Of course. I expected him to be with the delegation.

It doesn't bother you that he's here. That he might be spying on Sitia.

He's here for you. And I'm glad you had some time together.

But what if he killed Goel?

Goel was a danger to you. While I would have preferred to arrest him, I'm not upset by his demise.

"Go get something to eat. You look a little pale," Irys said.

"That's just great. I went from having none to having *two* mother hens."

Irys laughed. "Some people just need the extra help." She patted my knee and went in search of Bain.

Before I could leave, though, I saw Bavol Zaltana heading toward me. I waited for him.

"Ambassador Signe requests a meeting with you," Bavol said.

"When?"

"Now."

Bavol led me out of the great hall. "The Ambassador has been assigned some offices so she can conduct business while a guest here," Bavol explained as we walked through the Council Hall.

The entire Sitian government was housed in the vast building. Offices and meeting rooms hummed with the daily tasks of running a government. An underground record room stored all the official documents, although the local records remained at each clan's capitol.

I wondered about the Sandseed's moving capitol. Did they haul their records with them as they traveled throughout the plains? Remembering Irys's lecture about the Sandseeds, I realized they kept a verbal record, telling history through the Story Weavers. An image of Moon Man painted blue and sitting in the Council's underground room caused me to smile.

Bavol gave me a questioning glance.

"I was thinking of the record room," I said. "Just trying to imagine how the Sandseed Clan reports information to the Council."

Bavol grinned. "They have always been difficult. We indulge their…unusual ways. Twice a year, a Story Weaver comes to the Council and recites the clan's events to a scribe. It works, and keeps peace in our land. Here we are." Bavol gestured to an open door. "We will talk again later." Bavol dipped his head and shoulders in a half bow and left.

The invitation had not included Bavol. I walked into a receiving area. Adviser Ilom sat behind a plain desk. The scratches on his neck had stopped bleeding. Two soldiers guarded a closed door.

Ilom stood and knocked on the door. I heard a faint voice, and Ilom turned the knob. "She's here," he said, then pushed the door wider and gestured me inside.

I entered Ambassador Signe's office, noting the simple functional furniture and lack of decorations. Guards stood behind her, but she dismissed them. None of the soldiers had been Valek, and I wondered where he had gotten to. Ari and Janco were probably off-duty.

"You caused a considerable stir last night," Signe said when we were alone.

Her powerful eyes scanned me. I marveled at her appearance. She had the same delicate features as the Commander, yet the long hair and the thin lines of kohl around her eyes transformed his face into her ageless beauty.

"I hope your sleep wasn't interrupted," I said, sticking to a diplomatic approach.

She waved away comment. "We're alone. You may speak freely."

I shook my head. "Master Magicians have excellent hearing." I thought about Roze, she would consider eavesdropping on the Ambassador to be her patriotic duty.

Signe nodded in understanding. "Seems the Wannabe King has gotten hold of some *wrong* information. I wonder how that happened."

"A miscommunication between several parties."

"There will be no more false accusations?" Signe asked.

Her gaze pierced me as if she held a knife to my throat. She wondered at my ability to keep her disguise a secret.

"No." I showed her my palm, pointing to the scar she had made when I promised not to reveal the Commander's secret to anyone. Not even to Valek.

That thought reminded me of Irys's suggestion that Valek leave Sitia. I pulled my butterfly pendant out. "Some rumors tend to smolder, and it would be best to make certain there is no fuel left to ignite another fire."

Signe had to know about Valek. "I will take that under advisement. However, I had another matter to discuss with you." Signe pulled a sheet of parchment from her black leather briefcase. She rolled it up, and held it in her hand.

"The Commander has sent a message for you. He has thought in depth about your last conversation with him. He decided that the advice presented was valid and would like to thank you for the suggestions." Signe handed me the paper roll.

"An invitation to come visit us when your magical training is complete. We are planning on returning to Ixia in a week's time," she said. "Your response is required before we leave."

A dismissal. I bowed to the Ambassador and left her office. I puzzled over her words as I headed toward the Keep. The Commander had signed an order of execution, visiting Ixia would be suicide.

I waited until I had a warm fire lit in my rooms before unrolling the Commander's message. Staring at the dancing flames, I contemplated Commander Ambrose's offer. I held the order for my execution in my hands. But tossing it into the fire would not be a simple act. A brief note had been written on the document.

Prove my loyalties to Ixia and the order would be nullified. Show the benefits of having a magician working for Ixia to the Ixian generals and an adviser's position would be mine. Do these things and I could return to Ixia. Return to my friends. Return to Valek.

Without knowing it, Cahil had seen my possible future when he had called me a master spy at the Council's session.

29

I gazed at the fire as my conflicting emotions, my conflicting loyalties and my conflicting desires all burned and danced in my chest, mimicking the flames. Coming no closer to a decision, I hid the execution order in my backpack. It might be better to think about it later.

Remembering my promise to my parents, I headed toward the dining hall, hoping I would find them eating lunch. Along the way, I encountered Dax.

"Yelena," he said, falling in step with me. "Haven't seen you in days."

"I'm sure you're just dying to tell me all the campus gossip about me. Right?"

"I *do* have a life. Maybe I've been too busy to listen to rumors," he huffed, pretending to have hurt feelings.

I looked at him.

He sighed. "Okay, you win. I'm bored out of my skull. Second Magician is busy playing detective, and Gelsi is neck-deep in some project and I never see her anymore." Dax paused dramatically. "My life is so boring that I have to live vicariously through your adventures."

"And since the rumors are so accurate—"

"Your adventures have turned into legends." He swept his arms wide, laughing. "So where are you off to now? Going to slay a dragon? Can I tag along as your lowly squire? I'll polish your staff of power every night with my shirt. I promise."

"I'm glad my problems are keeping you entertained," I said with some sarcasm. "I'm searching for my...ah, for the Tree King and his Queen. We're going to plan our attack against the evil Tree Varmints who have assembled an invisible army in the Keep."

Dax's eyes lit up. "I heard about the Tree Queen's adventures this morning."

The game soured. I didn't want to hear the students' gossip about my mother. Before Dax could elaborate, I invited him to tag along.

I found my parents in the dining hall and we joined them. While we ate, Dax's presence worked to my advantage. The topic of conversation stayed on school and horses and mundane matters, giving my parents no chance to question me about the Council session. And when my mother offered to distill a special cologne for Dax, I knew she was glad I had found a Sitian friend.

After saying goodbye to Dax, I went to the guest quarters with my parents. As Perl brewed some tea in the small kitchen, I asked Esau about the Curare. Irys had told him about the drug when she feared Ferde had kidnapped me.

He ran a calloused hand over his face. "I never thought it would be used like that," he said, shaking his head. "When I discover something new, I always experiment with it until I know all the side effects and know how the substance could be used or abused. Then I weigh the good against the bad. Some discoveries never see the light of day, but for others, even though they might not be perfect, the benefits outweigh the risks."

Esau stopped speaking when Perl entered the room carrying

a tray of tea. The warning in my father's eyes told me that my mother didn't know about Ferde's gruesome use of the Curare.

She served the tea and sat close to me on the couch. She had worn her cloak during lunch, but had removed it when we entered their suite.

"What happened at the Council's session?" she asked me.

I gave them a watered-down version of Cahil's accusations against Adviser Ilom. Perl's hand flew to her neck when I mentioned Valek's name, but she relaxed when I told her Cahil had been proven wrong. Neglecting to mention Cahil's claims about my involvement with Valek, I informed them about Goel's murder.

"Good," Perl said. "Saves me the effort of cursing him."

"Mother!" I was astonished. "Can you do that?"

"Perfumes and scents are not the only things I can concoct."

I looked at Esau. He nodded his head. "Good thing Reyad and Mogkan were already dead. Your mother has quite the imagination when she's angry."

I wondered what other surprises I would discover about my parents. Changing the subject, I asked about their journey to the Keep and about the Zaltana family, spending the day with them as promised.

When the hour had grown late, Esau offered to escort me to my rooms. At first I declined. I hadn't been assigned guards since the episode with Goel. When he insisted and when Perl frowned, I remembered her comment about curses and not wanting to be a target of her ire, I agreed.

The campus atmosphere hung silent and empty. Moonlight glistened off the ice-coated trees. Only four more days until the full moon. My hand found Valek's snake and I twisted the bracelet around my arm.

When we were halfway to my rooms Esau said, "I need to tell you another thing about Curare."

"There's more?"

He nodded. "The stinging nettle plant was the reason I sent the shipment of Curare to the Sandseeds before I finished all my experiments on the drug. The plant grows in the Avibian Plains and the sting causes unbearable pain for many days. It's usually the children who wander into a patch without realizing it. In low doses, Curare is excellent for numbing the wound. It had never occurred to me that someone would use high doses of Curare to paralyze the entire body." Esau frowned, running a hand through his shoulder length gray hair. "Later I discovered another side effect that seemed minor at the time. But now…" Esau stopped and turned to me. "At high doses the Curare will also paralyze a person's magical abilities."

I felt the blood drain from my face. That meant Curare could render even a Master Magician completely helpless. Tomorrow night was the time of the secret exchange. Since I had taken over Goel's body with my magic, I planned to take over Ferde's, believing that, even if I was incapacitated by the drug, I could still use my magic. It now seemed imperative that I avoid getting shot with Curare.

My father must have seen the horror in my eyes. "There is an antidote of sorts," he said.

"Antidote?"

"Not a complete reversal, but it does free the magic and return some feeling, although it creates some new problems." Esau shook his head in frustration. "I haven't been able to experiment with it fully."

"What is it?"

"Theobroma."

That explained the new problem. Eating the brown sweet would open my mind to magical influences. My mental defenses would not work against another magician, even one weaker than me.

"How much Theobroma would I need?" I asked my father.

"A lot. Though, I could concentrate it," he mused.

A chill wind blew through me, shivering I pulled my cloak tighter as we continued our walk.

"It wouldn't taste as good, but it would be a smaller quantity," Esau said.

"Can you do it by tomorrow afternoon?" I asked.

He stared at me. A worried concern filled his kind eyes.

"Are you going to do something that I shouldn't tell your mother about?"

"Yes."

"Important?"

"Very."

My father considered my request. When we arrived at my rooms, he gave me a hug. "Do you know what you're doing?"

"I have a plan."

"Yelena, you managed to find your way home despite the odds. I'll trust that you'll prevail again. You'll have the antidote by tomorrow noon."

He stood in my doorway like a protective bear while I searched inside. Satisfied that I was safe, he said good-night and headed back to the guest quarters.

I lay in bed and mulled over the information Esau had given me. When my shutters swung wide, I sat up, grabbing my switchblade from under the pillow. Valek climbed through the window with a lithe grace, dropping without a sound onto my bed. He locked the shutters then joined me.

"You need to leave. Too many people know you're here," I said.

"Not until we find the killer. And besides, the Commander ordered me to protect the Ambassador. I would be remiss in my duties if I left."

"What if she ordered you home?" I turned so I could see his face.

"The Commander's orders overrule all others."

"Valek, did you—"

He stopped my question with a kiss. I needed to discuss many things with him. Goel's death and the Commander's offer. But once his body molded to mine and his musky scent reached my nose all thoughts of murder and intrigue evaporated. I pulled at his shirt. He smiled with delight. Our time together was limited and I didn't want to waste the night on words.

When I woke in the semidarkness of sunrise, Valek was gone. But I felt energized. My rendezvous with Ferde was scheduled for midnight so I reviewed the plan as I went through my day.

Irys had wanted me to try to move objects again with my magic for my morning lesson. I had yet to manage that skill. But I asked if we could work on strengthening my mental defenses. If I had to resort to using Esau's antidote, I wanted to be able to produce a strong enough barrier that might block his magic even while under the influence of the Theobroma.

Before dismissing me for the day, Irys asked, "Are you still feeling tired from your encounter with Goel?"

"A little. Why?"

She gave me an ironic smile. "You've been pestering me about the search for Opal every day for the last week. Yet no questions today."

"I assumed you would tell me any news."

"We've reached a milestone!" Irys declared. "You're learning to trust us." Then the humor in her eyes dulled. "No news. We don't think they are in the Citadel or the plains so now we're widening the search area."

Feelings of guilt squeezed my chest as I hurried to find my father. I had wanted to work with Irys and the others, but now I planned to meet Ferde with just Valek backing me up. Granted Valek equaled four armed men, but I hadn't confided our plans to her. A true Sitian would present the information to the Council.

But why didn't I trust Irys? Because she wouldn't let me go to the rendezvous. The danger to Sitia was too great, but trying to ambush Ferde wouldn't work without me there. Irys believed they would find him eventually and sacrificing Opal was a small price to pay for Sitia. I believed that risking all was the only way to stop him. Knowing the risks, and trying to minimize them would be the key.

Irys didn't believe in my abilities to capture Ferde, but I had kept Roze, the most powerful magician in Sitia, from extracting my innermost thoughts, I had healed Tula's body and found her consciousness, I had taken over Goel's body and would soon have an antidote to Curare.

Trust needed to go both ways. Loyalty, too. Did I feel any loyalty? To Irys, yes. But to Sitia? I couldn't say.

Even if we succeeded in rescuing Opal and capturing Ferde, Irys would cease my lessons. That grim thought led me to contemplate my future and the Commander's offer.

Irys would sever our relationship, and I would have no obligations to Sitia. I could tell the Commander about Cahil and his plans to build an army to overthrow Ixia. Cahil, that weasel, had no qualms about telling the Council of my connection with Valek.

My father waited for me outside the guest quarters. He had concentrated the Theobroma into a pill the same size and shape as a robin's egg.

"I coated it with a gelatin that will keep it from melting," Esau explained.

"Melting?"

"How would you eat it if you're frozen with Curare?" When my eyes widened in sudden understanding, he said, "You can hold this pill between your teeth. If you're pricked with the Curare just bite down on it and try and swallow as much as you can before your jaw muscles become paralyzed. Hopefully the rest will melt and slide down your throat."

Before learning about this antidote my main goal had been to not get hit with Curare at all. If I willingly went to Ferde, he shouldn't need to use it. Or so I'd hope. Esau's pill made me even more confident about the rendezvous tonight, and he had given me an idea. I borrowed a few other items from my father.

I spent the remainder of the afternoon practicing self-defense with Zitora, and after dinner with my parents I went to the barn. Everything about the day seemed odd as if I did things for the last time. Perhaps the feeling was due to the fact that my life would be different after tonight.

Kiki sensed my mood. *Lavender Lady sad.*

A little. I led Kiki from her stall and groomed her. Usually I talked to her, but tonight I worked in silence.

I go with Lavender Lady.

Surprised, I stopped brushing. I had thought my connection with Kiki only involved emotions and simple communication. She discerned my feelings, and possessed certain instincts like when I had been threatened by Goel, but until now I had believed she didn't know why.

It would be suspicious if I take you.

Take me to smelling distance. Lavender Lady needs me.

I pondered her words as I put the grooming brushes away. Cahil hadn't come to the barn for my lesson. I wasn't surprised. Guess I would practice on my own. But how to get onto Kiki's back without a saddle or a boost up?

Grab mane. Hop. Pull.

Kiki, you're full of advice tonight.

Smart, she agreed.

As we rode around the pasture, I realized the value of her offer. I would take her along and let her graze in the plains. The exchange site was set at the only location in the plains that I knew, Blood Rock. My skin crawled when I contemplated how Ferde had gotten that information.

Ferde's image and thoughts still frequented my nightmares, and I wondered if I had inadvertently formed a mental connection with his mind. His desire to possess me haunted my dreams. I no longer ran from the snakes. Instead, I waited for their tight embrace, welcoming the oblivion of their bites. My dream actions became as disturbing as Ferde's.

Kiki switched to a trot, jarring me from my thoughts. I concentrated on maintaining my balance. When my legs and back began to ache, she stopped.

After giving Kiki a quick rubdown, I led her back in her stall. *See you later*, I said, heading toward my rooms to prepare for the exchange. My confidence soured to nervousness as the darkness advanced over the sky.

Trust, Kiki said. *Trust is peppermints.*

I laughed. Kiki viewed the world through her stomach. Peppermints were good; therefore, trusting another was also good.

Valek waited for me in my rooms. His stiff expression resembled a metal mask. A cold sheen covered his eyes; his killer's gaze.

"Here." He handed me a black turtleneck shirt and black pants. "They're made of a special fabric that will protect you from airborne darts from a blow gun, but won't stop a dart if you get jabbed by one."

"These are great," I said, thanking him. At least I wouldn't be surprised, and hopefully, once Ferde was close enough to jab me, I would have the upper hand.

The new clothes hung on my small frame. I rolled up the sleeves and added a belt to keep the pants from falling down.

A brief smile touched Valek's lips. "They were mine. I'm not the best seamstress."

I packed my backpack with care, taking only critical supplies, which included the Theobroma, the items Esau gave me, my grapple and rope, an apple and my bow. Ferde hadn't specified to come unarmed. My lock picks went into my hair, and I strapped my switchblade onto my thigh through the hole cut into my pant's pocket. Valek had thought ahead. He might not be the best with a needle and thread, but he knew the art of combat like no other.

We reviewed our plan and I told him about Kiki.

"Sneaking through both the Keep's and Citadel's gates without a large animal is hard enough, love," Valek said.

"I'll manage. Trust me."

He gave me a flat stare, showing no emotion.

"I'll take Kiki out to the plains and give you time to get through the Citadel's gate before heading toward the meeting site," I said. "Once Opal is out of harm's way and Ferde is visible, that's the sign to move in."

Valek nodded. "Count on it."

I put on my cloak and left. Four hours remained until midnight. A few people moved about the campus. The torches along the walkways had been lit and students hurried through the cool night air, heading to an evening class or to meet up with friends. I was a stranger among them. A shadow, watching and yearning to join them, wishing that my worries only focused on studying for one of Bain Bloodgood's history quizzes.

Kiki waited for me in her stall. I opened the door and let her out. Getting onto her back with a cloak and loaded backpack became an impossible task. I pulled a step stool over and used it.

Need practice, Kiki said. *No stool in wild.*

Later, I agreed.

Kiki glanced back at Irys's tower as we started toward the Keep's gate. *Magic Lady.*

The guilt I had suppressed about not telling Irys about the exchange threatened to break free. *She won't be happy.*

Kicking mad. Give Magic Lady peppermints.

I laughed, thinking I would need more than peppermints to repair the damage.

Peppermints sweet on both sides, Kiki said.

Cryptic horse advice? *Are you sure Moon Man isn't your father? Moon Man smart.*

I pondered her words, trying to decipher the true meaning.

Before we reached the Keep's gate, I pulled a magic thread to me and projected my awareness. Two guards watched the gate. Bored, one guard thought of the end of his shift with longing; the other considered what he would eat for a late dinner. A magician dozed on a stool. I sent the magician into a deeper slumber, and using the guard's desires, I encouraged them to focus on something other than the horse and rider passing beneath the gate. As one soldier scanned the sky to see how far the South Star had moved, the other rummaged around the guardhouse looking for something to eat. Both failed to notice us and we soon passed out of sight.

Kiki walked quietly through the Citadel. No farrier would go near a sandseed horse, the breed's strong disdain for metal shoes was well-known. Four guards watched the Citadel's gates. Once again, I distracted the guards as we crossed. When we were out of sight of the gate, Kiki broke into a gallop and we headed into the Avibian Plains. When we could no longer see the road or the Citadel, Kiki slowed to a walk.

My thoughts returned to Kiki's words about peppermints. For the plan to work tonight, we each had to do our part. Both sides needed to be sweet. She had also claimed trust equaled peppermints. Did she refer to Irys instead of Valek?

The answer bloomed in my mind. I didn't know whether to feel smart for figuring out Kiki's advice, or feel like a simpleton for having a horse tell me the right thing to do.

Irys, I called in my mind.

Yelena? What's the matter?

I took a deep breath, steadied my nerves and told her my plans. Silence, long and empty, followed my confession.

You'll die, she finally said. *You're no longer my student. I'll link with the other Master Magicians and we will stop you before you get to him.*

I expected her response. Her anger and immediate censure were the reasons I hadn't wanted to tell her about the exchange.

Irys, you told me I would die before. Remember when we first met in Ixia's Snake Forest?

She hesitated. *Yes.*

I was in an impossible position. My magical powers were uncontrolled, you were threatening to kill me and I had been poisoned by Valek. Each course of action from that point seemed to lead to my eventual death. But I asked you to give me some time, and you did. You hardly knew me, yet you trusted me enough to let me figure a way out. I might not know the ways of Sitia, but I'm an old hand at dealing with impossible situations. Think about that before you call the others.

Another long painful silence. I withdrew my connection to Irys, needing to focus my attention on tonight's task. Kiki stopped within a mile of Blood Rock. I sensed the Sandseed's subtle magic. The protection lacked the strength of the one that covered their camp, but it resembled a thin web, waiting to catch its prey unaware. A magician with the proper magical defense in place could avoid detection by the Sandseeds, but if the clan intensified their power, they would then sense the magician's presence. Their magic would attack the interloper. I breathed a small sigh of relief, knowing Valek's immunity would make him undetectable.

I slid off Kiki's back. *Stay out of sight*, I told her.

Stay in wind. Keep smell strong, Kiki instructed.

I hid in the tall grass, giving Valek time to catch up. Kiki had reached this point in an hour, but it would take him an extra hour to get into position. When I felt I had waited long enough, I started walking toward Blood Rock, trusting that Valek would approach the exchange site from the opposite direction.

Rabbit, Kiki said. *Good.*

I smiled. She must have flushed a bunny from its burrow. The moon's bright light shone on the long stalks of grass. A slight breeze blew and I watched as my moon's shadow skimmed over the rippling surface.

Irys's voice reached my mind. *You're on your own.* Then her mental connection with me severed, destroying our student-mentor link. My head throbbed with the sudden emptiness.

My heart squeezed out little spikes of panic. I calmed my nerves with the reminder that both Valek and Kiki trailed me.

When I drew closer to the meeting point, I stopped and took off my cloak. I rolled the garment up and hid it in a clump of tall grass. Pulling Esau's Theobroma pill from my pack, I placed it between my back teeth. My mouth felt awkward, and I hoped I didn't accidentally bite into the pill.

I continued onward. The dark shape of the rock filled the land before me. Rays of moonlight filtered through the clouds as I peered into the semidarkness, searching for some sign of Ferde and Opal.

Relief poured through my body when I saw Opal step out from behind Blood Rock. She hurried toward me, and only when she left the shadows could I see the terror on her face. Her eyes looked swollen; her pale skin blotchy from crying. I scanned the area with my magic, feeling for Ferde as my gaze hunted for him.

Opal threw herself into my arms, sobbing. Too easy. Wouldn't he want my promise to go with him before releasing her? The girl hugged me so tight she pinched my skin. Ferde still didn't appear. I pulled her away, planning to guide her back to the Citadel.

"I'm so sorry, Yelena," she cried and ran away.

I spun around, expecting Ferde to be standing there gloating. No one. Confused, I moved to follow Opal but my feet would not obey me. Stumbling, I fell as my body lost all sensation.

30

I lay on the ground as the paralysis swept through my body with amazing speed. I had only a second to realize that I'd been hit with Curare before the drug froze all my muscles. Only a second to bite down on the Theobroma pill before my jaw seized, swallowing just a drop of the antidote.

Lying on my side, I saw Opal in the gray moonlight, running toward the Citadel. My helpless position was the direct result of my appalling overconfidence. By focusing on the danger from Ferde either from his magic or from the Curare, I didn't prepare for an attack by Opal. She had jabbed me, apologized and run off.

A muted fear pulsed in my body. The Curare seemed to dull my emotions as well as my magic. I felt as if I wore a heavy wet woolen cap around my head.

Behind me, I heard the slight crunch of footsteps coming closer. I waited for Valek. Would he pounce when Ferde drew closer to me?

The footsteps stopped and my view changed. Without feeling anything, I was pulled over onto my back. My head spun for a moment before I could focus on the night sky. I couldn't move my gaze, but I could still blink. I couldn't speak, yet I could breathe. I couldn't move my mouth or tongue, but I could swallow. Odd.

When a face entered my view, I remembered to be scared again. Until surprise eclipsed my fear for a moment. A woman with long hair peered down at me. She wore a robe and I could see faint lines had been drawn or tattooed on her neck. When she flaunted a knife and brought the metal tip close to my eyes, the air suddenly seemed thick and hard to draw into my straining lungs.

"Should I kill you now?" she asked. Her accent sounded familiar. She cocked her head to the side in amusement. "No comment? Not to worry. I won't kill you now. Not when you won't feel any pain. You need to suffer greatly before I'll end your pain for good."

The woman stood and walked away. I searched my memory. Did I know her? Why would she want to kill me? Perhaps she worked with Ferde. Her language matched his, but without the lilt.

Where was Valek? He should have witnessed my predicament.

I heard a rubbing sound and a thump then a strange disorientation made me realize that the woman dragged me. My world tilted and straightened. She brandished a rope, and I guessed by the brief glimpses and sounds that she had pulled me onto a cart and was tying me to it. She jumped off, and, after a moment, I heard her call to a horse.

The creaking of the wheels and steady clomping of the horse were the only indication that we moved. From the swish and whack of grass, I guessed we were headed deeper into the Avibian Plains. Where was Valek?

I worried and waited and even slept. Every time some of the melting Theobroma reached the back of my throat, I swallowed. Would I get enough to counteract the Curare? By the time the woman stopped, a pale sheen of dawn had wedged into the night sky. Feeling began to return to my limbs. I moved my tongue, trying to swallow more of the Theobroma.

Pain flared in my wrists and ankles. My hands and feet were stiff and cold. I had been tied spread-eagled on the hard cart. My ability to connect with the power source started to wake when the woman climbed onto the cart. My thoughts scattered when I saw her holding a long thin needle. I banished the fear and drew power to me.

"Oh, no, you don't," she declared then jabbed me with the needle. "We need to reach the Void before I let you feel. Then you can feel cold steel slicing into your skin."

I thought that this would be an excellent time for Valek to arrive. But, when he failed to appear, I said, "Who…" before the drug numbed all my muscles.

"You don't know me, but you knew my brother very well. Don't worry—you'll know the reason for your suffering soon enough." She hopped off the cart and the familiar sounds of movement started again.

Anytime now, Valek, I thought. But as the sun progressed through the sky, my hopes for a rescue faded. Something must have happened to keep Valek from following me. Perhaps Irys's message last night about being alone had been a warning.

Various horrible scenarios about Valek played in my mind. To distract myself, I wondered about Kiki. Was she near? Would she follow my scent? With my magic ability paralyzed, would she know I needed her help?

The sun hovered above the horizon when the cart stopped again. A burning sensation in my fingertips meant the Curare started to wear off. Soon enough cramps, pain and cold air wracked my body. I shivered and gulped the rest of Esau's antidote, preparing for another jab. But it didn't come.

Instead, the woman climbed onto the cart and stood over me. She spread her arms wide. "Welcome to the Void. Or in your case, welcome to hell."

In the fading light, I saw her gray eyes clearly. The strong features of her face reminded me of someone, but I couldn't think. My head ached and my mind felt dull. I reached for a thread of power, but found dead air. Nothing.

A smug smile spread on the woman's lips. "This is one of the few places in Sitia where there is a hole in the blanket of power. No power means no magic."

"Where are we?" I asked. My voice sounded rough.

"The Daviian Plateau."

"Who are you?"

All humor dropped from the woman's face. She appeared to be around thirty years old. Her black hair reached past her waist. She rolled the sleeves up on her sand-colored cloak, revealing the purple animal tattoos that covered her arms.

"You haven't figured it out? Have you killed that many men?"

"Four men, but I'm not averse to killing a woman." I gave her a pointed stare.

"You're really not in the position to be bragging or boasting." She pulled her knife from a pocket of her cloak.

I thought quick. Of the four, Reyad was the only one I knew well, the others I had killed in self-defense. I didn't even know their names.

"Still don't know?" She moved closer to me.

"No."

Rage flamed in her gray eyes. That expression jolted my memory. Mogkan. The magician that had kidnapped me and tried to rob me of my soul. He was known as Kangom in Sitia.

"Kangom deserved to die," I said. Valek had made the killing blow, but Irys and I had first caught the magician in a web of magical power. I had not included him in my count, but I admitted being responsible for his death.

Fury twisted the woman's expression. She drove her knife

into my right forearm, and then pulled it out just as fast. Pain exploded up my arm. I screamed.

"Who am I?" she asked.

My arm burned, but I met her gaze. "You're Kangom's sister."

She nodded. "My name's Alea Daviian."

That was not one of the clan names.

She understood my confusion and said, "I used to be a Sandseed." She spat the clan name out. "They're stuck in the past. We are more powerful than the rest of Sitia, yet the Sandseeds are content to wander the plains, dream and weave stories. My brother had a vision on how we could rule Sitia."

"But he was helping Brazell to take over Ixia." I found it hard to follow her logic when my blood poured from the stab wound.

"A first step. Gain control of the northern armies then attack Sitia. But you ruined that, didn't you?"

"Seemed like a good idea at the time."

Alea sliced her knife along my left arm, drawing a line from my shoulder to my wrist. "You'll learn to regret that decision before I cut your throat just like you did to my brother."

Pain coursed through my arms, but a strange annoyance that she had ruined Valek's special shirt tugged at my mind. Alea raised the knife again, aiming for my face. I thought fast.

"Are you living in the plateau?" I asked.

"Yes. We broke from the Sandseeds and declared a new clan. The Daviians will conquer Sitia. We will no longer have to steal to survive."

"How?"

"Another member is on a power quest. Once he completes the ritual he will be more powerful than all four Master Magicians together."

"Did you kill Tula?" I asked. When she squinted in confusion, I added, "Opal's sister."

"No. My cousin had that pleasure."

Alea had a family connection to Ferde. He must be the one

on the quest, which led me to the question. Who was Ferde targeting for the final ritual? It could be any girl with some magical abilities and he could be anywhere. And we only had two days to find him.

I pulled against the ropes with the sudden need to move.

Alea smiled in satisfaction. "Not to worry. You won't be around for the cleansing of Sitia. However, you will be around for a little longer." She pulled out her needle and jabbed into the cut on my arm. I yelped.

"I don't like wasting your blood on this wagon. We have a special frame set up so I can collect your red life and make good use of it." Alea hopped off the cart.

The Curare began to dull the pain in my arms, but full paralysis didn't grip my body. Esau's antidote must be working. The presence of Void meant I didn't have to worry about my mind being open to magical influences. However, being tied to the cart and unarmed, I didn't know if my body would be in any condition to fight Alea.

Searching for my pack and bow would reveal to her that I could move. So I clamped my teeth down to keep them from chattering and to remind myself to stay still.

I heard a thump and the cart tilted. My feet now pointed toward the ground as my head came up. With this new angle, I could see a wooden frame just a few feet away. Made of thick beams, the frame had manacles and chains hanging from the top with some type of pulley rigged to them. Under the frame lay a metal basin. I guessed that the victim stood in the basin.

Beyond the frame spread the vivid colors of the flat Daviian Plateau. The patchwork of yellows, tans and browns seemed so soothing in comparison to the torture device.

My heart began beating in a fast tempo. I kept my eyes staring straight ahead when Alea came into view. A few inches taller than me, Alea's chin reached my eye level. She had removed her cloak and revealed her blue pants and short-sleeved V-neck blouse that had white disks sewn onto it, making it look as if she wore fish scales. A leather weapon belt circled her waist.

"Feeling better?" she asked. "Let's make sure." She poked the tip of her blade into my right thigh.

Concentrating so hard on not reacting, I took a moment to realize the thrust hadn't hurt. The tip of Alea's knife had hit my switchblade holder. Still strapped to my thigh, I wondered if the weapon remained inside it. Alea considered my expression for many frantic heartbeats. If she suspected I could move, then all would be lost.

"Your clothes are strange," she said finally. "They're thick and resist my knife. I will remove them and keep them. They would make a fine reminder of our time together."

She stepped over to the frame and grabbed the manacles that hung down, pulling. The wheel on the pulley spun and let more chain through until the cuffs reached my cart.

"You're too heavy for me to lift. Good thing my brother added that pulley so I can easily yank you into place." She unlocked the metal cuffs and opened them wide.

My time to act approached. If she was smart, she would secure my wrists in the cuffs before untying my feet. Once my arms were locked into the frame, I would be helpless again. I would only have a brief window of opportunity. And I planned to risk everything on a guess.

She leaned over with her knife and cut the rope holding my right arm to the side of the cart. I let it drop to my side as if it were a dead weight, hoping she would untie my other arm before fastening them. Instead, Alea put her knife in her belt and reached for my arm.

I plunged my hand into my pocket and grabbed for my switchblade. Alea froze for a moment in shock. My fingers found the smooth handle and I almost laughed aloud with relief. Yanking the weapon out, I knocked aside her arm and triggered the blade.

She drew her knife. Before she could step back, I plunged my blade into her lower abdomen. Grunting in surprise, she aimed her weapon at my heart. She staggered a bit as she leaned forward to strike, and I felt cold steel bite deep into my stomach. Alea fell, sitting hard on the ground. She hunched over my switchblade.

I gasped for breath, trying to keep from passing out. Pain flamed up my back and gripped my insides like a tight vise.

Alea pulled my blade from her guts and dropped it onto the ground. Crawling over to her cloak, she retrieved a vial of liquid from one of the pockets. She opened it, dipped her finger in and rubbed the liquid into her stab wound. Curare.

Lurching to her feet, she walked back to me. She studied my condition in silence. The Curare she had used must have been diluted in order for her to move.

"Take my knife out to free yourself and you will bleed to death," she said with grim satisfaction. "Leave it in and you will eventually die. Either way you're in the middle of the plains with no one to help you and no magic to heal you." She shrugged. "Not what I had planned, but the results will be the same."

"What about your problem?" I asked, huffing with the effort.

"I have my horse and my people close by. Our healer will cure me and I will be back in time to watch your final moments." She moved past the cart. After some rustling and grunting, she clicked at her horse, and I heard the familiar thumping of hooves.

As my vision began to blur I had to agree with Alea. My position hadn't improved, but at least I'd denied her the satisfaction of torturing me. The intense pain made concentrating difficult. Do I pull the knife? Or keep it in?

Time passed and I drifted in and out of consciousness. I roused when the drum of a galloping horse reached my ears. I hadn't made my decision and Alea was returning to gloat.

Closing my eyes to avoid seeing her smug expression, I heard a whinny. The sound soothed my pain as if I'd been dosed with Curare. I opened my eyes and saw Kiki's face.

My prospects looked better, but I wasn't sure I could communicate with Kiki.

"Knife," I said aloud. My throat burned with thirst. "Get me the knife." Looking over to my switchblade on the ground, I then stared at Kiki. I let my eyes and head move from one to the other. "Please."

She turned an eye in the right direction. Then walked over and grasped the handle with her teeth. Smart, indeed.

I held out my free hand and she placed the weapon in my palm. "Kiki, if this works out," I said, "I'll feed you all the apples and peppermints that you want."

Fresh waves of pain coursed through my body as I twisted to cut the rope around my left wrist. When the strands severed, I fell to the ground, but had enough sense to land on my elbows and knees, keeping the knife from plunging deeper into my stomach. After an eternity, I reached back and cut the rope around my feet.

I probably would have curled up on the ground and given in to the release of unconsciousness, but Kiki huffed at me and nudged my face with her nose. Looking up, I thought her back seemed as unattainable as the clouds in the sky. No step stool in the wild. I laughed, but it came out as a hysterical cry.

Kiki moved away. She returned with my pack in her mouth, setting it down next to me. I gave her a wry smile. Whenever I rode her, I always had my pack with me. She probably thought I needed my backpack to climb onto her back. Pawing with impatience, she pushed the pack closer to me. I had mentioned apples. Perhaps she wanted the one inside.

I opened it. Smart girl. I found the Curare that I had forgotten about. Planning to use the drug against Ferde, I had packed one of Esau's vials. I rubbed a tiny drop into my wound. The drug soothed my pain. Sighing with relief, I tried to sit up. My arms and legs felt wooden and heavy, but they moved the right ways. The Theobroma in my body kept the Curare from freezing all my muscles. It was an effort to put my backpack on. Fear of Alea's return motivated me, and I stood on wobbly legs.

Kiki bent her front legs down to her knees. I looked at her askance. No step stool? She whickered with impatience. I laced my fingers in her mane and swung a leg over her back. She lurched to her feet and broke into a smooth ground-eating stride.

I knew the instant we left the Void. Magic encompassed me like a pool of water, but I soon felt drowned by the amount. An unfortunate side effect of the Theobroma opened my mind to the magical assault. On entering the Avibian Plains, the Sandseed's protective spells rushed me. Unable to block the magic, I fell.

Strange dreams, images and colors swirled around me. Kiki spoke to me with Irys's voice. Valek steeled himself as a noose wrapped around his neck. His arms tied behind his back. Ari and Janco huddled by a fire in a grassy clearing, alarmed and uneasy. They had never been lost before. My mother clung to the upper branches of a tree as it swung wildly in a storm. The smell of Curare filled my nose and Theobroma coated my mouth.

Alea's knife had been driven deeper into my abdomen when I had hit the ground. In my mind's eye, I saw the torn muscles, the tear in my stomach with blood and acid gushing out. Yet I couldn't focus my magic to heal the wound.

Valek's thoughts reached me. He fought the soldiers around him with his feet, but someone pulled on the rope and it tightened around his neck.

Regret pulsed in his heart. *Sorry, love. I don't think we're going to make it this time.*

31

No! I yelled to him. *Stay alive. Think of something!*

I'll stay if you will, he countered.

Damn frustrating man. In exasperation, I gathered the twisting images and magic that threatened to overwhelm me. I wrung them and wrestled the magic. Images swirled around me like snowflakes in a blizzard. Theobroma coursed through my blood and enhanced my perceptions, making the magic tangible. The threads of power slipped through my hands like a coarse blanket.

Sweating and panting with the effort to hold on to the magic, I yanked Alea's knife from my stomach and pulled magic toward the wound. Laying my hands over my abdomen, I covered the warm torrent of blood with power.

Concentrating, I sent my mind's eye toward the damage. I grabbed a thread of the magic swirling around me and used it to stitch closed the rip in my stomach. I repaired my torn abdominal muscles and knitted my skin together. A quick glance at my stomach revealed an ugly red ridge of puckered flesh that caused a sharp stab of pain whenever I drew breath. But the wound was no longer life threatening.

I kept my end of the bargain. I desperately hoped Valek kept his. Exhaustion tugged at my consciousness, and I would have fallen asleep, but Kiki nudged me.

Come, she said in my mind.

I opened my eyes. *Tired*.

Bad smell. Go.

We were out of the Void, but we must be close to Alea's people.

Grab tail, she instructed.

Clutching the long strands of her tail, I pulled myself into a standing position. Kiki knelt, and I mounted her back.

She took off, breaking into her gust-of-wind gait. I hung on and tried to stay awake. The plains blurred past as the sun set. The icy air bit at my skin.

When she slowed, I blinked, trying to focus on my surroundings. Still in the plains, but I saw a campfire ahead.

Make noise. Not scare Rabbit.

Rabbits? Sudden hunger made my stomach growl. I did have an apple, but I'd promised that to Kiki.

She snorted in amusement, whinnied and stopped. I glanced past her head and saw two men blocking the path. The moonlight shone off their swords. Ari and Janco. I called to them and they sheathed their weapons as Kiki drew closer.

Rabbit? Not Rabbit Man?

Too quick for a man.

"Thank fate!" Ari cried.

Seeing how I drooped over Kiki's neck, Ari pulled me off and carried me to their campfire, setting me down as if I was as fragile as an egg. The sudden wish that Ari was my real brother overcame me. Even as an eight-year-old, I'd bet Ari never would have let me be kidnapped.

Janco feigned boredom. "Going off and getting all the glory again," he said. "I don't know why we even bothered to come to this crazy land. Your trail marks didn't even have the decency to go anywhere but in circles," he grumped.

"Don't like being lost, Janco?" I teased.

He harrumphed and crossed his arms.

"Don't worry. Your skills are still keen. You're in the Avibian Plains. There's a protective magic here that confuses the mind."

"Magic," he spat. "Another good reason to stay in Ixia."

Ari sat me by the fire. "You look terrible. Here." He wrapped my cloak around my shoulders.

"Where—"

"We found it in the plains," Ari explained. Then he frowned. "Valek had asked us to back him up last night. We followed him, but they ambushed him at the Citadel's gates."

"Cahil and his men," I said.

He nodded then began inspecting the cuts on my arms.

"How did they know where to find him?" I asked.

"Captain Marrok is a tracker of some renown," Ari said. "Seems he had dealings with Valek before. He is the only soldier to have escaped from the Commander's dungeon. He must have been waiting for the perfect opportunity." Ari shook his head. "Valek's capture presented a dilemma."

"Help Valek or help you," Janco said.

"I think he suspected something might happen to him and didn't want you unprotected. So we stuck to the plan and followed you." Ari handed me a jug of water.

I gulped the liquid.

"Not that we did any good," Janco huffed. "When we reached the meeting site, the horse and cart were gone and we figured we would track you. She had to stop sometime. But—"

"You lost your way," I finished for him. Ari probed the deep gash on my right forearm. "Ow!"

"Hold still," Ari said. "Janco, get my med kit from my pack—these cuts need to be cleaned and sealed."

If I'd had any energy, I could have healed the wounds on my arms with magic. Instead, I endured Ari's administrations and admonishments. When he pulled out the pot of Rand's sealing glue, I asked him about the Commander's new chef to distract myself from the pain.

"Since Rand never made it to Brazell's for the transfer of cooks, the Commander promoted one of Rand's kitchen staff." Ari frowned.

I grimaced as Ari applied the glue to my cut more from remembering Rand than from the burning in my arm. Rand had lost his life protecting me, but I wouldn't have been in danger if he hadn't set me up for an ambush in the first place.

"The food hasn't been the same," Janco said with a sigh. "Everyone is losing weight."

When Ari finished wrapping my arms, he pulled something from the fire. "Janco got a rabbit." He broke off a piece and handed it to me. "You need to eat something."

That reminded me. "Kiki needs…" I moved to stand up.

Janco waved me down. "I'll take care of her."

"Do you—"

"Yeah, I grew up on a farm."

I had gnawed every bit of meat off the rabbit's bone when Janco came back covered with horsehair. He seemed to be in a better mood. "She's beautiful," he said about Kiki. "I've never had a horse stand so patiently to be rubbed down and she wasn't even tied!"

I told him about the honor she gave him by changing his name from Rabbit Man to Rabbit. "Unprecedented."

He gave me an odd look. "Talking horses. Magic. Crazy southerners." He shook his head.

He might have said more, but I could no longer stay awake.

The next morning, I told my friends about Alea and the clan on the plateau. They wanted to go after her, but I reminded them about Valek and the need to find Ferde. My heart lurched when I thought of Valek. Even with a night of sleep, I still didn't have enough energy to find out what had happened to him.

The rest had roused me. "We need to get to the Citadel," I said, standing.

"Do you know where we are?" Ari asked.

"Somewhere in the plains," I said, shouldering my backpack.

"Some magician you are," Janco said. "Do you even know which direction the Citadel is?"

"No." Kiki came and stood next to me. I grabbed her mane. "How about a boost?" I asked Janco.

He muttered under his breath, but offered his linked hands for my boot. When I had settled onto her back, I looked down at him. "Kiki knows where to go. Can you keep up?"

He grinned. "This rabbit can run."

Ari and Janco packed their gear and we set off at a trot. All those laps around the Commander's castle had kept them in top physical condition.

We reached the road, and I heard Janco curse and grumble about being lost only a mile away. When we approached the Citadel's gates, we encountered the four Master Magicians. They all sat on horseback. A well-armed Calvary team accompanied them.

I smiled at Roze Featherstone's look of astonishment, but sobered at Irys's cold stare.

"Why are you here?" I asked.

"We were coming to either rescue you or kill you," Zitora said. She flashed Roze an annoyed glance.

I met Irys's gaze, questioning. She turned away and blocked my efforts to reach her mind. Even though I had known she would shun me for going off alone, her actions still tore at my heart.

Not bothering to conceal the satisfaction in her voice, Roze said, "Because of your dangerous disregard for the well-being of Sitia, you have been expelled."

The least of my worries. "Is Opal safe?" I asked the magicians.

Bain Bloodgood nodded. "She told us a woman held her. Was she connected to the killer?"

"No. We still need to find Ferde. He doesn't want me. He must have taken someone else. Has anyone been reported missing?"

My announcement caused a considerable stir. Everyone had assumed that Ferde was holding Opal. Now they needed to change tactics.

"We've been searching for him for two weeks," Roze said, putting a stop to the chatter. "What makes you think we can find him now?"

"The last victim would not have been kidnapped," Bain said. "Let us go back and discuss this. Yelena, you will be safest in the Keep. We will talk about your future when this whole mess is resolved."

The Magicians headed toward the Keep. Ari, Janco and I followed. I thought about Bain's comment. My future would be nothing without Valek. I caught up to Bain and asked about him.

Bain gave me a stern look, and I felt his magic press against my mental barrier. I relaxed my guard and heard his voice in my mind.

Best not to talk aloud about this, child. Cahil and his men captured him two nights ago, but Cahil would not release Valek to the Councilors or Master Magicians.

I felt Bain's disapproval over Cahil's actions. And I had to quell my desire to find Cahil and skewer him with his own sword.

Cahil tried to hang Valek yesterday at dusk, but Valek escaped. Bain seemed impressed. *We have no idea where he is now.*

I thanked Bain and slowed Kiki, letting the others go ahead. I savored my relief that Valek was alive. When Ari and Janco caught up to me, I relayed the information to them.

When we reached the Council Hall, Ari and Janco headed

toward the guest quarters. Kiki picked up her pace and we joined the others.

I thought about where Valek might have gone. Back to Ixia seemed the safest and most logical course, but I knew Valek would stay nearby until Ferde was caught. That led me to consider who would be Ferde's next victim. He had been working in the Keep where there were many young female magicians just learning to control their magic. Since the full moon would rise tomorrow night, he would probably need a few days to prepare. The Master Magicians couldn't locate him with magic, but they might be able to contact the girl with him. But how to find her?

Just past the Keep's gate, the Master Magicians dismounted, handed their horses to the guards and started for the Keep's administration building. I followed, but Roze stopped me at the base of the steps.

"You're confined to your quarters. We will deal with you later," she promised.

I had no intention of obeying her, but I knew they wouldn't let me into the meeting room. So before Bain could mount the steps to the building, I touched his arm.

"The killer probably seduced one of the young first-years to come with him," I told him. "If everyone takes a barrack you can find out who's missing and try to communicate with her."

"Excellent," Bain said. "Now go rest, child. And do not worry. We will do all that we can to find the killer."

I nodded. Fatigue wrapped around me like a stone cloak, and Bain's order to rest made sense. Before heading toward my rooms, I made a slight detour to the Keep's guest suite.

My father answered the door. He crushed me in his muscular arms. "Are you all right? Did my pill work?"

"Like a charm." I kissed him on the cheek. "You saved my life."

He ducked his head. "I've made some more for you just in case."

I smiled with gratitude. Looking past his shoulder, I asked, "Where's Mother?"

"In her favorite oak tree by the pasture. She was doing so well until..." He gave me a sardonic grin.

"I know. I'll find her."

I stood at the bottom of the oak, feeling as if I'd been run over by a horse. "Mother?" I called.

"Yelena! Come up! Come up where it's safe!"

No place is safe, I thought. The events of the past two days began to overwhelm me. Too many problems, too much riding on me. My encounter with Alea proved that, even when I felt confident that I could take care of a situation, I really didn't know what I was doing. If Alea had checked me for weapons, I would be standing ankle deep in my own blood.

"Come down. I need you," I cried. I sank to the ground and wrapped my arms around my legs as tears poured from my eyes.

With a rustle and creak of branches, my mother appeared beside me. I transformed into a six-year-old child, flung myself into her arms and sobbed. She comforted me, helped me to my room, gave me a handkerchief and a glass of water. Tucking me into bed, she kissed me on my forehead.

When she went to leave, I grabbed her hand. "Please stay."

Mother smiled, took off her cloak and lay next to me. I fell asleep in her arms.

The next morning she brought me breakfast in bed. I protested about the extravagance, but she stopped me. "I have fourteen years of mothering to catch up on. Indulge me."

Even though the plate was loaded with food, I ate every bit and drained the tea. "Sweet cakes are my favorite."

"I know," she replied with a smug smile. "I asked one of the servers in the dining hall, and she remembered that every time they cooked sweet cakes your eyes would light up." She took the empty tray. "You should go back to sleep." Perl went into the other room.

I could have easily complied, but I needed to find out if the others had discovered who was missing. Unable to stay in bed, I decided to get a quick bath before finding Bain.

"Come to our suite when you're done at the bathhouse," Perl said. "Once your father told me what's been going on with this killer and the Curare, I thought of something that might help you. It may have aided you yesterday," she huffed. "I'm not a delicate sapling. You and Esau don't need to keep things from me. And that includes Valek." She put her hands on her hips, wrinkling the smooth lines of her blue-green dress.

"How—" I sputtered.

"I'm not deaf. The dining hall buzzed with conversation about you and Valek. And Valek's escape from Cahil!" She put a hand to her throat. But then she took a deep breath.

"I know I tend to overreact about some things and go running for the trees." She smiled ruefully. "Valek has the most horrible reputation, but I trust you. When you have some time, you need to educate me about him."

"Yes, Mother," I said and also promised to stop by their suite after my bath.

It was the middle of the morning so the bathhouse was almost empty. Washing, I thought about how much I would tell my mother about Valek. When I finished drying off, I changed and headed toward the guest suite.

Dax intercepted me. His usual jovial face was taut with worry, and the dark smudges under his eyes made it look as if he hadn't slept in a while.

"Have you seen Gelsi?" he asked.

"Not since the New Beginnings feast." So much had happened since that night. The semester had not gone as I had imagined. Nothing since coming to Sitia had gone as I had imagined. "Wasn't she working on some special project for Master Bloodgood?"

"Yes. She was experimenting with the Bellwood plant. But I haven't seen her in days and I can't find her anywhere."

His words struck me like Alea's knife. I gasped.

"What?" His green eyes widened in alarm.

"Plant? Where? With who?" The questions tumbled from my mouth.

"I already checked the greenhouses many times. She worked with one of the gardeners. Maybe we could ask him?"

Him. My heart twisted. I knew who Gelsi was with.

32

"Me? But I've never linked with Gelsi." Dax's drawn face took on a wild fearful expression.

I had taken Dax back to my rooms. We sat together on the couch. "Don't worry. I've only worked with her once, but you've known her for a year. I'll find her through you." I hoped. "Relax," I instructed. I took his hand in mine. "Think of her." Finding a thread of magic, I reached toward his mind.

A horrible vision of Gelsi, bloody and terrified, filled my mind. "Dax, don't imagine where she might be. Think of her at the New Beginnings feast."

The image transformed into a smiling young lady wearing a soft green gown. I felt Dax's thrill when he held her hand and guided her while they danced. I sent my magic to Gelsi, trying to see Dax from her mind.

She gazed up at him. They had always danced together at the feast, but this time felt different. Her skin tingled where he had touched her, and a warmth pulsed in her chest.

Gelsi, I called, pulling her into the memory.

What a lovely evening, she thought. *How things have changed. Dax seemed distant after that night. Preoccupied.*

Gelsi, where are you? I asked.

Shame flared. *I've been a fool. No one must know. Please tell no one.* Fear trembled through her mind.

You were deceived by a cunning sorcerer. No one will hold that against you. Where are you?

He will punish me.

She tried to pull away. I showed her Dax's concern for her. His hunt through the Keep. *Don't let your captor win*, I pleaded.

Gelsi showed me a bare room. She was naked and tied to metal spikes that had been driven into the wooden floor. Strange symbols had been painted on the floor and walls. Pain throbbed from between her legs and the multiple cuts along her arms and legs burned. He hadn't needed to drug her with Curare.

I loved him, she said. *I gave myself to him.*

Instead of the wonderful loving experience she had expected, Ferde tied her down, beat her and raped her. Then he bled her, collecting the blood in an earthen bowl.

Show me where you are, I instructed.

Beyond the room was the living area and outside I could see a courtyard with a white jade sculpture of fifteen horses.

Have faith, I said. *We'll be there.*

He'll know. He has surrounded the neighborhood with a magical shield, he knows when someone passes through and if he feels threatened, he'll complete the ritual.

Doesn't he need to wait until the full moon tonight?

No.

The note left by Alea had originally set the exchange for the full moon so everyone had not only assumed Ferde sent the note, but that the phase of the moon was critical for the ritual.

He had to move many times, Gelsi said. *I had thought it exciting. I didn't know he was the one the Masters were searching for. He led me to believe he was on a secret mission for the Master Magicians.*

We'll find a way, I promised.

Hurry.

I withdrew my awareness and sat back. Dax stared at me in horror, he had been able to see and hear our conversation.

"She will need you when this is over," I told him.

"We need to tell the Masters—"

"No." My mind raced through options.

"But he's strong. You heard Gelsi. He has a shield," Dax said.

"All the more reason to go alone. They have been searching for him and he knows them. I think I can get through undetected."

"How?"

"There's no time to explain. But Gelsi will need you close by. Can you meet me in the market in an hour?"

"Of course."

I jumped up and started gathering supplies.

Dax hesitated at the door. "Yelena?"

I looked at him.

"What happens if you don't stop him?" Fear shone in his green eyes.

"Then we find Valek. Otherwise, Sitia will be Ferde's."

Dax swallowed his fright and nodded before leaving. I packed my equipment and changed my clothes. Dressed in a plain brown tunic and pants I would blend in with the regular citizens of the Citadel. Covering my disguise with my cloak, I stopped at my parent's suite on the way out.

Leif sat with them in the living room. I ignored him. "Father, do you have those extra pills?" I asked, hoping he knew I wanted the Theobroma.

He nodded in understanding and went to retrieve them. While I waited, Mother remembered her little invention she had told me about. She handed me a strange device made of tubes and rubber and explained how to work it.

"Just in case," she said.

"This is great," I said. "You were right about it being useful."

She beamed. "That's what every mother wants to hear."

Leif had said nothing, but I could feel his penetrating stare as if he tasted my intentions.

Esau handed me the pills. "Are you coming to lunch with us?"

"No. I have something I need to do. I'll catch up with you later," I said, giving my father a hug and my mother a kiss on her cheek.

A queasy feeling rolled in my stomach. Perhaps I should tell the Master Magicians about Ferde and Gelsi? After all, it had been only pure chance that saved me from Alea. I was still discovering what I could do with my magic. And now that I had been expelled, would I be able to fully explore my potential?

My mother stopped me just past the door.

"Here," she said, handing me my fire amulet. "I think you need this. Remember what you endured to win it."

I opened my mouth to protest, but she shook her head, "I want it back." She squeezed me in a tight hug for a moment.

Examining the scarlet prize in the sunlight, I marveled at Perl's empathy. I tucked the amulet into my pocket and set a brisk pace for the Citadel.

After I had passed the Keep's gate, I heard pounding footsteps behind me. I whirled, drawing my bow. Leif halted a few feet away. His machete hung from his belt, but he made no move to grab it.

"Not now, Leif," I said, turning, but he clasped my shoulder and spun me around to face him.

"I know where you're going," he said.

"Bully for you." I shrugged his hand off. "Then you know time is of the essence. Go back to the Keep." I started to walk.

"If I do, I'll tell the Masters what you're doing."

"Truly? You're not very good at telling."

"This time I won't hesitate."

Seeing the stubborn set to his broad shoulders, I stopped. "What do you want?"

"To come along."

"Why?"

"You'll need me."

"Considering how helpful you were in the jungle fourteen years ago, I think I'm better off on my own." I spat the words at him.

He cringed, but the obstinacy remained in his face. "Either include me in your plans, or I'll follow you and ruin them."

I clamped down on my sudden rage. I didn't have time for this. "Fine, but let me warn you that you're going have to let me inside your mind in order for you to get through Ferde's shield."

His face paled, but he nodded and fell into step with me as I hurried to the market. Dax waited there. I left Leif with him and hunted for Fisk. He helped a woman barter for a bolt of cloth, but he finished as soon as he recognized me.

"Lovely Yelena, do you need help?" he asked.

I told him what I needed.

He smiled and said, "Sounds like fun, but—"

"It's going to cost me," I finished for him.

He raced off to gather his friends.

Once Fisk had assembled about twenty children, I explained my plan to them. "Make sure you don't go within a block of the courtyard until you hear the signal. Understand?" I asked. The children nodded. When I felt satisfied they knew what to do, Fisk's friends scattered and went to get into position. Fisk led Leif and me toward the white jade statue. Dax waited in a side alley far enough away not to touch Ferde's shield, but within sight of the second-story windows.

I kept my mind open, seeking for the edge of Ferde's magical barrier. About half a block away from the courtyard, Leif touched my arm, stopping me.

"It's just ahead," he whispered.

"How do you know?"

"I feel a wall of fire. Don't you?"

"No."

"Then it's good that I came."

I glared, but had no reply. Fisk watched us, waiting for our signal.

This was not the time for a fight. I looked at Leif. "You have to open your mind to me," I told him. "You have to trust me."

He nodded without hesitating. "Do it."

I pulled power to me, spinning it around me like a huge curtain. Reaching out, I made contact with Fisk's mind. "Think of your parents," I instructed, hoping this would work.

The young boy closed his eyes and imagined his parents. I linked to their minds through Fisk then reached for Leif's.

Leif's mind resembled a black labyrinth of pain. Guilt, shame and anger twisted together. I understood why Moon Man wanted to help him, but I felt a mean satisfaction at Leif's remorse.

Pushing his dark thoughts aside, I replaced them with Fisk's father's concerns about finding work and supporting his family. I pulled in Fisk's mother's thoughts about her sister's ailing health into my own mind. Holding their personalities and thoughts in Leif's and my mind, I gave Fisk the signal.

He barked like a dog. Soon other barks echoed on the marble walls in reply. Fisk's friends would begin the distraction, playing tag and running in and out of the courtyard and Ferde's magical shield as many times as they could.

I took Fisk and Leif's hands and the three of us continued on to the courtyard. As we crossed the barrier, I felt the probing heat of an annoyed and powerful magician. He scanned our thoughts, determined we were one of the local beggar families and dismissed us.

When we reached the statue, I released Fisk's parents. They would have an unusual story to tell their friends about how they had felt as if they were in two places at once.

"That's half the battle," I said to Leif.

He wouldn't meet my eyes. His face was flushed with shame. Irritated, I snapped, "Now is not the time for this."

He nodded, but still wouldn't meet my gaze. Fisk ran off to join his friends in the game, giving us a few more minutes to get into the house.

We approached the house from a side street. The door was locked. I pulled my diamond pick and my tension wrench from my backpack and began working on the lock. Once I had aligned the pins, the lock's tumbler turned and the door swung inward. I heard a surprised huff from Leif. Then we stepped inside the foyer and closed the door. I shoved my picks into my pocket.

Walking without sound, we entered a living area. The normal furniture and decorations seemed out of place. I guess I had expected something wild and weird; something that reflected a killer's mind.

Leif held his machete and I gripped my bow, but I knew they would not protect us. Magic filled the house. It pressed against my skin and I started to sweat. The sounds of the children faded and we heard the light tread of feet from the floor above us.

Connecting with Gelsi's mind, I saw Ferde approach her. He held a brown stone bowl and a long dagger. He wore his red mask and nothing else. She had been fascinated with the tattoos and symbols on his sculpted physique, but now she eyed them with revulsion.

I'm downstairs, I told her. *What's he going to do?*

He wants more blood. Wait or else he will kill me if he hears you.

I had to physically hold on to Leif when Gelsi started moaning with pain. Handing him one of Esau's Theobroma pills, I motioned that he should put it into his mouth. I placed my pack on the floor and quietly removed Perl's device from my backpack.

With my bow in one hand and the device in the other, I

waited at the bottom of the staircase with Leif. Finally, we heard Ferde moving again.

He's gone, Gelsi said with relief.

My stomach tightened with apprehension. I pulled power to me to strengthen my mental defenses. A mistake. Ferde felt the draw and I could sense his growing alarm.

"Now," I whispered to Leif. We rushed up the stairs, taking them two at a time.

Ferde waited for us on the landing. We skittered to a stop on the top step. An amused smile quirked Ferde's lips before he pressed them together with concentration. Revulsion and terror welled up my throat at the sight of him, and I thought I would vomit as Tula's horrible memories filled my mind.

The wave of his magic crashed against us. I grabbed the railing to keep from plummeting down the stairs. Leif jerked beside me but remained upright. Was that it? I glanced at Ferde. His eyes were closed. Moving toward him, I raised Perl's device.

"Yelena, stop," Leif said. His voice sounded odd.

I looked at Leif in time to see him swing his machete. Jumping back, I dropped Perl's device and blocked Leif's weapon with my bow.

"What are you—" I tried to ask, but with the pill between my teeth made it hard to talk.

Leif spat his pill out and moved to strike again. "When those men took my perfect baby sister, I thought I would reclaim my parents' undivided attention." Leif's machete sliced toward my neck.

I ducked. Had his shame and guilt all been an act? Was he working with Ferde this whole time? Pushing aside my stunned disbelief, I jabbed him in the stomach with the end of my bow. He hunched over and grunted. Magic pressed on my skin and Leif straightened with renewed vigor. But whose magic?

"Instead, I had to compete with a perfect ghost," Leif said and attacked.

Chunks of wood flew through the air as I blocked his wide blade. It was only a matter of time before he would destroy my bow and I was running out of room in the narrow landing. There was a hallway to my left, and an open doorway on my right.

"Mother refused to leave our house, and Father was never home. All because of you." Leif puffed with effort. "And you stayed away just to spite me. Didn't you? You're my strangler fig, and now it's time to chop you down."

Ferde had disappeared. I felt Gelsi's brief cry of alarm as Ferde entered her room. He planned to finish the ritual while Leif kept me occupied. And it was working.

With a loud crack, my bow splintered in two. Leif advanced and I formed a magical shield, but he walked right through. As a last-ditch effort I sent out my mental awareness, entering his dark mind.

Hate and self-loathing filled his thoughts. I felt another presence in Leif's head. Ferde had Story Weaver abilities and he had brought out all of Leif's raw emotions and used them against me.

As Leif sliced his machete toward me, I stepped to the left, bringing my awareness back. I couldn't defend myself physically while mentally gone; I just wasn't that strong. Leif pulled his weapon back and thrust at me again. I had nothing left to defend myself. Perl's device was out of reach.

Gelsi's pleas for help burned through my thoughts like a hot poker, energizing me. I projected myself into Leif's mind, taking control of his body like I had done with Goel. Halting the tip of his machete a mere inch from my stomach, I made Leif step back.

Pushing through the darkness of Leif's mind, I found the young boy who had watched his sister being kidnapped; untainted with the feelings of guilt and hate. At that moment he held only curiosity and disbelief. Two emotions that Ferde wouldn't be able to use against me. I sent Leif into a deep dreamless sleep. He crumpled to the floor as I went back to my body. Stopping Ferde was paramount; I would deal with Leif later. I hoped.

Picking up Perl's device, I sprinted down the hall, searching for Gelsi. Only the last door on the left had been closed. Locked. I yanked my picks out and unlocked the door. My fastest time yet. Janco would be proud.

The door swung inward and I stumbled into the room. Ferde had his hands around Gelsi's throat. I watched in horror as all animation left her face. Her eyes turned sightless and flat.

Ferde shouted and thrust his fists toward the ceiling in celebration.

33

Too late. With my heart sinking, I watched Ferde rejoice. But then I saw a strange shadow rise from Gelsi's body. Before logic could overrule, I dove. Knocking Ferde aside, I inhaled this shadow, gathering Gelsi's soul inside me. It felt as if the world paused for a moment so I could tuck her into a safe corner of my mind. Then, *snap.* Movement resumed and I fell on top of Ferde. Perl's device flew from my hand. It landed next to the wall.

After a brief struggle, Ferde pinned me to the floor, sitting on my stomach. "That's my soul," he said. "Give it back."

"It doesn't belong to you."

Yelena? I felt Gelsi's confusion in my mind.

Hold on, I told her.

Ferde reached toward my neck. I grabbed his hands, and using his forward momentum I pushed him further off balance with my left knee. I planted my left foot on the floor and twisted my hips, rolling him off me. I jumped up and assumed a fighting stance.

Ferde smiled and regained his feet with a panther-quick grace. "We are well matched. But I think I have the advantage."

I braced for an attack, but he didn't move. His red tattoos

began to glow until they burned my eyes. He caught my gaze with his own, staring at me with his dark brown eyes.

Ferde's face transformed into Reyad's. My world spun and I found myself back in Reyad's bedroom in Ixia, tied to the bed and watching Reyad dig through his chest of torture devices. After an initial moment of panic and fear that I would be forced to relive Reyad's torture, the scene jumped ahead to Reyad's stunned expression as hot blood gushed from his throat, soaking me.

You are a killer, too, Ferde said in my mind. Images of the other men I had killed flashed by. *You have the power to collect souls without the need for symbols and blood. Why do you think Reyad still haunts you? You have taken his soul, your first of many more. I see the future and yours doesn't improve.*

The images spun dizzyingly and Irys's cold eyes stared at me as I watched Valek swing from a noose. Leif's hatred pounded in my mind along with Cahil's desire to have me executed. The Commander smiling in satisfaction at my trial for committing espionage, because he had gotten what he wanted from me and now I would no longer be a problem for Ixia.

Look at what the Master Magicians did to that Soulfinder long ago, Ferde said.

A man who had been chained to a post was set on fire. His screams of pain vibrated in my mind. Ferde held that image until the man's skin had burned away. I struggled to regain control over my mind, but Ferde's magic equaled a Master and I couldn't push him away.

The Soulfinder only wanted to help, bringing the dead back to life for their family and friends. It wasn't his fault they were different when they awoke, Ferde said in my mind. *Panic and fear of the unknown condemned him just like the Council will condemn you, too. All that I have shown you will be your fate. I see it in your story threads. Moon Man isn't your true Story Weaver, I am.*

His logic was persuasive. He understood my desire to find my place. It was next to him. Soulfinder and Soulstealer.

Yes. I'll change your story and the Council won't burn you alive. Just give me Gelsi's soul.

A small corner of my mind resisted, yelling for action. *Stealing souls is wrong*, I said. *I shouldn't.*

Then why have you been gifted with the ability if you're not supposed to use it? Ferde asked.

I should use it to help people.

That's what the other Soulfinder wanted to do. See what happened to him.

Focusing my thoughts became difficult. Ferde's control began to spread and soon he would take Gelsi from me.

Give me the girl. If I pull her from you, you will die. You'll be the first victim of my new administration. Your parents will be the next two.

Images of Perl being mutilated and Esau being hacked into pieces filled my mind. Blood splashed as I watched in helpless horror.

Save them and you can have complete freedom for the first time in your life.

His strong spell enticed me. I found myself agreeing with him. Freedom. Ferde sent a wave of pleasure through my body. I moaned as an intoxicating mix of joy and gratification flushed through me. I wanted to give Gelsi to him. But he went too far when my soul filled with contentment. Because I already owned that feeling whenever Valek held me in his arms.

I swayed on my feet and sweated with the effort to keep Ferde from taking Gelsi. He had realized his mistake and launched a mental attack to get her soul. Wrapping my arms tight around my chest, I collapsed to the ground. Fire burned inside me. Tears and sweat stung my eyes, but I spotted Perl's device nearby before pain twisted my body. All I needed was a second.

Trouble, love? Valek asked.

I need your immunity to magic.

Yours.

A resistance to magic, unlike any barrier I could form, grew in my mind, blocking Ferde's control. I opened my eyes.

"You almost had me," I said to Ferde. I picked up Perl's device and stood on unsteady legs.

Ferde's surprise didn't last long. "No matter. The effort to repel me has weakened you."

In two strides, he closed the distance between us. His hands wrapped around my throat. He was right. While I didn't have the power to stop him, I could do something else. As his thumbs pressed into my windpipe, I lifted Perl's device.

Black and white spots began to dance in front of my eyes. Before Ferde could react to my movement, I aimed the nozzle at him and pumped the rubber ball, spraying Curare into his face. Invented to apply perfume, Perl's little device worked like a charm.

Ferde's face froze in horror. I pushed his hands away and he fell to the ground.

There will be others, was Ferde's last thought before the drug paralyzed his body and his magic.

Once satisfied that he was frozen, I entered his mind. Trapped within the darkness were all the souls he had stolen. I released them into the sky. Feeling a rush of movement, I briefly joined the freed souls, soaking in their happiness and joy, then I returned to my body.

Without a moment to lose, I scooted over to Gelsi. Resting the tips of my fingers on her neck, I concentrated on her injuries and repaired them, including the cuts along her arms and legs.

Go back, I told Gelsi.

She had huddled in my mind, frightened and confused during the battle with Ferde, but now she understood. Her body bloomed with life, and she drew in a long shaky breath.

I cut her bonds with my switchblade, and, after spitting out the soggy Theobroma pill, I lay next to her, feeling exhausted and spent. She clung to me. My throat blazed with each lungful of air.

After a long while, I summoned the energy to stand, pulling Gelsi with me. We found Gelsi's clothes and I helped her into them. Before guiding her down to the living room to rest on a comfortable couch, I waved a hand out one of the secondstory windows. Dax would be here soon.

"I will be expelled," she whispered.

I shook my head. "You'll be smothered with concern and understanding. And given all the time you need to recover."

Once Dax arrived to take my place next to Gelsi, I went back up to the landing where I had left Leif. Reluctance pulled at my legs. It felt as if they had been pricked with Curare.

I didn't have the strength to untie his twisted thoughts. My promise to Moon Man would have to wait a while longer. I drew Leif into a lighter sleep so he would rouse after I left. Ferde's last comment had made me realize that I still had some unfinished business to attend to.

Dax had a protective arm around Gelsi when I went downstairs.

"I sent a message to Master Bloodgood. The Masters are on their way with a battalion of guards to take Ferde to the Keep's prison," Dax said.

"Then I better go. I'm *supposed* to be confined to my quarters."

Dax shook his head. "Second Magician knows what you did."

"All the more reason not to be here when they arrive."

"But—"

I waved and hurried out the door, slinging my backpack over one shoulder. Since I had been expelled from the Keep's program, I knew I would soon be kicked out of my rooms. I planned to be long gone before giving Roze the satisfaction of evicting me.

Fisk ran over to me when I crossed the courtyard.

"Did we help?" Fisk asked. "Is everything okay?"

"You did great." I rummaged in my pack and handed Fisk all the Sitian coins I had. "Distribute these to your troops."

He smiled and dashed away.

A bone-deep weariness settled on me as I made my way through the Citadel. My surroundings blurred and I walked in a daze. When I passed the Council Hall, the group of beggars, who always hovered near the steps, began to follow me.

"Sorry. I can't help you today," I called over my shoulder. The group returned to the Hall, but one persisted. I turned around. "I said—"

"Lovely lady, spare a copper?" the man asked.

Dirt streaked his face and his hair hung in greasy clumps. His clothes were torn and filthy, and he smelled like horse manure. But he couldn't disguise those penetrating sapphire-blue eyes from me.

"Can't you spare a copper for the man who just saved your life?" Valek asked.

"I'm broke. I had to pay off the distraction. Those kids don't work cheap. What—"

"Unity fountain. A quarter hour." Valek returned to the steps and joined the other beggars.

I continued toward the Keep, but once I was out of sight of the Council Hall, I took a side street and headed to the Unity Fountain. The jade sphere with its holes and other spheres nestled inside it shone in the sunlight. The water spray from the circle of waterspouts sparkled in the cool air. My relief from knowing that Valek was unharmed warred with my concern that he should be far away from the Citadel.

A quick movement in a shadow caught my attention. I wandered over to the dark recess of a doorway and joined Valek, embracing him for a fierce moment before pulling back.

"Thank you for helping me against Ferde," I said. "Now go home before you get caught."

Valek smiled. "And miss all the fun? No, love. I'm going with you on your errand."

I could only produce a muted surprise. Valek and I didn't have a mental connection like the one I'd had with Irys, yet he knew my thoughts, and, when I had needed his help, he had always been there.

"There's no way I can convince you to go to Ixia?" My brief spurt of energy on seeing Valek safe faded.

"None."

"All right. Although I reserve the right to say, 'I told you so' should you get captured." I tried to say it in a stern tone, but my battered and tired soul was so filled with relief that Valek was coming with me that the words turned playful.

"Agreed." Valek's eyes lit up, anticipating the challenge.

34

Valek and I decided on the best course of action, and arranged to meet again at the edge of the Avibian Plains.

When I reached the Keep, I went straight to my rooms to pack. While I determined what to take along, someone knocked on my door. Out of habit I looked for my bow before realizing it had been destroyed by Leif. Instead, I grabbed my switchblade.

I relaxed a bit when I opened the door. Irys stood there, looking hesitant. Stepping back, I invited her in.

"I have some news," Irys said. When I just stared at her, she continued, "Ferde has been taken to the Keep's cells, and the Council has revoked your expulsion. They want you to stay so you can fully explore your magical abilities."

"Who would teach me?"

Irys glanced at the ground. "It would be your choice."

"I'll think about it."

Irys nodded and turned to go. Then stopped. "I'm sorry, Yelena. I had no trust in your abilities and yet you achieved what four Master Magicians could not."

There was still a faint link between us, and I felt Irys's uncertainty and her loss of confidence. She questioned her ability to handle future difficult situations. She felt her beliefs on what was needed to solve a problem had been proven wrong.

"In this situation, magic was not the solution," I told her. "It was the lack of magic that allowed me to beat Ferde. And I couldn't have done that without Valek."

She considered my words for a moment and seemed to make a decision.

"I propose a partnership," Irys said.

"A partnership?" I asked.

"I believe you no longer need a teacher, but a partner to help you discover just how strong a Soulfinder you are."

I winced at the title. "Do you think I'm one?"

"I've suspected, but didn't want to really believe it. An automatic response just like your cringe just now. And, it seems I need some guidance. I've found that the Sitian way is not always appropriate. Perhaps you could help me with that?"

"Are you sure you would want to learn the 'rush into a situation and hope for the best' method?"

"As long as you want to discover more about being a Soulfinder. Is it really against the Ethical Code? Perhaps the Code needs to be updated. And could you be considered a Master, or would you have to take the Master's test first?"

"The Master test? I've heard some horror stories." My throat began to tighten. I swallowed with some difficulty.

"Rumors, mostly. To discourage the students so that only those who feel confident in their abilities will be brave enough to ask to take the test."

"And if they're not strong enough?"

"They won't succeed, but they'll learn the full extent of their powers. This is better than being surprised later."

Irys fell silent. I felt her mind reaching toward mine. *Do we have a deal?* she asked in my mind.

I'll think about it. A lot has happened.

So it has, she agreed. *Let me know when you're ready.* Irys left my rooms.

I closed the door. My mind shuffled through the possibility of exploring my powers versus the risk of being condemned as a Soulfinder. Despite having to worry about poison in the Commander's food, I began to think life in Ixia had been easier. After my errand, as Valek so casually called it, I had some choices on where to go next. Nice to have choices. Again.

I moved through my rooms, checking if I missed anything. I had packed the valmur statue for Valek, the rest of my Sitian coins, my northern uniform and an extra set of clothes. My armoire remained filled with my apprentice's robes and a couple of Nutty's skirt/pants. Papers and books piled on my desk, and the room smelled of Apple Berry and Lavender. My stomach squeezed with longing and with a sudden realization. These rooms in the Keep had turned into my home, despite my resistance.

Shouldering my pack, I felt the weight of it drag on me as I left. Stopping at the Keep's guest quarters on my way, I visited my parents. I could hear Esau in the kitchen and Perl had a strange expression on her face. Her hand touched her neck so I knew something had upset her. She made me promise to stay for tea, pulling my backpack off, and she hovered over me until I sat in one of the pink overstuffed chairs.

Calling to Esau to bring another cup, Perl perched in the seat next to me as if she would spring into action should I decide to leave. Esau brought in the tea tray. She jumped up and handed me one of the steaming cups.

Seeming to be satisfied that I was anchored to my chair, at least until I finished the tea, Perl said, "You're leaving. Aren't you?" She shook her head before I could answer. "Not that you would tell me. You treat me like a delicate flower. I'll have you know that the most delicate flowers often produce the strongest scent when crushed." She stared at me.

"I have some unfinished business to attend to. I'll be back," I said, but the weak response failed to soothe her.

"Don't lie to me."

"I wasn't lying."

"All right. Then don't lie to yourself." She eyed my bulging pack that she had set on the floor. "Send us word when you're settled in Ixia, and we'll come visit," she said in a matter-of-fact tone. "Though, probably not until the hot season. I don't like the cold."

"Mother!" I stood and almost spilled my drink.

Esau nodded, seeming nonplussed by the topic of our conversation. "I'd like to find the Mountain Laurel that grows near the ice pack. I read somewhere that the plant can cure Kronik's Cough. Be interesting to find out."

"You're not concerned that I might return to Ixia?" I asked my parents.

"Considering the week you had," my father said, "we're just happy you're alive. Besides, we trust your judgment."

"If I do go to Ixia, will you promise to visit often?"

They promised. Not wanting to prolong the goodbyes, I snatched my pack and left.

Apple? Kiki asked with a hopeful tone.

No, but I'll get you some peppermints. I went into the barn's tack room to search for the bag of candy. I took two and returned to Kiki.

After she sucked the candy down, I asked her, *Ready to go?*

Yes. Saddle?

Not this time. The Keep provided tack for the students, but it was understood that once a student graduated, he bought his own equipment.

I pulled the step stool over and Kiki snorted. *I know. I know,* I said. *No step stool in wild. But I'm tired.*

In fact, what little energy I had left leaked away with an

alarming speed. Kiki and I didn't encounter any trouble at either the Keep's or the Citadel's gates. We took the road through the valley for a while. I refused to look back at the Citadel. I planned to come back, didn't I? Today wouldn't be the last time I saw the pastel colors of the sunset reflected in the white marble walls. Right?

As the light faded from the sky, I heard the pounding of hooves on the road behind me. Kiki stopped and spun to face the newcomer.

Topaz, she said with pleasure.

Though by the molten anger and murderous expression on Cahil's face, I knew this encounter would be far from pleasant.

"Where do you think you're going?" he demanded.

"That's not your concern."

Cahil's face turned a livid red as he sputtered in astonishment. "Not *my* concern? Not *my* concern?"

I saw him rein in his temper. Then in a deadly rumble, he said, "You're the heart mate of the most wanted criminal in Sitia. Your whereabouts are of the utmost concern to me. In fact, I'm going to personally see to it that I know exactly where you are at all times." He whistled.

I heard a rush of movement and turned in time to see Cahil's men move into defensive positions behind me. Trying to conserve my strength, I hadn't scanned the road ahead with my magic. Hadn't believed I would need to. Silly me.

Did you smell them, Kiki? I asked.

No. Upwind. Go past?

Not yet.

Looking back at Cahil, I demanded, "What do you want?"

"Playing the simpleton to delay the inevitable, Yelena? I guess it has worked for you in the past. You certainly played me for a fool," he said with an eerie calmness. "Convincing me *and* First Magician that you weren't a spy, using your magic to make me trust you. I fell for it all."

"Cahil, I—"

"What *I* want is to kill Valek. Besides getting revenge for the murder of my family, I will be able to show the Council my abilities and they will finally support me."

"You had Valek before and lost him. What makes you think you can kill him this time?"

"Your heart mate will exchange his life for yours."

"You're going to need more men to capture me."

"Truly? Take another look."

I glanced over my shoulder. Cahil's men had kept their distance from Kiki's hindquarters, but, even in the twilight, I could see that each one held a blowpipe to his mouth, aiming at me.

"The darts are treated with Curare," Cahil said. "An excellent Sitian weapon. You won't get far."

Fear replaced annoyance as my heart rate increased. I had some Theobroma in my pack, but I knew if I tried to take it off my back, I would become a pin cushion for Cahil's men.

"Will you cooperate or do I need to have you immobilized?" Cahil sounded as if he asked if I would like some tea.

Ghost, Kiki said.

Before I could understand what Kiki meant, Valek sauntered into our group from the tall grass of the plains. Everyone froze for a second in shock. Cahil gaped.

"That's an interesting choice, love," Valek said. "You'll need some time to think it over. In the meantime…" Valek held his arms away from his body as he moved closer to Cahil. He had changed from his beggar disguise into the plain brown tunic and pants that the local citizens wore. He appeared to be unarmed, but I knew better, and, it seemed, so did Cahil who transferred Topaz's reins to his left hand and pulled his sword.

"Let's see if I have this right," Valek continued, seeming unconcerned about Cahil's sword a few feet away. "You want revenge for your family. Understandable. But you should know that the royal family is not *your* family. One thing I have learned over the years is to know my enemy. The royal bloodline ended the day the Commander took control of Ixia. I made sure of that."

"You lie!" Cahil urged Topaz forward, lunging at Valek with his sword.

Stepping to the side with grace and speed, Valek avoided being trampled and cut.

When Cahil turned Topaz for another charge, I said, "It makes sense. Valek wouldn't leave a job unfinished."

He pulled back on the bridle, stopping in disbelief. "Your love for him has damaged your senses."

"And your hunger for power has affected your intelligence. Your men are using you, yet you refuse to see the obvious."

Cahil shook his head. "I won't listen to any more lies. My men are loyal. They obey me or else they will be punished. Goel's death helped me to reinforce that lesson."

I recognized that flatness in his pale blue eyes. "*You* killed Goel."

He smiled. "My men have pledged their lives to me. I committed no crime." He brandished his sword. "Ready," he called to his men. "Aim and—"

"Think about this before you gloat about *your* men, Cahil. They look to Captain Marrok for approval before following your orders. They gave you a sword that was too heavy for you, and failed to properly train you with it. You are supposed to be related to the King, who was a powerful magician. Why don't you have any magic?"

"I—" Cahil hesitated.

His men glanced at each other in either consternation or confusion. I couldn't tell, but it broke their concentration. And in that moment, Valek leaped onto Kiki's back behind me. She took off into the plains without being told. I grabbed her mane as Valek's arms encircled my waist, and Kiki broke into her gust-of-wind gait.

I heard Cahil yell fire, and thought I heard the whiz of a dart near my ear, but we were soon out of range. Kiki traveled twice the distance of a normal gallop without any obvious effort. When the moon had reached its apex, Kiki slowed then stopped.

Smell gone, she said.

Valek and I slid off her back. I inspected her for injuries before she snorted with impatience and moved away to graze.

I shivered in the cold air, searching my body for darts before wrapping my cloak tighter. "That was close."

"Not really," Valek said, pulling me toward him. "We distracted the men so when Wannabe King gave the order they didn't have time to aim."

Valek felt warm even though he wasn't wearing a cloak. Seeming to read my thoughts, he said, "I'll share yours." He smiled with a mischievous delight. "But first you need a fire, food and some sleep."

I shook my head. "I need you." It didn't take me long to convince him. Once I had divested him of his clothes, he elected to join me in my cloak.

I woke to the delightful smell of roasting meat. Squinting in the bright sunlight, I saw Valek crouched near a fire. He had set up a spit of meat over the glowing embers.

"Breakfast?" I asked as my stomach rumbled.

"Dinner. You've slept all day."

I sat up. "You should have woken me. What if Cahil finds us?"

"Doubtful with all this magic in the air." Valek peered into the sky, scenting the wind. "Does it bother you?"

I opened my mind to the power surrounding us. The Sandseed's protective magic tried to invade and confuse Valek's thoughts, but his immunity deflected the strands of power with ease. The magic seemed indifferent to my presence.

"No." I told Valek about my distant relationship to the Sand-seed clan. "If I came close to their village with the intent to harm them, I think the protection would attack me." Then I thought about Moon Man's magical abilities and his scimitar. "Either that or one of their Story Weavers would."

Valek considered. "How long will it take us to reach the Daviian Plateau?"

"It depends on Kiki. If she decides to use her gust-of-wind gait, we could be there in a few hours."

"Gust-of-wind? Is that what you call it? I've never seen a horse run that fast before."

I mulled over Valek's comment. "She only does it when we're in the plains. Perhaps it's connected to the Sandseed's magic."

Valek shrugged. "Faster is better. The faster we can take care of Alea, the better."

But exactly how we would take care of Alea remained the real question. I knew she would be a threat to me if she had survived her injury, yet I didn't want to kill her. Perhaps turning her over to the Sandseeds would be enough. I thought about Moon Man's remarks about the Daviian Vermin, and realized that Ferde's comment about the existence of others might not have been about Alea coming after me, but about the other Daviians.

Valek pulled the meat from the fire and handed the spit to me. "Eat. You need your strength."

I sniffed the unidentifiable lump. "What is it?"

He laughed. "You're better off not knowing."

"Poisons?"

"You tell me," he teased.

I took an experimental bite. The juicy meat had an odd earthy taste. Some type of rodent, I thought, but no poisons.

When I had finished my supper, we began to pack up our meager supplies.

"Valek, after we deal with Alea, you must promise to return to Ixia."

He grinned. "Why would I do that? I'm beginning to enjoy the climate. I might build a summer home here."

"It's that cocky attitude that got you into trouble in the first place."

"No, love. It was you. If you hadn't gotten yourself captured by Goel, I wouldn't have tipped my hand to the Wannabe King."

"You didn't tip your hand. I'm afraid I did that when I was fighting with Cahil."

"Defending my honor again?" he asked.

Back in Ixia, I had inadvertently exposed one of his undercover operations by standing up for him. "Yes."

He shook his head in amazement. "I know you love me, so you can stop proving it. I really don't care what Wannabe King thinks of me."

I thought about Cahil. "Valek, I'm sorry for believing you killed Goel."

He waved away my apology. "You would have been right. I went back to take care of him for you, but he had beaten me to it." Valek's angular features grew serious. "The Wannabe King remains a problem."

I nodded. "One that *I'll* deal with."

"Now who's cocky?"

I started to protest, but Valek stopped me with a kiss. When he pulled away, I noticed that Kiki's head was up and her ears pointed forward.

Smell? I asked her. Then I heard the sound of hoof beats, heading toward us.

Rusalka, Kiki said. *Sad Man.*

My first reaction was annoyance that Leif had followed us.

But the thought that, if he could find us, then so could Cahil filled me with apprehension.

Anyone else? I asked.

No.

Valek disappeared into the tall grass just as Leif's horse seemed to materialize from a cloud of dust.

Leif's green eyes were wide with shock. "She's never done that before."

My annoyance transformed to amusement. Rusalka's black coat gleamed with sweat, but she didn't appear to be stressed.

"I call that Kiki's gust-of-wind gait," I told Leif. "Is Rusalka a sandseed horse?"

He nodded. Before he could say another word, I saw a blur of motion to his left as Valek leaped out of the grass and knocked Leif from his horse. They landed together with Valek on top of Leif's chest. He held Leif's machete to Leif's throat as my brother struggled to get his breath.

"What are you doing here?" Valek asked.

"Come. To find. Yelena," Leif said between gasps.

"Why?"

By this time, I'd recovered from my surprise. "It's all right, Valek. He's my brother."

Valek moved the blade away, but remained on top of him. Leif's face twisted into an expression of astonished terror.

"Valek? You have no smell. No aura," Leif said.

"Is he a simpleton?" Valek asked me.

I grinned. "No." I pulled Valek from Leif. "His magic can sense a person's soul. Your immunity must be blocking his power." I bent over Leif and examined him, looking for broken bones with my magic. I didn't find any serious injuries.

"Are you all right?" I asked Leif.

He sat up and glanced nervously at Valek. "That depends."

"Don't worry about him, he's overprotective."

Valek harrumphed. "If you could keep out of trouble for one

day, protecting you wouldn't be so instinctive." He rubbed his leg. "Or so painful."

Leif had recovered from his shock and stood.

My annoyance returned. "Why are you here?" I asked.

He looked at Valek then at the ground. "It was something Mother said."

I waited.

"She told me that you were lost again. And only the brother that had searched for you for fourteen years could find you."

"*How* did you find me?"

Leif gestured a bit wildly at his horse. "Kiki had found Topaz in the plains, so I thought, since Rusalka was bred by the Sand-seeds, I asked her to find Kiki. And… And…"

"She found us very fast." I mulled over what Leif had said about our mother. "Why does Perl think I'm lost? And why send you? You weren't any help the last time." Now, I had to suppress the urge to punch him. He had almost killed me with his machete at Ferde's house.

Leif cringed with guilt. "I don't know why she sent me."

I was about to tell him to go home, when Moon Man walked into sight. "A good guy," I said to Valek before he could attack him.

"This seems to be quite the meeting place," Valek muttered under his breath.

When Moon Man came closer, I asked, "No mysterious arrival? No coalescing from a sunray? Where's the paint?" The scars on his arms and legs stood out against his dark skin, and he wore a pair of short pants.

"It is no fun when you already know those tricks," Moon Man said. "Besides, Ghost would have killed me if I had suddenly appeared."

"Ghost?" I asked.

Moon Man pointed to Valek. "Kiki's name for him. It makes sense," he said, seeing the look of confusion on my face. "To magical beings, we see the world through our magic. We see him with our eyes, but cannot see him with our magic. So he is like a ghost to us."

Valek listened to Moon Man. Although expressionless, I could tell by the rigid set to Valek's shoulders that he was prepared to strike.

"Another relative?" Valek asked.

A broad smile stretched Moon Man's lips. "Yes. I am her mother's uncle's wife's third cousin."

"He's a Story Weaver, a magician of the Sandseed clan," I explained. "And what are you doing here?"

Moon Man's playfulness faded from his face. "You are on *my* lands. I could ask you the same thing, but I already know why *you* have come. I came to make sure you keep your promise."

"What promise?" Leif and Valek asked at the same time.

I waved the question away. "I will, but not now. We need—"

"I know what you intend to do. You will not succeed with that unless you untangle yourself," Moon Man said.

"Me? But I thought you said…" I stopped. He had made me promise to untie Leif, but then I remembered that Moon Man had said our lives twisted together. But what did helping Leif have to do with going after Alea? "Why won't I succeed?" I asked.

Moon Man refused to answer.

"Do you have any more cryptic advice?" I asked.

He held out his hands. One toward Leif and the other to me.

Valek huffed in either amusement or annoyance, I couldn't tell, but he said, "Looks like a family affair. I'll be close by if you need me, love."

I studied Leif. His reaction to the Story Weaver the last time we had met him had been one of fear. Now, he stepped forward and grabbed Moon Man's hand, shooting me a look of stub-born determination.

"Let's finish this," Leif said, challenging me.

35

I slid my hand into Moon Man's. My world melted as the warm magic of the Story Weaver took control of my senses.

We traveled to the Illiais Jungle to the place Leif had hidden while watching Mogkan kidnap me over fourteen years ago. The three of us viewed the events through Leif's eyes and felt his emotions. In essence, becoming him.

A mean approval that Yelena got what she deserved for not staying close to him spiked Leif's heart. But when the strange man put her to sleep, and pulled his pack and sword from under a bush, sudden fear of getting taken by the man kept Leif in his hiding place. He stayed there long after the man had carried his sister away.

Moon Man manipulated the story's thread for a moment, showing Leif and me what would have happened if Leif had tried to rescue me. The ring of steel rolled through the jungle as Mogkan pulled his sword from its scabbard and stabbed Leif in the heart, killing him. Remaining hidden had been a good decision.

The story then changed and focused on Perl and Esau's despair and anger when Leif had finally told them that I was lost. Leif believed he would be in worse trouble if he had told them the truth and they knew he hadn't done anything to stop the man. Leif had been convinced that the search parties would find the man and his sister. Already he felt jealous of the attention she would get for just being rescued.

When the search parties failed to find her, Leif began his own quest. He knew they lived in the jungle, keeping out of sight just to spite him. He had to find her, and maybe his mother and father would love him again.

As the years passed, his guilt drove him to attempt suicide, and, eventually, the guilt transformed into hatred. When she finally came back into their lives stinking of blood and of the north, he wanted to kill her. Especially when he saw for the first time in fourteen years the pure joy on his mother's face.

Cahil's ambush, while unexpected, gave Leif a receptive audience about the need to get rid of the northern spy. But watching her get hurt caused a small rip of concern in his black cloak of hate.

Her escape from Cahil was proof he had been right about her, but then she came back, insisting she wasn't a spy and therefore would not run away like one. Roze then confirmed her claims, puzzling Leif.

His confusion and conflicting emotions only grew when he saw her try to help Tula. Why would she care about another? She hadn't cared about him or how he suffered while she was gone. He wanted to keep hating her, but when she struggled to bring Tula back, he couldn't bear the guilt if he stood by and did nothing again.

When they traveled to the plains and Story Weaver approached, Leif had known his sister would discover the truth about him. He ran, unable to face the accusations that would fill her eyes. But when he calmed, he thought, would the truth be that difficult for her? She weathered so much in Ixia. Perhaps she could overcome this hurdle, too.

But after she had returned from the plains, Leif knew it was impossible. Her anger and censure flamed on her skin. She didn't want him or need him. Only his mother's pleas that he help his sister made him seek her out.

Story Weaver let the strands of the tale fade. The three of us stood on that dark plain I remembered from my last encounter with Moon Man. His coloring matched a ray of moonlight. Leif glanced around with wonder.

"Why did Mother ask you to help me rescue Gelsi?" I asked Leif.

"She thought I could assist you in some way. Instead, I had tried to—"

"Kill me? You can join the 'I Want to Kill Yelena Guild.' I hear they have six members in good standing. Valek is president since he had wanted to kill me twice." I smiled, but Leif stared at me with guilt in his eyes. "It wasn't you. Ferde tapped into your memories and used them."

"I did want to kill you before you helped Tula." Leif hung his head.

"Don't feel ashamed for having those feelings and those memories. What happened in the past can't be changed, but they can be a guide for what happens in your future."

Moon Man radiated approval. "We could make a Story Weaver out of you if you were not already a Soulfinder." He flashed me a wide smile.

"Truly?" How many people would I need to hear it from before I believed it or felt it? Perhaps it would be best not to declare myself a Soulfinder and just be regular old Yelena.

Moon Man raised an eyebrow. "Come visit me when you are ready."

Then the world spun and I shut my eyes against the feelings of vertigo. When they stopped, I opened them, finding myself back in the plains with Leif. Moon Man was talking to Valek.

I digested what happened on the stony plain. Leif had been in the process of untying himself. His road had smoothed when he made the decision to help me with Tula. So why had Moon Man asked me to help him? I looked for the Story Weaver, but he had disappeared.

Then the answer came to me, and, along with it, my own guilt. Without truly understanding Leif, I had treated him badly, holding the actions of an eight-year-old boy against a grown man and failing to see how he tried to amend them.

Leif watched me.

"How come they never schedule a New Beginnings feast when you really need to start over?" I asked.

Leif smiled at me. The first genuine one since I had returned from Ixia. It warmed me to the core of my soul.

"That's okay. I don't dance," he said.

"You will," I promised.

Valek cleared his throat. "Touching as this is, we need to go. Your Story Weaver is providing us with some soldiers to aid against Alea's people. We're to rendezvous with them at dawn. I take it your brother…"

"Leif," I filled in.

"…is coming along?"

"Of course," Leif said.

"No," I said at the same time. "I don't want you to get hurt. Mother wouldn't like it."

"And I wouldn't be able to face her wrath if I didn't stay and help." Leif crossed his arms over his chest. His square jaw set into a stubborn line.

"Your mother sounds like a formidable woman," Valek said into the silence.

"You have no idea," Leif replied with a sigh.

"Well, if she's anything like Yelena, my deepest sympathies," Valek teased.

"Hey!"

Leif laughed and the tense moment dissipated.

Valek handed Leif his machete. "Do you know how to use it?"

"Of course. I chopped Yelena's bow into firewood," Leif joked.

"You took me by surprise. I didn't want to hurt you," I shot back.

Leif looked dubious.

"How about a rematch?"

"Anytime."

Valek stepped between us. "I'm beginning to wish that you were an orphan, love. Can you both manage to focus on the task at hand without trying to catch up on fourteen years of sibling rivalry?"

"Yes," we said in unison, properly chastised.

"Good. Then let's go."

"Where?" I asked.

"In keeping with his cryptic nature, all your Story Weaver said was, 'The horses know where to go.'" Valek shrugged. "It's certainly not a military strategy I would use, but I've learned that the south uses its own strategy. And, strangely enough, it works."

The horses did know where to go, and, as the sun rose over the plains, we encountered a group of Sandseed soldiers on a rocky outcropping surrounded by tall grass. A dozen men and six women dressed in leather armor and equipped with either scimitars or spears waited. They had painted red streaks on their faces and arms, creating an impressively fierce countenance.

There were no other horses. Valek and I jumped off Kiki and Leif dismounted Rusalka to join us. The two horses began to graze. I shivered in the cold morning air, feeling naked without my bow, wishing I had another weapon besides my switchblade.

Moon Man greeted us. He had dressed like his clansmen, but

he was armed with his scimitar and a bow. The bow he held was no ordinary staff of ebony wood. It had been carved with symbols and animals, revealing a gold-colored wood under the black surface. And I felt that, if I could just stare at it long enough, the carvings may reveal a story. I shook my head, trying to stay focused on Moon Man's words.

"I sent a scout last night," Moon Man said. "He found the blood-letting apparatus in the Void just as Yelena described. Then he tracked the Daviian Vermin to a campsite about a mile east of that location. We are on the edge of the plains about two miles north of that site."

"We'll wait until dark and launch a surprise attack," Valek said.

"That will not work," Moon Man said. "The Vermin have a shield that will alert them to intruders. My scout could not get too close to their camp for fear of discovery." Moon Man appeared to scan the horizon. "They have strong Warpers, who can hide their whereabouts from our magic."

"Warpers?" Leif asked.

Moon Man frowned. "Magicians. I refuse to call them Story Weavers for they manipulate the threads for their own selfish desires."

I glanced at the group of Sandseeds, noting again the array of weapons. "You don't plan to use your magic?"

"No."

"And you don't plan to take prisoners?"

"That is not the Sandseed way. The Vermin must be exterminated."

I wanted to neutralize the threat of Alea, but I didn't want to kill her. Esau's vial of Curare still remained in my backpack. Perhaps I could paralyze her and take her back to the Keep's cells.

"How are you going to prevent the Daviians from using their magic?" Valek asked.

A dangerous glint flashed in Moon Man's eyes. "We move the Void."

"You can do that?" I asked, surprised.

"The blanket of power can be repositioned only with the utmost care. We will center the blanket's hole directly over the Vermin's camp and then we will attack."

"When?" Valek asked.

"Now." Moon Man walked over to his soldiers.

"I'd hoped to use the Sandseeds as a distraction," Valek said to me in a low whisper. "This will work. Once Alea is dead, we leave. This isn't our fight."

"I think capture and incarceration would be a harsher punishment for her," I said.

Valek studied me for a moment. "As you wish."

Moon Man's group shouted a war cry, then disappeared into the tall grass. He came back to us. "They will position themselves around the camp. The signal to attack will be when the Void is in place. You are to come with me." He glanced at the three of us. "You need weapons. Here."

He tossed his bow to me. I caught it in my right hand.

"That is yours. A gift from Suekray."

"Who?"

"A horsewoman of our clan. You must have made an impression on her. Her gifts are as rare as the snow. Your story is etched into it."

Mother, Kiki said with approval. And I remembered the short-haired Sandseed woman who had taken Kiki for a ride the day I had met with the elders.

I marveled at the bow. The balance and thickness felt perfect in my hand, and, despite the carvings, the black wood remained smooth and strong. By the time I pulled my eyes from the beauty of the bow, I saw that Valek clutched a scimitar and Leif wielded his machete.

"Let us go."

I took off my cloak and made a few quick preparations before we followed Moon Man into the tall grass.

From our position near the Daviian camp, I could see some activity around their tents and campfire. The air hovering over their site seemed to shimmer and it distorted the images of the people inside as if a massive pocket of heat had been trapped over them.

The grasses of the plateau grew in small clumps and had turned brown from lack of rain. I crouched with Valek behind a small bush. Leif and Moon Man were five hundred feet to our right huddled in a slight depression. I wondered how the other Sandseeds had fared in finding hiding spots. The Daviians had chosen a wide-open area for their camp and cover was minimal.

I felt the hair raise on my arms as power pressed against my skin. Seeking out with my awareness, I felt Moon Man and three other magicians tug the blanket of power. They applied equal pressure so the blanket would not gather in one location, but would move smoothly. Their magical abilities impressed me, and I thought, if I did stay in Sitia, the Sandseeds would make powerful teachers.

The Void's arrival felt like all the air had been sucked out of my lungs. My awareness of my surroundings reduced to the mundane senses of sight, smell and sound. Before I could adapt to my magical loss, another war cry sounded. The signal to attack the camp.

I jumped to my feet and followed Valek toward the camp. And stopped dead in my tracks when the scene in front of me registered in my mind.

The Daviians shield had been destroyed and, with it, the illusion. Instead of a few people milling about the campfire, there stood over thirty. Instead of a handful of tents, there were rows and rows of them. Granted most of the Vermin stared in shock at the loss of their magic, but we were outnumbered four to one.

Too late to retreat. We had the element of surprise and nineteen battle-thirsty Sandseeds, who cut wide bloody swaths through the Daviians. I could see Moon Man's bald head above the fighting, and Leif's powerful strikes kept a couple Daviians busy. Valek shot me a grim look. Find Alea, he mouthed to me before joining in the fray.

Great, I thought, edging around the outskirts of the battle. Find Alea in this mass of confusion. I ducked as a Daviian swung his scythe at me. I swept his feet from under him and hopped onto his chest before he could raise his long weapon. Ramming the end of my bow into his neck, I crushed his windpipe.

I paused for a heartbeat. He was the first person I'd killed since coming to Sitia. I had hoped never to take a life again, but if I wanted to survive this melee, I couldn't afford to be compassionate.

Another Daviian attacked. My melancholy thoughts disappeared as I defended myself and searched for Alea. Dodging and fighting, I lost all track of time as the series of matches began to blur together. In the end, Alea found me.

Her long black hair had been pulled back into a knot and she wore a simple white tunic and pants that were splattered with blood. She held a bloody short sword in each hand. Alea smiled at me.

"I planned to find you," she said. "How nice that you saved me the trouble."

"That's just how I am, always thinking of others."

She crossed her swords in a mock salute and lunged. I stepped back, and brought my bow down on the top of her blades, deflecting them toward the ground. She took a step forward to regain her balance just as I shuffled closer to her. We touched shoulders. Our weapons pointed down.

But mine remained on top. I yanked the bow up, hitting her in the face. She yelped as blood gushed from her nose. My strike failed to stop her, and she tried to swing her swords toward my stomach. I moved next to her; too close for large weapons. We dropped them.

I triggered my switchblade as she pulled a knife from her belt. She turned and stabbed at me. I blocked her blade with my arm. Pain burned as the knife bit into my flesh, but the move allowed me to grab her hand. I pulled her toward me and sliced her forearm with my blade then released her.

Alea staggered back in confusion. I could have plunged my knife into her stomach, killing her. Her expression turned to horror as she realized what I had done.

My switchblade had been treated with Curare. All I had needed to do was prick her skin with the tip of the weapon. When she fell to the ground, I stood over her.

"It's not fun being helpless. Is it?" I asked.

I looked around. Valek had maneuvered himself so that he stayed between me and the Daviians, keeping the others from interfering with my fight with Alea. Leif fought a short distance away, hacking with his machete. I couldn't see the other Sandseeds, but I spotted Moon Man just as he took a man's head off with his scimitar. Yuck.

Moon Man sprinted for us. "Time to retreat," he called.

"Next time," I said to Alea. "We'll finish this."

Then the Void moved and the magic came back for half of the campsite, creating a diversion. We were bathed in power, and I felt Moon Man encompass us in a shield of protective magic as we began our retreat. Valek, though, paused over Alea's still form. He knelt beside her, picked up her knife and said something to her.

Before I could call to him, he cut her throat in one smooth move. It was the same lethal strike that he had delivered to her brother, Mogkan.

When Valek caught up to me he said, "We can't afford to play favorites."

★ ★ ★

We raced back toward the plains. The Vermins ceased chasing us at the border of the Avibian Plains, but we kept our pace until we reached the rocky outcropping where Kiki and Rusalka waited.

"No doubt they will move their camp farther into the plateau," Moon Man said. The effort of running had not winded him, although his skin gleamed with sweat. "I will need to bring more soldiers. To have deceived my scout and me means their Warpers are more powerful than we suspected. I must consult with the elders."

Moon Man inclined his head in farewell and I soon lost sight of him in the grass.

"What now?" Leif asked.

I met Valek's gaze. What now, indeed.

"You go home and so will I," I said to Leif.

"You're coming with me to the Keep?" Leif asked.

"I…" Back to the Keep and to the feelings of isolation? Back to being feared for my abilities? Or back to spy on Sitia so I could eventually return to Ixia? Or just being on my own, exploring Sitia and spending time with my family?

"I think you're afraid to go back to the Keep," Leif said.

"What?"

"It will be much easier for you to stay away, and not have to deal with being a Soulfinder, being a daughter and being a sister."

"I'm not afraid." I had tried to find a place in Sitia, but I kept getting pushed away. How many hints did I need? I wasn't a glutton for punishment. What if they decided that a Soulfinder equaled evil and they burned me alive for violating their Ethical Code?

"You *are* afraid," Leif challenged.

"Am not."

"Are too."

"Am not."

"Then prove it."

I opened my mouth, but no sound came out.

Finally, I said, "I hate you."

Leif smiled. "The feeling is mutual." He paused for a moment. "Are you coming?"

"Not now. I'll think about it." It was a delay tactic and Leif knew it.

"If you don't come back to the Keep, then I'll be right. And every time you see me, I'll be insufferably smug."

"And how's that different from now?"

He laughed and I could see the young carefree boy he had been in his eyes. "You've only had a small glimpse of how insufferable and annoying I can be. As the older brother, it's my birthright."

Leif mounted Rusalka and galloped away.

Valek and I walked with Kiki toward the north. Toward Ixia. He held my hand and I felt content as my thoughts mulled over the last few hours.

"Valek. What did you say to Alea?"

"I told her how her brother had died."

I remembered how I had trapped Mogkan with magic, immobilizing him so Valek could cut his throat. Alea died the exact same way.

"We had no time to take Alea with us, love. I wasn't going to let her have another chance to hurt you."

"How do you always know when I need you?"

Valek's eyes flamed with an intensity that I had rarely seen. "I know. It's part of me like hunger or thirst. A need that must be met to survive."

"How do you do it? I can't connect my mind to yours with my magic. And you don't have magic. It should be impossible."

Valek remained quiet for a moment. "Perhaps, when I feel your distress, I relax my guard and allow you to connect with me?"

"Perhaps. Have you ever done that for anyone else?"

"No, love. You're the only one who has caused me to do the oddest things. You have truly poisoned me."

I laughed. "Odd, eh?"

"It's a good thing you can't read my mind, love."

A sapphire-blue fire smoked in his eyes, and I noticed a tightening in his lean muscles.

"Oh, I know what you're thinking." I stepped into his arms, putting my hands under his waistband to where his thoughts had traveled, making my point.

"I can't. Hide. From you," Valek panted.

I heard Kiki snort and move away as my world filled with the feel and smell and taste of Valek.

Valek and I spent the next several days walking the plains and enjoying being together without any worries or problems hovering over our heads. We would discover small caches of food and water along our path. And while I didn't have the feeling that someone watched us, I felt that the Sandseeds knew where we were, and the provisions were their way of extending their hospitality to a distant cousin.

Eventually, we left the plains. Skirting east of the Citadel, we headed north through the Featherstone clan's lands. Careful to travel at night and hide during the day, it took us three days to reach the Ambassador's retinue.

I had lost track of the days and been surprised to see their camp, but Valek had known they would be about a half-day's walk to the Ixian border. After determining where the Sitian "spies" hid, Valek changed into his Ilom disguise, and slipped into the camp in the middle of the night. I waited and approached the next day. There was no reason for me to hide, and, if I went back to Ixia, the Sitian spies could report back to the Keep and the Council that I had left.

The Ixians had begun to pack up their equipment when I

rode in on Kiki. One tent still stood, but Ari and Janco rushed over to greet me before I could reach it.

"Didn't I tell you, Ari? She's come to say goodbye, after all. And you were pouting and miserable for days," Janco said.

Ari just rolled his eyes, and I knew if anyone was miserable it was Janco.

"Or have you decided that you can't bear to be parted from us and are going to disguise yourself as a soldier and come back to Ixia?" Janco's smile was hopeful.

"Beating you in a bow fight every day is really tempting, Janco."

He scoffed. "I know your tricks now. I won't be so easy to beat."

"Are you sure you want me to come? I have a tendency to cause trouble."

"That's what I'm counting on," Janco said. "Life has been *so* dull without you."

Ari shook his massive head. "We don't need any more trouble. The diplomatic niceties started falling apart between the Ambassador and the Sitian Council toward the end. Before we left, one of the Councilors had accused the Ambassador of bringing Valek to Sitia to assassinate the Council."

"Not good," I said. "The Sitians are constantly worried the Commander will want to take control of their lands. And I would be, too, knowing that Valek possessed the skills to assassinate the Councilors as well as the Master Magicians, creating enough chaos so there is little resistance to an Ixian attack."

I shook my head, sighing. The Ixians and Sitians viewed the world so differently. They needed someone to help them understand each other. A strange feeling churned in my stomach. Fear? Excitement? Nausea? Perhaps all three; it was hard to tell.

"Speaking of Valek," Janco said, "I take it he's well?"

"You know Valek," I said.

Janco nodded, grinning.

"I'd better talk to the Ambassador." I slid off Kiki. Before I could move, Ari's large hand grabbed my arm.

"Just make sure you say goodbye to Janco," Ari said. "You think he's annoying when he's in a good mood—he's worse when he's in a bad mood."

I promised Ari, but as I walked to the Ambassador's tent, that odd feeling in the pit of my stomach became almost painful. Goodbye seemed so final.

One of the two guards outside the tent ducked inside to announce me. He came out and held the flap for me to enter. Ambassador Signe sat at a canvas table, drinking tea with Valek still dressed as Adviser Ilom. Signe dismissed him and I caught a look and the word "tonight" from Valek before he left the tent.

Bypassing the pleasantries, Signe asked, "Have you decided if you're going to visit us?"

I took the Commander Ambrose's order of execution from my pack. My hand trembled slightly and I took a breath to steady my nerves. "With this unfortunate clash of opinions between Ixia and Sitia, I believe you both will need a liaison. A neutral party who knows both countries and can facilitate negotiations, assisting them in understanding each other better." Meaning I wouldn't spy for Ixia, but I offered to help. I handed Signe the order. The Commander must decide what to do with it.

And there he stood in Signe's uniform, studying me with his powerful gold eyes. I blinked several times. The transformation from Signe to Commander Ambrose was so complete that I could only see a faint resemblance to the Ambassador in his face.

The Commander rolled up the execution order and tapped it on his palm as his gaze grew distant. Considering all the options, I thought, he never made a hasty decision.

"A valid point," he said.

He stood and paced the small area. I saw a bedroll on the

floor behind him and a lantern. The tent and table appeared to be his only luxuries.

Commander Ambrose stopped then tore my execution order into small pieces, sprinkling them onto the ground. Turning, he held out his hand to me. "Agreed, Liaison Yelena."

"Liaison Yelena Zaltana," I corrected as we shook hands.

We discussed the Commander's plans for Ixia and how he wanted to expand trade with Sitia. He insisted I finish my magical training before becoming the official liaison. Before I left, I witnessed Ambassador Signe's return. It was then that I felt, for a brief moment, that two souls resided within one body. That would explain why he had been so successful at keeping his secret.

I mulled over the interesting idea to keep my mind off the startling fact that I was going to return to the Keep. The Ambassador's retinue finished packing. I told Ari and Janco that I would see them again.

"Next time, your ass is mine," Janco sang.

"Keep your skills sharp," Ari ordered.

"It was bad enough having two mothers, now I have two fathers," I teased.

"Send word if you need us," Ari said.

"Yes, sir."

I headed south as the Ixians traveled north. Pulling a thread of magic, I projected my awareness. One of the Sitian spies followed me in hopes that I would meet up with Valek. I sent the man a confusing array of images until he lost all sense of what he was supposed to do.

Remembering Valek's promise, I didn't travel too far. I found an empty wooded area between two farms and set up a small campsite. As the sunlight faded, I projected my awareness into the surrounding woods. A few bats began to wake and a couple rabbits crept through the underbrush. All was quiet except for the steady approach of Cahil and his men.

He didn't try to mask his movements. Bold and cocky, Cahil left his men guarding the edge of the wood while he continued toward me. I sighed, more annoyed than scared, and reached for my bow.

I glanced around. Nowhere to hide on the ground, although the tree canopy might offer some protection. It might work except Marrok waited with Cahil's men. And I was certain the Captain's tracking skills had led Cahil to me. I would have to resort to using magic in my defense. Projecting, I reached toward Cahil's mind.

His emotions boiled with hate, but he had tempered them with a cold calculation. He stopped at the edge of my camp and inclined his head. "May I join you?"

"It depends on your intentions," I said.

"I thought you could read my intentions." He paused. "I see you have decided to stay in Sitia. A bold move considering the Council will know about your involvement with Valek."

"I'm not a spy, Cahil. And the Council needs a liaison with Ixia."

He barked out a laugh. "You're a liaison now? That's funny. Do you really think the Council will trust you?"

"Do you think the Council will go to war for a commoner?"

Cahil sobered for a moment. He glanced over his shoulder in the direction where his men waited. "I will find out the truth about that. But it really doesn't matter to me anymore. I've decided to take matters into my own hands."

Even though he hadn't moved, I could feel a renewed sense of threat from him. "Why are you telling me this? You know you can't get to Valek through me. Besides, he's back in Ixia by now."

He shook his head. "As if *I* would believe *you*. A beautiful day for riding and you stop here?" He gestured to the surrounding woods then took two steps toward me. "I'm here to give you a warning." Another step.

I brandished my bow. "Stop right there."

"You once said you thought Goel was decent for warning you about his intentions. I thought I would do the same. I know I can't beat you or Valek—even my men don't have a chance—but someone, somewhere has that ability. I'll swear I'll find him and, together, we'll make it our mission to see you and Valek dead." With that, Cahil spun around and headed for his men.

I didn't relax my grip on my bow until Cahil mounted Topaz and rode away. His men followed behind, running to keep up. As I broke my connection with Cahil's mind, I dipped into Marrok's mind. He was scared and worried about Cahil's odd behavior. That made two of us.

That night, my campfire seemed lonely until Valek arrived. He appeared by the fireside, warming his hands over the flames. I decided not to ruin our last night together by telling him about Cahil's visit.

"Forgot your cloak again?" I asked.

He smiled. "I like sharing yours."

Long after the fire had died, I fell asleep wrapped in Valek's arms. When the sun intruded, I burrowed deeper under my cloak.

"Come with me," Valek said.

It wasn't a plea or an order. An invitation.

Regret ached in my heart. "I still have much to learn. And when I'm ready, I'll be the new liaison between Ixia and Sitia."

"That could lead to serious trouble," Valek teased.

"You would be bored if it was any other way."

He laughed. "You're right. And so was my snake."

"Snake?"

He pulled my arm out to expose my bracelet. "When I carved this, my thoughts were on you, love. Your life is like this snake's coils. No matter how many turns it makes, you'll end up back where you belong. With me." His sapphire eyes held a promise. "I'll look forward to your first official visit. But don't wait too long. Please."

"I won't."

After another kiss, Valek rose and, as he dressed, I told him about Cahil.

"Many have tried to kill us. All have failed." He shrugged. "We've thrown him a curve. Either he'll sulk over his lack of royal blood and disappear, or he'll make himself believe we lied and will have a renewed determination to attack Ixia, which should make life interesting for the new liaison."

"*Interesting* isn't the word I would use."

"Make sure you keep a close eye on him." Valek smiled ruefully. "I have to go, love. I promised the Ambassador I would catch up to her at the border. If there is going to be any trouble from the Sitians it would be near there."

I regretted my decision to stay the moment he left and utter loneliness overcame me. But Kiki's cold nose against my cheek intruded on my morose thoughts.

Kiki stay with Lavender Lady, she said. *Kiki help.*

Yes, you're a big help.

Smart.

Smarter than me, I agreed.

Apple?

You've grazed all night. How can you still be hungry?

Always room for apple.

I laughed and fed her an apple before we began our two-day trip back to the Keep.

When I arrived at the Keep's gate, the guard instructed me to go directly to the Master's meeting room. As I gave Kiki a quick rubdown at the stables, I wondered what had been going on in my absence.

Students hurried from one building to the next as an icy wind blew through the campus. They gave me only a fleeting surprised glance before increasing their pace. The gray sky darkened and sleet cut through the air. An ominous start to the cold season. I pulled my hood up to protect my face.

I had arrived in Sitia at the beginning of the hot season. The two seasons I had lived here felt more like two years.

When I entered the conference room, three neutral expressions and one livid greeted my arrival. Roze threw a ball of furious energy at me. It hit me square on the chest, and I stumbled back before deflecting her attack. Pulling power to me, I projected my awareness toward her. Her mental defenses were impenetrable, but I aimed lower. Through her heart and into her soul. A much more vulnerable spot.

Now, now, I said. *Play nice.*

She jumped. *What? How?*

I have found your soul, Roze. It's dark and nasty in here. You've been hanging around those criminal types too long. You better change your ways or this soul won't fly to the sky.

Her amber eyes burned into mine with all the hate and loathing she could muster. Underneath, though, she was terrified. Hate and loathing didn't bother me, but fear was a powerful emotion. Fear causes the dog to bite and Roze was one bitch.

I released her. Roze sputtered and glared at me with a poisonous gaze. I stared back with calm patience. Eventually, she stormed from the room.

"So it is true," Bain said into the sudden silence. "You *are* a Soulfinder." He seemed more thoughtful than scared.

"What made her so upset?" I asked.

Irys gestured for me to sit down. I sank into one of the plush chairs.

"Roze thinks you and Valek are part of a plot to assassinate the Council." Before I could respond, Irys went on, "There's no proof. But what is more alarming is Ferde's escape from the Keep's cells."

I jumped to my feet. "Ferde escaped? When? Where?"

Irys exchanged a knowing glance with Bain. "I told you she had nothing to do with his release," she said to him. Then to me, "We're not sure when. He was discovered missing this morning." Irys gave me a wry grin. "We think Cahil rescued him."

"Cahil?" Now I was confused.

"He is gone. Captain Marrok was found brutally beaten. Once Marrok regained consciousness, he told us Cahil had tortured him until Marrok had told him the truth." Irys stopped, shaking her head in astonishment.

"That Cahil doesn't have royal blood," I said.

"You knew?" Zitora asked. "Why didn't you tell us?"

"I suspected. But Valek just confirmed my suspicions."

"Marrok told us that Cahil's mother had died in childbirth and he was the son of a soldier slain during the Ixian take-over. When they fled to Sitia, they took him along," Irys explained.

"Where is he now?" I asked.

"We don't know," Irys said. "And we don't know what his plans are now that he has learned the truth, and why he took Ferde with him."

So much for Valek's sulk-and-do-nothing theory about Cahil's reaction to his origins. "I guess, we'll just have to find him and ask," I said.

"But not yet," Irys said, and sighed. "The Council is a mess. Since you released all those souls, Ferde is weak and will be unable to do any magic for quite some time. And…" She hesitated, and I had the unpleasant feeling that I wasn't going to like what she said next. "They want you to explore your Soulfinder capabilities and perhaps become a Council Adviser."

Discovering my abilities matched my own wishes, but if I

wanted to be a neutral liaison, I couldn't be attached to the Council in any capacity.

"They don't need a Council Adviser," I said. "They need a liaison with Ixia."

"I know," Irys said.

"We should go after Ferde and Cahil today."

"I know. You'll just have to convince the Council of that."

I stared at Irys. My Story Weaver had to be laughing his blue ass off right now. My future appeared to be a long twisted road fraught with knots, tangles and traps.

Just the way I liked it.

★ ★ ★ ★ ★

Acknowledgments

A wholehearted thank-you to the one who holds down the fort while I'm doing book events, who gets the dishes done and the kids to soccer, who has been my biggest fan and supporter from the very beginning, my husband, Rodney.

To my Seton Hill University critique partners, Chun Lee, Amanda Sablak, Ceres Wright, thanks for all the help. Also, many thanks go to my Seton Hill mentor, Steven Piziks. I hope you find enough descriptive details!

I couldn't forget to thank my Muse and Schmooze critique group for their continued support and guidance. Your help has been wonderful, and our biannual retreats and coffee bar conversations are much loved.

Many thanks and praise go to my excellent editor, Mary-Theresa Hussey. Despite her busy schedule, she always finds time to answer my million questions. Thank you so much!

And a heartfelt thanks to Susan Kraykowski and her horse Kiki. Without them both, I wouldn't have learned how to ride, and I wouldn't have discovered the unique bond between horse and rider.